PLAYING THE PUCKING GAME

LA VIPERS
BOOK 2

TRACY LORRAINE

Model - Storm S

Photographer - Wander Aguiar

Development Editing by Pinpoint Editing

Content Editing by Rebecca at Fairest Reviews Editing Services

Proofreading by Lisa Staples

ABOUT PLAYING THE PUCKING GAME

Lincoln Storm.

Hockey god.

My brother's best friend.

And that's only the beginning of it because now, he's also my roommate and my colleague.

The New Year brings a new chapter to my life, and after years of working my ass off to prove myself in a man's world, I've landed myself my dream job as an assistant athletic trainer for the LA Vipers.

But days before I start, my life goes up in flames. Or more specifically, my apartment.

With little choice, I take my brother's best friend up on his offer to crash at his place.

It makes a lot of sense.

We've known each other almost all our lives. We work at the same arena. We'll be travelling together.

There's just the itty-bitty problem of the teenage crush I've never been able to banish.

To outsiders, it appears that I hate him. I mean, I do, I hate his playboy ways and happy-go-lucky persona.

The problem is, there is a lot more to Lincoln Storm than he allows the rest of the world to see.

And living with him...

I'm going to experience it all.

I'm a strong, independent woman who knows exactly what she wants in life.

There's only one thing I've never been able to resist.

Him.

PARKER

"You owe me," I slur, throwing my arms around my best friend.

I've barely had a chance to speak to her tonight; if she hasn't been attached to her hot hockey playing boyfriend's hip, then she's been chasing around after his sassy little girl, Sutton.

It lights me up inside, seeing my best friend so happy. Seeing her smiling like she is now.

But it also exposes just how fucking lonely I am.

"Why do I owe you?" Casey asks.

"We made a bet, remember?"

Her brows pinch.

"Uh...did we?"

"Yep. At the beginning of the season, I said something like, 'I bet that by the end of the season, you'll have fucked Kodie again.' Well, Missy. It's New Year's, the season is far from over, and you have just moved in with him. You owe me."

Casey quirks a brow, her smile growing as she thinks about her man.

Ugh, there's that happiness again.

It's a good thing I love her so much.

"That doesn't constitute as a bet, and it certainly doesn't mean I owe you anything."

I narrow my eyes at her.

"Why aren't you as drunk as me? If you were, you'd agree."

She shakes her head. "What is it you want for winning?"

I blow out a long breath as I think.

"I don't know."

"Okay, so the point of bringing it up was…"

"Proving a point that I was right, I guess."

"Well, congratulations, Miss Donnelly. You were right. Now, have you figured out who you're going to be kissing in…" Casey checks the time. "Six minutes?"

I groan.

"This room is full of hockey players."

"So? It's New Year's. It's all about new starts, remember?"

Excitement stirs in my stomach as I think about what the next year holds for me already.

Casey wasn't the only one to have her dream come true this year.

By some miracle, I've managed to achieve mine, too.

In three days, I am officially starting my new position as the LA Vipers' newest—and obviously hottest—athletic trainer.

"My new job is even more reason why I shouldn't be kissing any of these guys," I point out.

Drunk or not, I will not be forgetting the promise I made to myself all those years ago.

No hockey players. Not again.

Ever.

"Baby, it's almost time," Kodie says, stepping up behind my best friend so he can steal her away for their midnight kiss.

"Please, Parker," Casey begs, her eyes all soft and pathetic. "Next year is your year, I can feel it. Please don't start it alone."

"Go, just go," I say, waving them off before turning to the bar and gesturing to one of the servers for a new drink.

My spine stiffens as someone steps up beside me.

I don't need to turn around to know the looming presence belongs to a hockey player; I can tell by the expensive scent of their cologne.

My only question is...which one?

"Thank you," I say as my double Jack and Coke is placed in front of me.

"Something wrong with all the champagne that's being passed around?" His familiar deep, raspy voice rolls through me, igniting irritation everywhere it goes.

Closing my eyes, I silently will the man next to me away. This is not how I want to spend the end of this year and the beginning of the next.

But I already know I'm not that lucky.

Lifting my drink to my lips, I swallow a gulp, hoping it'll help me deal with the man beside me.

My skin heats under his attention, but I refuse to give him the satisfaction of knowing he affects me in any way other than annoying me.

"I guess this is the problem with the parties the team owner throws. He doesn't invite bunnies," I taunt, finally twisting around to look at the player who dared to come over and ruin the last few minutes of this year.

The smirk that pulls at Lincoln Storm's lips makes my teeth grind.

He thinks he's so special. So hot and...okay, fine. He is hot. But the fact he knows it counteracts the whole situation. That along with a whole list of other things.

He's always been the same. Although, it never used to annoy me as much as it does now.

I guess that's what happens as you get older.

You get wiser.

"It's not really an issue when you're in the room, sweetheart." My top lip curls.

"If you think that kind of line is going to get you anywhere with me, you really need to think again."

"It's almost midnight, Donnelly."

"And that means what, exactly? You going to turn back into a pumpkin?"

One side of his mouth kicks up in amusement.

"I didn't have you down as a fairy tale fan."

I sneer at him.

"You're even hotter when you're drunk."

"I'm done here," I say, lifting my glass from the bar and walking away.

I make it four steps before everyone around me begins counting down.

Ten.

Nine.

Eight.

I look around the room at the couples and groups of friends excited to welcome in a new year.

I understand why the Vipers are happy. They're having their best season in years. There is a very good chance that this is going to be the first time in almost a decade that they make it to the playoffs.

Seven.

Six.

Five.

Fletcher has his arms around his wife Reese's waist. Kodie is gazing into Casey's eyes.

The other couples on the team are ready.

Four.

Three.

Two.

And I'm standing here with only my drink to celebrate with.

Fuck. I hope Casey is right. I hope next year is my year.

One.

Cheers erupt as kids pull party poppers, shooting confetti everywhere. I'm about to lift my drink to my lips in a private celebration with myself when a hand wraps around the back of my neck.

Before I know what's happening, a warm pair of lips presses against mine.

It takes me a second for my brain to catch up, and the second it does, I raise my glass higher and dump the contents all over Lincoln Storm's head.

"The fuck, Donnelly?" he barks as my Jack and Coke soaks his hair and runs down the sides of his face.

"Happy New Year, Storm. It can only get better from here."

He stares at me, his eyes wide with disbelief, his chest heaving. He shouldn't look as good as he does right now with my drink dripping from his chin, soaking his white button-down.

Amusement explodes inside me, but I smother it, the slight tugging at the corners of my lips the only evidence.

His gaze darkens as his jaw tics.

My heart pounds harder, unable to drag myself from his intense stare.

He's the only thing I can see. The party and celebrations around us cease to exist as we both wait to see what the other is going to do next.

We're at a standoff, one I desperately need to get away from.

Lincoln Storm is dangerous. He always has been.

I remember that very first time my big brother brought him home for a playdate.

I was only eight. But even then, I felt this weird pull toward Linc.

He was a sweet kid. Arrogant as fuck. Nothing has really changed there. But for the first few years of their friendship, he was nice to me. He'd allow me to play with them and chastise Rett when he tried to shove me aside.

I got it. I was a little girl who lived and breathed ice hockey just like they did. But I wasn't one of them. I was never going to be.

Discovering that fact as a young girl with big dreams of playing hockey for a living was a bitter pill to swallow.

The truth is, it doesn't matter how well we play, how good we are at our jobs. Hockey has always been a male-dominated sport. Sure, things have slowly been getting better over the years. The PWHL is growing in popularity, and I really hope it continues.

Casey and I didn't manage to live out our childhood dreams.

But there's a chance that in ten years' time, Sutton will.

Linc suddenly takes a step toward me, ripping me from my thoughts and back to reality.

He's no longer that sweet little kid. He's a huge, brutal hockey player with a smile that makes panties drop left and right.

He acts like the world of women owes him something. And I, for one, am not giving him a single fucking thing.

"The fuck do you think you're doing?" I seethe, taking a big step back.

My lips are still tingling from that kiss.

That unwanted kiss...

Thoughtlessly, my hand lifts, my fingers brushing over my bottom lip.

His signature smirk appears as he takes another step.

"You're still thinking about it, aren't you?" he drawls, making my hand sink like a rock.

My eyes narrow, irritation flaring to the surface once more.

"You need to back the fuck up before I do something I'll regret."

"Aw, babe, I think we both know you'd never regret anything when it comes to me."

"Don't call me babe," I snap. "I'm your colleague now; it's about time you learned some respect."

Amusement glitters in his eyes.

"Babe, you were my friend long before you were my colleague," he taunts.

My top lip peels back.

"We've never been friends."

His smile widens. "Sure, you keep lying to yourself, Donnelly. We both know it's only a matter of time before you end up in my bed."

Fury erupts, and this time I'm the one who surges forward. He might be a six-foot-four giant who could squash me like an annoying fly, but I've had enough alcohol tonight to delude myself into thinking I'll have any kind of impact on him.

"You're a fu—"

"Let's dance," my best friend suggests loudly, wrapping her hand around my upper arm and dragging me away from the irritant who seems to want to press every one of my buttons tonight.

"What are you doing?" I cry as she drags me all the way to the middle of the dance floor. "I was just about to tell him what I think—"

"He already knows, Parker," she assures me as we come to a stop.

She steps in front of me, her body already swaying to the music.

Happiness radiates from her.

"He's such an asshole," I mutter, crossing my arms and pouting like a petulant child who didn't get her way.

What did I want, though?

"Let it go, P. It's a new year. A fresh start."

A little bit of hope trickles in.

"And on top of that, you're about to start your dream job. You did it, Parker," she says, her smile growing impossibly wide. "Have I told you how proud of you I am?"

My arms drop, and the resentment I was clinging to begins to ebb away.

"Maybe," I murmur. "But I could hear it again."

Casey laughs before throwing her arms around my shoulders. "I'm so fucking proud of you, Parker Donnelly. You are going to be the best athletic trainer in the NHL, and you're going to look hot as fuck doing it."

Excitement tingles in my belly. Of course, I'm fucking terrified about landing the job I've been working toward since I was fifteen, but I can push that aside for a few days in favor of celebrating. Something tells me that I've got plenty of opportunities ahead of me where I'll question my place in a man's world.

"Fuck Storm. Fuck all of them. This is about you right now," Casey says, swaying her hips as she loses herself in the music.

Her ability to forget everything for a few minutes helps me to do the same, and for a few songs, we dance together as if we're the only two people in the room.

I startle as a small person bumps into me, and when I look down, I find Sutton beaming up at me.

"Can I dance with you?" she asks, looking between me and Casey as if we're the most incredible women in the world. Man, this kid does good things for my confidence.

"Of course!" We take her hands in ours, lifting them above her head, dancing together as she giggles in delight.

Sutton may only be seven, but she is a force to be reckoned with. She's going to go far, I know it. Her grit and determination are up there with the ice hockey players we're surrounded by. I have no doubt that the name Sutton Rivers is going to be hitting headlines in the years to come for her contribution to women's ice hockey.

We dance and laugh until I have sweat dripping down my back.

Sutton is doing her best, but she's getting tired.

Looking up, I spot Kodie, her dad, heading our way with a drink in his hand.

"Parker," he says, handing me the glass. "I understand that someone is wearing your last one," he teases.

"What?" Casey asks, a frown marring her brow.

Kodie barks a laugh as he lifts his daughter into his arms. She immediately snuggles against him, resting her head on his shoulder.

A few months ago, I wasn't sure this man was capable of laughing. But since getting with my best friend, he smiles more than any of the Vipers' family thought possible.

"Didn't you notice Linc was wet?"

Casey spins around, searching for the man in question.

She stills when she finds him before turning back to me with a curious look in her eyes.

"What did you do?"

"Nothing you need to know about," I say, trying to wave it off.

"Parker," she warns, amusement twitching at her lips. "Did you dump your drink on Linc's head?"

"He kissed me," I blurt.

"W-what?"

"At midnight. The ball dropped, and he thought...god, why is he such a fucking idiot."

"He kissed you, and to thank him, you dumped your Jack and Coke all over him?"

"What else was I supposed to do?" I ask, not seeing the issue here.

"Uh...I don't know. Kiss him back?"

I balk. "There is not a chance you'll ever catch me kissing Lincoln Storm," I state firmly, my hand on my hip for good measure.

She stares at me, her eyes bouncing between mine before she asks, "Do you want to bet?"

2

LINCOLN

My hair and shirt are dry by the time I watch Parker march across the huge room the team owner booked for tonight's party.

I was expecting her to disappear when Casey, Kodie, and Sutton left. But she surprised me by hanging back and continuing dancing with Reese and a few of the other wives and girlfriends.

"We should head out," Killer says beside me.

The single guys and I planned to head to a club and continue the party.

I was buzzing for it earlier in the night, but now...not so much. I can't put my finger on why, but I fear it might have something to do with the redhead currently making her way to the exit.

Invite her, a little voice says in my head.

A laugh bubbles up at the thought. I haven't spoken to her since she was about five seconds away from causing me physical harm earlier.

I shouldn't do it. I shouldn't rile her up any more than she already is, but I can't help it.

The sight of her eyes flaring with irritation, knowing that I'm getting a reaction out of her, is just too much to deny.

Sadly, Casey dragged her away earlier before I could discover what ideas were playing out in that pretty little head of hers.

Dragging my hand down my face, my skin still slightly sticky from the drink that ran down it earlier, I make a rash decision.

"I'm gonna call it a night," I tell the guys. "See you at practice." I push to my feet and march away before anyone has a chance to question me.

I'm never first to leave the party, especially on a night with as much to celebrate as New Year's.

I follow Parker out, keeping my distance so she doesn't realize who's behind her.

When she gets into the elevator, I hit the stairs.

The two drinks I allowed myself earlier in the night have long worn off. I can't say the same for Parker, though. I've watched her movements on the dance floor become more and more erratic.

She's wasted and is apparently going to go stumbling out onto the street where she could be picked up by anyone.

Yeah...I don't think so.

The elevator is still descending when I hit the ground floor, my heart racing with exertion.

I wait in the shadows for the elevator doors to open, allowing her to spill out.

The second they do, and she stumbles forward in her skinny jeans, sequined tank, and heels, a smirk curls at my lips.

Parker Donnelly is hot. And while she might know she's attractive, I don't think she understands the half of it.

She has every single man in her orbit under her spell, and she has no idea.

The excitement that rolled through the dressing room when news got out that she's going to be our assistant athletic trainer was something I'll never forget.

And what happened next probably taught a number of my teammates a lesson they'll never forget, too.

I crack my knuckles, remembering how it felt to slam my fist into Marcus Sutherland's jaw when he made a comment he instantly regretted about our new colleague.

I'm pretty sure everyone thought it was because Parker is my best friend's little sister, and of course, that's a part of why I'm protective of her. But I'd have done the same for any woman in our world. Hell, in any fucking world. I can only imagine how fucking hard it's going to be for Parker to walk into the arena, and the training room, in a few days. She's the only woman on staff. The last thing she needs is our fourth-line winger shooting his mouth about her abilities to help us relax after a game.

As far as the team should be concerned, she's no different to Jarad or Dillion, our other trainers.

Funnily enough, I haven't heard a single word said about her from Sutherland since. Maybe he isn't such a stupid motherfucker after all.

I'm not naive though. His opinion will only be the first of many.

I fucking hate how hard Parker is going to have to work to prove herself just because she's a woman.

It's fucking wrong, and I'll stand up for her and any woman who is following their dream and trying to break into a male-dominated career.

The second she steps onto the sidewalk, her arms lift in a pathetic attempt to cover herself from the rain.

She looks up and down the street as if she's looking for her Uber, sighing in defeat when she doesn't see it.

Pushing my hand into my pocket, I pull my keys free and march forward, ready to make my presence known.

I'm aware that this could be an even worse idea than kissing her at midnight, but apparently, I'm a glutton for punishment.

"Come on," I say, stepping up behind her, the raindrops

hitting my face. She tenses at the sound of my voice. "I'll drop you home."

"I'm waiting for my lift," she almost shouts so she can be heard over the rain.

"And I'm right here, and my car is right...there," I say as I press the unlock button, watching as the light illuminates the street a few cars down.

"I'm fine. Thank you."

"Parker." I sigh. "It's raining, and you're wasted. Let me just get you home safe."

"Who says I'm going home?" she taunts, finally turning to look at me. "Maybe I'm going to my boyfriend's house."

The word hits me harder than it should.

Parker has dated a few guys over the last couple of years, but none of them have lasted. There are only two that I know of who've hung around long enough to earn the term "boyfriend," but both of them fucked up and lost what was undoubtedly the best thing in their life.

Refusing to take the bait she's dangling, I step a little closer.

"Then I'll drop you there. Just give me an address."

Pressing my hand to the small of her back, I find the fabric already damp as I gently push her forward, more than ready to get out of the downpour.

My shirt is already soaked through and stuck to my body. Now that I've decided to leave, I'm ready to get home.

Fuck. I'm getting old.

It's New Year's, and I'd rather be giving Parker a ride and then going home than continuing the party.

I guess it hits all of us eventually.

"Cancel your ride," I instruct as I successfully move her forward. To be fair, it's not exactly hard. I'm sure I bench press more than her body weight daily.

I'm under no illusion, though. Parker is a beast.

Her strength and endurance have always been outstanding.

I remember training with her as a kid. Rett and I would never admit it out loud, but she was always faster and more agile than us. And she's hella strong.

I might not have worked with her yet, but I already know that she possesses the strength to make all of us weep in pain.

Something tells me that she's excited about it too.

My sexy little sadist.

"What the fuck has gotten into you tonight?" Parker asks as we close in on my car.

I snort a laugh. "Funny. You're usually hassling me about who I've gotten into."

Parker gags dramatically.

"You know, for someone who claims not to like me, you sure are interested in my love life."

"Love life?" she balks.

"Okay, bad choice of words," I reason.

"I don't give a fuck who you fuck," she drunkenly shouts. "But I can't get away from it. Every time I open my socials, there's some story about your wayward dick."

"Aw, babe. Look at you worrying about me not being able to control my dick."

"Get over yourself, Storm. I've never worried about a single part of you, least of all your dick."

Car lights shine from behind us, and Parker halts.

"That'll be my ride."

"I said, cancel it," I hiss, giving her little choice but to continue forward.

"B-but—"

"Don't be a pain in the ass, Donnelly."

She huffs as we come to a stop beside my car.

Reaching around her, I pull my passenger door open and wait.

"Don't make me put you in there."

Sliding my hand from her back to her hip, I crowd her. She can either get into the car, or press herself against me, and I know which she isn't going to do willingly. Such a fucking shame.

"You drive me fucking crazy, Storm," she seethes before dropping into my car with a huff of irritation. I smirk as she puts her belt on and then sits with her arms crossed over her chest, her eyes staring straight ahead.

I don't know what it is about Parker, but her defiance gets me every fucking time.

Shaking my head, I slam her door and jog around to the driver's side to join her.

"So," I start once the engine is purring and I have the heat cranked up to help dry us off.

"So," she repeats.

"If you want to go to your boyfriend's, you're going to need to give me his address." I fucking hate saying the words. Even if she's lying, they taste bitter on my tongue. But I need her to tell me what I already suspect.

There is no boyfriend. There hasn't been for some time.

She glances at me out of the corner of her eye, and I immediately want to celebrate.

"I hate you," she mutters under her breath.

"I know. And isn't it so much fun?"

She makes a weird noise at the back of her throat that I can't decipher, and my obnoxious smile grows wider.

Fuck, I love riling her up.

"I bet it didn't take you this long to tell your Uber driver where to go."

"No, and he'd have given me less shit, too."

Taking matters into my own hands, I put my car into reverse and back out onto the street before taking off in the direction of Parker's apartment. She lives on the same side of town as me. Our apartments aren't all that far apart, something I've thought about more times than I've actually been there— which is all of once, when Rett and I helped move her in a couple of summers ago.

She used me for my muscles and then sent me on my way.

She didn't even invite me for a thank-you meal, which I think is rude, but whatever.

"Just take me home," she finally says, although it's so quiet, if I weren't paying attention, I'd miss it.

"I'm sorry, what was that?" I ask like an asshole.

"Fuck's sake, Linc," she mutters. "I said, just take me home."

"But your boyfriend will be so disappointed."

"I'm sure he'll get over it."

"Yeah," I muse, desperately trying to hold back a laugh.

Silence falls as I continue driving to her place. The roads are dead. Everyone is either still partying or sleeping.

Parker shifts, and I glance over as she twists my way, pulls her legs up to her chest, and rests her head against the seat, her eyelids lowering.

Her features almost instantly relax, leaving her looking peaceful and beautiful. I mean, she's always beautiful, but it's different when she's not throwing barbs at me.

Her red hair is wild after a night of partying and drinking; her makeup is smudged and sexy, and her lips are full and unbelievably kissable.

I think back to midnight, and fire shoots through me.

Only once has a kiss ever affected me so potently. But the less I think about that right now, the better.

"Shit," I hiss, swerving sharply to miss a parked car.

Parker mumbles something, but I'm pretty sure she's passed out.

I drive with her snoring lightly next to me, lost in my own world, but it all comes crashing down as I turn the final corner and drive straight into a scene of devastation.

"Fuck. Parker," I say, reaching out to wake her. "Parker, you need to—"

"Are we here?" she murmurs sleepily.

"Uh...yeah. You need to—"

"Fuck."

3

PARKER

I blink, unable to believe what I'm seeing.

Sleep and alcohol make my vision blurry, but sadly, it's not enough to make me think I'm dreaming.

I wish I was.

The street before us is clogged with fire engines and ambulances. Lights are flashing, and sirens are blaring. People are rushing around everywhere, either trying to help or to escape.

Ripping my eyes from the people, the knot in my stomach tightens as I take in my building.

Bright orange flames are licking up the sides, black smoke billowing into the sky.

"Oh my god," I gawp, unable to process what I'm seeing.

"Your apartment is at the back, right?" Linc asks, his voice full of disbelief.

"Uh...y-yeah."

Fear rips through me as I think about my neighbors. About the young family next door. The elderly man with the softest dog I've ever met who live opposite me.

I press my hand to my stomach as the food and drink I've overindulged in tonight threaten to make a reappearance.

"It's going to be okay," Linc assures me, although his voice is lacking conviction.

He can't make me promises like that, and he knows it.

My gaze returns to the carnage before us, and the second I see a familiar face, I throw the door open and run for her.

"Maddie," I cry as she watches her husband and a paramedic help her young son and daughter into the back of the ambulance.

They're walking, so that's a relief.

Maddie twists, and the second she sees me coming, she bursts into tears.

Instantly, I gather her up in my arms, my eyes locked on her husband, George, over her shoulder as he lowers his daughter to the gurney.

"It all happened so fast," Maddie cries, clinging to me like a lifeline.

"You're okay," I assure her through my own tears. "You're okay, and so are your babies."

At the mention of them, she rips herself from my hold and races toward the ambulance.

Both of them sit there listening to every single word the paramedic says. Their cheeks are black with smoke, and their eyes are heavy and tired, but they're okay.

George gathers Maddie in his arms, and they cling to each other.

Lifting my hands, I wipe my tears away, feeling utterly alone.

My world has just gone up in smoke—quite literally—and I've got no one to hold me like that.

I might be on the cusp of getting everything I've ever wanted career-wise, but what about everything else?

It's New Year's, and I was about to return home to my apartment alone, yet again.

I suck in a ragged breath, and a cough erupts. I'm standing out on the street, and the smoke is affecting me. I can't even begin to imagine what Maddie, George, and the rest of my neighbors have been through.

Fuck. I hope they all made it out.

I stumble back, staring up at my building as it burns.

The firefighters are already trying to tackle it. They might be succeeding, but to my untrained eye, there seems to be more fire than water, even with the rain, and that isn't a good sign.

A sob breaks free as I think about my home.

Sure, it was never my forever home, but it was my safe place all the same, and I loved it.

It's stupid and I feel materialistic as fuck, but thoughts of all my things make the tears fall faster. The clothes and decorations I've purchased while on shopping trips with Casey. Silly gifts that Rett sends me from his travels around the country for games. Christmas and birthday gifts from my parents. The drawing Sutton did for me that I have pride of place, pinned to my fridge.

As I break down, a set of arms wrap around me.

I startle, not expecting anyone to be comforting me when they're all living their own nightmare right now.

But then his rich, manly scent hits my nose a beat before my cheek presses against his firm chest, and the tears fall faster.

Line.

With one hand banded tight around my back, his other hand sinks into my hair, holding me tighter than I think I've ever been held before.

It's...too nice. Too much.

But at the same time, I'm powerless but to accept it.

Voices float around me, but I don't have the energy to pull my head from his chest. The image of our building burning is seared into my head; I don't need to look up and see it all over again.

I'm pretty sure I've already seen enough to ensure the image will haunt my nightmares for the rest of my life.

Linc's chest vibrates as he says something, but I don't make out any words.

The next thing I know, we're moving.

"W-what—"

I look up and find we're walking back toward his car. His arm is locked tightly around me, and I shamelessly cling to him. If I don't, there's every chance I'll end up in a pile on the damp ground. At least that's what I tell myself because I can't cope with any other reason right now.

"There's nothing we can do here but get in the way," he explains, his voice soft.

Another sob bubbles up my throat when he releases me to open the passenger door, and thankfully, I manage to catch it before it erupts.

He helps me get in as if I'm a child. He pulls back, and I expect him to move out of the way and close the door, but he doesn't.

Instead, he lingers, his eyes bouncing between mine as if he's searching for something.

I blink, forcing another tear to fall.

Without missing a beat, Linc reaches out and catches it with his thumb.

"It's going to be okay, babe," he says softly before leaning forward and pressing the sweetest kiss on my forehead.

It does very little for my fragile state.

He pulls back, checks on me again, and offers a sympathetic smile before backing away and closing the door.

Coldness washes through me the second we're separated. I hate it, but I'm powerless to stop it.

It only lasts five seconds because then he's back, dropping into the driver's seat and starting the engine.

He spins the car around, putting the devastation behind us.

Relief rushes through me, but it's quickly followed by guilt.

All of my neighbors are back there in the thick of it, and I'm being driven away unharmed.

I have no concept of time, but as we drive in silence, a thought hits me. I sit upright.

"Where are we going?" I bark, my heart racing.

"My place," Linc says, as if it's the most obvious thing in the world.

"No, Linc. I can't. Just..." I rack my brain for a place I could go.

Casey would always be my first port of call. But she's just moved in with Kodie, and it's New Year's. It wouldn't be fair to insert myself into their life. Casey would tell me it's okay, and Kodie probably would too, but that doesn't mean it's right.

"Take me to a hotel. I'll get a r-room a-and..." My voice breaks. I hate it.

"Fuck that, Parker. I'm not leaving you alone with nothing."

"I won't let Rett kick your ass," I muse, trying to ignore the way my chest swells at his words.

"Even if he could kick my ass, I'm not worried about him."

"I can't stay with you," I argue. "I'm about to be your trainer. That's—"

"Parker," he sighs, lifting his hand from the wheel to comb his damp hair back from his face. "Like I said earlier, we've been friends far longer than anything else. And plus, loads of the guys have roommates. It's not a big deal."

"I'm not being your roommate," I state as he takes the final turn toward his building.

I might know where he lives, but I've never been inside. Honestly, I dread to think what I'll find. It's probably the epitome of a bachelor pad. Fucking hell, there are probably women's panties and bras everywhere. Beer cans. Dirty dishes.

I shudder at the thought.

I'm not a neat freak. But I do like my home to be at a

certain level of clean and tidy—something that I can't imagine Linc sharing.

I've heard stories about the team hanging out at his place.

I bet it's all giant couches, huge TV screens, and more game consoles than one man should possess.

I'm going to hate it.

"Okay, so where are you going to go?" he asks, an amused lilt to his voice that pisses me the fuck off.

"A hotel, like I said."

"It's New Year's, Parker. Everywhere decent will have been booked up months ago."

"Okay, so take me somewhere that's not decent. I'm not a flashy hockey player who expects the finer things in life. I don't give a shit if I have to live out of a shitty motel for a few weeks."

"Absolutely not," he states before turning toward his underground garage.

I suck in a deep breath as the roller door rises for his fancy Porsche. I want to keep fighting, but as he pulls into one of his many parking spaces—benefits of owning the penthouse—my body is shutting down faster than I can control.

My eyes are locked on the white wall of the garage as he kills the engine.

He doesn't move or say anything for long seconds. They're agonizing, but I can't do anything about it.

"Come on, let's get you into bed," he finally says before pushing the door open.

His words drag me back to reality almost as much as the slam of his car door. What he said to piss me off at the party earlier rings out in my head, and a little bit of my previous frustration edges its way in.

"I'm not sleeping in your bed," I hiss the second he opens my door.

"Whoa," he says, rearing back a little as if I just slapped him. "I was gone for like, three seconds," he reasons.

"Earlier, you said about getting me into your bed. That is not what is happening."

He rubs the back of his neck awkwardly. "Jeez, I was just trying to have a laugh with you earlier, babe. I hate to say it, but you looked sad. That's why I came over to perk up your New Year's."

"Oh great. So not only was it a midnight kiss I didn't want, it was a pity kiss at that."

He sighs. "It wasn't out of pity, Parker."

"Then why?" I probe.

He's Lincoln Storm. The Joker, the Playboy, the guy you go to if you want a good time.

He saw an opportunity to fuck with me, and he went for it.

It wasn't the first time, and I'm sure it won't be the last.

His playful grin drops, and his eyes soften. "Because no one should start a new year feeling sad, Parker. Least of all you, when you've got so much to look forward to."

My mouth opens to say something, but I quickly discover I have no words.

He's right. No one should go into a new year feeling how I was in the seconds leading up to the ball drop. But is being irritated by your best friend's brother when he decides to kiss you unannounced any better?

I'm yanked from my thoughts—literally—as he reaches in, grabs my hand, and effortlessly pulls me from the car.

On any other day, I might fight him, especially as he doesn't seem to be in a rush to release me.

I breathe a sigh of relief when his hand finally drops mine, but it only lasts a second, because as we wait for the elevator to take us to his penthouse, he throws his arm around my shoulder and tugs me into his body.

"Come on, Little P. I hate seeing you sad."

"My life just went up in flames. I'm allowed to be sad," I mutter as we enter the enclosed space.

/
4

LINCOLN

Parker doesn't say anything else as we rise through the
building.

I'm aware that she's never been up here before,
and all I can think about is the state I left it in before heading
out earlier.

I shouldn't care what she thinks, not that she's in any kind
of state to notice, but I do.

Parker already has enough opinions about me and the way
I live my life. I don't need her adding more reasons to be
irritated by me.

Unease prickles at me as I think about what I'm doing
here.

I have never had anyone else stay with me before besides
Rett or my little sister, every now and then, when she needs a
break from her life.

I certainly have never had a woman stay here.

In fact, other than my mom and sister, no woman has ever
been here.

I don't even think Reese has been inside.

Something flutters wildly in my stomach as the elevator
dings and the doors open to my private hallway a few seconds
later.

Without glancing at her, I know what she's thinking.

That I'm a flashy, arrogant motherfucker.

Hell, she's said it to me so many times that I can hear it as clearly as if she were saying the words to me right now.

She's right, of course.

I don't need this huge penthouse. It's too big for me.

But...I fell in love with it when my realtor showed it to me, and I couldn't help myself.

We spend so much of our year on the road, sleeping in hotels and waking up not knowing where the fuck we are, that I wanted something special for when I'm at home.

This place is my haven. And, of course, a place where I can hang out with my teammates, my brothers, and we can kick back and forget about the pressure constantly weighing on our shoulders.

Dropping my arm, I press my hand to the small of her back and lead her into my apartment.

The bare skin of her back burns my palm, and I can't help but brush my thumb against her soft skin.

I ensure she's a step ahead of me so I can watch her reaction.

But to my surprise, she doesn't give one.

She looks around, sure. But I can't tell if she's impressed, disgusted, or something else entirely. She's...indifferent.

It's something I really don't like.

Parker is always quick to let me know how she feels.

We step into the huge, open-plan living, kitchen and dining room, and I send a silent prayer up that it isn't as messy as it could have been.

"The guest bedroom is down here," I say, pointing farther down the hallway.

She nods and keeps walking.

Opening the door for her, I allow her to step in first before following her inside.

I close the blinds, put the bedside lamp on for her, and place her clutch on the dresser.

She stares at it with a frown on her face.

"You dropped it when you jumped from the car," I explain.

She just continues to stare.

"The bathroom is through here. It's all yours."

She watches me step toward the attached bathroom, but she doesn't make a move to check it out. It's a shame because I think she might like the size of the tub hiding in there, but whatever.

If it weren't so late, I'd offer to run it for her.

"Do you want a drink? Are you hungry?"

She shakes her head, her arms locked around her middle.

She looks utterly defeated.

I want to help, to do something...anything. But there isn't anything I can do or say to make this situation any less dire.

I stand there, feeling useless.

My cell burns a hole in my pocket.

I should ring Nova. My sister would know exactly what to do.

Casey would as well, but I don't want to disturb them. If Parker wanted to go there, she'd have directed me there.

I run my eyes down the length of Parker's body, and it suddenly hits me that she has nothing.

Only the clothes on her back and the clutch I placed on the dresser.

"The bathroom is fully stocked. I know it's not your usual, so just send me a list and I'll get whatever you need."

"No, you don't need—"

"I'll go and grab you something to wear for tonight."

Before she can say anything, I dart out of the room and straight into the one next door.

After a quick rummage through my closet, I grab one of my old Vipers T-shirts and a brand-new pair of boxers. I swing by the kitchen for a bottle of water and some crackers, just in case, and make my way back to her.

I knock, because every now and then I can be a gentleman, but when I don't get a response, I let myself in anyway.

I half expect to find her curled up in bed already, but instead, I discover a pile of discarded clothes on the floor and the bathroom door ajar. The sound of the shower running fills the air, my grip on the clothes in my hand tightens.

There is a naked woman in my apartment.

And not just any woman. Parker fucking Donnelly.

I knock on the bathroom door before continuing to the bed and lowering my T-shirt and boxers to it.

"There are some clothes on the bed," I call through to her.

I don't know if she hears me or not; I don't hang around to find out. I don't need any more temptation to crack the door a little wider to see if I can catch her reflection in the mirror.

I shake my head as I walk away.

It's the Parker Donnelly effect.

No other woman on the planet drives me wild the way she does.

And what have I done?

Invited her into my home.

⸻

TWENTY MINUTES LATER, I'm showered and in bed naked, staring up at the ceiling and questioning my life choices.

Parker Donnelly is in my home with nothing more than the clothes on her back.

Well, no, that's not true.

Right this moment, she is probably wearing a Vipers T-shirt that has my name across the back.

My teeth grind at the thought.

In all the years I've known her, I have never, ever seen her wear my jersey. She was there the day I played my first Vipers game. Even then, my name didn't grace her shoulders.

There's this determined part of me that wants to figure

out a way to make it happen. I want to see what she looks like with *Storm* written across her back like I own her. But there's also this other part of me that refuses to think about it.

I can't. It…it's too much.

So instead, I force those kinds of thoughts from my head and focus on more rational things like what Parker is going to need to do tomorrow, and what I can do to make all this easier.

She might be adamant that we've never been friends, but I have a very different opinion.

She's been a part of my life for almost as long as I can remember. I might be closer to her brother, or at least I was growing up. Hell, the two of us were inseparable, both on and off the ice. We were until the day we got drafted. Sure, we're not worlds apart with him up in Seattle and me living out my childhood dream of playing for the LA Vipers, but we're not as close as we once were.

Parker is still here, though. She's still a part of my life in a way Rett isn't. And with her new job, she's about to become an even bigger part of it.

My skin prickles as I consider how I'm going to cope with her running her hands all over me on the daily.

She's a professional, I have no doubt about that. She's worked too damn hard to secure this role, beating out all the men who applied. There isn't a single chance in hell of her doing anything to put that at risk.

Me though…I'm an entirely different story. I live for the adrenaline rush, and having Parker rub me down is undoubtedly going be to a high of the very best kind.

I continue lying there for the longest time, creating a mental list of all the things that need to happen next.

Hours pass, and I'm still wide awake. I tell myself that it's because I'd been prepared to be out partying all night. But I know that's bullshit. I can't sleep because I'm on high alert. Parker is right on the other side of the wall, and our headboards are almost touching. Every single noise has me hyper-focused in case something is wrong, in case she needs me—which will never happen, but a guy can hope.

Right now, as far as I know, I'm the only one aware of what's happened tonight, and I want to be there for her.

My legs twitch with my need to go and check on her.

Is she sleeping? Or is she pacing the room, trying to get her head around what's happened? And if it's the latter, does she need someone to talk it out with? Does she need my shoulder to cry on again? Because I'll loan that motherfucker out time and time again for her to make use of.

Eventually, the not knowing gets too much, and I roll out of bed, pull on some boxers, and silently pad toward her door.

Everything is silent, leading me to believe that she's sleeping. Just like the bathroom door earlier, I find it ajar, and when I poke my head around the door, I quickly find that I'm right. She's curled up on her side, facing away from me with the covers bunched at her waist.

But my eyes only focus on one thing.

My name.

My heart rate increases and my fists curl at my sides.

Finally, after all these years, Parker Donnelly is wearing my name and number.

Lifting my hand, I rub my chest, right above my racing heart.

Fuck, that is a sight to behold.

I stand there for a good minute before I realize that I'm acting like a total creep and back out of her room.

I'd be lying if I said that my boxers weren't a little tighter on the return journey. The image of her wearing my name and number is ingrained in my brain, and I'm pretty sure it's going to live there rent-free for the foreseeable future. I'm equally sure my wild imagination will also get a hold of it. I groan, sinking my hand into my boxers and squeezing my length.

It's wrong. She's just experienced probably the worst night of her life, and here I am getting hard over the fact she's in my space and wearing my clothes.

I'm hardly surprised, though.

It's Parker.

She's been under my skin since I was eleven, and after all these years, I've resigned myself to the fact that I'm never going to get her out.

I grab my cell the second I'm safely back in my room, flop back on my bed, and set about knocking off a few things on that to-do list I created.

I don't doubt that Parker will be annoyed with me for it, but that's always been our love language, so why change that now?

5

———

PARKER

I barely got a wink of sleep.

Despite my shower, the scent of smoke still lingered in my nose. Every time I closed my eyes, all I could see was my building being engulfed by flames.

I fought the tears with everything I had, but it was pointless. The more I thought about my home, about the things I've collected over the years that I love to surround myself with, the faster they fell.

I don't know how much time had passed before I heard Linc push my door wider and step into the room. All I do know is that I kept my breathing as heavy and as even as possible, hoping he'd be convinced that I was sleeping.

What he did last night...well, it was more than I ever could have asked of him.

It was New Year's; I'm sure he had plans to be out partying and pulling bunnies. Yet instead, he was here with me in his apartment, ruining any chance he had of bringing a woman back.

When I finally throw the covers off this morning, my body aches and my eyes are swollen and sore. I can only imagine how I look.

But unfortunately, as tempting as lounging around in bed all day is, I've got shit to deal with.

Just thinking about all the calls I need to make, all the things I need to replace, is making my head spin. I need to make a physical list and figure it all out. Then, I'll work through one at a time.

Linc was right last night: it will be okay. It's just going to take some time.

I pad through to the bathroom and kick the door so it almost closes behind me before dropping my ass to the toilet.

I stare at Linc's boxers around my thighs and groan.

How the hell did I end up here?

Once upon a time, this would have been my ultimate fantasy. Wearing his clothes, being with him alone in his apartment.

I shake my head. That was the dream of an innocent teenager with a crush.

I'm a woman now who knows a hell of a lot better than to crush on my unavailable brother's best friend.

Hell, I've learned a lot of lessons about men over the past few years.

The biggest of which, is that they can't be trusted.

Okay, sure, there are a few out there who break the mold.

Kodie, Fletcher, a couple of others who prove on the daily that they truly love their women and are nothing but loyal.

I just...I haven't met one who might be interested in being loyal to me.

Finishing up, I walk toward the sink and scan the counter.

It's empty, save for a crappy bar of soap.

In desperate need for a toothbrush, I pull the vanity door open and peer inside.

A relieved sigh spills from my lips. Linc wasn't lying; everything I could need really is in here.

In a rush, I rip at the packaging, squirt some toothpaste onto the brush, and freshen up.

I feel marginally better once I'm done, but sadly, the light pounding at my temples doesn't lessen. Nor does the ache in my chest.

Wiping my mouth with the hand towel, I stand to full height and stare at myself in the mirror.

You are a strong, independent woman, Parker Donnelly.

You are about to be the LA Vipers' first female athletic trainer.

This is not going to break you.

If anything, it's an opportunity.

New job. New you.

Buy new clothes. Test out new makeup.

You got this.

I force a smile on my lips, my eyes tracking down my body that I work so hard to maintain, but the second my eyes land on a big number seven, everything I just told myself crumbles to the ground.

I don't need to twist around to see my back to know what's there.

"Motherfucker," I hiss before racing from the bathroom and then seconds later, the bedroom.

"Lincoln Storm, why the fuck am I wearing your name and number?" I shout as I march toward the living area he briefly showed me last night.

It was all a blur, so when I step into the room, I immediately come to a stop. And not because of the half-naked man sitting at his kitchen island, sipping on coffee.

Motherfucker, indeed.

His eyes lock on mine, and a smile pulls at his lips. "Good morning, Little P. How did you sleep?"

Irritation shoots through me. How can he be so...so...blasé about this?

"Oh, wonderful. It was almost as if my entire apartment building didn't go up in flames last night and I haven't lost every single thing I own," I snap, my hands on my hips for good measure.

His smile falters, but only for the briefest of moments before it's back to full wattage again.

Asshole.

"So like a baby, then?"

"I need coffee if I have to deal with this," I mutter, stalking toward the kitchen, and sadly, closer to him.

Why is he only wearing a pair of athletic shorts, and why does his hair have to be wet, dripping onto his shoulders and sending little rivers running down his chest and abs?

Stop fucking looking, Parker.

He doesn't say a word as I come to a stop in front of his coffee machine.

My independence is soon squashed when I realize I have no idea where the pods or mugs are.

A deep chuckle rumbles around me.

"What?" I snap, whirling around to glare at him.

"You look hot with my name on you, Donnelly."

"Bite me, Storm."

He smirks. "Just give me the chance, babe. You know I'll make it sting so good."

I fucking hate that his words have my lower stomach tightening.

It wouldn't be so bad if I thought he was bullshitting, but I know he's not. His reputation alone is enough to prove that any bite—or anything for that matter—from Lincoln Storm would be more than good.

His lips part, and I internally groan in preparation for whatever lewd remark is going to spill free next. I swear, if he offers to make my day better by allowing me to ride his dick, I'll forgo the coffee and launch the machine at his fucking head. There are coffee shops for a reason.

But what he does say makes me pause the very vivid images playing out in my head of the moment he tumbles to the floor, clutching his head.

"In the refrigerator."

I narrow my eyes, confused by the words.

"Huh?" I say eloquently.

His expression turns smug, and it makes me want to punch him.

Why didn't I force him to take me to a hotel last night?

"In the refrigerator," he repeats.

Ripping my eyes from his, I scan the kitchen before focusing on the appliance in question.

Walking over, I pull the door open.

It's practically empty, telling me what I already guessed: Linc isn't much of a cook. But there, right in front of me, is a glass with what looks like a double shot of coffee in it.

"W-what's this?"

He chuckles again, the deep rasp sending a shiver racing down my spine.

"Coffee, babe. Iced coffee, to be exact. Or at least, it will be once you add some creamer and ice. There are options in the door; I wasn't sure what your preference was, so I ordered a few."

Looking to my right, I scan the row of bottles.

Holy shit.

With the refrigerator door still open, the coldness rushing over my bare legs, I spin around and stare at Linc.

"You made me coffee and put it in the fridge?"

"I also ordered you creamer," he states proudly. "At least tell me that one of them is right."

My previous attitude vanishes, and my entire body deflates as emotion hits me out of nowhere. My nose itches and my eyes burn. I beg for the tears not to fill my eyes, but I'm powerless.

My sight gets blurry, but he's as clear as day before me. "All of them are perfect," I confess quietly. "Thank you."

"I'm sorry," he says, teasingly cupping his hand around his ear so he can hear better. "Can you repeat that?"

"Thank you, Linc. I really appreciate it."

Our eyes hold for a moment, but the second I fear he can see more than I'm willing to share, I twist back around, grab the glass and one of the bottles of creamer, and complete my coffee.

Silence falls around us, but I know he's watching. My skin is burning with his attention.

When I'm done, I rest my ass back against the counter opposite him and lift my glass to my lips.

Closing my eyes, I breathe in the scent of my coffee, letting it ground me for a moment before taking my first sip.

Shit. Linc has good coffee.

"Why?" I finally ask once I've savored my first taste.

"Why?" he echoes. "Because everyone deserves to start the day with good coffee."

"Well, yeah. That's a given. But I could have just come out here and made my own. Why go to the effort of making it earlier, putting it in the fridge, and ordering creamer?"

He laughs in disbelief, his hand lifting to rub the back of his neck.

"You have no idea, do you?"

"I'm too tired to talk in riddles, Storm," I warn before taking another sip.

Damn, it's good.

"You had a shitty night, and I can't imagine today is going to be much better. I just...wanted to help, I guess."

"Hmm...do you do this for all the women who spend the night here?"

Pushing his empty mug back a little, he rests his threaded forearms on the counter. He laces his fingers together, and it makes the muscles ripple and his veins become more pronounced.

I clear my throat and force my eyes back to his.

"So, what's the plan for today?" he asks, completely ignoring my question.

I shrug one shoulder.

"I don't even know who I need to call for information. The fire marshal?"

"And your insurance company," he suggests, making me

grimace. "If your things need replacing, then—what's that look for?"

"Fuck's sake," I groan, tipping my head back and closing my eyes.

"Parker, please tell me that you had renters' insurance."

"Yeah, of course," I say, looking back down but staring past him and into the living room. "I just...didn't renew it the other week when it ran out."

"You're shitting me."

"Do I look like I'm fucking shitting you? With the stress of the interview process, the holidays, I just...fucking hell." I drop my face into my hands as pain and guilt war within me.

I can't afford to replace everything I own.

I have some savings, and sure, my new position comes with a pay increase, but still...I don't have a multi-million-dollar contract and more money than I know what to do with, like the man staring at me with disappointment etched into every feature of his face.

Oh god. Mom and Dad are going to be so disappointed in me.

Rett too.

"Parker," Linc says, his voice closer this time.

I jump when his warm fingers wrap around my wrists, dragging my hand away from my face, stopping me from hiding from my massive fuck-up.

"There's no point dwelling on something that can't be fixed. Are you sure the policy ended?"

"Yes," I whisper weakly.

"Okay, so let's see if we can determine the extent of the damage. It might be okay. They could have stopped the fire before it got to the back of the building. Everything might be safe."

I want to share his hope, I really do. But let's be honest, it's not going to be my reality. It's just too good to be true.

"Go get your cell. Let's get some answers before you start freaking out."

6

PARKER

"Have you got a charger?" I ask, returning to the kitchen only minutes after leaving with my dead cell in my hand.

"Of course," Linc says before stalking across the room.

His athletic shorts sit low on his hips, so low that I can't help but wonder if he's wearing anything beneath.

As he turns away from me, I find my eyes running down his back. His skin is tanned despite the fact that we're in the middle of winter, and his muscles ripple and pull in the most delicious way.

Man, I'd love to dig my fingers into those and see how much he can take.

My fists curl as I think about how much pain I'd like to deliver to his well-worked muscles for all the torment I've suffered from him over the years.

He bends over, showing off that firm, round ass, and I almost swallow my tongue.

Being here is a bad idea.

I need to get my shit together and get the hell out as fast as I can.

The second he stands with the charger in his hand, I look

away. The last thing his ego needs is to catch me checking him out.

"Here," he says, handing it over.

"Thanks," I mutter as his fingers brush mine.

"Plug it in there," he says, pointing toward a socket in the kitchen. "Go and shower and freshen up. I'll make more coffee. Then, we'll tackle it."

"Why are you being so helpful?" I accuse.

"Uh...because I'm not an asshole. Would you rather I kick you out like a hookup I don't give a shit about?"

I know it sounds stupid, but if he did that, at least I'd know where I stood. This right now? It's throwing me for a loop.

I think about it for a moment, knowing that he's right but desperately wanting to fight it.

"I don't have any clothes," I mutter quietly. It's bad enough that I'm standing here wearing a pair of his boxers with the waistband rolled over more times than I can count, and a T-shirt with his name and number on it.

"I'll lay something out on your bed."

"I need to go shopping. I need—"

"We'll figure it all out," he assures me before I descend into a full-blown panic attack.

My life has gone to hell in a handbasket, and I'm starting a new, demanding job in two days. How the hell am I supposed to focus on that when I'm homeless and don't have so much as a pair of panties to my name?

Placing my cell on the charging pad, I immediately take a step back.

I have no idea what is going to be waiting for me on it, and I'm not sure I'm ready to find out.

When I booked my Uber last night, I had a million notifications, but I naively assumed they were all Happy New Year messages.

If I'd just looked, maybe I'd have discovered what was going on before we drove headfirst into it. Not that it would have made it any less devastating.

"Thank you," I murmur before walking away and heading straight for the guest room.

Leaving the door ajar, I march straight into the bathroom and push that door to as well.

I hesitate. Linc is going to come in here with fresh clothes. I should shut and lock the door, but unease races down my spine at the thought.

Deciding it's safer to leave it open slightly, I strip out of his clothes and turn the shower on.

I had one not so long ago, but I can't help craving its solace.

Stepping under the powerful spray, I wince as the too-hot water burns my scalp and shoulders, but I don't turn it down. Instead, I welcome the burn.

Making use of the products he has in here, I wash my hair, finger brushing while the conditioner is in, in the hope it leaves it somewhat smooth when it dries.

I don't hear anything from the bedroom, but I can only assume Linc has done as he said and brought me some replacement clothes.

Once I'm done, I step out and wrap one towel around my body, tucking it under my arms, and another around my head. Without any face care products, or even any deodorant, I slowly pull the bathroom door open and step out. Part of me expects to find him waiting for me, so I'm surprised to find my bedroom empty, although that relief soon turns to confusion when my eyes land on the bags sitting on my bed.

"What the—"

Rushing over, I pull the first one open, peering inside.

Women's clothes.

"What? How?" I breathe as I pull out three pairs of leggings and three matching sports bras, all in the right size.

The next bag has a brand-new pair of sneakers and sports socks inside, also the right size. The third bag has two hoodies in it, but it's the final bag hiding at the back that really gives me pause.

La Perla.

I shake my head.

Lincoln Fucking Storm brought me lingerie. I don't know whether I'm impressed or utterly creeped out.

Reaching into the bag, I pull out a tissue-wrapped parcel and lay it on the bed.

My hands tremble as I begin to open it, wondering what he'll have chosen for me.

Will it be something I'll be able to wear, or some slutty little thing that his hookups usually turn up in, in the hope of being the one to tie him down?

My stomach knots at the thought. Needing to know, I continue ripping into the paper.

"Oh my god," I gasp when I finally discover what's hiding inside.

I lay each set out on the bed, both in love and in awe that he chose such beautiful and wearable items for me. And not only that...they're the right size.

"How?" I ask again. How on earth does my brother's best friend know my bra size?

A lot impressed and equally as curious, I drop my towel and pull on a soft pink lace thong before stepping into the navy leggings—my favorite brand—and then wrestling the sports bra over my head.

It's warm enough in here to forgo the hoodies, and after finger-combing my hair again, I double-check my appearance in the mirror and head out feeling a little more prepared to deal with this shitshow head-on.

I'm hit with déjà vu when I step into the kitchen and find Linc sitting exactly where he was earlier, still only in his shorts, with a coffee beside him. Only now he's dry and has his cell in his hand.

He lowers his hand as I approach and looks over. His eyes widen before running down the length of me as one side of his mouth curls up in a half-smirk.

"You look better," he surmises.

"Wearing clothes that fit will do that for you," I point out, making him roll his eyes. "I don't know how you did it so fast, but thank you, Linc. I really appreciate it."

His expression softens as he accepts my thanks, and when his lips part, I really think that something nice, thoughtful even, is going leave them.

Oh, how wrong I am.

"I'm Lincoln Storm, babe. I can make anything happen."

"Of course. How could I forget," I mutter. "I'm not even going to ask how you know my bra size."

His smirk grows.

"And I don't want to know about your vast experience with women's bodies that means you can guess on sight alone."

"Man, I wish. What a superpower that would be."

"Life changing," I deadpan as I take a sip of my fresh iced coffee before picking up my cell.

"It's been lighting up like crazy," Linc tells me, but it isn't necessary; I can see all the notifications.

I don't know where to start.

But then I see that I've had a missed call from Maddie, and I figure that's as good a place as any.

"Hey, how are you all?" I ask the second the call connects.

She sighs. "We're all okay. Kids have a cough, but the doctors assured us that it'll pass in a few days. The only lasting effects will be the memories."

"God, I can only imagine."

Taking my coffee, I walk through to the living room and curl up on one of Linc's huge couches.

He watches me go, but he doesn't attempt to stop me.

With my legs curled under me, I listen to Maddie as she recalls their night before going on to explain what she knows.

The long and the short of it is that the building is fucked.

Thankfully, everyone who lives there has been contacted, and they either made it out or they weren't at home.

I guess that's one good thing about it being on a night when most of the city is out at parties. Maddie tells me the building has been condemned and that no one is allowed in until they've secured it and deemed it safe, so we have to wait to discover the state of our homes and our possessions. She thinks it could be weeks.

As awful as this is for me, I think of all the families in our building. Those who've lived there all their lives. It must be beyond devastating.

Maddie checks in with me, making sure that I have somewhere to stay and support around me.

They're at George's parents', which is close enough to both their work and the kids' school so they can attempt to continue with some kind of normal life, but I can't imagine everyone in our building is that lucky.

After promising to send me a number I can call for updates, she promises to stay in touch and offers to help me out with anything I need, which I appreciate but will never act on. Her life has been turned upside down just like mine has. She has to look after her own family before even considering anyone else.

"That didn't sound overly promising," Linc says after I've hung up and lowered my cell to my lap, clearly not giving a shit about eavesdropping on my half of the conversation.

"It wasn't. She didn't say it for a fact, but I'm pretty sure I've lost everything." My voice is cold and hollow as I say the words.

I know things could be worse. No one has died. It's just a building and a few possessions. But I'm pretty sure the tightness in my chest is grief.

"I've got something that might cheer you up," Linc says.

"More than buying me lingerie?" I tease.

"Babe, trust me: that was all for me."

"You say that as if you'll ever get to see them."

"I'm confident," he says before footsteps race my way.

I look over just in time to see my best friend barrel around the corner.

7

LINCOLN

I take a step back as Parker jumps to her feet, Casey racing around the corner as fast as her legs will carry her. The two collide, instantly wrapping their arms around each other.

A small smile plays on my lips as I watch them embrace. The sight also solidifies that I did the right thing by calling Casey, even if it is weird as fuck to have not just one but two women in my space.

I first picked up my cell long before Parker woke up. I was in desperate need of help, and thankfully, after a barrage of questions I mostly refused to answer, Casey gave me the information I needed to ensure Parker had something to wear when she got out of her shower.

So, while Parker might be confident in my abilities to look at a pair of tits and immediately know what size they are, it's not actually true.

Did I need to buy her lingerie from La Perla? Absolutely not. I could have gotten panties from the same store I got the leggings from. But I couldn't stop myself. The thought of treating her, of giving her a little bit of luxury while her world is falling apart, was too much to ignore.

As was the thought of knowing exactly what she's wearing beneath those sexy leggings.

Jesus.

I drag my hand down my face as the two of them drop onto the couch.

The sound of Parker's sobs fills the room, and it tugs at my chest. The urge to rush over there and be the one to comfort her is all-consuming. But I can't.

I'm pretty sure I've already massively overstepped in my role of annoying-big-brother's best friend. But I can't stop myself. I want to help. I want to make things better for her. And damn it, if I'm being honest with myself, I want to be the one to make her smile on her worst day.

"You want coffee, Watson?" I ask, ripping my attention from them and stalking into the kitchen. Pain shoots through my groin, but I ignore it like I have for weeks now.

It's weird as fuck, having women here.

"That would be great. Kodie and Sutton are waiting downstairs. They want to know if you fancy a spin around the rink."

I glance back, and both women are looking at me with tear-stained cheeks and red eyes.

Christ, I don't just have women in my apartment. I have *crying* women in my apartment.

Yeah, I need to get the fuck out of here.

Grabbing my cell from my pocket, I fire off a message to Kodie, letting him know that I'm gonna make his girl a coffee, then I'll be down.

I set the machine going, then head to my bedroom to pull on some clothes.

I'm out the door as soon as I've delivered Casey her coffee. However, I make sure to tell them to call me if they need anything.

I find Kodie with his engine running, waiting just outside the entrance to my building.

"Storm!" a little voice shouts excitedly from the back as I drop inside.

"Hey, little Riv. How's it going?"

"We're going to skate; things are fantastic."

I can't help but chuckle at our little hockey addict.

"What are you drawing?" I ask, looking at her upside-down piece of art.

She lifts it from the makeshift desk of her lap and shows me a drawing of two women and a girl, all kitted up and standing in the middle of an ice rink.

"It's for Parker. I did one before, and she had it on her fridge, but it's gone now." Hearing the sadness in her voice for one of the most important people in her life makes my chest tighten.

"Aw, she'll love that. If you get it finished, maybe you can take it up to her after our session."

"You mean, after I've beaten you," she counters with a fierce look in her eye.

"Yeah, Lil Riv. After you've beaten us."

Kodie puts the car into drive, forcing me to turn back around and pull my seat belt on as a heavy sigh spills from my lips.

"That bad?" Kodie asks, looking over at me with concern written all over his face. It's not something I'm used to seeing from him.

Sure, Kodie and I struck up a friendship when he was first traded to the Vipers last season, but it's only been in the last few months that he's really allowed me into his life. Casey unlocked something in him, and it's only making him a better person and player.

"It's...not great," I say after a moment of hesitation. I'm achingly aware that Sutton is sitting right behind me and probably listening to every word I'm saying. "It doesn't sound like anything is going to be salvageable."

"That sucks. At least insurance will cover it. That could take ages to come through, though."

I bite down on my bottom lip, not wanting to spill what Parker told me earlier. Something tells me that she isn't going to want everyone knowing about her little oversight. She's already beating herself up about it as it is; the last thing she needs is judgment from the rest of us.

She's left herself in a pretty shitty position, but we'll figure it out.

"Casey is pissed at her dad," Kodie suddenly says, snapping me out of my thoughts.

"Uh...why?"

"He's already promised her old apartment to a new social media intern. Parker could have moved in there if this happened two days ago."

"That sucks. It's not Coach's fault, though. It's not like he could have seen this coming. I tried bringing her to you last night," I explain. "She refused point-blank. Wanted me to take her to a hotel."

"The fuck?"

"Daddy," Sutton warns, making him roll his eyes.

"Why didn't she want to come to us?"

"Because it's your family home. Because Casey just moved in. She didn't want to intrude."

"She'd have been more than welcome. She always is."

I smile at my friend and teammate. He never would have offered his home out to anyone a few months ago. Hell, it took me long enough even to get his address, let alone to come for a visit.

"She's thinking of you guys," I reason.

"Parker is a good person."

She's the fucking best, I think, but keep the musing to myself.

"How did you end up involved in all this, anyway? Last we saw, she was scowling at you from across the party, and you were heading out with the guys."

"Yeah, my plans changed. I ended up giving Parker a lift home, and..."

"You changed your mind about going out?" Kodie asks as if it's the most absurd thing he's ever heard.

"Yeah, I wasn't feeling it. I was sticky from her Jack and Coke and tired from our week, so…"

Kodie glances over at me, but he's not buying a single word of it.

"What?" I snap.

"Nothing," he mutters before focusing back on the road as the arena comes into view in the distance.

"You like her," Sutton pipes up, making Kodie snort a laugh.

"Of course—she's my best friend's little sister."

Kodie makes a weird noise.

"She's awesome, and she needs a boyfriend," Sutton continues. "Maybe you can be her boyfriend."

"Can't risk it, Lil Riv. Rett would end me, and then what would the Vipers do?"

She thinks for a moment. "Good point."

"Hey," Kodie says. "We could manage without Storm."

"Possibly, but you must admit that he does bring a lot to the team. I can think of maybe a couple of others who could take his spot. I think Andrey Petrov would probably be my top choice?"

"The fu-dge?" I correct quickly, remembering who I'm talking to.

Kodie's grip on the wheel tightens at the mention of the Bandits winger. A little earlier in the season, Petrov was pictured dancing with Casey on a night out after a game. The next time we have a match-up, I'm pretty sure Kodie is going to make him pay for that little stunt.

"What? I'm just saying," Sutton mutters as if she hasn't just dismissed my presence on the team.

Kodie just laughs.

"You can shut the hell up," I sulk as he pulls into the parking garage and finds his space alongside a few other familiar cars.

"I see this wasn't a special invite, then," I tease as we get out.

"Aw, aren't you feeling like my number one, Storm?" Kodie taunts. "I love all my teammates equally."

Punching him in the arm, I take off, leaving the annoying father and daughter behind me.

I love them dearly, but what is this, National Chirp on Lincoln Storm Day?

The guys' voices hit my ears long before I see them.

Today is a day off, but I'm hardly surprised they all jumped at the chance to get on the ice.

We're having a great season so far, and none of us wants to risk losing the momentum we've gained.

We're going into the new year at the top of the division and second in the Western Conference. It's better than we've achieved for years, and a really good sign about where this season could take us.

Playoffs, here we come.

Images of lifting the Stanley Cup alongside my brothers fill my head.

Fuck, I want it so fucking badly.

It's what we've all worked for since we were little boys with a dream. And we're the closest we've ever come.

Barely five minutes later, we have our skates on, Sutton in full pads and helmet, and we're stepping onto the ice with our captain, Fletcher Ferguson, our goalie Cole Hansley, aka Handsy, our first line defensive pair Calvin Kellar, aka Killer, and Milo Makenna, aka Brit, and our second line defensive rookie, Hayden Monroe, aka Marilyn.

"Happy New Year," Marilyn shouts like the overexcited puppy that he is. "We're gonna win the cup this year."

"Kid, you're not even gonna be able to lift it," Killer teases as he skates past him.

"Screw you, old man. I'm stronger than all of you and you know it."

"Enough, children," Fletch snaps once we've all had a

chance to warm up a little. "Let's set this up. Lil Rivers, you ready to face off?"

"You ready to lose?" Sutton taunts as if she's not talking to a six-foot-three brute of a man.

I fucking love watching her hold her own with these guys. It's funny as hell.

Fletch holds the puck between them, their eyes locked, their chests heaving.

"Come on, Lil Riv, you've got this," I call.

She nods, accepting my encouragement, but other than that, she's solely focused on the task at hand: winning.

Fletch drops the puck and Sutton steals it, shooting off to successfully score our first goal of the morning.

Ignoring the fact that he just failed to save a goal shot by a seven-year-old, Handsy grabs her and lifts her high in the air in celebration. She squeals as he does a victory lap with her before placing her back on center ice to start over again.

We play for thirty minutes before we all hit the bench, sweaty and out of breath, but with smiles on our faces.

"Fuck, I love you guys," Marilyn says, earning himself a slap on the head from Kodie for swearing around Sutton.

"We love you too, Monroe, even if you're like our annoying little kid," Fletch states.

After a bit more banter, talk turns toward our upcoming games—both the Vipers and the Polar Bears, the girls' team Sutton plays for.

She has no idea, but we're all going to watch one of her games soon. We've had it planned for ages, and I'm eager to see her reaction.

She does it for us, so why shouldn't we do the same for her?

Eventually, we say goodbye to the guys.

"Ready to head home?"

"To the crying women on my couch? No, not really." I laugh, although it's a lie. I'm more than ready to check on Parker.

But before that can happen, I need a favor.

"Can we head to a store on the way back?" I ask.

"Sure, which one?""

"Sephora?" I ask hesitantly.

"Sephora?" Kodie echoes. "You need some more blush, Storm?"

"Something like that," I mutter, shaking my head as I contemplate what I'm about to do.

8

———

PARKER

"Move in with us," Casey begs after listening to me relay the horrifying events of the night and my bleak reality.

"I can't, Case. You and Kodie are just starting your life together. It's not fair. He's already on the road half the time."

"You will be, too," she points out.

"Yes, but we'll be together at the same time. If I were with a different team and on a different game schedule, then maybe. I'm not putting myself in the middle of your relationship like that."

She stares at me, silently begging for me to cave. Deep down, though, she knows I'm right.

"What will you do?"

Anxiety twists up my stomach. "I don't know. But I'll figure it out. Someone out there must need a temporary roommate while I get on my feet again."

"I can ask Hailee," Casey says, referring to the Vipers' PR Director. "She always knows everything about everyone."

"Maybe," I muse, hating the idea of already needing help from my new employer before I've even started.

I wanted to walk into the arena on day one in my new

uniform with my head held high, like I could take on the world.

Right now, I don't even have a uniform to fucking wear, let alone be able to hold my head up high.

"I need to do something, though, I can't stay here."

"I'm sure Linc won't mind you staying for a bit. You're both going to be on the road as much as you're here over the next few months."

"Even more reason to get out of his hair. He doesn't need me cramping his style."

"He'll just have to take his conquests elsewhere for a while. He'll cope."

"But he shouldn't have to. This is his home," I reason.

"If he didn't want you here, he wouldn't have brought you here last night."

"Linc's a decent person," I say. He might annoy the shit out of me most of the time, but I can't deny this. "He was doing what he thought was right."

"And making sure you had clothes first thing this morning?"

"Okay, so that went a little above just being nice. It's New Year's Day. How did he even manage it?"

Casey shrugs. "It's probably for the best we don't know. But talk to him about you staying. He might surprise you."

"And what if I don't want to stay here?"

"Parker, I love you, but right now, you don't have much of a choice."

Tears burn my eyes again.

"Talk to Linc and then take things one day at a time. You'll soon be sucked into the excitement of the season, and before you know it, you'll be out apartment hunting and starting over. By the time the boys win the cup, you'll have a whole new life.

"You're already making a name for yourself. Do you know how many female athletic trainers there are in the NHL?"

She doesn't need to ask that question. Of course I know.

It's why I thought I had as much chance of securing this job as finding unicorn shit.

But I did it.

And not only that, I can get through this, too.

Rolling my shoulders back, I push to my feet and march toward the kitchen.

"More coffee?"

"I thought you'd never ask."

As much as I know I need to go out to replace things, when Casey offers to call an Uber, I turn her down.

The thought of stepping outside and pretending everything is okay is just too much.

Tomorrow. I'll do it tomorrow.

She'll be back at work, Linc will be at the rink, and I can start rebuilding before my first shift the day after.

I just need today to wallow.

Casey stays with me, chatting about everything and nothing for hours. We order lunch, and she keeps me distracted from reality until voices filter down to us a few hours later.

Light footsteps race our way, and I smile.

"Parker," Sutton cries before jumping into my lap and wrapping her arms around my shoulders.

The sound of paper crinkling hits my ears as she holds me, and my chest tightens.

"What have you got there?" I ask as she pulls back.

"I made you a new one," Sutton says with a wide, proud smile as she holds her replacement drawing between us. "And I think this one is better."

I stare at it, tears blurring my vision.

"It's beautiful, Sutton," Casey says.

"I love it," I force past the lump in my throat. "Thank you so much."

"Linc said you can put it on the fridge," Sutton informs me.

"Oh, is that right?" I ask, twisting to look over my shoulder just as the man in question places some bags on the kitchen island. "What's all that?"

Linc spins around, his eyes locking on mine.

"I'll show you later," he says, and I swear his cheeks get a little pink.

I hold his gaze for a beat before focusing on the bags.

"Did you go to Sephora?"

"Umm..." Linc hesitates, rubbing the back of his neck.

"We should go," Kodie says to Casey.

"Ow," Sutton complains. "I like Linc's place. Can I see your gym?"

Linc looks from her to Kodie before promising, "Next time you come over, you can totally check out my gym."

Sutton looks a little disappointed, but she doesn't argue.

"I'll call you tomorrow," Casey says as she pulls me in for a hug. "But if you need anything, if you change your mind about moving in with us, call me, yes?"

"Yes, Mom," I tease.

"Oh, and call your parents. It'll only get worse the longer you leave it."

"I know, I will," I promise. The prospect of confessing my failings to my parents fills me with dread.

They're going to be so disappointed. They raised me to be more responsible.

I know they'll help me out if I ask. Dad's hockey career might have been cut short due to injury, but my parents have never struggled for money. He coached after retiring, but two years ago, he decided he was done for good. They downsized their house, and they've pretty much been travelling the world ever since, enjoying the time they have left and the money Dad worked so hard to earn.

I'm beyond happy for them, and I love getting postcards from each place they visit. I need to tell them I'm no longer at my apartment if I want to receive any more.

Casey walks away while I'm deep in thought, and it's not until she speaks again that I come back to myself.

"Look after my girl."

I turn around to see Casey giving Linc the look. She's known him just as long as I have, but they don't have the love-hate relationship we have. I guess it helps that Linc didn't used to team up with her big brother with the sole intention of tormenting her.

I shake my head, refusing to think about those times.

We're not kids anymore. A lot has changed.

Like the fact that you're currently living with him.

There was a time when he showed me another side of himself. A time I've fought so fucking hard to forget. But in only a few hours, it's becoming painfully obvious that it's still there.

Lincoln Storm might be an egotistical, self-absorbed asshole. But he's not just those things. He can also be sweet, supportive, and...as much as I hate to admit it, a good friend.

After another round of goodbyes, Casey, Kodie, and Sutton leave.

The silence that descends is deafening.

"What?" Linc asks, and it's only when his voice hits me that I realize I'm staring at him. "You're looking at me like I'm a stranger."

I think you might be.

"S-sorry. Everything is just...a lot, you know?"

"Yeah," he muses, rubbing the back of his neck again.

It's a move he's done when nervous for as long as I can remember. I also remember thinking it was incredibly hot once upon a time.

Not now, though.

Nope. Not hot at all...

"Did hanging out with Casey help?"

I smile. "Hanging out with Casey always helps. Thank you for calling her. She tried to convince me to move in with them."

"Are you?" Linc asks a little too quickly.

I knew he didn't want me here, but seeing that reaction, that hope that I might be leaving, is like a slap to the face.

"Not if I can help it. Casey suggested talking to Hailee to see if she knows of anyone who needs a roommate."

"If anyone will know, it'll be her. Maybe one of the girls in the front office is looking."

"Yeah, maybe," I muse, hating how much I hate the idea of living with a stranger. What if they have really annoying habits or a dog that barks at night or—

I cut my own thoughts off. I shouldn't be talking myself out of this.

"I can ask around as well, if you want. The sooner you get your own space, the better, right?"

"Uh-huh. Yep. So, what's in the bags?"

"Umm..." He starts rubbing his neck again, and my curiosity builds. "If any of it is wrong, tell me and I can exchange it. Casey gave me a list, but honestly, I had no idea what the fuck I was looking at. Sutton helped a bit, but..." He trails off as I peer into the first bag.

"Linc," I breathe as shock rocks through me.

"Are they right?" he asks nervously as I stare at the bottles.

Bottles of my favorite hair products.

"Yes, they're perfect. Thank you," I say, praying I don't sound like I'm moments away from breaking down.

"There's more," he says, sliding another bag closer.

Inside that one are my face care products and a selection of makeup in my favorite brands.

"The color Casey gave me for the lipstick didn't exist. We spoke to a lady who works there, and she said—"

"That it's been discontinued."

"Y-yeah. She suggested that one as the closest alternative."

A laugh bubbles out of me.

Before I know what I'm doing, I launch myself at him, jumping so I can properly wrap my arms around his shoulders.

"Whoa." He grunts, catching me before I slide down his

body and no doubt crumple into an emotional heap on the floor.

"Who are you and what have you done with Lincoln Storm?" I ask brokenly as I cling to him, my tears embarrassingly soaking into his T-shirt.

He holds me tighter as his chest rumbles with laughter. "I'm pretty sure you're the only one who knows this side of me exists, babe. No other woman has seen it, that's for sure."

His words and the reminder of the past they drag up are like a bucket of ice-cold water thrown over me.

I release him and drop to the floor as if I've been burned.

"Parker?" he asks, confused by the sudden change.

"Thank you so much for this. You don't know how much I appreciate it."

"I've got practice and a strength and conditioning session tomorrow, but I can be done early afternoon if you need company for anything else," he offers.

"I think I'll be fine. I'm just gonna..." I gather up the bags, needing to get as far away from him as I possibly can while inside his apartment. "Hang out in the guest room, get out of your hair. Forget I'm even here. Just...you do you, yeah?"

9

LINCOLN

I t's been hours since Parker disappeared into my guest room. She told me that she was going to get out of my way, and she's certainly done that.

I should be relieved she's allowing me to continue my life as if she's not here, but I'm not.

When Killer messaged in our group chat earlier, asking if we were doing anything tonight, I put them off. Usually, I'd be the first to invite everyone here to hang out and play Xbox. But tonight, it felt wrong.

Parker is suffering, and the last thing she needs is an apartment full of hockey players.

So instead, I hit my home gym for the second time today before falling onto the couch to watch game tape.

Everything is moving in the right direction, but we've still got a long way to go if we're going to keep our place in the league and secure our playoff position.

Hours pass, but eventually, my stomach begins growling, demanding food.

I glance toward my kitchen. Usually, I cook. I'm not the best at it, but I try my best. What I really need is a chef like some of the other guys have, but that means having someone I don't really know here a lot of the time, and to be honest, I'd rather just manage myself.

But tonight, the prospect of cooking is even more unappealing than usual.

Pulling up a delivery app, I scroll through, searching for something that catches my eye.

Unfortunately, nothing healthy or well-balanced does, and I quickly find myself looking at a menu for a Thai place, my mouth watering at the prospect of the flavors it would deliver.

I figure that if we were to share it, it wouldn't be so bad. I push to my feet and pad toward my occupied guest room.

I hesitate when I'm standing in front of the door. Just like before, it isn't fully closed. It feels like an invitation, but I know that it's not. Parker is just used to living alone, I guess.

She doesn't want to speak to me. That's why she's hidden herself in here.

But I've never been one to second-guess my actions, and I don't intend to start now.

Lifting my hand, I knock.

Silence.

"Parker?" I call.

There's movement inside the room, but she doesn't say anything.

"Parker?"

"What?" she huffs.

Well, okay then.

"I was thinking about ordering Thai and wondered if you wanted to join me."

Silence again.

"Can I come in?" I ask. I'm pushing my luck, I know I am, but I can't help it.

She sighs. There's some rustling, and then she finally responds.

"Yes."

A silly rush of excitement goes through me as I push the door open wider and step inside.

I find Parker sitting in the middle of the bed with the covers up to her waist, her cell resting on her lap. But none of that steals my attention. She's wearing the T-shirt again with my name and number on.

Fans—bunnies—wear my jersey every single game, and I barely pay any attention. But Parker pulls on a T-shirt, not even a jersey, and I'm on the verge of losing my shit.

I've always understood the concept of a girl wearing your jersey; I just never really thought it mattered. Seeing her right now, though...it matters.

She isn't even mine, and it matters.

"Did you actually want to talk to me about dinner, or did you just come to gawp?"

"Thai," I blurt. "Did you want any?"

"I could be convinced. Do I get to choose dishes?"

"Yeah," I say, pulling my cell from my pocket and moving closer so I can hand it to her. "Select whatever you like."

I stand awkwardly beside the bed as she scrolls through the menu.

This room has barely changed since she moved into it last night, but it feels different. It smells different. It smells like girl, and somehow, it's more welcoming.

"There," she says, dragging my attention back to her as she holds my cell out for me.

I'm about to take it when what's lit up on her screen catches my eye.

"Are you watching me play?" I ask, a teasing lilt to my voice.

"Oh yeah, I just can't get enough. I'm obsessed with you, Lincoln Storm, and I watch every move you make."

"Alright," I mock. "There's no need for that."

"I'm watching game tape."

I frown. "Why?"

She barks a laugh.

"Fucking hell. Is this what I should expect in the coming

days and weeks? Everyone underestimating me because I've got a fucking vagina?"

"You're working," I mutter, feeling like the world's biggest moron for not putting it together sooner.

"Yeah, asshole. I'm working. And do you know what I've learned?"

Her narrowed, angry eyes hold mine. She's desperate to tell me whatever it is.

"Go on," I encourage.

"You're struggling on the ice. That groin injury you picked up after Thanksgiving hasn't healed properly, has it?"

My chin drops. The need to lie to her surges through me. But what's the point? She knows. She's seen it with her own eyes.

"You're favoring your left side when your right is usually dominant."

"Parker," I warn.

"What was your treatment plan?"

"Do we have to do this right now?"

She tilts her head to the side, her gaze turning a little patronizing. "Do you want to retire early?"

"Wow," I say with a laugh. "Say it like it really is." Absently, my hand lifts to the back of my neck, kneading the tight muscles there.

"What? Would you prefer I fob you off with a half-assed treatment plan that sees you underperforming in games and risking your career?"

"No, of course not."

"Who did your treatment plan, and what was it?" she demands again.

When I still don't say anything, she makes a very accurate guess.

"You didn't tell anyone how bad it was, did you?"

"We'd won five games in a row. We were on the best winning streak in years. I couldn't risk being the reason it ended."

"Lincoln."

"I did what I had to do to ensure I wasn't benched."

"You should have been," Parker states flatly.

There's no point arguing. She's right. Of course she's fucking right. But she needs to learn the stubbornness of the men she's about to start working with.

We have one focus and one focus only: lifting that cup.

We play injured more often than not. We lie about how much it hurts, do our best to cover the evidence, and we grit our teeth and get on with our fucking jobs.

Parker and the rest of the medical team just have to get used to the fact we're going to butt heads on the daily.

"It is what it is," I say with a shrug as I finally lift my cell and place our order. "It'll be here in twenty. Are you going to come out and eat with me?"

"Will you continue to be a pig-headed asshole?"

"Is the sky blue?"

"Fucking hell. I've worked so hard to get this job, and sometimes I can't help but wonder why. You're all going to make my life a million times harder, aren't you?"

"If dealing with us is the worst of it, then I think you'll cope."

"What do you mean?"

I shake my head. "I will make sure that every player on our roster respects the fuck out of you, Parker. But there are so many other men in our world that will have opinions you're not going to like."

"Do you really think I'm not aware of this?" she says, putting her cell to sleep and throwing the covers off.

Unlike last night, my boxers don't show beneath the T-shirt. Instead, I'm greeted with nothing but long, bare legs.

My mouth runs dry, and I make the stupid mistake of trying to swallow.

I cough, choking on nothing but air as she throws her legs off the side of the bed and pushes to stand.

She's only wearing a pair of the panties I chose for her, and

I'll be fucked if I don't want to know which color she picked. But before I get a chance to find out, the fabric of my T-shirt falls around her thighs.

Combing her long, red hair back with her fingers, she twists it up into a knot on the top of her head with one of the hairbands I got for her earlier.

I want to say those were my ideas, but honestly, Sutton really came into her own during that shopping trip. Between Casey's list and Sutton's help, I walked out of Sephora feeling successful. I haven't been told otherwise, so I'm taking it as a win.

Dragging my eyes from her legs, I pause when I get to her chest.

Holy shit, she's not wearing a bra.

My teeth grind, and I swear to God, her nipples harden even more under my attention.

"Linc."

They'll be so pretty.

"Lincoln?"

Rosy pink against her milky skin.

"Storm?"

My eyes jump to hers. "Huh?"

She shakes her head before shoving past me. "The sooner I get out of here the better," she mutters as she stalks out of the room, leaving me standing there with nothing but her sweet scent surrounding me.

By the time I join her in the kitchen, she's got her head in the fridge, searching for something.

"Do you have anything to drink?" she asks without looking back.

"There's soda and juice in there. Water too."

"I meant, a real drink."

"Uh...no. I don't drink at home."

"Of course you don't," she mutters under her breath, her grip on the side of the fridge tightening until her knuckles turn white.

"I try to follow a strict nutrition plan," I explain as she grabs a can of soda and spins around.

"Is that why you ordered Thai?" Cracking the top, she lifts the can to her lips and takes a sip.

I watch her neck ripple as she swallows, and no sooner does she pull it away from her mouth does her tongue sneak out and lick across her top lip.

Goddamn.

"A treat. I think you deserve it, don't you?"

"I think you've already done enough. I'm going to start thinking you want some kind of payment for all of this."

"I don't." Although I'd be lying if I said her words don't inspire some thoughts I really shouldn't be having.

"Good to hear because you won't be getting anything other than my appreciation. Now, tell me about your injury."

"Are we still doing this?"

She nods before taking another sip.

"It's my job to ensure you're in a fit playing state, and right now, I don't believe you are." My mouth opens to argue, but she quickly shuts me down. "Lie to me, Storm. I fucking dare you." Her eyes narrow on mine, and my heart rate picks up speed at the same time my dick jerks in my sweats.

Fuck, Parker's fire always gets me going.

"Your employment doesn't start for another day. Right now, my health is none of your concern."

"Fine," she states, crossing her arms under her tits and pushing them up in the most tempting way.

She'd be so fucking sweet.

"Eyes up here, Storm," she warns firmly.

Doing as I'm told, I hold her intense glare.

"Have it your way, but rest assured, you are going to be the first person on my bed in the training room."

A smirk kicks up the corners of my lips.

"If you want to get me into bed and have your hands on me, Donnelly, all you have to do is ask."

It's a good thing she's nowhere near my knives because, if

she were, I'm pretty sure one would have been flying toward me the second those words left my mouth.

"That is never, ever going to happen."

10

PARKER

I can't knock him. Living with Linc does have its advantages. For example, when he came back from practice yesterday with five new Vipers polo shirts and a zip-up for me so I could turn up this morning actually looking like I belonged.

And it's that little logo sitting above my left breast that I find myself staring at in disbelief just over thirty minutes before I need to be at the arena to start my first day.

I've had four weeks to get used to the idea of having my dream become reality. But now it's here, I don't feel like it's settled in at all.

Puffing out my cheeks, I let out a long, slow breath.

This is it. It's really happening.

"You've got this," I say to myself before pulling on my zip-up and hooking my purse over my shoulder.

Casey finished work early yesterday and swung by to pick me up so we could go shopping and collect my car, which was still sitting in the parking lot of my building. Thankfully, I had a key in my purse; otherwise, it would have been sitting there until I'm able to get into my apartment to see if it was useable or not.

At least I can be a little bit independent now and not rely on everyone else for every little thing.

Linc has been fantastic. Better than I could have ever hoped for. But it's time for me to stand on my own two feet.

He has a job to focus on. Hell, so do I.

With butterflies rioting in my stomach, I make my way to the kitchen to grab a cereal bar I bought yesterday when I did some grocery shopping, and when I open the fridge for a bottle of water, I stop dead in my tracks.

There on the middle shelf is a travel cup with a Post-it note stuck to it.

Good luck today.

Pulling it free, I twist the top and find an iced coffee inside.

Shaking my head, I lift it to my lips and take a sip, too desperate for my morning hit now that it's in my hand.

"Goddamn you, Lincoln Storm," I complain after I swallow.

I slept like shit last night. Not only did I have the stress of rebuilding my life like a boulder in my stomach, but I also had the nerves for today.

Of course, it helps that I know almost every member of the team. I've hung out with them after most home games this season. And I trust what Linc said the other night—he'll make sure that not a single one of them steps out of line. He doesn't have the same kind of control over the other staff, though.

It'll be fine.

No one is going to care you're a woman.

They'll all see you like a professional who is just as capable of doing her job as every man in the league.

With that little pep talk out of the way and my coffee in hand, I head toward the elevator to make this happen.

The drive to the arena passes in a heartbeat. As I pull into the lot I've been instructed to park in, I realize that I don't remember a single second of the journey. Killing the engine, I rest my head back and close my eyes, trying to commit the moment to memory.

You did it, Parker.

You fucking did it.

Pulling my cell from the charger, I find a stream of notifications waiting for me.

> Mom: Good luck today. Go smash it and call
> me later x

My stomach knots even tighter. I still haven't called them.

> Casey: Go and be the baddest bitch in the
> NHL. Make them all cry like little babies. Even
> Kodie. Just don't tell him I said that.

I burst out laughing.

> Rett: Good luck today. But don't do too good
> a job. The cup is ours this year.

I roll my eyes. My brother is so predictable.

He might play for Seattle right now, but his heart belongs to the Vipers. It always has and always will. He'll be stoked if the guys make it all the way. He might not have said anything, but when his contract with the Bandits ends in a few years, I don't doubt that he'll instruct his agent to try to do whatever it takes to get him on the Vipers' roster.

As I'm sitting there, another message comes through.

> Storm: You got this, Little P. See you later

I blow out another breath before putting my cell on do not disturb and slipping it into my purse.

As I approach the arena's main entrance, my entire body trembles with nerves.

But the second I step inside and the familiar scent floods through my nose, I relax.

I've spent almost as much time here as I have in my own home.

From as early as I can remember, I'd be in the stands with Mom and Rett, and it hasn't stopped since. All my life, I've either been supporting the Vipers or playing my own games with Casey by my side.

Fuck, I used to love playing together.

The highs from the wins used to be so incredible. And losing wasn't so bad either because I had my best friend to commiserate with.

"Parker," a friendly female voice calls, and when I look over, I find Esme Clifton, the Vipers' senior HR manager, waiting for me with a smile playing on her lips.

"Hey," I say, making my way over.

"It's so good to finally have you here," she says, sounding genuinely excited.

"It's good to be here."

"I hope you're ready; we've got a full day planned for you."

"Bring it on." I need a distraction right now more than I ever have.

"We're going to head up to my office to finalize paperwork. I'll get you set up with your passes and equipment before handing you off to Jarad Lennon, so he can give you a tour of the facilities and get you settled. Brooke Owens has then requested that you join her to make some content so that she can announce your arrival on socials. If you're still with us at that point, Jarad wants you to join him and Dillion at the team's afternoon practice session before meeting the guys."

"Okay," I breathe, already feeling a little overwhelmed by it all. Especially the social media element.

Sure, I post on my socials, and I'm as addicted as the next person, but I don't have any kind of following. Something tells me that is about to change if the Vipers' social media team is going to get their hands on me.

Am I really ready for this?

The role itself, yes. I've been training for it for years. But everything else that goes with it? I'm not so sure.

"Ready?" she asks.

Forcing a wide smile onto my lips, I nod. "Lead the way."

She chats away about the holidays as we ride the elevator to the fourth floor, where her office is located. I answer questions where necessary, but she mostly talks about returning to New York to see her family for a few days.

As we get closer to her office, I know my time holding things back is coming to an end. I'm going to have to update her about my temporary address change; it probably also needs to go on record that I'm living with one of the players.

"Come in and take a seat," Esme says, holding the door open for me.

"Oh, wow," I breathe as I take in the view across town from her large windows on the other side of the room.

"Stunning, isn't it?" she says as I move closer and just stare out.

"Oh, um..." I startle, taking a step back, embarrassment heating my cheeks.

"It's okay, I might have been here a few years now, but every now and then, I still stand there like that, wondering how I ended up here. Take a moment," she says understandingly as she takes a seat behind her desk and wakes up her computer.

I allow myself ten seconds before I sink into the seat across from her.

"I've moved in with Lincoln Storm," I blurt, needing to get the words out.

Esme pauses, moving her mouse before ripping her eyes from her screen and focusing on me.

"Don't worry, he's already let me know. I've updated your contact details already."

"Oh," I say, deflating a little. "It's only temporary, and I don't actually want to be there. I don't like him very much and

—" I cut myself off when an amused smile spreads across her lips. "Sorry, you don't need to know any of that."

"It's okay." She laughs. "I'm sorry to hear about your apartment. If you need our support with anything, please just ask. We might be a sports franchise, but we're also a family, and you're a part of that now. We look after our own before anything else."

"That's..." Emotion burns up my throat and tickles my nose. "Thank you."

"Anytime. Hailee, our PR Director, is the one who knows everything around here. She's the best one to ask if you need to know anything."

"Funny, you're not the first person to say that."

Esme chuckles. "She'll be glad to know she's got a reputation as a busybody."

"All a part of the job, I guess."

"Okay, so," Esme starts as she scrolls through whatever is on her screen.

"Personal details, emergency contact, ID...all good. Okay, next thing is passes." She pulls her drawer out and retrieves an ID card, sliding it over to me. "This will give you access to everywhere you need in the building. Keep it on you at all times, and if you lose it, you must report it immediately."

"Okay," I say, taking it and studying the awful mug shot gracing the front.

After passing me a holder and lanyard, she moves on to my new laptop and iPad.

After ensuring I can log onto both and am successfully into my email, almost an hour has passed.

A firm knock sounds on the door, and after Esme calls out, another familiar face pokes his head inside.

Jarad Lennon is the Vipers Head Athletic Trainer. He's probably in his fifties, with salt and pepper hair and beard, and glasses that make his eyes look a little larger than I'm sure they are. Along with the General Manager and the team's Head Physician, he was in all my interviews. From the very first moment, I felt like he was on my side. Without knowing, he helped put me at ease right from the very beginning, and it's no different now.

"Are you finished with my new trainer, Es?" Jarad asks.

"Parker, are you happy with everything? Do you have any questions before I set you free?"

I shake my head, thinking for a moment. "No, I think I'm good."

"Okay then. I hope you enjoy the rest of your day, and if you do think of anything, you know where to find me."

"Thank you," I say, standing and clutching my new IT equipment to my chest.

I walk silently beside Jarad as we move toward the elevator that will take us down to where the medical staff offices and training rooms are.

"So we haven't scared you off yet then?" he teases.

"It'll take more than a few hockey players to do that," I shoot back.

"Glad to hear it, Donnelly."

He walks me through everything. I may have been back here numerous times before, but it's good to see it all with fresh eyes. He introduces me to everyone we pass—some of whom I already know, but many I don't. He shows me where my desk is, and my locker for my things. We're about to hit the training room where Dillion is working with some of the guys when an excitable blonde comes racing toward us.

"Parker Donnelly," she announces. "By the end of the day, everyone is going to know your name."

I groan, making Jarad chuckle.

"Good luck with this one," he says. "She tried to convince me to do some viral dance last week. Do I look like a man who dances?"

"Parker, I'm Brooke," she says, holding her hand out that's not clutching a cell. "Content creator. Are you ready to let the world know about your new position?"

"Absolutely not. But something tells me I don't have a choice."

Brooke studies me for a beat, and I worry I may have said the wrong thing.

"Oh, I think I'm going to like you. Although not as much as the guys, of course."

11

LINCOLN

I've been distracted all morning, wondering what Parker is doing. It's ridiculous and not something I've ever experienced before. Usually, my mind is on the game and nothing else. But suddenly, there she is, taking up thoughts in my head when I should be focused on winning our next matchups.

We've got a stretch of three away games that we need to win. We might be sitting pretty right now, but we all know that it can change on the flip of a dime. And having my mind drifting, wondering if she's in the training room rubbing down one of my teammates, isn't going to fucking help.

Stepping out of the shower, I wrap a towel around my waist and walk toward my stall, water dripping from me.

"The fuck was up with you today?" Handsy asks as I drop to my ass, my elbows on my knees and head in my hands.

"Off day," I grunt, hoping it'll be enough to pacify him.

"You sick or something? Because if you are, I don't want you anywhere fucking near me. Hammond isn't ready," he says, mentioning our second-line goalie.

"No, I'm not sick." Just...distracted by a woman I know is walking around here in those goddamn leggings that make her ass look insane.

Every motherfucker inside this building is going to be looking. The knowledge causes something red hot to rise up inside me.

I fear it might be jealousy, but I'm refusing to think about it.

"Right, well, whatever it is, fix it before we hit the ice this afternoon. I've got a meeting with Coach," he says before disappearing from the dressing room. The other guys in here shoot me looks, but none of them dare says anything.

You just need to see her, a little voice says. *Once you know she's here and settled, you'll relax.*

Pushing to my feet, I make quick work of getting dressed, my groin pulling as I step into my shorts. I swear it's been hurting worse ever since she brought it up. She's punishing me, and she doesn't even know it.

With my hair still wet and my athletic shirt sticking to my back, I march out of the dressing room in search of her.

I don't have to look very far, because as I'm approaching the training room, her voice floats down to me.

The hairs on the back of my neck lift as she talks passionately about how grateful she is to be allowed to do a job she loves with a team she's supported all her life.

I pause at the doorway and just listen. I'm hardly surprised when another familiar female voice speaks up. Of course, Brooke has gotten her hands on Parker because having a female athletic trainer is marketing gold. I just hope Parker is ready for what's going to follow it.

Being in the public eye can be incredible. I have met some unbelievable people because of it, and my reach has helped many good causes over the years. But there is a dark side to it all. The trolling, the hate-filled comments. And I hate to even think it, but I have a feeling the ones that are going to be directed at Parker are going to be a lot worse than the kind the guys and I get after a shitty loss.

Despite hearing Parker's voice, my need to see her grows again, and my feet move before I've registered the decision.

A huge breath leaves me as my eyes land on her. She's sitting on the edge of the treatment table, her focus fully on Brooke as she asks another question, completely oblivious that she's got the attention of every other person in the room.

Monroe, Killer, Fletch, and Kodie have all stopped what they were doing to watch and listen.

But as much as I want to bark at them to get back to work, I don't want to announce my presence yet. I just want to watch.

"And what is it that you're looking forward to most in your new role?"

"Being a part of something I love. Being able to support the team, ensure that they're all in peak condition, so that they can bring the cup to LA this year."

"Amen to that," Brooke says.

I don't know what I do—I swear, I don't move—but suddenly, Parker's eyes lift, instantly finding mine.

My hand rises, and like a fucking moron, I give her a little wave.

What the fuck is wrong with you, Storm?

Brooke notices where Parker's attention has wavered to, and she looks over her shoulder.

"You've been a part of the Vipers' family for a long time, haven't you, Parker?"

"I have. My dad played for them for a short time back in the day. He moved us here, and it's where we stayed. My brother and I grew up supporting our home team, and while he might have moved on—" A round of boos sound out, making Parker laugh. "I'm still here supporting my boys every chance I get."

"You're friends with Casey Watson, our coach's daughter, and Kodie River's new girl, is that right?" Brooke asks, shooting Kodie a look. He does everything he can to avoid her questions or demands for content, so she'll take any mention of him as a win.

"Yes, Casey and I grew up together. We also used to play on the same team."

"Ice hockey?"

"Of course. It runs through our blood. She was always better than me, though."

"Ah, yes, of course. And while we don't like talking about our rivals, it would be rude not to point out that you're Everett Donnelly's little sister."

"Please, don't remind me," Parker says with a laugh. "Rett and his best friend Lincoln Storm," she says, her eyes locking with mine again, "spent their formative years tormenting me."

Brooke, following Parker's attention, turns toward me.

"And we have the man in question right here. So, you and our new athletic trainer have history, and it seems, sorry if I've misjudged, that she might have some revenge to take."

I chuckle, rubbing the back of my neck.

"Nah, it's all water under the bridge now. Isn't that right, Little P?"

Parker glowers at me. "I guess that's between me, you, and the table, Storm."

"Okay, cut," Brooke shouts before barking a laugh. "That was gold. Fans are going to eat this up. Brother's best friend. Childhood rival. It's got "going viral" written all over it."

I shake my head, walking deeper into the room. After all, I'm not just here to stalk Parker; I do actually need to put some work in.

"Okay, I'd really love to get some shots of you at work. Do we have any volunteers to—"

"I will," Marilyn pipes up, jumping to his feet faster than any grown-ass man should be able to move after a grueling training session.

In a flash, he's kicked his sneakers off and he's on his front on the bed.

"My hamstring is acting up. It could really use some TLC."

"Motherfucker."

All eyes turn on me as I apparently say that out loud.

"Problem?" Marilyn asks, grinning up at me like a fucking fool.

"Of course not. You know what it's like when Dillion really gets to your muscles?" I ask.

"Yeah..." Marilyn agrees hesitantly.

"Well, you've felt nothing yet."

Honestly, I have no idea if that's true or not. I've offered up my body for Parker to practice on for years, but she's always refused. Equally, she wouldn't have gotten this job if she didn't know what she was doing—and sadly, that means pain.

Marilyn shoots a look at Parker, who rubs her palms together, warming them up.

"I promise to go easy on you."

"Whoa." Marilyn rears back. "I might be a rookie, but I'm no pussy."

"We'll see," Parker says before getting into position and sliding her hands up the back of his thigh.

Every single muscle in my body tenses at the sight of her touching him.

"See, that's nice," Marilyn says.

"Yeah?" Parker asks, something wicked flashing in her eyes. "What about this?"

Marilyn's yelp echoes around the room as Parker finds the sore spot. I swear, his entire body leaves the surface of the table.

Laughter ripples through the air, and he whimpers in pain.

"Aw, was that a little too much for you?" Parker teases, causing more laughter.

Oh yeah, she's going to fit right in here.

"Little bit," Marilyn forces out, tears in his eyes.

"Okay, I'll take it a little softer. We'll get this fixed up in no time."

He relaxes back and we all watch for a few minutes as she lessens her pressure and begins a hypnotic rhythm up and down Marilyn's hamstring.

"This isn't prime-time TV," a deep voice booms around the room. "Get some work done. We're on the ice in two hours," Coach barks before disappearing as fast as he arrived.

"You heard the man," Fletch says, continuing with the stretches he was doing before turning his attention to Parker.

"You good?" Kodie asks when I step up beside him, still watching Parker and Monroe out of the corner of my eye.

"Yeah, of course. Why?"

"You look like you want to be the one up there."

"Being put in that much pain? No, thank you."

"Hmm."

"If you have something to say, Rivers, just spit it out."

"How is living together going?"

"Wait, what was that?" Fletch asks. "Linc is living with someone? A woman?"

I shoot a look over at Parker, but she's too distracted with Monroe to hear us. Something tells me that she doesn't want the entire team to know about her current living arrangements.

"Just helping out a friend. It's nothing like that," I say, narrowing my eyes at Kodie.

He holds his hands up in surrender.

"Whatever you say, man. Just be aware that Fletch and I know what that look means." He points at me, circling his finger around my face.

"What look?"

"Yeah," Fletch muses. "I see it."

"See what?" I demand.

Kodie slaps me on the shoulder. "You'll figure it out. When you do, you know where we are."

"What? What are you talking about?" I shout as he marches from the room.

Fletch continues stretching, laughter rumbling in his chest.

"You're not funny," I mutter before dropping to the mat on the floor.

She might be on the other side of the room, but at no point do I forget she's there. It's not until Jarad calls her away that I can finally fully focus on what I'm doing.

It's becoming more and more obvious that having Parker here is going to be a fucking problem for me.

And it only gets worse a little while later when we all take the ice, and there, standing in front of the player bench, is none other than Parker Donnelly with an iPad in her hand and her eyes on us. It's not unusual; Jarad and Dillion are always watching our performance, looking for injuries and weaknesses.

The problem is that when they turn their attention on me, I don't feel it all the way down to my toes.

12

―――――

PARKER

I love watching ice hockey.

Every game I attend, I'm just as excited for the action as I was the one before.

Nothing changes, and I hope it never does.

But standing on the sidelines, wearing an LA Vipers' team-issued polo shirt with an iPad in my hand and the head athletic trainer standing beside me, having an intellectual conversation about the men shooting around the rink before us, hits in an entirely different way.

I'm a part of it now.

Ice hockey runs through my veins. But now, I'm not just a player. I truly am a part of the family, and I will be forever grateful for this opportunity.

The need to prove myself as a woman in a man's world burns through me. I'm competitive—I always have been. You have to be if you're going to be successful at any sport. But while I might no longer strap on skates or shoot a puck around, the need to be the best I can be hasn't ever left me.

I have worked my ass off to be here, and I'm not going to waste a moment of it, or give anyone even a second to question my skills, knowledge, and ability.

"Storm," Jarad starts, pointing at our first-line winger as he shoots around the back of the goal.

"Favoring his left side when his right is the strongest. I suspect his groin pull from last year hasn't healed properly."

"It has," a deep voice barks from behind me.

I don't need to turn around to know who it belongs to.

Dillion Mitchell, the other assistant athletic trainer, and my new colleague.

I don't know all that much about him. We've only met a handful of times, but while most of the team takes the time to acknowledge me, and chat with me, he never has. Don't get me wrong, I have no issue with him not wanting to talk to me. Just because I'm often at games, and best friends with the head coach's daughter, it doesn't mean I expect any member of the Vipers' organization to know who I am and want to interact. What bothers me is the look in his eye. It's a look that makes me uncomfortable.

I want to ignore it and convince myself that I'm being silly. But I learned a few years ago that I should trust my gut feeling. If I'd done it more then I might not be so jaded when it comes to dating and relationships.

I'm getting better. If I see a red flag now, I'm out that door faster than a winger on a breakaway.

But this isn't a place where I can walk away from bad eggs. I'm going to have to be professional and work with them. I just pray that I'm wrong and he's not going to make my life here harder than it needs to be.

"Okay," I muse, turning to look at him with a calm expression. I really don't want to piss the guy off on day one. "Then he's picked up something recently that isn't being treated correctly. I know how Storm plays and—"

"And you think we don't?" Mitchell snaps, his hackles up like a pit bull about to attack.

"That isn't what Parker is saying," Jarad assures him.

Mitchell's eyes drill into me. He's silent for a second before conceding.

"I'll pull him in after practice and see what's happening."

"No need. Storm is on Parker's list now."

What?

"What?" Mitchell balks. "He's one of our most vital players. He needs more than—"

"Careful," Jarad warns. "It might be Parker's first day, but she is just as qualified and capable of doing this job as we are. It doesn't matter which players are on whose list. All will receive the same high level of treatment they deserve.

"I emailed lists earlier. Most of yours are the same as previously, but I've made a few adjustments." Jarad's tone is firm, not leaving any space for argument.

Mitchell nods, aware that he hasn't got a leg to stand on.

I, however, stand there internally freaking out that my life currently seems to contain a hell of a lot more of Lincoln Storm than I'd like.

At home—his home. In the trainers' room.

My fingers twitch as I think about working on his body. Getting up close and personal.

I can't. It's got disaster written all over it.

My lips part to say something that might get Storm moved back to Mitchell. But then, my eyes find his angry ones a beat before Linc shoots around behind him, clearly struggling with a lingering injury, and I realize that I can't.

Mitchell is the reason Linc is in pain and not playing at his best. I can't allow that to continue.

Jarad continues discussing each player with us, taking notes before he instructs us to attend a meeting after we've met with our athletes after practice.

He leaves us standing by the boards to watch the rest of practice, and the second he's out of sight, I swear the tension ramps up.

It isn't the good kind.

It takes long, painful seconds, but eventually Mitchell speaks.

"Storm is at the top of his game right now."

"He's playing well," I agree, because he is. But he can be better.

I know Linc better than any other guy out there, and I know exactly what he's capable of. Right now, he's not at his peak. He's still really fucking good, sure. But he's been better.

"You're—shit," he hisses, cutting himself off as one of our third-line defensemen trips over his partner and hits the ice hard.

Mitchell takes off to help.

I don't know which trainer's list the guy is on. I leave Mitchell to deal with it as I open the email app on my iPad.

My heart pounds harder the second my eyes land on Jarad's name.

I already know that I'm going to find Lincoln Storm as one of my athletes. But who else am I going to get the pleasure of working on?

"PARKER DONNELLY, WE MEET AGAIN," Linc taunts as he saunters into the trainers' room almost two hours later, his hair still wet from the shower and cheeks flushed from exertion.

We're not alone. Mitchell is already working with one of his players, and we have a few others stretching on the mats, but the second Linc moves closer, his eyes locked on mine, it may as well be just the two of us in here.

"I can't seem to escape you," I mutter.

"And why would you?" he asks, holding his arms out wide. "You might try to hide it, but deep down, we both know that I'm your favorite person."

"Mmm," I mumble, refusing to dignify that with an actual response. "Hop up, Storm. I want to look at that injury you're carrying."

"Still on that, huh?" he asks, although surprisingly, he does as he's told. He even hikes his athletic shorts up high, giving me the access I need to his groin.

"I'm not likely to forget. You might have the others fooled, but I know you, Linc. I know the way you play."

My hands are cold. Usually, I'd rub them together for a little more comfort for my athlete, but today, I don't give him the courtesy.

"I always knew you only came to games to watch me play," he states smugly.

"You wish," I mutter as I reach out and gently run my thumb and forefinger up the adductor muscles on his inner thigh, watching him closely for a reaction.

When he doesn't give me one, he smirks in accomplishment.

"Lie back, Storm. We're only just getting started."

"No problem, Doc."

My teeth grind at his new nickname for me. I should probably be happy about it. It's a hell of a lot better than babe.

It takes me longer than I was hoping for, but eventually, I find the spot that's giving him issues.

"Motherfu—" He abruptly cuts himself off, realizing that I've just proven my point. And not only to him, but also to my colleague, who heard it loud and clear on the other side of the room.

Everything is fine, my ass.

"I don't want to say I told you so, but—"

"Just get it fixed up, Donnelly," Linc demands.

His chest expands as he prepares to embrace what I'm going to unleash on him.

As much as I might want to be rough, I'm not. We need him healed as fast as possible. The Vipers are having a record season so far, and I don't have any intentions of changing that anytime soon.

Other players come and go, but I don't let Linc up for longer than I think he was expecting.

"When you get home, you need to ice this," I tell him firmly when I finally lift my hands from his thigh.

"Yes, Doc," he teases.

"I'm serious. I'm pulling you from morning skate tomorrow, and I'll only let you play if I'm confident you've been looking after it."

"You threatening to bench me, Donnelly?" he asks, his eyes wide with shock.

"You fucking bet I am. You're going to lift that cup this year, Storm, but it won't happen if you don't let this heal. Monroe is waiting for me, but once I've seen him, I'm going to talk to Coach."

"Well, shit," he mutters, combing his still-damp hair back from his brow.

"What?"

"You're even hotter when you're being all dominant."

"Get your head in the game, Storm." I take a step back, his eyes following. "And listen to me. I'm not having any of my athletes putting themselves at risk."

"Okay," he agrees, pushing to sit on the table.

"Okay?" I ask, blinking.

He never agrees with anything I say, so it throws me for a loop.

He chuckles as he jumps to his feet and steps closer.

"Loved having your hands on me, Donnelly. Celebrating your new gig tonight, yeah?"

I roll my eyes.

"Of course. Gotta celebrate working with you assholes on the daily."

I sense Monroe join us before I see him.

"See, Marilyn," Linc says, throwing his arm around the rookie's shoulder. "I think she likes me."

"I just watched the faces you made as she tried fixing up your groin. I beg to differ."

"Give it time. Just give it time."

Ignoring him, I keep my attention focused on my next patient.

"Your shoulder, right?"

Marilyn blinks at me.

"Y-yeah. Right one."

"Great. Face down, then. Let's see what we're working with."

With a wicked grin at Linc, Monroe does as he's told and settles onto my trainer's table.

"Go and ice your groin, Storm," I state when he lingers, watching us.

"Love when you talk dirty to me."

"Get out of here," I demand, feeling Monroe's rumble of laughter as I trace his muscles.

"There," he states. "Old high school injury that flares up every now and then."

Linc's attention lingers a little longer before the heat of his gaze disappears.

"So, you and Storm close?" Monroe asks.

"We grew up together," I say, probably stating the obvious. "I was just the annoying little sister. We've never been able to stand each other."

"Is that right?"

"What are you trying to say?"

"Nothing." He answers too fast, and my brows pinch. "Did you know he ripped Sutherland a new one the other week when he said something about you joining the medical team here?"

"Linc has always been protective of those around him. He'd have done the same for Casey, Reese, or any of the other females on staff."

"If you say so."

I want to ask more, but I find myself biting on the inside of my lips, stopping any words spilling free.

Instead, the conversation turns to other things as I help him stretch out his lateral head.

Before long, the trainers' room empties out. Mitchell thankfully disappears, although he leaves me to tidy up his shit.

I'm bent over, straightening the mats, when a familiar, welcome voice hits my ears.

"Should we be worried about our boys getting injured on purpose just to get the hot new trainer's hands on them?"

I spin around with a wide grin stretched across my face. My best friend is in the doorway, leaning a hip against the doorframe, her arms folded in front of her chest.

"Ready for that Mexican I promised you?"

"Been ready all afternoon," I say, my stomach growling at just the thought of food alone, let alone tacos and margaritas. "Let's go."

I head toward the back of the room, which leads to our offices, and pause when Jarad's voice hits my ears.

"Yes, sir?" I ask, stopping in his doorway.

"Less of the sir, please. It makes me feel old."

"Sorry," I mumble.

He waves me off. "Great work out there today. Your knowledge of our athletes is really going to help make this transition smoother."

"I'll do everything I can to make this as easy as possible."

"I know Mitchell can be a little standoffish. He's feeling threatened by your arrival, I don't think that's a secret. But he'll relax. Just focus on your job. And just know, you can come to me about anything. My door is always open."

"Thank you, si—Jarad. I appreciate that."

"Now go out and celebrate. Things are about to get wild."

Butterflies flutter in my belly. I can't wait to get on the road and sucked in during games.

It's going to be busy and exhausting, but I can't think of anything better right now. It'll push thoughts of my lost home, and the new one I've found myself in, far from my mind.

Arm in arm, Casey and I walk out of the main arena entrance and out into the evening sun toward my car.

After heading to our favorite Mexican, we eat our body weight in our favorite dishes and force ourselves to be sensible by only having two margaritas. It's a school night, after all.

We have the best evening together, and she allows me to forget my worries in a way that no one else can.

But all too soon, I have little choice but to drop her off at her new home before heading to mine.

"The offer is still there to move in with us," she says before getting out of the car, her eyes focused on my face, searching for signs that I'm going to agree.

"I appreciate it, but no. I'm okay where I am for now. After this away stretch, I'll start figuring out my options."

"Okay, well, the offer will still stand."

She leans over the center console to kiss my cheek.

"But in the meantime, give that boy hell, P. He deserves it."

You don't know the half of it...

I watch her go, jealousy trickling through my veins when Kodie pulls the front door open a few seconds before she gets to it as if he was waiting for her, missing her.

One day...

Maybe...

With a wave and a forced smile, I spin out of their driveway and head home.

Home.

Linc's home.

The temptation to drive around for a bit to waste time is strong, but I'm exhausted and my bed is calling.

I park in the garage and get into the elevator in record time. Silently, I count the floors as I climb through the building, trying to distract myself from wondering if Linc will be there. If he'll be entertaining.

I'm not sure what's worse: the thought of having the entire team up there or him being with a woman.

Shoving the unwanted feeling that thought threatens to

drag up, I hitch my purse up higher on my shoulder and step toward the doors.

The second they open into his private hallway, the most incredible scent hits me.

I'm full, but still, my mouth waters.

Making my way toward the kitchen, I try to figure out what it is.

There's tomato, garlic—lots of garlic—and cheese. It smells delicious and drags up an image of Linc standing in his kitchen, wearing an apron and cooking. It's at complete odds with everything I know about my brother's best friend.

All of those thoughts immediately leave my head though as I step around the corner and see him sitting at the dining table with an empty plate in front of him and another full one opposite him. There's a bottle of unopened wine in the middle of the table, and a huge, beautiful bouquet of flowers.

Holy shit, he's on a date. And from the hard, irritated expression on his face, he's not happy about being interrupted.

I'm about to excuse myself when he speaks.

"Where have you been?"

13

———

LINCOLN

I stare at Parker, my entire body tense, my fingers gripping the base of my chair to stop me from getting up and marching toward her and...I don't want to think about what could follow that.

"Where have I been?" she echoes in confusion.

"Yes. Parker. Where have you been?"

"Out with Casey. We went for Mexican. Why? What's— shit, didn't your date turn up?" She balks. As if that's an issue I ever have. And no, not for the reason you're thinking. Women always turn up; I don't date. Ever.

A self-deprecating laugh falls from my lips as I push my chair back and stand.

"Yeah," I muse. "Something like that."

She watches me like a hawk as I round the table and move closer to her, reality still not hitting her.

I feel like a fucking fool.

I did this. I did all of this for her. To celebrate the first day of her new job, to say thank you for noticing what I've managed to hide from all the others and force me to deal with it. But she didn't come.

I have never, ever gone to this much effort for anyone else

before, and she didn't fucking turn up until the food was cold and the evening was over.

Maybe you should have invited her properly, a little voice shouts, but I ignore it.

I did mention it, and really, do I need to invite my roommate to dinner in our own place?

Apparently, I do.

"Linc, what's—" She cuts herself off as I step into her space.

Emotions riot within me as I stare down into her eyes. The worst is the embarrassment. I should let her think I got stood up; it would be better than confessing that I did all of this for her.

But I want her to know. As she said earlier: she knows me. She'll know the significance of my actions.

Shit, I'm not even sure I'm aware.

Was this...did I...did I plan a date?

No. I just wanted to hang out with my roommate, with the girl I grew up with.

We're...friends. Kind of.

"There's a card with the flowers," I state before stepping aside and moving around her.

I'm out of the room and kicking my bedroom door closed before she has a chance to say anything.

As I move, my groin hurts, and I curse myself for not grabbing an ice pack on the way.

I could go back out there, but I refuse to see the moment she figures out what that really was out there.

"Fucking idiot," I mutter as I drag my T-shirt off and stalk toward my bathroom.

I don't need another shower, I had one when I got back, but the need to shut myself in my own little rainfall heaven is too much. It's easier to forget reality when there is nothing but the sound of falling water around you. It's the same with the rain, but there doesn't seem to be much chance of that tonight.

Kicking my pants from my legs, I leave a pile of abandoned

clothes behind me before turning the shower on and stepping under the water long before it's warm enough.

A shudder races through me, but I don't shy away. It's nowhere close to being as bad as an ice bath.

I like the pain, embrace it, and use it to help me focus, to push me forward.

My eyes fall closed as I think about who I'm doing all this for now.

Sure, at the beginning, I played hockey because I loved it. Because I got to hang out with my best friend and have a laugh. I wanted to be like my dad. But as I got older and truly began to understand the legacy he left behind, the more I wanted to do him proud. And that need only got stronger when he passed.

It was too soon. He wasn't ready. We weren't ready. He wasn't even sick, for fuck's sake. But none of that matters because he's no longer here. All that's left is his legacy, and I have every intention of keeping it alive.

He was one of the greats. He won three back-to-back Cup finals and all of the prestigious awards. He held records for years that others have struggled to beat.

Honestly, I can only ever dream of being as good as him. He was incredible.

Regardless of how good I was, he always supported me. He was the best coach a little boy with stars in his eyes could get.

I just hope he's up there somewhere now, looking down on me with his proud smile.

Everything I do is for him, because of him. I just wish he'd gotten to see more.

My heart is in my throat as I think back over times gone by with my dad. Hell, our whole family.

The thought of Parker plucking the card from the flowers and reading the truth is enough to have me hiding in here a little longer.

When my skin is wrinkled, I figure I need to man up and face reality.

Turning the dial, I step out and grab a towel.

After wrapping it around my waist, I pull the bedroom door open, leaving little puddles of water behind me.

"The fuck?" I bark, my heart lurching at the sight of someone sitting on the edge of my bed.

Parker's eyes widen, and she jumps to her feet. "Shit, I'm sorry. I shouted. I thought you heard me."

"Clearly fucking not," I mutter as I rip my eyes away from hers in favor of walking toward my dressing room for a clean pair of boxers.

"I'm sorry." The sincerity in her voice makes my steps falter. I don't look back, though. I can't.

"It's fine. It was a stupid idea anyway."

"No, it wasn't," she says in a rush, moving closer.

Goose bumps prick my skin as I spot her in my periphery. She's close enough to touch me. She won't, though.

"It was so thoughtful. I really appreciate it. I just...I wish I knew. I'm sorry I didn't and messed it up."

"Don't worry about it. Dinner wasn't all that nice, anyway." It's a lie. I pulled out the big guns and made her my specialty, parmesan chicken. I might not be a great cook, but that dish...I nail it every time, even if I do say so myself.

"That can't be true; it smelled amazing."

"Garlic and tomato always smell good," I mutter, forcing myself to continue.

She lingers behind me as I pull out a pair of underwear.

I consider my actions for almost a full second, but I quickly decide that she's the one who invited herself into my room, so screw it.

Her breath catches as my towel hits the floor, leaving me standing before her bare.

I've never been one to be shy about my body. It helps that women throw themselves at me daily and that I'm on more billboards than I'd care to count. But knowing that I'm naked with Parker hits differently from every other woman I've ever been with.

Heat courses through my veins, awareness making my hairs stand on end.

"Linc," she warns.

"What? You invited yourself in here. Just be glad I didn't walk out of the bathroom naked."

I step into my boxers and tug them up my body before spinning to face her.

Her cheeks are rosy, and I swear there's desire in her eyes.

I wonder how long it's been since she saw any action.

"None of your business."

I rear back, blinking at her in surprise. My hand lifts to the back of my neck, massaging my tight muscles.

"What?"

Shit. I didn't mean to say that out loud.

"We don't all sleep with every willing candidate."

"Nor do I. I'm selective."

"How discerning of you."

"I know what you think of me, Parker," I point out. "As you said earlier, you *know* me."

Her eyes immediately drop to my inner thigh. I grit my teeth, trying to convince my body that she's only interested in my adductor.

"How is it feeling?"

"Fine."

"Liar," she hisses.

"Wha—"

"You can try and tell me all you want that it's not hurting, but I watched you walk over here. I *know*, Storm."

"Damn you, Donnelly."

"I'll go and get you some ice."

"You don't have to do that."

"It's the least I can do for screwing up your night."

"You didn't. Eating alone was much more peaceful."

Her mouth opens and closes, but she swallows down whatever comment she wants to make.

Instead, her entire body relaxes and her voice softens. "If you'd have just told me—"

"I thought I had. Clearly, I fucked that up."

"Linc," she starts, but I don't let her continue.

I've been vulnerable enough tonight. And after where my head went in the shower earlier, I'm done. I'm exhausted. I just want to fall into my bed and crash.

"Are you getting ice or not?" I ask a little harsher than I intended.

I've shown her a side of myself tonight that I'm really regretting.

It's only ever happened once before, and the exact same thing happened.

I was shut down and reminded of the person everyone thinks I am.

The player, the life and soul of the party.

The fun one without a care in the world.

If only that were true.

And it just goes to prove that Parker was wrong earlier. She doesn't know me. Not really. She knows Lincoln Storm, LA Vipers' number seven. She doesn't know Linc, the guy who's been there right under her nose since we were just kids.

"Y-yeah. I'll get your ice."

I stand frozen on the spot, watching her go, my head spinning with thoughts and feelings. Most of which I shoved down a long time ago.

Six years ago, to be exact.

Thankfully, Parker returns with an ice pack from my freezer before I make the mistake of losing myself in memories that are best kept in the past.

"Get comfortable," she instructs, jerking her chin in the direction of my bed.

"I've got it, Donnelly," I say, practically snatching it from her.

She watches as I fall onto my bed, pressing the ice pack

against my inner thigh. It's cold—freezing, actually—but I don't react.

"You're not benching me for our next game," I state, my eyes closing as I rest my head back.

"We'll see," she warns.

I don't look as she moves, and my eyes don't open for long minutes after the sound of my door closing fills the room.

But it doesn't matter that she's gone. She's still the only thing I see.

14

PARKER

My eyes are sore and my body is sluggish as I climb up the stairs to the team's private jet the next afternoon.

I stood my ground this morning with Linc and told Jarad, and then Coach, that he wasn't partaking in morning skate, nor is he playing tomorrow night.

Coach didn't look too impressed, but he had no choice but to agree. He needs his best players healthy, and right now, Linc is struggling, even if he won't admit it.

But while I might have won Coach over, the player himself is another issue entirely.

He's pissed. Not that I care. Not about pulling him from a game, at least.

I still feel awful about last night.

I had no idea. Not a single fucking clue that he'd organized anything.

I spent ages lying in bed, trying to remember our conversation in the trainers' room. The only thing I recall him saying was "celebrating tonight?" But I took that as a question about my plans for the night, not an invitation to celebrate with him.

When I think back to the set table, the homemade food, the flowers, the note, I struggle to believe it was real.

Those aren't the actions of the Lincoln Storm I know.

He doesn't buy women flowers. Hell, I don't think he's even bought his mom flowers.

The inside of the airplane is already in chaos. Despite being lost in my memories of the disastrous night before, my eyes are everywhere, taking it all in.

"Parker," a soft voice calls, and when I look over, I find Brooke in the row behind the coaches and a free seat beside her. "I saved you a seat."

My eyes lift to the rows behind her and find them almost full of the team.

I've been around ice hockey players long enough to know the airplane protocols and how seriously they all take their seating positions. I don't dare go back and mess with their pre-game rituals.

However, I also don't really want to be in the middle of the coaches' discussions either. My other option is Mitchell, who's sitting alone on the other side of the aisle.

Hell no.

Good to know no one else wants to sit next to the guy, either.

"Thank you so much," I say, making a decision before someone else can snag the seat.

After placing my carry-on into the overhead bin, I drop into the seat. And holy hell, it is so much better than any airplane seat my ass has ever hit before.

I shouldn't be surprised by the luxury the guys travel in, but I am.

"This is crazy," I breathe as I rest my head back and allow a smile to pull at my lips.

I did it.

I fucking did it.

"Are you ready for your first road games?" Brooke asks.

There's excitement glittering in her eyes, but nowhere as much as I'm feeling.

"Yeah, I think so. I'm pretty sure I packed too much, though," I confess.

"Standard. You'll get used to it. It becomes second nature after a while."

I nod, confident that she's right. I'm going to be spending a significant amount of time on this plane and away from LA in the coming months. I'm buzzing for it. Not only am I getting to do a job I've dreamed of for years, but I'm getting to travel and see new places. It might be early days, but I think I might have made a friend, too.

"It's so good to have a girl to travel with," Brooke muses as a few more players walk down the aisle to find their seats. "Sometimes Hailee joins us, but more often than not, it's me and a plane full of men."

"You and a whole team of ice hockey players. I guess every job has its hardships," I tease.

"You know what happens on a hockey team plane, right?"

I can't contain my smile.

"Oh yeah, I'm aware."

"Best part of every trip," Brooke says as Monroe steps onto the plane and begins walking toward me.

"Donnelly," he says with his signature smile.

"Monroe," I greet. "How's that shoulder?"

"Almost as good as new," Monroe says happily. "You've got the magic touch."

As he says this, there's a grunt of disgust from behind him.

I grit my teeth to stop from saying anything. Mitchell wants attention, but I'm not going to give him any. Neither is Monroe, it seems, when he keeps his eyes on me.

"You've got a good seat here," he continues, a flirtatiousness I'm more than used to in his tone.

"Is that right?"

"Yep," he says with a wink before taking another step

forward and lifting his carry-on above his head into the bin behind me. "If you need anything, I'll be right behind you."

Of course. Rookies at the front, vets at the back.

Without meaning to, my mind wanders to Linc. Where does he sit? He's been a Viper since his rookie year; he might not be classed as a vet yet, but he has to be pretty far back. And that's a good thing; the farther he is from me, the better.

I don't need the next four hours to come complete with his glare.

You're doing the right thing, I remind myself. *Linc will thank you for it in the long run.*

As if I summoned him, he appears at the front of the plane, his face set in the same scowl as earlier.

He was gone before I got up this morning, but I soon found him in the trainers' room where he was told not to get dressed for morning skate. The second the words rolled off Coach's lips, his glare turned on me.

He was embarrassed last night. Pissed off that I'd accidently stood him up. It would have been easy to let it go and allow him to play. But as a professional, whose main focus is his health, I have to do what's right for him, his body, and his future playing career.

He scans the plane as if he's looking for someone, and I hate myself for sinking down a little in the hope he won't see me. It's pointless—not even a second later, he finds me.

His eyes narrow and his jaw tics.

Yeah, he's really pissed.

He also looks hot as fuck.

Forcing myself to ignore that second observation, I smile at him before dropping my gaze to the back of the seat in front of me.

Monroe lingers as Linc moves closer. I don't need to be looking to know he's closing the space between us. I feel it. The air gets thicker, making it harder to breathe.

"Good to see he's taken the news well," Monroe teases.

"Shut the fuck up, Marilyn," Linc barks. "Sit the fuck down and stop flirting with our trainer."

"Someone's feeling extra sensitive today," Monroe taunts, although when I glance back, I notice he's stepped out of the aisle and out of Linc's way.

Linc glares at the rookie. But Monroe being Monroe, he just shakes it off and smiles back.

"I'd go and rest that leg, if I were you," I state, hoping to get him to move on. I've had more than enough of his surly ass today.

I spent almost the entirety of morning skate working on him. He barely said a word to me, and those he did were barbed and full of frustration. Somehow, though, the silence was worse. It allowed my mind to wander, to drift back to last night and all the sweet things he'd done for me.

No guy has ever bought me flowers before, let alone gone to the effort of writing a handwritten note. And the home-cooked dinner. As disappointed as I am that I missed the invitation, I'm also relieved. I don't need to be around that side of Linc. It's dangerous.

I'm better off remembering that he's an arrogant manwhore who doesn't care about anything but the game.

There was a time I allowed myself to see past that and let my fantasies run away with me. But I'm not that naive eighteen-year-old anymore. Instead, I'm an almost-twenty-four-year-old cynic who knows finding "the one" is reserved for only a few special people. The rest of us are destined to spend our lives searching and forever failing.

With one more silent glare, Linc continues toward his seat.

Don't look back. Don't look back.

Squeezing my eyes closed, I chant that over and over.

Nothing good can come from watching his ass as he walks down the aisle.

"Are you okay?" Brooke asks quietly.

Her attention makes the right side of my face burn, but I don't respond immediately.

I count to five, and when I'm confident that I can keep my attention focused forward, I open my eyes and smile.

"Yeah, of course. I've been dealing with Linc almost my whole life. I know how to handle him."

An amused scoff comes from the other side of the aisle, and this time, I can't stop myself. My head whips around to stare at Mitchell.

"Is there something you'd like to say?" I bark, my hackles rising.

I fucking hate this guy.

"Who, me?" he asks innocently. "Nope."

"Ignore him," Brooke urges, and I do, because I don't have the energy to spar with the asshole.

The last few players arrive and quickly take their seats. Both Fletch and Kodie stop beside me for a quick hello. But before long, the flight attendants are locking the doors and giving the signal that the guys have been waiting for.

Movement erupts behind our heads, and I can't help but smile as I think about the amount of skin that's about to be on display.

"Best job ever," Brooke giggles beside me.

I jump when a pair of pants land in the aisle next to me, and I make the stupid move of turning around.

Oh, holy hell.

Inches upon inches of toned muscle, tanned skin, and tight boxers greet me.

But while my eyes scan the bodies, it's not until they find one that they linger.

I recognize him instantly. And it's not just because of his ink that I've seen more than enough times over the years, or because I had my hands on him less than six hours ago.

I know I should turn back around, but I can't. Much like last night when he walked out of the bathroom in only a towel, my eyes are glued to him.

You're his trainer.

Be professional, Parker.

The second I spot the hourglass on his arm, my breath catches, and I look up.

Our eyes collide, and that familiar electricity crackles between us.

He makes a show of opening his pants and letting them drop to his ankles, but I keep my eyes on his face.

The second the arrogant motherfucker blows a kiss, I twist back into my seat and cross my arms over my chest, silently chastising myself for being so weak.

"Did you want to talk about it?" Brooke asks.

"Nothing to talk about," I lie, instantly feeling bad about it.

I might only be on day two, but Brooke has been nothing but friendly and supportive.

I haven't even spoken to Casey about this. Whatever this is.

"Okay," she says lightly, although I doubt she believes a word of it. "The offer is there, though. If you need it. Us girls have to stick together."

After a few more minutes, the guys settle back into their seats, the flight attendants do their safety demonstrations, and we're taxiing toward the runway.

The young female flight attendant makes her way down the aisle, checking for seat belts, and pauses the second she gets to me.

"Welcome aboard," she says, holding her hand out for me to shake. "I'm Leah, one of the team's crew." Her smile is friendly, and there's a fun air about her that instantly pulls me in. Her skin is dark and beautiful, her hair has been artfully styled away from her face, and her makeup is flawless. And her curves...damn. I bet the guys love flying with her taking care of them.

"Hey, I'm Parker. The team's newest athletic trainer."

Her smile grows. "I was stoked when I saw the post

announcing your new position. Congrats. Freaking love it when we sneak our way into a man's world. We should go out and celebrate tonight."

"Yesss," Brooke agrees happily.

"Uh..." I hesitate, unsure of the rules while we're on the road.

"It's perfect. The guys will be having an early night ready for the game tomorrow. We won't have to worry about bumping into them."

"I should also be doing the same."

"We won't stay out late," Brooke assures me. "Some food. Some cocktails. You deserve it for putting up with Storm today."

"Uh oh, getting on the wrong side of the players already?" Leah teases.

"Only Storm," Brooke explains for me. "But from the sounds of it, she's been on his wrong side for years."

I can't help but groan.

"Sounds like there's a story there," Leah says, curiosity burning in her eyes. "Listen, I've got work to do. But I'll message you when we land and make a plan," she says to Brooke before making her way to the back of the plane.

15

LINCOLN

"You're driving me crazy. Go and find a bunny or something to blow off some steam," Kodie says as I pace the length of our room.

"I don't want a bunny," I mutter.

Out of the corner of my eye, I see him sit upright.

"Are you sick?" he asks in a teasing tone.

"No, I'm just—"

"Pissed?"

Finally, I pause, my eyes locked on the wall ahead as my heart continues to thump heavily in my chest and the knot in my stomach tightens.

It's been the same since last night. Since I sat at my own dining room table with the dinner I painstakingly made in front of me. Alone.

I thought that I'd wake up this morning, forget all about the whole embarrassing event, and move on.

But I woke up with images of Parker on repeat in my head, and mortifyingly, a raging boner that I had no choice but to do something about.

And when I came...yeah, it was to an image of her laid out on my dining table as if she was going to be my next meal.

Heat surges through me now just from the memory alone.

It was nothing more than a fantasy, but it's fucking me up.

The last thing I wanted to do was see her at the arena this morning. I knew without doubt that I'd end up on her table; I just didn't think she'd have had me benched before that even happened.

I get it. I've been playing injured, lying to Lennon and Mitchell. I'll only hurt myself more in the long run, but I told myself that if I can just get through the season, I'll have the summer to rehab it, and everything will be good. It was a solid plan. I just had to hide the pain. It was working. Until she walked in.

Now I'm missing practice and our next game.

I'm angry at her, but if I'm being honest, I'm mostly angry with myself. And worst of all, I know that Dad would be ashamed of me.

If we weren't playing our best season for decades, then I might have gone about it all differently. But that's not the case. There are still a lot of games to play, but right now, we're on track for the playoffs, and I refuse to do anything to lessen our chances.

I want it.

I want it so fucking badly.

"Yeah, I'm fucking pissed," I hiss, finally letting it out.

He questioned me more than once on the flight here, but I kept my lips shut and pretended to sleep. I'm pretty sure he knew I didn't sleep a wink. How could I when Parker was only a few rows away? What made it even worse was when Marilyn stood in the aisle and spent a good thirty minutes flirting with her. The need to go up there and drag his ass back was all-consuming. I fucking couldn't, though.

Not only is she Rett's little sister, but she's now my trainer.

Off-limits has never been so tempting.

"I know it doesn't feel like it right now, but you know she's doing the same thing. Really, you should be pissed that Lennon or Mitchell hasn't benched you already."

"They didn't know I was carrying this."

Kodie rolls his eyes.

"Don't sit there trying to be the big man. You know for a fact that you'd do the same thing. We're having our best season in forever. We need me."

"We need you healthy. We'll cope for a couple of games without you if it means we get the rest of the season with you in your best form."

He's right, but it doesn't lessen my anger at all.

"Parker really gets under your skin, doesn't she?" he asks, pulling his cell from his pocket before smiling at the screen. No doubt it's Casey, and he's going to request I leave the room any minute so they can have some time alone.

Of course, I don't mind. The two of them are cute as fuck, and I've never seen Kodie happier. But there's a selfish part of me that doesn't want to share him tonight.

There's also the risk of what I'll do when I leave this room.

I may not know where hers is, but it wouldn't take too much detective work to figure it out. And unlike us, she'll have a room to herself.

To do what in, Storm?

I shake my head at my stupid thoughts.

"She's always been annoying," I finally say, dragging his attention back to me.

He studies me for a beat. "That wasn't what I meant," he mutters. "It's okay to admit you like her."

My chin drops. "I don't like her. That's the whole issue here. I'm proud of her for securing this job, but I'm not all that pleased with the fact that she's now on my ass practically twenty-four-seven, watching for every twitch and limp."

"Maybe you shouldn't have invited her to live with you," he points out.

No, I probably shouldn't have. But it's a bit fucking late.

"Her building was burning. Her apartment...what else could I have done?"

"Brought her to us."

"She didn't want me to," I argue, much to his amusement, if his quirked brow is anything to go by.

"And since when did you start listening to what people tell you?"

My lips part to argue, but I quickly find that I don't have a response.

He's right.

I could have ignored her and taken her to Casey that night. Hell, I could have even done what she suggested and taken her to a hotel. But I couldn't. The only place I wanted to take her was my place, even if I knew she would drive me to the brink of insanity. Not only is she a part of my professional life, but she's also a huge part of my personal life. And...I like it more than I'm willing to admit to anyone.

"It was New Year's Eve."

"Uh huh," he agrees as he taps out a message.

"I'm...uh...gonna go for a walk. Give you some time with Casey."

He stills before looking up.

"You don't have to do that, man."

"It's fine. Honestly. I could use some fresh air. Maybe it'll give me some clarity."

Last year, I felt like I had everything under control. Now, only a few days into the new year and everything seems to be spiraling already. It's not the start I wanted.

Stuffing my feet into my sneakers, I pocket my cell, AirPods, and hotel key card before stalking toward the door.

"Message me when it's clear to return. I have no intentions of walking in on you jerking off again."

"Don't worry, it wasn't my idea of a good time either."

I glance over my shoulder before I pull the hotel room door open to find Kodie completely distracted by his cell, or more specifically, the woman on the other end of it.

I'm happy for them, I am. But there's something else there, too. Something I can't quite put my finger on.

I inhale a deep breath as I step out into the hallway, but it's too small, too restrictive. I need to move and be free.

Usually, when I'm feeling antsy like this, I'd go for a run, but I'm pretty sure that'd end with me spending even more time on Parker's torture table.

I'm not sure why that thought excites me. I should be running in the opposite direction, not wondering how her hands would feel on more parts of my body.

Shaking my head, I force myself to focus on something else as I pop my AirPods in and hit play on an exercise playlist as I walk toward the elevator.

With my cap pulled low, I exit the hotel to a chilly Texas evening.

A shiver races through me, making me wish I'd put a coat on. But not wanting to go back up and interrupt anything, I focus on moving. If I walk fast enough, I'll warm up in a few blocks.

I WALK FOR HOURS, lost in a million different thoughts, from work to family and everything in between. But no matter where my mind goes, somehow it always drifts back to her.

Memories of times gone by that I've forced to the dark depths of my mind begin to emerge. They're dangerous and lead me down a road I told myself I'd never venture again. But I can't help it.

Kodie was right. She is firmly under my skin.

What he doesn't know is that she always has been.

By the time I head back toward the hotel, the streets are almost deserted. There are a few drunken people spilling out of clubs and bars, but it's nothing like being at home. And thankfully, everyone is either too drunk or distracted to pay much attention to me.

Kodie messaged me hours ago, letting me know that it was

safe to return. But even that didn't have me turning around to find my bed.

If I'm not playing tomorrow, what's the point?

Honestly, I'm not even sure why I'm here. They might as well have left me at home, for all the help I'm going to be.

My heart aches and my muscles are lagging as I shuffle through to the hotel foyer. I'm freezing but numb enough to ignore it.

There are a couple of people loitering around, but no one pays me any mind as I make my way to the elevator. I've just pressed the call button when a familiar giggle hits my ears.

Spinning around, my eyes widen when I see Parker and Brooke stumbling into the hotel with hot dogs in one hand and takeout coffee cups in the other. Both have wide, genuine smiles on their faces. They're dressed as if they've been in a club, only Parker isn't wearing any shoes. On closer inspection, I find them in a carrier bag hanging from her wrist.

They don't see me as they get closer, too lost in whatever they're talking about.

"I can't believe you turned him down," Brooke shouts. "He was so fucking hot."

My entire body tenses.

"Then you could have had him. Not my type."

"Girl, you need to have a word with yourself if fine isn't your type."

"He was an athlete," Parker reasons.

"So? What's wrong with having a hot night with an athlete?" Brooke finally looks up, her glassy eyes finding mine.

"Yeah, what is so wrong with having a hot night with an athlete?" I ask, waiting for the moment a drunk Parker recognizes my voice. And I'm so glad I did, because her reaction is everything I needed tonight.

16

PARKER

Everything is great, until *his* voice rocks through me.

Lincoln Storm. The man who's been a constant in my thoughts recently. Of fucking course he's in the hotel foyer, looking like the hot ice hockey god that he is.

Images I don't want erupt in my head as I stare at him, seeing him not as the man and professional athlete he is today, but the young man with stars in his eyes he was six years ago.

It takes a few seconds for my slightly buzzed and exhausted brain to catch up with me.

"Shouldn't you be in bed?" I snap.

His eyes run down the length of me, taking in my fitted little black dress. It was an emergency purchase the other day in case of an impromptu night out like this. Honestly, I didn't think I'd get a chance to wear it, but I'm glad I did. I felt like my old self tonight, getting dolled up and going out.

Brooke and Leah are the best.

We started our night with tacos and margs—the only way to start a girls' night, in my opinion. And then we hit up a club. Leah knew the bouncers, and we were allowed straight in and then directed to the VIP section, where we found a football team to hang out with.

113

I've only had a few drinks. I have work tomorrow, so I cut myself off earlier than the other two. But it didn't matter. I didn't need to be wasted to have the time of my life with them.

I may have only met Leah today, and known Brooke for a short time, but we all connected in a way I often don't with other girls.

I can't remember the last time I laughed until my throat was sore and my stomach hurt with anyone but Casey. It felt so fucking good, even if a little guilt lingers because my best friend didn't get to experience it with me.

My feet ache, and my muscles are tired and ready for bed. It's late, and I need to call it a night so I can be fresh for the game tomorrow, so we dropped Leah off at a hotel a few blocks away before promising to catch up with her tomorrow.

Linc shrugs one shoulder but doesn't speak until his eyes meet my narrowed ones.

"What's the point? It's not like I'm going to be any use to anyone tomorrow."

His accusation isn't lost on me, but I don't have the energy to spar with him. Now that we're back, the only thing I can think about is stripping out of my dress and falling into bed.

"Your team needs you, Storm. Even if it is support from the bench while you recover."

Thankfully, the elevator doors open before he can respond, and Brooke and I race forward.

She pushes the button for her floor as Linc joins us and presses the one for the floor above.

We ride in silence, the air thick around us, and it doesn't help that Brooke stares at me the entire time as if she's hoping I'll do something.

I'm not sure what she's expecting, but she's going to be disappointed. After the death glares I've received from our first-line winger all day, the last thing I want to do is hang around and have a conversation with him.

Come on, I silently beg, desperate to get out of this elevator.

When the car finally stops and the doors open, Linc steps out.

"It's okay, I'm right here," Brooke says, pointing to a door just a little farther down.

She taps her key to the panel and opens the door as Linc holds the elevator doors open so he can see she's safe.

How very gentlemanly of him.

"I'm not a total asshole, you know," he mutters after Brooke waves and lets her door click closed.

"U-uh..." I stutter, not realizing I said that out loud. Maybe I'm drunker than I thought.

"What floor?" he asks, ignoring my previous comment.

"Same as you," I confess quietly. Why I couldn't have been next door to Brooke, I have no idea. Maybe I should have pretended I was, just so we didn't have to be stuck together in this enclosed space for the next two minutes.

"Okay then," he says, jabbing his finger into the door closed button repeatedly.

The second they slide together, I take a deep breath, praying it'll be enough because something tells me all the air is about to be sucked right out of this car.

The elevator jolts as it continues its ascent.

Silent seconds pass. If it weren't for Linc's stare burning the side of my body, I'd think he didn't care.

But it seems that he can't take his eyes off me, and that does things to my insides that it really shouldn't.

"How much have you had to drink?"

"Not enough to forget this exchange in the morning."

"Huh."

"What?" I snap.

"Nothing."

Fired up by his attitude all day, and with a little extra confidence thanks to the cocktails tonight, I step a little closer.

"If you've got something to say, Storm, I suggest you just—"

The elevator dings and the doors open.

"I don't have anything to say, Donnelly," he says a beat before he presses his hand to the small of my back and gives me a gentle shove to get me moving. "What number?"

"Excuse me?" I balk as my feet hit the carpet. I very nearly let out a loud sigh. My feet really are hurting.

"What is your room number?"

"I'm more than capable of getting myself to my room. I don't need you to protect me. I've never needed you."

His hand slips away as those final words erupt. I didn't mean to say them, but it's too late; they're in the universe now.

"No, I got that memo."

"Number?" he demands again.

"Twelve-twenty-two."

"Of course," he mutters under his breath as we continue down the hallway.

"What does that mean?" I ask.

"It means the universe is fucking with me, that's all."

"What—"

"Here you go," he says, stopping outside my room.

I glance at the number and then at the keypad before my eyes finally land on my purse hanging over my shoulder.

"Fuck's sake. Hold these," I demand, thrusting my cup and hot dog at him. But he doesn't move an inch. Well, apart from his brows, which shoot up. "Please?"

With an unnecessarily dramatic eyeroll, he takes my late-night treats, allowing me to dive into my purse for my key.

Once I have it, I tap it to the panel and push the door open. Spinning around, I almost knock the cup clean out of his hand because he's followed me in as if I've invited him.

"What are you doing?" I cry.

"Uh...bringing these in?" he says, looking between the cup and hot dog with his brows pinched.

"I'm more than capable of handling it from here."

Dropping my purse at my feet, I hold my hands out to take everything back, so he has no excuse to stay.

"You're bleeding."

"I'm what?"

"Your foot, Parker. You're bleeding. There's fucking loads of it."

Suddenly, he's storming past me, and I have to stand and watch as the door swings closed, leaving us alone in my hotel room.

One second, I'm standing there, apparently bleeding all over the carpet, and the next, my feet are leaving the floor and I'm being carried into the bathroom.

"Linc, get the hell off me." I wriggle and kick, but he's too strong.

Twisting me in his hold, he sits me on the counter before dropping to his knees before me. The sight makes my head spin, but all of that confusion is forgotten when my eyes lock on my foot.

"Oh fuck," I gasp, watching as blood drips to the floor. He wasn't joking; it really is bleeding.

I watch, enthralled, as he takes my foot in his hands and carefully inspects it.

"I think you might have some glass in it," he explains.

"I didn't walk far. It's probably just a—" His determined eyes find mine, and my words die on my lips.

"I'm going to call for a first-aid kit. If I can't get it out, then—"

"Just get it out. I'm not going to the ER."

He quirks one brow but chooses not to argue. I fear that if he can't get the glass out, I might not have a leg to stand on, figuratively and metaphorically.

"Don't move," he demands before pushing to his feet and marching from the room.

"Where the fuck am I going to go?" I mutter to myself before his voice fills the hotel room as he demands to have a first-aid kit brought up immediately.

"Don't you think this is all a bit overdramatic?" I ask when he returns. His eyes drop to the puddle I've no doubt made on the floor before running up the length of my bare leg, and all the way to my face.

My blood turns to lava at the possessive and protective look in his eyes, and it takes everything in me not to squirm on the counter.

It's Lincoln Storm. We don't want him, I silently remind my body.

It doesn't matter how long it's been. He isn't the one to end our dry spell.

"No, Donnelly. I don't think I'm being overdramatic. I'm also not leaving until this is patched up, so don't even try it."

I tilt my head to the side in an attempt to look innocent, because the thought of demanding he leave so that I can deal with this alone never crossed my mind…

"You want to tell me off, don't you?" I ask, hating that judgmental look in his eyes.

He remains silent.

"Go on, say what you've got to say."

He shakes his head, as if he needs to clear his thoughts.

"I'm not going to tell you off," he states.

"But," I urge.

"But…I fucking hate that you've been out and got hurt." The second the words are out, he slams his lips shut.

My fuzzy brain works overtime, trying to decipher what he means, as he holds a tissue against my foot to catch the blood.

"Because I'm Rett's little sister?" I ask quietly.

Linc being protective isn't new. He and Rett used to be overbearing nightmares when I was growing up. Things have been different in the last few years, and I'm not sure how I feel going back to having him watch over my every move.

He clears his throat. "Yeah. It's my job to make sure you're safe, especially now that he's out of town."

"Hmm."

Thankfully, a knock sounds out, and in a flash, Linc is on his feet and racing toward the door.

When he returns, he's got a first-aid kit in his hand and determination in his eyes.

"You know, we could just call Eddie," I say, mentioning the team doctor.

17

LINCOLN

The thought of someone else touching her—seeing her — right now sends a wave of something hot and unwelcome racing through me.

I grit my teeth as I lower myself back to the bathroom floor beside the little puddle of blood she's created.

Keeping my eyes focused on the first-aid box, I flip it open and rummage through to find what I need.

"Or anyone more qualified to be digging around in my flesh," Parker continues, pushing the knife a little deeper.

"I've got it," I mutter, my voice sharper than I was hoping for. "Just...let me fix you up."

Wisely, she keeps her mouth shut as I rip open a wipe and begin cleaning her up so I can get a better look at the situation.

It soon becomes clear that I was right: she's got glass in her foot.

The need to chastise her for being thoughtless enough to walk around the city barefoot is almost too much to deny, but somehow, I manage to keep it inside.

I'm in a great position to be kicked in the face here, and I'm already carrying one more injury than I'd like right now.

"Do you have any tweezers?" I ask when I fail at moving the shard, so I can grab it.

"In my toiletry bag," she says, nodding toward a floral bag on the other end of the counter.

Walking over, I open it up and instantly feel like I'm violating her privacy when I'm greeted with tampons.

I still, and she giggles behind me.

"Problem?" Parker asks, sounding way too amused for my liking.

Look, I love women. I think they're fucking incredible, and their bodies...mind-blowing. But seeing as I'm a fuck-it-and-chuck-it kind of guy, I've never really experienced periods or everything that comes with it. I was already at college when my sister, Nova, hit that part of her life, and I escaped it there, too. However, I am more than familiar with her hormonal mood swings.

Suddenly, the need to know more surges through me. When is Parker due? What symptoms does she get and what does she like to do to make herself feel better? Hot water bottle? Chocolate? Snuggle in bed with trashy TV?

I shake my head, wondering where the hell that came from. I've certainly never considered it with any other woman I've spent time with.

Why does it suddenly matter?

Because it's Parker.

Tweezers.

I came here for tweezers.

Without responding, I rummage through the sanitary products, on a mission to find what I came here for.

The second I locate them, I pull them free and return to my previous position, kneeling at Parker's dangling feet.

I can't lie, I've thought about being here numerous times over the years, although there were never bloody feet and first-aid kits involved.

Thoughtlessly, my eyes drift up her calf before continuing up her thigh.

Her dress is short and stops just an inch before I'd like it to.

What color are her panties?

"Lincoln," she snaps, dragging me back to the moment. "If you can't finish the job, go and find someone who will."

"I always finish the job, Parker," I state before getting back to the task at hand.

"Ow, fuck," Parker squeals as I pull the glass free.

"Christ. Didn't that hurt to walk on?" I ask, staring at the bloody shard that's a lot bigger than I was expecting.

"Why the hell do you think I was limping?" she quips.

Shaking my head at her, I place the glass on a Kleenex before cleaning the wound again and bandaging her up.

"You're going to feel that in the morning."

"Wonderful," she mutters as I clean up.

Once I have everything put away, I sit back on my haunches and stare up at her.

Her fingers are curled around the edge of the counter, her knuckles white with her tight grip.

Once again, my attention shifts to her thighs; only with my new position, I can see all the way.

Black.

They're black.

"You can leave now," she snaps, ensuring my attention jumps to her face.

She's exhausted.

Any joy from earlier has drained from her now. Her eyes are heavy; her shoulders slumped.

"I'm not leaving you sitting up there."

"I'm more than capable of looking after myself," she argues, earning her an "oh really" look from me. "I stood on one piece of glass accidentally. I'm not a child who needs putting to bed, Linc. I'm a fully grown adult who, before this week, lived alone without drama."

"What if I like looking after you?" I blurt before I can think better of it.

"Then you need to have a good word with yourself because I don't need or want it."

Her words sting, but I refuse to let her see that.

"Please just let me help you to bed, then I'll go."

"I need to take my makeup off."

Looking back toward her toiletries, I spot a packet of face wipes and quickly grab them.

"Here. Do your thing."

She stares at them before glaring up at me.

"You're a pain in my ass, Storm."

"I think the words you're looking for are thank you."

"Mmm," she hums as she wipes her face.

"Anything else?"

"Everything else."

I glance back at all the products I've never heard of.

"I need to double cleanse, then serum and—"

"Okay, okay," I say digging out each bottle and watching as she meticulously works her way through each one.

"Teeth?" I finally ask, locating her toothbrush and toothpaste when it looks like her routine might be coming to an end.

She nods, and after helping her slide closer to the sink, I stand in the doorway, watching like a creep.

The second she's done, I hand her a towel to wipe her mouth before lifting her from the counter.

"This isn't necessary," she argues, wriggling in my hold.

"You'd rather hop to bed?" I ask with a laugh.

"Do you have to look so smug?" she sulks.

"Smug? I was going for sexy."

"Sorry to burst your bubble."

"Pajamas?" I ask once I've placed her on the edge of the bed.

Her eyes shoot toward her suitcase, which is at least double the size of mine for this short trip.

"I can take it from here," she assures me.

I want to argue, but I figure I've probably already overstayed my welcome. Not that I'm sure I was ever really welcome in the first place.

Reluctantly, I take a step back.

"Okay," I concede. "But message if you need anything. I'm not far away."

"I'll be fine."

With a nod, and one final look at her, I spin around and move toward the door.

She shuffles around behind me, but I keep my focus ahead and try not to think about what she's doing.

I have my fingers wrapped around the handle when her voice hits my ears and the hairs on the back of my neck stand on end.

"Linc?" she asks quietly.

"Yeah?"

"Could you...um..."

At her hesitation, I spin around and find her with her back to me.

"Could you unzip me?"

A heavy breath rushes past my lips as I think about undressing her.

"Of course," I say, hoping like hell it doesn't sound as enthusiastic as I feel.

Stalking forward, I stop just a beat from her body, close enough that her heat burns down my front and her sweet scent fills my nose.

I went out earlier to get some fresh air, but I think deep down, what I really needed was this.

Reaching out, I pinch the zipper between my thumb and forefinger and begin pulling it down.

The sound fills the air, and I pray it's loud enough to hide my increased breathing.

Inch after inch of pale skin appears before me.

She isn't wearing a bra.

Unable to stop myself, I let my finger slip behind the fabric, allowing my knuckle to graze her skin.

The second we connect, she shudders and goose bumps erupt across her skin.

I take in every mole and freckle I discover until I hit the bottom, right above her ass.

"Thank you," she whispers, her breathing almost as labored as mine.

"I'll undress you any time, Donnelly. All you need to do is ask."

"Goodnight, Storm."

At the dismissal, I take a step back.

"And...thank you."

A wide smile pulls at my lips.

"You're welcome, Little P. If either your foot or your body needs redressing in the morning, you just let me know."

She chuckles but doesn't say anything, and this time, when I walk away, I do so backward so I can continue getting my fill of her.

My breath catches when she drops her dress. The top half falls, but sadly, it catches on her hips, so I don't get a shot of her in just her panties.

"I thought you were leaving," she shoots over her shoulder, aware of my lingering attention.

"I am. Going right now," I say, as I blindly search for the handle behind me.

"Great," she says, pulling an oversized T-shirt over her head. "And anyway, it's not like you haven't seen them before."

Her words are like a slap upside the head, and it only gets worse when I discover the T-shirt she's pulled on is one of Rett's.

His name and number are impossible to miss on the back as she shimmies her dress down, letting it drop to her ankles.

Your best friend's little sister.

And yeah, I have seen her tits before. They're the things dreams are fucking made of.

"Goodnight, Little P," I finally say as I pull the door open.

"Night, Linc. Be a good boy and go and ice that leg."

A self-deprecating laugh falls from my lips as I force

myself to walk away, images I don't need in high definition in my head.

In six years, she's never said even a word about what happened that night.

Honestly, I thought she'd forgotten.

But maybe she hasn't.

And maybe, just maybe, she's suddenly thinking about it again.

Or maybe I'm just crazy and reading into things I shouldn't be.

The room next door is in darkness when I silently slip inside. I'm hardly surprised; it's late, and Kodie has a game tomorrow.

I should have a game tomorrow...

Shutting myself in the bathroom, I come to a stop in front of the sink and rest my hands on the counter.

With my eyes closed, I replay the events of tonight over in my head. Only as I get to the part where I unzip Parker's dress, my imagination begins to take over.

Rett's shirt doesn't exist, and when she dropped her dress to the floor, there wasn't anything covering the small lace G-string she was wearing.

And when she spoke, it wasn't to say goodnight but to call me back over.

Shamelessly, I shove my sweats and boxers to my knees, letting my hard dick spring free.

A groan spills from my lips as I wrap my hand around myself and stroke from root to tip.

Closing my eyes, I focus on her, on the dip of her waist and the fullness of her hips and ass.

My hand moves faster as I think about stepping up behind her and gripping those full tits.

She sighs, leaning back against me as I pinch her hard nipples.

"You like that, babe?"

"More, Linc. Please."

I work myself harder, faster, as I picture my hand sliding down her stomach and into her panties, finding out just how wet she is for me.

"Soaked," I groan in her ear as she coats my fingers.

"All for you. It's always for you."

Tingles erupt at the base of my spine as my release approaches.

"Get on the bed. Hands and knees, and drag your panties aside. I want to see that pretty pussy."

It has to be a fantasy because Parker immediately follows orders and crawls onto the bed.

The moment she exposes herself to me, I come.

It hits me hard and fast, but as my cum drips to the floor, I discover it's nowhere near enough to even take the edge off.

I need more.

I need...

Things I can't have.

18

———

PARKER

Eight years ago...

"**E**verett, you jerk," I wail a second after crashing to the ground outside our house.

For the last hour, Rett, Linc, and I have been playing basketball in the front yard. The summer sun is beating down on us and sweat drips down my spine. It's been a really good day. Or at least it was until Rett's shoulder-cheked into me in his attempt to get the ball. Granted, I tripped over my own feet, but I'm placing the blame for the whole situation purely at his.

"Don't be a pussy, PK," my big brother barks.

Like most little sisters, I have a love-hate relationship with my big brother. In many ways, he's the world's most irritating person. But in others, he's sweet and thoughtful. He also doesn't see me as an incapable girl.

He may be faster and stronger than me, but he's never stopped me from playing sports with him. Whether it be on the ice or on a court, he lets me join and sometimes even chooses me for his team. It's rare, but it does happen sometimes.

"I'm bleeding," I point out after twisting around so I'm

sitting on my ass in the middle of the driveway. Both of my knees are scraped, and from the pain in my right elbow, I'd say that took a beating, too.

"Nothing a wipe won't fix," he calls before sinking another basket.

"Asshole," I mutter under my breath.

"Need a hand?" Linc asks, gazing down at me with a little more concern for my injuries than my brother.

He holds his hand out, and I hesitate.

Lincoln Storm is hot. All the girls at school want him. Well, either him or my brother, but I really can't see the attraction with the latter.

I want to hold his hand more than I want my next breath, but not in this way.

"I'm fine," I huff, placing my palms to the scorching-hot asphalt beneath me and pushing myself to my feet.

I don't care how hot he is. I don't need a man to look after me.

I'm a strong, independent woman; a grazed knee or two isn't going to keep me down. I've suffered way worse hits on the ice and don't take a second to think about it before getting back to it.

"I'm gonna go and clean up," I mutter as I stalk toward the house.

"Linc," Rett barks, annoyed that he's now playing alone.

Linc's brow creases as he looks between the two of us.

I don't know what his problem is—it's not like he's ever going to choose to hang out with me over Rett. Those kinds of situations are reserved for my late-night fantasies.

"Do you need some help?" he asks, ignoring my big brother's demands for attention.

A laugh tumbles free, making his frown deepen.

"Oh, it wasn't a joke," I say when genuine hurt flickers through his eyes.

"Parker, I—"

"I'm fine. It's just a graze. Nothing to cry about, right?" But despite my words, my nose itches and my eyes burn. It hurts, sure, but not enough to cause tears. It's the embarrassment that's making emotion rise within me.

I need to get away before I lose the battle with them because I refuse to cry over a graze in front of Lincoln Storm.

"Right," he mutters as I flee toward the house.

I make a pitstop in the downstairs bathroom for the first-aid kit before running up to my room and swinging the door closed. It bounces back from the doorframe like it always does, since I demanded that Dad take the latch out because of my fear of being trapped.

Usually, when I want to hide, I'll push my chair against it to stop anyone coming in, but I don't bother right now because no one is going to be following me.

Mom isn't due home for hours, and Dad is currently at a summer camp on the other side of the country.

I sniffle as I walk across my room and give up fighting my tears.

As much as I'm grateful that Rett includes me, it's impossible to forget that I'm not like him. No matter how hard I train, how much practice I put in, I'll always be weaker.

He's going to make it. I can already picture him living the high life in the NHL. His dream is to play for our hometown, the LA Vipers. He'll probably do it, too. I love him, but that asshole gets everything he wants. Everything seems to fall into his lap; whereas, I have to work my ass off for everything I have.

I fall onto the end of my bed with a heavy sigh, tears streaking down my cheeks.

It's pathetic. I don't have a reason to cry, not really, but they fall regardless.

Sometimes, I really hate being a girl.

I wish Casey were here. She's been gone on vacation with her dad for a little over a week, and I miss her like crazy. She'd understand how I'm feeling right now. She knows what it's like to grow up in a man's world, and the work we have to put in to making ourselves stand out.

I don't want to be Everett Donnelly's little sister. I want to be Parker Donnelly: kickass ice hockey player and all-around decent person. But everything I do gets overlooked because of him. I don't want to be bitter about it. My brother is the best—not that I'll ever tell him that to his face. I am proud to be his little sister. I just...I want to be more than just that.

I want...I want to stand on my own two feet and make waves in the world like I know he's going to.

Maybe it would be easier if I were interested in something other than sports, or more specifically, ice hockey. It's my life, just like it is his. The only difference is that I'm not good enough to go all the way like he is. If I want to dedicate my life to the sport, I'll have to go about it a different way.

It's not going to be easy. Hell, it's going to be the opposite of easy. But I'm going to do everything in my power to make it happen.

One day, I'm going to be an athletic trainer in the NHL.

My eyes flick to my desk, where I've pinned my vision board for the future.

Hard work, determination, and focus. That, along with a whole load of luck, and I might just do it.

It's either that or I resign myself to a life of being a little sister.

My teeth grind at the thought alone.

Finally, I flip open the first-aid box and pull out a wipe to clean myself up.

I have blood trickling down both of my legs, soaking into my socks. Sitting here feeling sorry for myself isn't going to fix anything.

I'm wiping up my shin when a knock sounds on my door. I startle, but before I can say anything, an intimidatingly large body slips into my room.

"I thought you—what's wrong?" Linc asks, his eyes widening with horror when he sees my tears.

Fuck's sake.

Dropping the wipe, I drag the backs of my hands across my cheeks, trying to clear them away.

"Nothing. I'm just being stupid."

"Does it hurt that bad?" he asks as he invites himself in and moves closer.

He might only be sixteen, but already, he looks like a hockey player. Gone is the scrawny boy I remember from childhood, and in his place is what is going to be a professional athlete. I let my eyes wander for a moment, taking in the definition of his abs and those V lines that—

Shit.

"N-No, it's just...it's nothing."

He moves closer still, not put off by my emotional breakdown.

"Let me," he says, snatching the abandoned wipe from my lap and dropping to his knees at my feet.

"Oh, no you don't need to—ow shit," I hiss when he touches the wipe to my scrape.

"Sorry. Should have warned you."

I'm no virgin when it comes to cleaning up wounds. It comes with the territory of being an ice hockey player, even as a girl.

"It's fine," I whisper, my eyes locked on where he very carefully cleans me up.

Silence falls between us as he works. Every brush of his fingertips makes my heart beat a little faster and my skin erupt with goose bumps.

I'm fifteen. But thanks to my title as Rett's little sister, I'm yet to have a boyfriend or kiss anyone like most of the girls at school.

I want to. I'm ready to experiment, but all the boys are too scared to go anywhere near me.

A heavy sigh slips past my lips, and Linc looks up with his bright blue eyes.

"Penny for your thoughts, Little P."

That nickname makes something light up inside me. It reminds me that sometimes, he does see me as a person. Maybe even a girl.

I shake my head. I couldn't possibly tell him my thoughts. He'd laugh in my face. He has girls falling over themselves to get to him at school. They both do. And I'll never admit it, but I've overheard them talking about what they've been getting up to with said girls.

Something uncomfortable and unwanted stirs within me.

Jealousy.

I want him to look at me like he does those girls.

"Does Rett know you're up here?" I ask, changing the subject.

"Your mom called, reminded him that he promised to go to the store for her."

"You didn't want to go?"

"Does it look like it?" he says, switching to my other knee. "Thought I'd check on you. Grab a drink and chill for a bit."

"You don't need to check on me," I argue.

"What if I want to?"

I stare down at him, my mouth opening and closing as I try and fail to find any words.

"Okay," I squeak.

His eyes hold mine for a beat before he gets back to work.

"Rett was an asshole for checking you like that," he mutters as he places Band-Aids on both my knees.

"Tell me something I don't know."

He chuckles before demanding I show him my elbow.

"Jesus," he mutters, taking in the mess.

I hold my arm in front of my chest, allowing him to repeat the process of cleaning it up and checking for debris. He opens a Band-Aid and applies it, but as he smooths the underside down, his knuckles brush against my breast.

I might be wearing a padded sports bra, but his touch is like an electric current that zaps straight through me.

No one has ever touched them, but that one graze is

enough for me to know that I'd like it if someone—okay, if Linc —did.

"Shit, I'm sorry. I didn't mean—"

"It's okay," I breathe, noticing how raspy my voice is.

Holy cow. Am I...am I turned on?

I focus on my body, on the new sensations racing through me, and how everything seems to start and end between my thighs.

My chest heaves with my increased heart rate as we continue to stare at each other.

Nothing happens, yet at the same time, I think everything does.

Linc pushes higher on his knees, bringing us closer together.

His eyes bounce between mine as if he's trying to read something within them.

And when they drop to my lips, I swear I stop breathing altogether.

He wants to kiss me.

Lincoln Storm wants to kiss me.

Me.

He moves closer, and my head begins to spin; the room around me disappears. But just before I think he's going to take the final plunge, his cell begins ringing.

He jumps back as if he's been slapped, and my entire body sags in disappointment.

"Fuck," he mutters under his breath as he climbs to his feet and pushes his hand into his pocket to retrieve his cell, but as he does, I notice something. Hell, it's not exactly hard to miss, especially when his hand helps to pull the fabric tight across his crotch.

He's hard.

Heat floods south, and I rub my thighs together.

As he swipes the screen, he glances down at himself, and then very briefly at me. His cheeks are pink, yet his eyes are darker than I've ever seen them. It's the weirdest mix of cute and sexy I've ever seen.

But no sooner do our eyes collide than he opens his mouth.

"Rett," he barks before racing from the room as if the place is on fire.

19

PARKER

I wake with a start, that memory so vivid in my mind it might as well have just happened.

That was the day my childhood crush on Lincoln Storm turned into something much more serious.

He became something of an obsession.

But as much as I wanted more, he seemed to want the opposite because he backed right off, leaving me yearning for another innocent touch.

Casey returned with tales of her vacation and a boy she had a little fling with. Jealousy threatened to burn me to ash when she told me about kissing him on the beach.

I wanted a summer kiss.

But it wasn't to be.

The holidays passed, we all went back to school, and I only really ever saw Linc in passing or when he was hanging out with Rett. Hockey took over all our lives, as it always does when the season starts every fall, and time just ran away from us.

I watched him from afar, of course, but I eventually lost any hope that that afternoon meant anything to him.

I mean, why would it?

He could have any girl at school he wanted. Why would he choose me over all of them?

They know what they're doing. I was yet to be kissed.

Eventually, I got bored of wanting something I couldn't have, so when one of Rett's teammates was brave enough to stick his head above the parapet and ask me out, I said yes, knowing it would probably result in me getting some experience.

If only I knew where it would lead...

When my alarm begins to blare, I throw my covers off and swing my legs over the side of the bed.

I silence it and push to my feet.

That's when everything from the night before slams back into me.

I crash back to the bed and clutch my aching foot as the memory of having Linc on his knees, cleaning me up, comes back in technicolor.

I guess that explains the dream.

"Motherfucker," I mutter before gingerly pressing my foot to the floor again.

He warned me that it was going to hurt today. I hate that he was right.

I take a breath and steel myself to stand again.

I hobble pathetically to the bathroom and lower my ass to the toilet, feeling like an idiot.

It's my third day on the job, we've got a game this afternoon that I've benched one of our best wingers for, and I can barely stand.

This is going to be fantastic.

If Mitchell wasn't already questioning my appointment, then he really will be today.

I'm not sure how much help they'll be, but I swallow a couple of painkillers before I get dressed. I figure I'm going to need all the help I can get.

Everything is somewhat okay until I have to put my sneakers on.

Red-hot tears burn my eyes as I push my foot inside the snug shoe.

I sit on the edge of the bed and attempt to breathe through the pain for a few minutes.

Checking the time on my cell, I find I've got a few minutes before our call time.

> Parker: I might have had an accident last night.

Casey: Oh my god, are you okay?

> Parker: Yeah. I'm fine.

Casey: Are we talking physical accident or something else?

> Parker: I didn't sleep with anyone who wears a Vipers' uniform, if that's what you're getting at.

Casey: But did you sleep with anyone?

> Parker: Sadly, just me, myself, and my throbbing foot.

Casey: Throbbing…foot?

Deciding against typing the whole ordeal out, I tap for a voice note and relay the entire experience.

Casey: Linc is so sweet.

"What?" I blurt.

> Parker: Is that all you have to say about it?

Casey: I'm glad your foot is okay. I'm sorry you're in pain today, and it's going to be a long day.

Casey: But Linc is really sweet for looking after
you like that.

Parker: He's an overbearing asshole who
needs to butt out.

Casey: If you say so.

Guilt knots up my insides as I consider what to reply.

All my life, I've told my best friend everything...or at least, she thinks I have.

She doesn't know it, but I have a very big secret that only one other person on this planet knows. And as guilty as it makes me feel for not sharing, I convinced myself long ago that keeping it was for the best.

Parker: I gotta attempt to get down to the bus.
Wish me luck today.

Casey: You don't need it, you'll be the best
trainer the team has, even with a dodgy foot.

Parker: Thanks. Have a good day.

Casey: Love you x

Sliding my cell into the side pocket of my leggings, I get to my feet with a wince and grab my bag.

I'm almost at the door when my cell buzzes.

Assuming it's Casey again, I pull it free.

I quickly discover my mistake.

Storm: How's the foot? Need any help?

Shaking my head, I put my cell back to sleep, shove it deep in my pocket, and continue hobbling out of my room.

"Oh shit, what happened to you?" Cole Hansley—aka Handsy—asks the second the elevator doors open on my floor to reveal him and Calvin Keller—Killer—occupying the small space.

"I had a fight with a shard of glass. It won," I mutter as I join them.

"Let me take that," Handsy says, unhooking my bag from my shoulder and throwing it over his, along with his own.

"That's what happens when you agree to party with Brooke." Killer laughs.

"I wasn't even drunk. I stopped after three. It was stupid."

"Do you need it looked at? I'm sure Eddie could—"

"It's fine. It's been cleaned up, and the glass is gone."

"Well, if you need it checked, just give him a shout."

"I will. Thank you. Ready for today?" I ask, needing to change the subject.

"As ready as we'll ever be. It'll be good to see if Reeves can hold his own in Linc's absence," Killer says, mentioning the Vipers' second-line winger.

"I'm sorry that—"

"Don't be," Handsy says firmly. "Never apologize for putting our health first."

"You won't be saying that when it's you on the bench," Killer teases.

"I'm good. And I have every confidence that Parker will keep me limber and ready for every game."

I smile up at him. "I'll give it my best shot," I say as the doors part, revealing the rest of the team waiting for the buses to arrive in the foyer.

I scan the mass of bodies, and it only takes a second for my eyes to lock on a pair of familiar blue ones.

They narrow in question as I walk—or try to—between Handsy and Killer.

Linc moves closer, his eyes darting among the three of us.

"Thank you for the help, but I can take my bag from here," I say, holding my hand out.

"I've got it," Linc says, intercepting it and successfully turning all eyes on him.

"Shouldn't you be focused on your pregame ritual right now?"

He rolls his eyes.

"How's the foot? Bandage okay?"

I don't look over, but I know that Handsy and Killer are exchanging a look.

"Parker," a female voice calls, and when I glance over, I find Brooke racing toward me. "Oh my god, that was such an awesome night."

A wide smile spreads across my mouth. "It was."

"My head is pounding. Why didn't I follow your lead and stop earlier?"

Someone snorts a laugh behind me—clearly someone who knows Brooke better than I do.

"Gutted we're travelling tonight. We're totally going out after the game tomorrow night, though, before we head home. What do you say, boys?" she asks, looking around at the players surrounding us.

"Sounds good," Killer states. "We're always up for a night with some bunnies. Isn't that right, Storm?"

My breath catches in my throat. I shouldn't care about his response or the fact that he'll probably spend tomorrow night rolling around with some bunny.

"Damn straight. It's been too long."

Turning around, I glare up at him. "Contrary to popular belief, it doesn't actually fall off if you don't use it every night of the week."

His lips press into a flat line. "Well, that's good to know, considering I spent last night bandaging up your foot instead of getting any action."

"I didn't ask you to."

He's about to respond, but someone calls that we're to move out, and he turns around to head to the bus instead.

Brooke lingers, threading her arm through mine.

"What happened?" she asks, looking concerned.

"I must have stepped on some glass between the Uber and the front doors. It was nothing."

She quirks a brow. "Enough to have a hot hockey boy playing doctor. Your night certainly ended better than mine."

I don't agree, but I also don't say anything.

I'd much rather have just curled up in bed last night and been able to walk this morning.

THE REST of the morning and afternoon pass in a blur, working on the guys, getting them ready for the game, and then standing just a few feet away from a scowling Linc as everything gets underway.

He's barely spoken to me since we arrived at the arena. It seems his concern over my foot allowed him to forget his irritation for a while, but it's back in full force now.

Whatever.

The less we interact, the better.

It's a tough game. Lloyd Reeves plays the first line like his life depends on it. He manages two assists, but he fails to find the back of the net. We walk away with a 2-0 win, though. You'd think that score would mean Linc lightens up a little, but when we all make our way onto the airplane a few hours after the game, he's still wearing the same scowl he has been all day.

"Oh my god." I sigh as I sink into my seat beside Brooke.

I'm exhausted, and my foot feels like it has its own heartbeat.

"The guys killed it tonight," she says without looking up from her cell, where she's editing footage from tonight's game, ready to post.

"They did. And another shutout for Handsy. Coach is going to have offers coming in left and right with his performance this season."

"He'd be stupid to let him go."

"I can't see it happening. But we're getting toward that time of year."

She mumbles her agreement as the final few people take their seats.

Brooke switches her cell off as the doors are closed, and she finally turns toward me.

"Ready for the next leg?" she asks, excitement glittering in her eyes.

"Please try not to break me this time."

A shadow falls over me, and my heart sinks, but when I turn around, I find Leah smiling down at me.

"How's the head?" I ask.

"Better than your foot, by the sounds of it."

"I'm pretty sure if I take my sneaker off, I'll never get it back in."

"As soon as we're in the air, get it elevated. No excuses for tomorrow night," she teases before taking off to get started.

"You two are going to be the death of me."

"There are worse ways to go, don't you think?"

20

LINCOLN

e lose our next game. Badly.

It was embarrassing.

But no matter what I said to Coach, he wouldn't go against Parker's recommendation to bench me.

Instead, I was forced to sit there and watch as Colorado annihilated us.

I've had plenty of bad games in my career, and I know I've got plenty more in me. But while being a part of a loss is devastating, watching one from the sidelines is fucking torturous.

By the time the final buzzer sounds, the guys out on the ice lower their heads and move toward the tunnel, utterly defeated.

We've had injury after injury tonight. And while our opponents might have spent plenty of time in the box for it, we still couldn't pull out even a single goal.

It fucking hurts.

If I'd have been allowed out there, maybe, just maybe, I could have helped turn things around.

We're heading toward the second half of the season; we can't afford to have games like this if we want to secure our playoff position.

The second Monroe is off the ice, Parker is on him, checking his shoulder, while the others pass by, ready to put this whole night behind us.

I want to say something encouraging as I step up beside Kodie, but there are no words, and anyway, he isn't exactly giving off, "please talk to me about how I fucked up tonight" vibes.

So, like the others, I keep my gaze locked on the ground and prepare myself for the impending dressing down.

The air is thick with disappointment as we come to a stop at our stalls and begin stripping out of our uniform.

There are mumbled curses and more than a few thrown pieces of athletic equipment as everyone battles to restrain their frustration.

As Coach steps into the room, silence descends. We might have disappointed ourselves tonight, but I know I'm not the only one who feels worse about disappointing James Watson.

He's done incredible things since becoming our head coach. Not only is the man a fucking legend in his own right, but he's an incredible coach. Our respect for him is endless. As much as we want to win games for ourselves, we want to win for him more.

"I'm not going to stand here and bleat on about where we fell down tonight," he starts. "You all already know where your weaknesses were. You all know what you need to work on.

"But what I will say is that winning doesn't make a top-class athlete. Of course, it's a part of it, but it's how we deal with the losing that really makes us.

"It sucks. I get it. It hurts.

"But I urge you to let tonight go. What's done is done. Focus on the future. Focus on our next game and how incredible it's going to feel when we get back out there and show the world what we're really made of."

Agreement ripples around the room.

"We're having our best season in years, but that doesn't

mean there won't be lows. Use this loss to fuel everything that comes next.

"Now, we've got an afternoon flight home tomorrow, followed by two days off. Use this time to let your hair down, put this loss behind you, and come back to training ready to lift that cup."

Cheers sound out, and the atmosphere in the dressing room shifts.

"Onwards and upwards, right?" Kodie says, making Coach's solemn expression soften.

"Go out tonight, blow off some steam. But hear this...you miss the flight tomorrow, you'll walk your sorry asses back to LA. Got it?"

"Yes, Coach," we all agree.

He looks around the room, meeting each of our eyes, silently reassuring us, before he pauses on Fletch.

"Let's go, Ferguson. The press waits for no man."

We all watch as the two of them disappear, each of us grateful not to be the ones trying to put a positive spin on tonight's game for the press.

"We're going out tonight, right?" Marilyn asks.

"After that monstrosity? Hell yes," Killer agrees.

"I could drink," Handsy mutters, although there's no excitement on his face.

Everyone might have sucked tonight, but Handsy always takes it worse when he's the one letting the opponents get pucks past him.

"On us, man," Killer says, slapping him on the shoulder.

"You coming, Big D?" I ask, turning to Kodie, who's unlacing his skates beside me.

"Nah, I'm not feeling it."

"Fuck that," Killer barks. "Those who lose together, party together."

"And I know exactly where to go," Brit pipes up.

"Oh Christ," Handsy mutters. "It better not be like the last place you dragged us to."

Brit holds his hands up. "It's not a country bar, I swear. No line dancing."

I can't help but laugh as I recall the night in question.

"We need a do-over because Kodie didn't come. I think he'd look killer in a cowboy hat and boots."

"Fuck off, Storm," Kodie grunts.

"If we can promise no cowboys or dancing, will you come?" Killer asks with a pathetic pout.

"If your girl was here, you know she wouldn't take no for an answer."

"She would if I promised to make a night in my hotel room worthwhile."

"Our hotel room," I point out.

"Not when Casey is here," Kodie mutters.

"Whatever. You're coming, end of."

Kodie shakes his head before stripping down and heading toward the showers.

"Well, I think he's excited," I state once he's disappeared.

IT'S ALMOST three hours later when I'm dragging Kodie out of our hotel room, on the promise that he can leave early to have phone sex with Casey before I get back and ruin his game.

"I hate nightclubs," he mutters as the elevator descends.

"Oh, really? You've never mentioned it before," I quip.

When we spill out into the hotel lobby, we find the team waiting for us. Killer and Monroe have done a solid job at stopping them all from moping in their rooms tonight.

"What are we waiting for?" I ask, more than ready to put today—hell, this whole trip—behind me.

If it weren't for Parker, then it could have ended very differently.

So could the season, if your injury got worse...

"Ubers are outside; we're just waiting for our last few," Killer announces.

"Who?" I ask. Everyone's here.

But then, behind me, the elevator dings and the doors open.

"Oh fuck," I gasp as a limping Parker and Brooke move our way, both looking like freaking models.

"Oh, hell yes," someone—probably Monroe—cheers, and the girls' faces light up.

"I thought it was just the guys tonight?" I mutter.

"What's wrong, Storm? Against partying with our new trainer?" Kodie asks, a knowing smirk playing on his lips that I desperately want to wipe off.

"I want to let my hair down."

"And Parker being here stops you from doing that how exactly?"

Lifting my hand, I rub the back of my neck as Parker and Brooke join us. I have no idea what Brooke is wearing; I've barely spared her a second glance. But Parker...Parker is wearing a white tank that is thin enough to show the lace pattern of her bra beneath, and a navy skirt that is so short I'm not even sure it can be classified as a skirt.

"Damn, did Donnelly's legs get longer?" Monroe asks.

Reaching out, I smack him upside the head.

"Aw, what was that for?"

"For looking. Parker is your colleague. Show her some respect."

Kodie snorts beside me but doesn't say anything else.

"Where are we going then, boys?" Brooke asks as she marches through the middle of us like she's suddenly the leader, with Parker's hand clutched in hers.

Multiple sets of eyes follow them. Horny fucking bastards.

"This is a bad idea," I mutter under my breath.

"Oh no, you got me to agree to this. You're not backing out now," Kodie says, throwing his arm around my shoulder and moving us toward the exit and the row of waiting cars.

Thankfully, Parker is already in the first car by the time we get outside and climb into another.

The conversation is kept light during the short drive to the club. We talk work, but we don't mention our game tonight; instead, we focus on how others in the league have done.

Before long, we're pulling up out front of a club we've been to before. I'm pretty sure I hooked up with two bunnies the last time we were here.

I shake my head as I climb out of the car. I'd been excited—buzzing to find some girls to spend the night with. We had come off a win, and I was ready to celebrate the best way I knew how.

How things have changed.

Not only are we suffering the pain of a loss, but the thought of hooking up with one, let alone two, bunnies really doesn't appeal.

Somewhere over the last few months, something has broken inside me.

Things that used to fuel me into action no longer appeal.

I just wish I could put my finger on what it is so I could get rid of it and go back to those days.

The line to get in wraps around the building, but the second I step onto the pavement, I see those ahead of us being allowed through the rope, each member of the team thanking the bouncer with fist bumps.

I remain frozen on the spot as the others disappear into the building.

"Are you okay?" Fletch asks, coming to stop beside me.

I give myself a second before turning toward him and forcing a smile on my face.

"Yeah, of course. Why wouldn't I be?"

I expect him to mention something about being benched, but he doesn't.

"I don't know. You just...seem different."

"Just tired, I guess," I admit quietly.

"Ah, it happens to the best of us," he says, understanding

in his tone. "Next thing you know, you'll have found a girl and settled down."

I almost choke on my own spit.

"I don't think that'll be happening anytime soon."

Fletch laughs. "We'll see," he says before marching forward.

I follow, not wanting to be left out here alone.

The second I step inside, the deep bass of the music hits my ears, and some of my previous worries melt away.

"This way," Fletch shouts, moving toward the sectioned-off VIP area.

"Brit really pulled out all the stops, huh?" I mutter as we climb the stairs, the music getting quieter with each step we take.

No sooner do we get to the top than a tray of shots is thrust in front of us.

Needing something to take the edge off, I take a glass and swallow the bright pink liquid in one go.

"Ugh, the fuck was that?" I ask.

"Toxic," Fletch agrees.

Thankfully, another server follows with beer, and we both take a glass, immediately drinking half of it to wash away the taste of the shot.

The team quickly separates and finds seats, and I follow Fletch toward a cluster of couches and sit with him, Killer, Handsy, Brit, and Monroe.

"This place is sweet," Monroe says, his eyes wide in awe.

It's easy to forget sometimes that he's only a rookie and hasn't experienced life on the road like we all have.

"And did you see the girls as we came in?" He bites down on his knuckles.

"Just wait until someone drops our location on socials and the bunnies descend."

"Can't fucking wait, man."

"Aw, is Marilyn going through a dry spell?" Handsy teases.

"Fuck you," Marilyn snaps while I scan the VIP section, looking for the girls who travelled with us.

I shouldn't care. Parker is a grown woman who can look after herself.

But despite telling myself that, I still search for her.

"Where did Brooke and Parker go?" I ask, interrupting Killer as he attempts to get details out of Monroe about his love life.

"They stayed downstairs. Said they wanted to dance," Handsy states.

Instantly, my eyes dart toward the balcony that looks over the dance floor below.

Don't do it, Storm.

Just stay where you are.

21

PARKER

"Drink and put it all behind you," Brooke says, pushing two shots of tequila toward me.

I nod, wishing it was all that easy.

My mom called as I got back to my hotel room after the game. I've been avoiding talking to her for days. But my time hiding from her, from both of them, was over.

I fell back in my bed, swiped the screen, and set about confessing all my sins.

They were obviously concerned as I explained about the fire and losing my home and possessions, but as much as they tried to cover it, I could hear the disappointment in their tone, see it on their faces through the screen.

Disappointing them always hurts. They've always given us everything we could ever wish for, and yet I'm still fucking things up.

They offered to help me out financially, like I knew they would, but I told them I have it all under control. I hate taking money from them. I am an adult with a good job. I shouldn't need bailing out, even if I know they have more than enough.

I also may have failed to mention that I've temporarily moved in with Linc.

I didn't lie, not really, when I explained that I was living with a colleague while I get things sorted.

When Brooke knocked on my door, I wasn't ready, and she took one look into my eyes and knew something was wrong.

I had little choice but to open up and tell her what was going on with my life right now.

We sat on the edge of my bed, and she silently listened to everything. She didn't judge or tell me that I was stupid for not renewing my renters' insurance; instead, she just gave me a hug. It reminded of Linc the night we discovered the fire. He knew what I needed and gave it to me.

That's exactly how I feel as I take the shot from the bar, tap it against Brooke's, and swallow it down in one.

"Oh my god," I gasp as the liquid burns down my throat.

"So good," Brooke says before reaching for the second glass. "Leah is on her way," she says after checking her watch. "But she says she's not drinking."

I laugh, wondering how long that will last, before drinking my second shot.

The alcohol warms all the way down to my stomach, and I realize Brook is right. It is helping me forget.

We made the right decision to stay down here while the guys went up to the VIP section. I've had enough death stares from Linc today to last a lifetime.

I'm not stupid. I'm aware that letting him play tonight might have changed the result. But it was never going to happen.

He's making progress, and I'm hoping with another two days of rest, I'll be able to clear him for our next home game.

I keep telling myself that he'll thank me in the long run, but I'm believing myself less and less.

It's bearable while we're on the road. I don't have to see him all that much. But tomorrow, we're going home. Back to his penthouse. Then what?

"How's your foot holding up?"

I glance down at my sneakers. My foot has been throbbing

all day, but I figure it's got to be easier to deal with than some of the hits the guys took tonight, so I swallow the pain and keep moving forward.

"It's fine."

"You're such a little liar."

"Fine. It hurts. But it isn't going to stop me from dancing."

"Cheers to that," Brooke says, holding up her glass of Jack and Coke.

"Cheers," I say, tapping my glass to hers.

"And if we're really lucky, we might just find some guys to dance with."

I try to think back to the last time I hooked up with a guy in a club. It's been a while.

I've been dabbling with online dating, but I'm yet to find anyone who doesn't have some serious issues. I'm starting to think that all the decent men have already been taken. Which is sad, considering I'm only twenty-three.

"Last hookup?" Brooke asks, and I grimace.

"Guy from Tinder. He seemed okay. We had dinner, then he invited me back to his place. I agreed, and we were standing on the sidewalk waiting for an Uber when he kissed me."

"Okay, so far so good."

"Oh no, there was nothing good about it. He had so much tongue. I swear, a dead fish could have done a better job." Brooke giggles. "I turned away, desperate to get away from the assault, and do you know what he did?"

Brooke stares at me, biting the insides of her lips as she shakes her head.

"He stuck his tongue in my ear. IN MY EAR," I shout, pointing at my violated body part in case she isn't aware where an ear is situated.

"Oh my god. What did you do?"

I can't help but laugh.

"His Uber came, and being the gentleman that he was not, he climbed in first, so I closed the door behind him, rapped my knuckles on the roof for the driver to go, and watched him and his wild tongue sail away. I blocked him and then called my own car. Okay, your turn."

"Well, my guy was a great kisser. In fact, I thought he had it all. Until I did go back to his place, and no sooner had I walked through the front door than I was introduced to his mom and little sister."

"W-what?" I blurt.

"Turns out, he was religious and there would have been no sex before marriage."

"And I'm assuming that there will be no marriage?"

"Hell no. I fully respect those who want to wait. Fair play to them. But it's not for me; I need to test out the goods before I commit."

"Amen to that, girl," I say, lifting my glass again. "When we get back, we need to arrange a night out with Casey and our friend Freya."

"Just tell me when and I'm there."

Leah joins us a few minutes later, looking like a knockout in a leopard print jumpsuit, and true to her word, she orders a soda. I can't say the same for me and Brooke. I was good last night, knowing that I had work in the morning. Tonight is a different story.

"That guy down there hasn't taken his eyes off you for about five minutes," Leah tells me, jerking her chin toward the other end of the bar.

I take a sip of my drink before slowly looking around.

My breath catches when I find a cute blond guy staring right at me.

He's about as far away from a hockey player as you can get. And that's exactly what I need in my life.

He probably works in finance or law. Something stable and reliable.

"He's cute," Brooke says. "I'm pretty sure I'd eat him alive, but he'd be great for you."

"I reckon he could handle more than you think," Leah says. "It's always the quiet ones, remember?"

"Let's go dance. See if he's brave enough to make a move." Brooke finishes her drink and grabs my hand. "Let's go and find you a man."

"What about you?" I ask.

"Oh, don't you worry about me." Her eyes shoot over my shoulder, and I figure she's already got a target in mind.

"Is it true what they say about flight crew?" I ask Leah as Brooke drags us to the dance floor in full sight of the cute guy.

"Depends on which rumor you're talking about," she teases.

"That you have a lover in every place you visit."

She smirks, telling me everything I need to know.

"Well, put it this way: it isn't only the players who have little black books of names and numbers."

"You do not?" I gasp.

She laughs. "Of course not. That's old school. I have them in my phone, ranked by performance."

"Shut up."

"She does," Brooke assures me.

"Yes, girl," I cry. "I fucking love that. Where is your best state?"

"Well, there are a couple at the top of my list."

"I'm going to need to hear all the details on a quieter night."

Leah smiles. "You got it."

Brooke's plan to lure the cute guy over works perfectly, because we're barely two songs in when both my dancing buddies look over my shoulders and watch someone approach.

Hands land on my hips as the heat of a body burns down my back.

"Can't take my eyes off you," a deep voice murmurs in my ear.

Goose bumps race across my skin as a smile pulls at my lips.

"Oh yeah?"

"Yeah. You're mesmerizing."

Brooke gives me a wink, and I spin to face him.

My smile grows when I discover that he's even hotter up close.

Throwing my arms over his shoulders, I continue to move to the beat of the music. He follows my lead, and we begin to move together like we've been doing it for years.

Good sign. Very good sign.

"Are you single, pretty boy?" I ask. I've learned over the years that it's pointless, cheaters are generally the best kind of liars, but some have tells that give them away.

This guy, though...there's nothing suspicious as he tells me that he's very much single.

"Good to hear. So am I, by the way. And, I'm only in town for the night."

His eyes flash with excitement. "Is that right?"

"Yep, one night to make the most of this city before I fly home."

"And where is home?"

"Oh no, that isn't the kind of conversation we need to be having," I chastise. "One night, first names only. You in or you out?" His grip on my hips tightens, pinning our bodies together.

He chuckles. "Where have you been all my life?" he asks.

"Waiting for tonight, obviously."

"My lucky night," he muses before rolling his hips against mine.

Oh yeah, I can work with this.

Song after song passes as we dance together.

His hands begin to roam, but neither of us makes a move to push it further—not yet, anyway.

I'm too busy enjoying moving to the music and letting go.

Spinning back around, I wiggle my ass against his crotch, loving what I'm feeling behind the fabric.

When I look up, I find that both Brooke and Leah have found guys to dance with, and thankfully, I don't see any other familiar faces.

If I'm lucky, the team has already moved on. Or even better, headed back to the hotel.

The song changes again, and so does the lighting, plunging us into darkness for a moment.

My eyes jump to the second floor where those in VIP can look down at us mere peasants dancing.

I freeze the moment Linc's eyes collide with mine.

"Are you okay?" Pretty Boy asks, his hand tugging at my hips to keep me moving.

A heartbeat later, the lights come back on, and when I look up, Linc's gone.

Was he even there in the first place?

I shake my head, fully feeling the effects of the alcohol consumed tonight.

"I need another drink," I shout, hoping the girls can hear me.

They both look up and nod.

The six of us make our way to the bar, but despite finding the balcony empty, my skin continues to prickle as if I'm being watched.

22

LINCOLN

My knuckles are white with my grip on the balcony railing.

I managed to hold myself back for a while, but eventually the pull to search her out in the crowd is too much to ignore.

I'm just checking on her, I tell myself.

Doing my duty as her big brother's best friend.

But it's all bullshit.

I'm searching her out because I need to.

Trying to find her because of some weird compulsion I've had for...far longer than I'm willing to confess to.

I expect to find her dancing and enjoying herself. And that's exactly what I find when my eyes finally land on her in the crowd. Only, she isn't just dancing. She's dancing with a guy. Rolling her hips against his, letting his hand roam over her body. Losing herself in him and the beat.

How I remain standing here is beyond me. All I want to do is race down there and drag him away from her. Replace him with myself and discover what it would feel like dancing with her...

Get it fucking together, Storm.

Closing my eyes, I tip my head back, but the second darkness sets in, all I see is her dancing with him.

The alcohol swimming in my veins does very little to wash it away.

I don't drink that often anymore. Being focused and ready for a game is more important. But everything was different tonight. I needed something, anything, to take the edge off of everything I've been feeling the last few days. It's been...a lot.

Forcing myself to take a few deep breaths, I try to empty my mind. Forget the irritation of not being able to play and support my team tonight, lose the annoyance I've forced myself to feel toward Parker. Truthfully, I'm grateful. But I can't let her see that. It's easier to pretend I'm annoyed with her. It helps to keep a barrier between us. If that slips, then...

I can't go down that road.

Not again.

When I finally open my eyes and scan the gyrating bodies below me, I don't find her.

My heart jumps into my throat.

What if she left with the guy?

What if he takes her back to his place? Or worse, what if she brings him to our hotel and I'm forced to see him leave in the morning? I guess I should be thankful that her room isn't next to ours this time.

I couldn't listen to that...

I don't want to know what she sounds like when she's getting fucked by someone else. I don't want to know how hard he makes her come, or how good she is for him.

Frantically, my eyes dart around, searching for them as panic floods through my veins.

I don't breathe until I spot her.

"Thank fuck," I breathe, watching her, Brooke, and Leah at the bar.

For the briefest moment, I don't think the guys are with them, but then they step closer.

He smiles down at her as if she's just hung the moon as he runs his hand down her back, and I fight to take a breath.

I can't even say they don't look good together because, quite honestly, they do.

I can't tear my eyes off them as the bartender slides their drinks over. The six of them chat and drink. At no point does he break contact with her, and it makes me want to rip his arm off.

"What's caught your...ah," Kodie says, coming to join me and immediately spotting the car crash I'm watching. "And here I was, thinking you were enjoying yourself."

"Someone is," I mutter.

"Dude, you've got it bad."

"I don't have anything. I'm just keeping an eye out is all. What if he's a murderer?"

"What if he's her soulmate?"

"The fuck, Rivers?" I bark.

He shrugs, not giving a shit. "You've been spending too much time with Casey."

"I'm in love, man. What can I say?" His eyes go all soft as he thinks about her. It's cute as shit.

I'm happy for him, I really am. He's certainly less grumpy now that he's getting laid regularly, and that's good for all of us.

It's just a shame that he's upped his level of action, and mine seems to have fallen off the face of the Earth. It's not for lack of trying; it's just that over the last few months, no one has really stolen my attention. The girls who approach me are all hot, sure. But no one is sparking that match.

My eyes shoot to Parker again. Okay, so maybe not no one.

I think back to jerking off in the bathroom at our previous hotel. Yeah, there was fire in my veins then, for sure.

"I'm heading out. I—"

"What's happening over here?" Killer barks as he and Handsy join us.

"Ah, scoping out the possibilities. Shit, she's hot," he says, jerking his chin in the direction of a group of girls I completely passed by earlier. "I think it's time to get dancing, boys."

"I'm actually leaving," Kodie says again, taking a step away. His eyes find mine, silently asking if I'm going with him.

I should. Staying here is dangerous. I either get to watch Parker continue to grind on that guy and then eventually leave with him, or I go down there and do something about it. Both sound like disasters in the making.

But then I look at Killer and Handsy. They're expecting me to be the one to lead the way.

Making a snap decision, I spin around and march toward the stairs with Kodie at my side.

"I just need to talk to her, then I'll meet you outside."

He glances at me, ready to argue, but the second he gets a look at my determined expression, he agrees.

"Five minutes or I'm leaving."

"Fine by me."

I look back as we get to the bottom of the stairs and find half the team following us with excitement etched onto their faces. They need this after tonight.

Coach was right: we need to get it out of our systems so we can move on.

The second the rope to the VIP section is pulled back, chaos ensues.

Safe to say our location has been leaked.

Girls scream our names and the braver ones move closer.

I brush a few off, not even bothering to look at them as I keep moving toward my destination.

Just before I turn toward the bar, I spot Kodie escaping through the exit, but the others have been swallowed into the crowd. Good for them. I hope they all have a good night. Something tells me I won't be.

"Hey," I say, stepping up to Parker and none too discreetly forcing her new friend to take a step back.

She turns to me, her eyes wide with shock.

"Oh, you are not serious," she seethes.

"What? What did I do?" I balk.

"All day you've done nothing but scowl at me. And now, of all moments, you decide it's time for a chat?'

"Well, no. I was just—"

"Holy shit, you're Lincoln Storm," the guy Parker was dancing with announces, his eyes wide with awe. "Fucking sucks you didn't get to play tonight. Whoever made that call was wrong, in my opinion."

I nod in agreement before turning my attention back to Parker, raising a brow.

Usually, I don't have a problem interacting with fans, but tonight, this guy...no. Just no.

She rolls her eyes but refuses to point out that she's the one who kept me on the bench to her little buddy.

"We're heading back to the hotel. Did you want a ride?"

Parker's lips part, but no words spill free. She looks at Brooke, then Leah, and finally the guy with stars in his eyes.

"No, we're okay here," she says confidently.

Holy shit. So this is what it feels like to be turned down.

Sure, I wasn't propositioning her, but still.

"But—"

"No buts, Storm. Go back, ice your leg. Get some rest. Who knows, that idiot who benched you tonight might change their mind for the next game."

I narrow my eyes, hating the way she's talking about herself. I might have given her a hard time over the last few days, but we both know she made the right call. And as much as I hate to say it, my leg feels so much better. With her working on it and a more regimented icing regime, it's almost as good as new.

"Don't do—"

"Go back to the hotel," she insists. "I don't need, and never have needed, a babysitter. I'm a big girl. I can look after myself."

Fuck. She is. I know she is. She's dated plenty over the years. Just…not right under my nose.

I really don't fucking like the idea of this douche getting to spend the night with her.

"But—"

Brooke steps in front of me, her eyes holding mine despite the fact that she's barely five feet tall.

"She told you to leave," she states fiercely as someone steps up behind me.

"Come on, let's go," a familiar deep voice rumbles as a hand curls around my shoulder.

"Fletcher Ferguson. I'm a massive fan," Douche says, holding his hand out for Fletch to shake.

Because Fletch is one of the best people I know and a fantastic captain, he shakes the guy's hand and accepts his condolences over tonight's loss.

"Our Uber is here," Fletch says the second he can get a word in. "Let's go."

"But—"

"No buts," he warns in my ear before practically dragging me away from Parker, leaving her with Douche.

Just before we walk around the corner to leave, I look back.

My heart jumps into my throat because Parker hasn't forgotten all about me and turned back to him. Instead, her eyes are locked on mine.

The moment she realizes what she's doing, she looks away and turns back to the group, a fake smile pulling at her lips.

"Fuck," I breathe.

"You're doing the right thing," Fletch assures me.

But as we walk out of the club and hit the cool night air, I can't help feeling like I'm doing the opposite.

The short drive back to our hotel is in silence. Both Kodie and Fletch have their noses in their cells, no doubt messaging their women, letting them know they've got minutes to be phone sex ready.

Ripping my eyes from them, I focus out the window, watching the city pass by outside.

A heavy sigh passes my lips as the hotel approaches. Heat burns down the side of my face, letting me know that they're studying me, but I don't look over. I can't; I'm too busy wondering what it must be like to be able to go home to someone who means the world to you, even if home means a hotel miles away.

"I'm gonna get another drink, give you some time," I say as we move toward the elevators.

"You don't have to do that," Kodie says.

"Nah, it's fine. I'm not ready to crash yet." I want to wait here and see if Parker comes back, and if she does, I want to know if she's alone or not.

"Okay," Kodie concedes, more than happy to have some alone time with his girl. "Please, don't do anything stupid."

"What, me?" I ask, faux-horrified. "It's like you don't know me at all."

"We know you too well. Why do you think he's saying it?" Fletch laughs.

"Enjoy the rest of your night," I say, dismissing them. "See you in the morning."

They watch me for a moment, words dancing on the tips of their tongues, but they both decide against saying anything.

"Goodnight," they finally say before disappearing into the elevator.

I grab myself a soda from the bar before sitting into a shadowed corner that faces the entrance to the hotel, and I wait.

Time passes slower than I've ever known. I picture Parker and the rest of the guys still partying hard.

It's what I should be doing. That or icing my leg like I was instructed, but I can't find the energy to do either.

I just need to know she's back and alone.

I almost give up waiting when my eyes begin to close, but I'm glad I don't, because only ten minutes later, headlights illuminate the entrance to the hotel before two familiar figures come stumbling into the building trying to smother their giggles.

The need to go to her and help her to the room again burns through me, but I don't. I force myself to sit there and watch them disappear, happy that she isn't spending the night with another man.

23

PARKER

I'm exhausted by the time we walk into Linc's penthouse the next afternoon. My hangover lingered until well after lunchtime, and I can't say that flying made it any easier.

I still don't regret last night, though. I needed it.

Was I a little disappointed in how my evening went with my potential orgasm deliverer? I'd be lying if I said I wasn't. But after Linc and Fletch left, all he could talk about was ice hockey and the guys. He no longer seemed excited about spending time with me and only wanted to know about my friends. And of course, his comment about the idiot who benched Linc stung a little. He had no reason to know it was me, but he also didn't need to belittle the person who made the decision as if his opinion was more important than a professional's.

Thankfully, Brooke and Leah could read my body language, and when he was distracted, we headed out. We debated going to another club, but in the end, we settled with a bar that served arguably the best margaritas I've ever had and almost enough carbs to soak up all the alcohol we consumed. We laughed until our sides hurt, and eventually we got kicked out. In a repeat of the night before, we dropped Leah off first and then made our way back. Thankfully, there was no sight of Linc. I really didn't need a repeat of the night before, even if the sight of him on his knees before me has since become a permanent fixture in my head.

I need to forget about the whole situation and how he looked at me like he used to. Those times are long gone. Everything has changed. He's not that boy anymore, and I'm not the same girl who used to doodle his name in my textbooks and put our initials in hearts.

I was a sap back then who believed in romance, happily ever afters, and soulmates. It's laughable, really, that I thought he could have been it.

Silly, naive little girl.

The temptation to take a pit stop on the way home so I didn't have to lock myself in an apartment with him was strong, but all I really wanted to do was fall face-first into his guest bed and have a nice, long afternoon nap.

Linc and the guys might have the next two days off from practice, but I'm not so lucky. I have meetings with the team to review training and rehab programs moving forward. I also have a couple of sessions with members of the team, Linc included. So, despite wanting a break from him, it seems that until I get my shit together and move out, it's not going to happen.

"Plans for the afternoon?" Linc asks as we climb through the building.

"Sleeping. Last night was a lot."

"Uh-huh," he grunts. "That guy you met was a jerk."

"Well, he seemed to love you."

"Not as much as he liked you," he mutters.

There's something in his voice that makes me glance over at him.

I regret the move the second my eyes land on his face. He hasn't shaved since we left, and the added scruff to his jaw only adds to his good looks.

He hasn't said much about last night, but something tells me that he assumes I spent the night with the guy. Seeing as I don't have to justify my actions to him, I allow him to continue thinking what he likes.

If Linc hadn't come over, there was a chance I could have spent the night with him. And who knows, it could have been the best sex of my life. Or maybe he saved me from yet another disappointment when it comes to men. To be honest, that outcome is probably the most likely, but now I'll never know.

I haven't had a man in…well, ever, who hasn't turned out to be a disappointment.

"Jealous that I had some fun while you spent the night listening to Kodie snore?"

"Who says I didn't have any fun?" he asks, making something bitter and uncomfortable bubble up inside me. "I have girls ready and waiting in every city we go to. Look," he says, pulling his cell from his pocket and opening up Instagram.

His inbox is flooded with messages from girls.

"You haven't opened them," I point out.

He chuckles at my confidence. "These are new girls trying their luck. I have a few trusted regulars who make life easier. Sometimes, it's better the devil you know."

"Ugh, you're a dog."

"Call me what you like, Little P. As far as I see it, I have a stressful job, and I need some stress relief every now and then."

"Every now and then?" I echo. "Daily isn't every now and then."

He shrugs as if he has no cares in the world.

"Doesn't it get boring?" I ask as the doors open and we move into his apartment.

"I could ask you the same about dating," he points out. "The difference is, I'm only looking for some fun."

"So am I," I argue, although it's a lie.

"Is that why you let them take you out to dinner so you can get to know them first?" he asks, quirking a brow. "If you're only after fun, it doesn't matter what his job is or if he's funny.

You just need a decent-sized dick and a man who knows how to use it."

"Oh, I'm sorry for not wanting to fuck every asshole out there."

He smirks. "Didn't know you were into that. But each to their own."

"That's not what I meant," I argue. "There's nothing wrong with wanting to spend time with decent people."

"You might not want to admit it, but you're looking for more, Parker."

I roll my eyes, irritated that he can see through my bullshit.

"And you're not?"

"No," he states confidently. "I don't have time for more. Hockey is my life. I have things I want to achieve, and having a woman in my life would be a distraction."

"Is that what you think Casey is to Kodie?" I ask, offended on her behalf.

"No, that's different. She makes him a better person, a better player."

"And you don't think there's someone out there who could do that for you?"

He falls silent, his eyes dropping to the floor and his hand lifting to the back of his neck.

"Maybe I did once upon a time, but things change. Excuse me," he says before marching forward with his bag thrown over his shoulder. Not five seconds later, his bedroom door slams closed, leaving me standing there alone.

"Well, okay then."

Abandoning my bags, I take off for the kitchen to grab a drink and some snacks before heading to my room for a much-needed nap.

MY AFTERNOON NAP ends up being a little longer than I

was expecting. When I eventually wake up, my room is in darkness despite the fact that the curtains are wide open.

I blink in confusion, trying to remember where the hell I am. I need to get used to that, with all the travelling I'm going to be doing in the coming months.

After checking the time, I throw the covers off and pad toward the windows and stare out at the star-filled sky.

It's beautiful and an unusual sight in the city. I guess being this high up does have its benefits.

Minutes tick by as I lose myself in thoughts, both of the past and the future. I run treatment plans through my head and think about how the upcoming team meetings are going to go.

Jarad seems to respect me and my opinions. Mitchell is another story, though.

I get it. I'm young and female—probably the very opposite of the person he was expecting to fill the vacant trainer role. Trust me, I was as shocked as anyone when I got the call to tell me I got the job.

I have experience working with athletes and ice hockey teams, but not at the NHL level. But they saw something in me. Something I'm not going to question because I'm here. I made my dream a reality. And I'm not going to let any chauvinistic bastard question my place on the team.

We all have to start somewhere, and I'll thank my lucky stars every single day that I get to start here.

After freshening up, I pull on a sports bra and a pair of shorts before silently slipping out of my room and heading toward Linc's home gym.

I've wanted to spend some time in it since I first found it, but life has gotten in the way. But this morning, while the rest of the city sleeps, is the perfect time to test it out.

I'm not really a gym person. I prefer Pilates, or a bit of yoga if I'm feeling tired. But seeing as it's here for the taking, I figure it would be rude not to indulge.

I start off on the treadmill. I take it slow and steady, but before long, my face is red and I've got sweat running between my shoulder blades.

I move to his weight bench and work on my arms a little. But as good as the burn feels, it's not my chosen type of exercise.

So instead, I abandon the equipment and walk toward the wall. I don't need a fancy reformer to practice. I find a rolled-up mat, get it into position, and get to work.

With my back on the floor and my feet on the wall, I lift my ass off the ground, loving the pull of my muscles as I do so.

I work through a series of exercises that I've honed over the years.

I'm pushing up on my hand, my knees spread on the mat, and my feet against the wall when a figure appears in the door before me.

I gasp as Linc's eyes run the length of me, but I don't miss the way they linger on my ass.

"The fuck are you doing?"

"Pilates," I state as I right myself and climb to my feet, not wanting to be at a height disadvantage.

"I have all this equipment and you're using my wall?"

"Yeah, problem?" I quip, my hands on my hips.

Without trying to hide it, he drops his eyes again, taking a leisurely stroll over my body.

My chest heaves from exertion, and my skin is glistening with sweat. I don't need to look into the mirrors that cover an entire wall to know I look a mess.

"Nope. No problem here."

"Pig." I scoff, reaching for one of his rolled-up towels on the rack beside his head and wiping my face.

"I thought you were in better shape than to be sweating from some wall stretches."

My eyes widen at his assumption.

"You've never done Pilates?"

He chuckles. "No. Isn't it a woman's thing?"

I nod, an idea forming in my head.

"Yeah, I'm sure you'd find it a walk in the park."

"I'm a professional athlete, Parker. Peak condition here."

My eyes drop to his thigh, and I regret it immediately. The shorts he's wearing are short enough to show almost every ripped muscle of his thick thigh.

"Is that so?" I ask, tilting my head to the side.

"You like looking at my crotch, don't you, Little P," he teases.

"I go to classes two to three times a week. Once I've cleared you, you should join me. Show me how it's done."

"Okay," he states, his confident smirk firmly in place.

"Great. I'll book you in. I'm going to shower and get to the arena," I say before walking around him.

"What? You mean I don't get to watch you do weird sex positions while I work out?"

"Pilates, Storm," I correct. "And get any thoughts of me and sex positions out of your head. You've got plenty of bunnies waiting in your inbox for that, remember?"

I walk off with my body burning and an image of him in some of those positions with me.

Inviting him to a class with me was a very bad idea.

But I refuse to let him think that just because I'm a woman, I can't do the hard shit.

24

LINCOLN

It's only been a few days, but the difference Parker has made is incredible. She might be driving me to the brink of insanity, but after this, I have no doubt that I'm going to play better than ever.

"How does that feel?" she asks as I push my right knee to the floor in a butterfly stretch.

"Very much like you staring at my dick," I quip.

"For fuck's sake, Storm. Will you take this seriously?"

"Trust me, my career is at stake here; I couldn't take this any more seriously if I tried."

"Didn't stop you from playing injured, though, did it?"

"Can we drop that now? You found me out. You're working your magic."

She shakes her head as I continue to bounce my knees.

"How does that feel?" she asks again, her eyes holding mine in warning.

"Perfect. You'd never know anything was wrong." I smile at her, and her eyes narrow. I don't think she believes me.

"Level of pain?"

"One."

She holds my stare for three seconds before her lips twitch into the most incredible smile.

"Alright, there's no need to be so smug."

She drops onto her ass in front of me on the mats. It's been just the two of us in here for an hour, and honestly, it's been the best part of my day so far.

I love watching her work. Seeing the little frown line that appears between her brows when she's concentrating and the small twitch of one side of her lips when something goes to plan or she discovers her therapy has had the effect she was hoping for.

But this, her smile right now...I wish I could bottle it and keep it forever.

"I'm sorry, it just...it feels really fucking good to be right."

"And there I was thinking you're always right."

She shakes her head, her smile softening, but it's no less breathtaking. "So you do listen to me occasionally."

"I'm fixed, aren't I, Doc?"

"Not quite, but you're almost there."

"You mean I still need these one-on-one sessions? Damn, not sure I'll cope."

"You know you enjoy them."

Yeah, I do.

"I know you haven't exactly enjoyed the start of my time here, but..."

"But what?" I ask when she trails off, not finishing her thought.

"Thank you."

"I haven't done anything other than be pissed off."

She laughs. "I can handle that. I just...I needed this win. I know it's only been a few days, and most people have been so welcoming and supportive, but I'm aware that not everyone thinks I deserve my place here. But this...spotting your injury and having the chance to work with you and prove myself right? Well...it helps."

As she speaks, my frown gets deeper, and anger begins to simmer inside me.

"Who's said something?" I ask.

"It's nothing," she says, trying to brush her comment under the carpet.

"If that were true, you wouldn't have said anything."

"I'm just aware that I'm a young woman in a man's world. I want to prove my place, and this...you've helped."

"You're welcome. Maybe it was worth missing two games."

"You know I was right."

"Just so you know, I've never doubted you. We're lucky to have you working with us, and if anyone, I don't care how high up their position is, says anything that makes you question your position or your worth, you tell me."

"Linc," I warn.

"I'm serious, little P. You deserve this. You've worked your ass off, and you're better than any other trainer I've ever worked with."

"It's been four days."

"Yeah," I muse, but honestly, she's been taking care of me for much longer than that. From the day she decided to focus on becoming an athletic trainer, she's been there in the background asking questions, practicing her technique, and soaking up as much information as she could.

It's been an honor to watch her excel in her field. I never had any doubt that she'd make it. She was destined for this, and I can't wait to see how far she goes.

"You're going to get us to the Cup finals this year, Donnelly."

"Shut up. You guys are going to do that."

"We can't if we're injured," I counter.

She smiles again, her eyes dropping to her lap. "It's going to be a great second half of the season."

"It is."

Silence falls between us. Only our breaths and the distant whirr of the air conditioning can be heard as we lose ourselves in our thoughts.

"Parker?"

She looks up, her eyes colliding with mine. "Yeah?"

"What are you—"

"Knock, knock, knock," a voice booms before Monroe bounds into the room like an overexcited Labrador. "I come bearing gifts," he says with a shit-eating grin on his face and a takeout coffee tray in his hand. "Oh shit," he gasps when his eyes land on me. "I didn't know you'd be here, Storm."

"Good to see you too," I mutter under my breath.

"I didn't know what your poison was, so I called Casey. She told me to get a venti skinny iced latte with a caramel shot. I hope that's right."

"Are you fucking blushing?" I balk when his cheeks brighten.

"Fuck you, Storm. What did you bring with you, other than your shitty attitude?"

"Oh shit, someone is feeling brave."

"Enough, you two," Parker says as she climbs to her feet. "Thank you, Hayden. That's really thoughtful of you."

"Kiss ass," I mutter, also getting to my feet.

"Ignore him. He's leaving."

"And I thought we were bonding there for a moment."

"I've known you since I was ten. I think we're long past that, Storm."

"Nine."

"W-what?"

"I've known you since you were nine," I correct.

I remember the day as if it were yesterday.

Rett and I had started middle school a few weeks earlier, and he'd invited me to shoot a puck around his backyard. And there she was. Red pigtails, freckles over her cheeks and nose, in a pair of cute-as-hell overalls. I'm not ashamed to admit that I tripped over my own damn stick when she carried a tray of cookies and milk out for us.

I didn't understand my reaction to her that day, or for quite a few years, but as we all grew up, it started to get a little more obvious.

That first day I saw her, I thought she was the cutest girl

I'd ever seen. By the time I was fifteen and she' turned fourteen, I thought she was the hottest girl on the planet. And now, as a woman, well...fucking breathtaking.

"Right, okay."

"You two are cute," Marilyn states as he kicks his sneakers off and drags his long-sleeved Vipers shirt over his head. "Got romance novel written all over you."

"Excuse me?"

"You don't read; I wouldn't expect you to get it," Marilyn deadpans.

"Hey, I can read."

"I never said you couldn't, just that you don't."

Parker giggles behind me. The sound makes the hairs on my neck rise.

"And you do?"

"My sister and I have a book club," he explains. "Each month we take turns choosing something to read. We've been doing it for years."

"That's so cute. What are you reading at the moment?"

My eyes get wider and wider as Marilyn begins explaining the basic plot of some dark stalker romance he's in the middle of.

Honestly, it sounds beyond fucked up, but I can't deny that I'm curious.

"I haven't read a book for pleasure in years," Parker confesses.

"We've got plenty of flights coming up. I can give you some recommendations. We read all kinds of genres. Not just romance."

"Have I just entered the twilight zone?" I ask.

"Ignore him. Storm is just jealous you can read an entire book. He gave up trying in sixth grade."

"That's not true," I argue. "I read..." My words trail off when I realize I can't name a single book I've read since leaving school. "Well, I could if I wanted."

When both of them laugh at my expense, I shove my feet into my sneakers and drag my hoodie over my head.

"I guess I should leave you to it," I mutter and reluctantly move toward the door Marilyn walked through a few minutes ago.

"That would be wonderful," Marilyn says with a smirk. "It's my time with the hot doc now."

"Monroe," I warn.

"Chill out, Storm. I'm just teasing. Parker knows that she's my favorite." He winks at her before hopping onto her table on his front.

Refusing to leave just yet, I rest my shoulder on the doorframe and watch as Parker moves around the bed and grabs her iPad from the side. She wakes it up and begins typing, oblivious to my attention.

"What are you plans tonight?"

"Well, I'm glad you asked," Marilyn barks.

"Not you, Rookie. Parker, what are your plans for the night?"

She pauses what she's doing and looks up.

"Oh, um...I'm busy."

"Busy? Doing what?"

"I'm going out," she says, continuing to skirt around the truth.

"Out where?"

"A restaurant."

"Any one in particular?"

"I'm not sure. Jeez, what's with the twenty questions?"

"Stop being evasive, and I'll stop asking."

"Fine, I've got a date. He hasn't sent me the location yet."

Fire erupts within me.

A date?

I know she's been dabbling with online dating, but I haven't heard about her meeting anyone in a while, so I assumed that...

Fuck.

"You need the location. That'll help you decide if he's worth your time," Marilyn says.

"Who's the guy?"

"Storm," she warns.

"Donnelly," I counter.

"It's none of your business."

"No, yeah. You're right, it's not. I guess I'm just being selfish because we want your whole attention on us right now."

Marilyn twists around and stares at me with a knowing smirk on his lips.

"I appreciate the concern, but no man is going to distract me from doing my job."

I blink at her as my brain runs away with me.

She didn't mean that as a challenge, but damn, I really want to make it into one.

What would it take for her to break? And could I be the one to do it?

"Good to hear. Good luck with her, Monroe. Her fingers are extra probing today."

"I can handle her," he says confidently.

Trust me, kid. I really don't think you can.

"I'll see you later then."

Parker stops typing again and glares at me.

"Tomorrow. For your appointment," she forces out, letting me know exactly how she feels about anyone knowing we live together.

"Of course. I promise not to be late."

"This is fun and all, but you're holding us up," Monroe pipes up.

"Fine. Make it hurt, Doc," I say before giving her a salute and walking out the door.

I should walk straight to the exit and head home, but something has me lingering just a few feet away.

"Is he giving you shit?" Monroe asks.

"Of course he is. But he wouldn't be Linc if he weren't," she responds, her voice light and happy.

"If it gets too much, all you've got to do is say."

"That's sweet. But you don't need to worry about me. I've known Linc long enough to know how to put him in his place."

My brows shoot up.

Is that right?

The need to accept that unspoken challenge earlier gets even stronger. So does the need to somehow intercept her date tonight.

It was bad enough that I was left wondering if she went back with that douchebag in the club the other night. I can't sit back and watch her go out with assholes from Tinder night after night.

With my fists curled at my sides, I finally march toward the exit with ideas spinning around my head.

25

———

LINCOLN

Seven Years Ago...

Rett's house is silent when I let myself in. Exactly how I hoped it would be.

There's only one person here right now, and she's upstairs, getting ready.

My heart thunders in my chest, and my hands tremble on my lap as I sink into the couch.

I don't know why I'm here.

I shouldn't be here.

But I couldn't not be.

From the moment Seth came marching up to Rett in the dressing room the other day, it's been all I can think about.

Rett was pissed, rightly so, but for some reason, he agreed that tonight could happen.

I guess he could only hold off the inevitable for so long.

Parker is going to be seventeen soon. She deserves to be living the life all her classmates are. She deserves to experience the same things.

But with Seth?

I shake my head. He's not good enough for her.

Rett has to know it, but he's letting it roll regardless.

He's on our team, and…he's one of us. For that reason alone, he should be kept far, far away from Parker.

She should turn her back on hockey players and look at the guys hanging out in the library, maybe even in the music department. I know I'm dragging myself into this, but hockey players can't be trusted. We're too competitive, too busy craving the high of the next win, and it doesn't just have to be while on the ice.

Movement above my head has me looking up.

I wonder what she's wearing?

It doesn't matter what she's chosen; she'll look beautiful regardless. She always does.

I glance at the clock, and my heart rate increases. He'll be here soon.

I understand that Clark, her dad, is busy. Her mom, too. But someone should be here for this. It's a big moment.

Her first date.

And I'm going to be sick.

But there's no time to wallow in self-pity, because not a second later, her footsteps begin descending the stairs.

I'm pretty sure I stop breathing as I wait for her to appear in the doorway, and the second she does, all the air rushes from my lungs.

"Wow," I breathe, but I don't think she hears it. She's too busy screaming in fright.

"Linc, what the hell?" She has her hand pressed against her chest as if she's physically trying to keep her heart inside, and her eyes are wide as saucers.

"Sorry," I mumble, unable to stop my eyes from feasting on her.

She's wearing a long, floral dress that shows off her new curves perfectly. And I suspect that if she were to turn around, I'd find her back exposed.

That asshole is going to touch her.

My teeth grind at the thought of Seth brushing his fingers down her spine, resting his palm on the small of her back.

I don't know where the image comes from, because it's certainly not a move I've pulled with any of the girls I've been hanging out with. I guess it's because Parker deserves better than any of them.

She deserves to be dated, adored, and made to feel special. She's not just there for a good time.

"You look…"

Heat blooms on her cheeks and races down her neck to her chest.

I've tried my best to keep my distance from her since that afternoon in her bedroom.

It made me want things I can't have, and the easiest way to deal with it was to back off. I figured if she wasn't so present in my life, I could forget about it all and move on.

It was bullshit.

It doesn't matter how much distance I put between us. She's still there.

"Thanks," she whispers, struggling to accept my attempt at a compliment. "Rett isn't due back for a couple of hours yet," she points out, assuming that I'm waiting for him.

"No, I know. I'm not actually here to see him."

"Oh, okay. Well, I'm heading out in a minute," she says, as if I'm not aware.

"I know that, too. I just…" I trail off as my hand lifts to the back of my neck, rubbing at my tight muscles.

Why are you here, Lincoln?

She stares at me, waiting for me to say something.

There's a part of me that wonders if she's waiting for me to tell her not to date him and to hang out with me instead.

But I can't do that. Not only would Rett kick my ass into next year, but she deserves so much better.

Not Seth, but definitely someone better than me.

Her eyes narrow, waiting for me to finish my explanation.

"I just thought someone should see you off on your big night," I say lamely.

She shakes her head. "We're just going to the movies. It's no big deal."

But it is. I haven't taken a girl to the movies.

I just...

The less you think about that right now, the better.

"It's your first date, little P. Someone needs to be here to warn Seth to treat you right."

"I'm sure Rett has slammed him into the boards enough times already for him to be aware of what'll happen if he screws this up."

And yet, he was still brave enough to chance his luck.

Plexiglass is going to be the least of his worries if he fucks this up.

My words dry up as she moves closer—although I soon discover it isn't me she's getting closer to, but the window.

As she stands there, I can see the excitement glittering in her eyes for what the night might hold.

"He's not good enough for you," I finally blurt.

"Oh, and did you have someone in mind who might be?"

She turns to me and holds my eyes.

Is she...is she begging for me to say yes, to tell her to go out with me instead?

No, that's just my twisted imagination.

"I don't think there's anyone walking this Earth who is worthy of you, Parker Donnelly."

Her breath catches at the honesty in my words.

Her reaction is everything, but it isn't going to change anything.

She's still going out with him tonight, and I'll spend all evening wondering what they're doing, guessing if he made a move and kissed her.

"That's sweet. But even if it's true, I'm not going to sit around the house experiencing nothing. So..."

She fully turns to the window this time, and I get to see that I was right. Her dress exposes her entire back.

Her skin is flawless, her shoulders covered in the same cute freckles her nose and cheeks are, although they've lessened over the years since I met her.

The fabric begins just above her ass, and my fingers twitch to reach out and drag my knuckles along the seam.

I glance at the clock. He's due to pick her up any minute.

Is there any point in hoping that he's going to stand her up?

Nah, he'll be here. I'm not that fucking lucky.

There's a rumble of an engine outside and I panic, thinking our time together is over.

I shoot up from the couch, but a shot of pain goes up my leg as I press my foot to the floor.

I cry out in pain before crashing back down, clutching my leg.

"Linc, what's wrong?" Parker asks in a rush, her attention turning back to me.

"Crap," I force out, my leg continuing to spasm.

"Shit. It's okay. I've got you. Can you stretch it out for me?"

When I open my eyes, she's on her knees before me, her hands wrapping around my lower leg and gently pulling it from my hold.

"That's it. Rest it there," she says softly, placing my heel on the coffee table before me.

Then...then she does something so fucking magical, I feel something tumble in my chest.

She presses her thumbs into my calf, and instantly, I feel relief.

"Okay?" she asks as she continues massaging my muscles.

"Fuck," I gasp as warmth rushes up my leg, spilling through my entire body.

Sure, Parker has touched me before. But never, ever like this.

Holy shit.

I relax into the sensation, enjoying it far too much considering she's about to spend the night with someone else.

As she slides her hands up toward my knee, the fire inside me only burns hotter, and I can't stop my dick from reacting.

It hardens beneath the fabric of my sweats.

Shit. She needs to stop.

She needs—

There's a blare of a horn outside and it bursts my bubble, sending me crashing back to Earth with a bang.

My head falls back against the couch, and my eyes close while my hands rest in my lap. I pray that they cover the evidence of what her touch did to me.

One moment her warm hands are there, and the next, they're gone. The air that rushes over my skin is like ice, cooling my blood and reminding me of everything I shouldn't be doing, like being here right now.

Dragging my eyes open, I find her on her feet and checking herself in the mirror.

"It's him. Are you sure I look okay?" she asks before spinning toward me, holding her hands out from her sides so I can take her all in.

"Y-yeah, you look—"

The doorbell rings, cutting off my words, and she rushes past me to answer it.

She pauses with her fingers on the door handle.

"Are you okay? Is your leg…"

"Yeah. I don't know what you did, but it helped. A lot."

"I've been researching," she explains. "I think I want to be an athletic trainer one day."

"Well, in that case, I volunteer to be your patient anytime."

She giggles, and the sweet sound worms its way inside my chest.

"I might just take you up on that. Enjoy your night," she says before finally opening the door to reveal Seth on the other side.

"Oh shit, Parker," he gasps.

"Hey." She giggles again, but this time it's like a knife straight through my heart because it's not directed at me.

I shift on the couch to get a better view, and he spots me.

"Oh hey, Linc. How's it going?"

"Yeah, it's...going. Watch yourself tonight," I warn.

He smirks and rolls his eyes.

"Yeah, yeah. I got it. She'll be home safe and sound by eleven."

"Good to hear it."

"See you later," she calls over her shoulder. "Have a good evening."

And then the door closes behind her, and she's gone.

Have a good evening. As if that'll be possible.

The urge to follow them burns through me, but I can't.

I might not want Seth to have her, but I can't have her either.

I just have to hope that one way or another, he royally screws this up, so I have a really fucking good excuse to teach him a lesson.

A really fucking painful lesson.

Because Parker Donnelly is mine.

26

———

PARKER

I lied to Linc. I don't have a date tonight.

That's the last thing I need.

It's nothing more than a hookup.

After the stress of the last few days, and then the way he was looking at me in the gym this morning, I realized that I need a release.

Sure, I could go and replace my favorite vibrator. Hell, I'm definitely going to do that. But I need more than that.

I need a man. One who can take everything away for a few minutes and leave me feeling sated and limp and tingling with aftershocks.

I have a few regulars for when my itch needs a decent scratch. Guys who are only interested in a good time when a girl needs it.

And thankfully, when I opened Tinder after the gym incident this morning, it seemed that my luck was in, because there was a message waiting for me from a guy I only see a couple of times a year when he comes to town.

He's a businessman, although I have no idea what he does. He clearly does it well, because he always stays in the best hotels and orders the most expensive alcohol for us. Neither of which I complain about. He also knows what he's doing in the bedroom.

All I need is the name of the hotel he's staying at tonight and I'm set.

Hopefully, once that is done, I'll be able to focus on what I really need to do.

Find an apartment and get the hell away from Linc.

My session with Hayden passes quickly. He's the youngest guy on the team, fresh from college, but while he might be a little green and overexcited about life, he's so easy to get on with. His enthusiasm for life is infectious. I think we could all do with being a little more like him.

When I get home, Linc is lying on the couch, watching game tapes, but when he doesn't look over or say anything, I hurry down to my room to get ready.

I have a message burning a hole in my pocket with a location for tonight, and I need to shower and shave every inch of my body.

I don't feel the pressure with this hookup as I would with someone new, or even someone who could potentially be more than just a night of fun, but I still have some standards.

Henry has money, and very good taste, from what I can tell. I'd hate to disappoint him and walk away empty-handed.

Henry...I laugh to myself as I kick my door to. I don't even know if that's his real name. And do you know what? I don't even care if it's not.

I take my time getting ready, my stomach growling as I do so. The bagel I grabbed on the way to the arena earlier is long gone. But with the promise of a delicious meal before we get to the good part tonight, I held off having anything this afternoon.

I style my hair in loose waves before pinning the left side away from my face with a pretty clip, then I pull on a tiny pair of panties and the little black dress I wore out the other night. It's not like I have a lot of options in my wardrobe right now.

It's another reminder that I should probably be focusing on

my clusterfuck of a life instead of my libido, but fuck it. There's always tomorrow.

With a spritz of perfume, I grab my purse from the bed and stare down at my shoes.

My foot might be healing, but that doesn't mean there isn't any pain. But I can hardly turn up to this "date" wearing sneakers.

"Fuck's sake," I hiss as I bend down and snatch them from the carpet. I figure that I'll put them on at the last minute and then slip them off again the second I'm at the table.

Without my shoes tapping against the wooden floor, Linc doesn't hear me coming, so when I step into the kitchen, I see his entire body jerk in shock.

"Shit, you scared me."

"Sorry," I mutter.

"It's...fuck. Parker, you look—"

Thankfully, I've got my back to him, so he doesn't see the moment I squeeze my eyes closed as flashbacks from our past hit me out of nowhere.

He's not worthy of you, little P.

As much as I hate to say it, Linc was right.

Seth wasn't good enough for me. Although, to be fair, I'm not sure I've ever met a man who is.

None of them ever step up when needed.

Okay, that's a lie. Some do, just...not for me.

"Thanks," I mutter, my cheeks burning.

"Where is he taking you?"

The temptation to say the movies is strong, but I swallow down the nostalgia.

"The Carlton."

Linc whistles. "Fancy."

I shrug one shoulder and finally spin around to face him. I discover my mistake instantly.

He's on his feet and only a few feet away, wearing nothing but a pair of athletic shorts.

His torso is in full view, as are his tattoos.

At the arena, when I have an athlete on my table, they're nothing but muscles and joints. A machine that needs fixing up. I'm basically a mechanic for a very complex car. I pride myself on being professional.

But with Linc...

Well, he came before the trainer's table and the experience.

He was one of three men who allowed me to test things out on them. To hone my skills. And as much as I want to say that I saw him no differently to working on my dad or Rett, I'd be lying.

Having him lying before me and at my mercy has always hit differently.

He's always been more than a machine.

More than just Rett's best friend.

"He's a lucky guy, getting to spend the night with you. I hope he knows that," Linc muses, his eyes taking in every inch of me.

His appreciation is more measured, more considered than it was all those years ago. But we were just silly kids back then. Now, we're adults who are meant to know what we're doing.

A laugh rumbles up my throat, but I manage to catch it before it breaks free.

"Only time will tell, I guess," I muse, hitching my purse up higher on my shoulder.

My cell buzzes, letting me know that my ride is here, and I take a step to the side—only, Linc doesn't let me escape. Instead, he moves with me, blocking me.

"W-what are you doing?" I ask, my voice weaker, quieter than it was only moments ago.

Linc lifts his hand, and I startle the second his fingertips brush my cheek, the pair of shoes in my hand crashing to the floor, before he tucks a lock of hair behind my ear.

A shudder rips down my spine as his fingers graze my sensitive skin before his thumb purposefully rubs over the sweet spot beneath my ear.

My eyes drop from his to his mouth.

How would it feel if it were his lips there?

"Linc?" I whisper, not trusting myself to speak any louder as I stand frozen in place.

Anyone would think that this is the first time he's touched me, from how I'm acting.

But that's far from the truth.

"I hope he's worthy of you, little P."

A rush of air passes my lips as he steps even closer.

Without my heels on, he towers over me.

Heat rolls through my body like a wave, and I attempt to discreetly rub my thighs together when my clit begins to beg for attention.

You just need to get laid.

An hour of mindless sex will make all of this better.

Get out of the apartment.

Now, Parker.

Now.

A laugh erupts from me. "I'm yet to meet one that is, but I guess tonight could be my night. Wish me luck," I say, as I force myself to move away from him. "I could be about to meet my future husband."

Linc grimaces as I walk backward toward the elevator.

I don't know why I haven't turned around and marched away.

No, that's a lie. I do.

I want him to tell me to cancel.

I want him to—

No. Stop.

He watches me retreat without saying a single word.

"Have a good night, Linc. Don't do anything I wouldn't do."

He snorts as his hand lifts, but I spin around before I get to see the way his abs ripple as he rubs his neck. I don't need the visual; I've seen it so many times over the years that I have it committed to memory.

I'm almost at the elevator when he calls out.

I freeze on the spot as all the things I secretly want him to say play out in my mind.

But when he does speak, he doesn't say a single one of them.

"Your shoes."

Spinning around, I find him stalking over with my heels swinging from his fingers.

He drops to his knees before me and places them on the floor so I can slip my feet into them.

I swear to God, the sight of him down there makes my brain misfire.

"Get up," I demand when he doesn't even attempt to move.

"Humor me."

With a huff of fake irritation, I lift my good foot and slip it into my shoe. Linc's gaze burns up the length of my leg, and when he gets to the short hem of my dress, I should move, but I don't.

Instead, I shift my weight to my other foot and slip my bad one into the other shoe, aware that he can probably see everything right now.

I mean, I'm wearing panties, so it's not like he can see anything really, but the way my heart is racing and my blood is simmering, I may as well be naked.

I wince in pain but quickly swallow it down. No pain, no gain.

Linc stays on his knees, with his hands resting on his lap. As I take a step back, he swallows thickly before dragging his eyes up to mine.

"Have a good night, little P. Make sure he's worthy before you give him anything he doesn't deserve."

I walk away with my head spinning.

Damn him.

The second I'm settled in the back of my Uber, my eyes

roll up the tall building beside me, all the way to the penthouse sitting on the top.

Even if Linc were standing at the window, I wouldn't be able to see him, but that doesn't mean goose bumps don't erupt across my body, making me think that he is.

The driver drags me from my thoughts when he confirms our location and takes off.

Unease builds within me as we make our way through the city toward the hotel where I have a man waiting for me.

A man who won't hold back.

A man who will give me everything I ask for and never break my heart in the process.

As we get closer, the unease turns to a giant knot sitting heavy in my stomach, making me feel physically sick.

"Umm...could you go around the block again?" I ask my driver, not ready to get out.

"Yeah, sure," he agrees before taking off.

And when we get around the front again, I ask the same thing.

My cell buzzes, and when I look, I find a message from Henry, checking that I'm still coming.

I'm never usually late, but when I look at the clock, I discover that I am.

My hand trembles as I think about what I'm doing.

This morning, when I made this date, I was so sure of myself.

But now...

Now, going into that hotel and falling into bed with a man is the last thing I want to do.

I quickly tap out an apology and hit send. The second I see it's read, the pressure lifts, and I swear I breathe for the first time since I climbed into this car.

"Are you getting out, Ma'am?" my driver asks.

"Um...no. Could you carry on driving around for a bit? I'll give you a new location soon."

His eyes find mine in the mirror.

"You did the right thing," he assures me, despite the fact that he has no idea what just happened.

27

LINCOLN

"Argh, you motherfucker," Killer shouts as I run him off the road and leave him in my dust.

"Fuck's sake. How did you win again?" Marilyn complains, sulking like the toddler he is.

"Because clearly, I'm the most talented player in the room. Hey," I complain when Handsy throws an empty water bottle at my head.

"Let's not get into that argument," Brit mutters. "You all know I'd win."

After Parker left me kneeling on my own goddamn floor like a horny teenager with a raging hard-on, I called in the guys for a distraction.

We ordered pizza and fired up the Xbox.

This is what a normal night off looks for us during the season. Sometimes there are more of us, sometimes fewer, but we kick back and try to forget about the pressures that are on us from every direction.

I fucking love my job. Playing ice hockey in the NHL is the only thing I've ever wanted to do. From as early as I can remember, I wanted to be just like my dad.

With a shitload of hard work and determination, I did it,

and it's the best fucking job in the world. But that doesn't mean it can't get overwhelming at times.

We've got not only the entire city watching us, but the entire country. There are thousands of fans out there relying on us, desperate for us to do the unthinkable and bring the cup home. That kind of pressure can get too much if you don't find a way to push it all aside for a while.

Thankfully, I have the best kind of family around me.

My teammates are my brothers, and when one of us is struggling, we band together and do what we can to make things right.

No one understands the life we live, other than the men skating beside you night after night.

We win together. We lose together. And we do everything else in between together.

Tonight, I need them to take my mind off what Parker might be doing with the guy who booked a table at The Carlton.

It's a solid choice, and it certainly makes a statement.

The guy either has money, or he's the world's biggest liar. It really could go either way.

But it doesn't really matter which way it goes, as long as it goes badly.

Guilt twists up my insides for wishing a bad date on her. But I can't help it. I'm selfish like that.

I got so fucking close to demanding she didn't go out and instead spent the night here with me. But I swallowed down the words.

She'd have only rejected me.

She doesn't want me.

I'm everything she doesn't want.

I remember that all too well.

The rejection stings just as much now as it did all those years ago.

You'd think I'd be over it at this point. But it's still there, reminding me that I'm not good enough for the only woman I've ever truly wanted.

"Linc? Storm?"

"Hey," I complain when a cushion hits my head.

"Where did you go?"

"Nowhere, just thinking about—"

"Pussy, no doubt." Killer laughs.

"I dunno. Rumor has it that the legendary Lincoln Storm is going through somewhat of a dry spell," Handsy teases.

"Fuck off. I'm just...I dunno, feeling a little picky."

"Shit. If Linc is getting fussy over the women he beds, that must mean we're getting old."

"Speak for yourself. Thirties are gonna hit you." Killer laughs, as if Handsy needs to know what his next birthday is. "Fuck. We're doing something epic for that."

"Oh yeah, like what?" Handsy asks, sounding anything but excited by the prospect of spending his big day with us.

"It's in the off-season, so I say we need a vacation. Europe? We could eat our weight in pizza and pasta," Killer suggests.

"You might get some decent home-cooked food there," Brit mocks, earning himself a scowl from our goalie.

It's no secret that Cole Hansley can't cook for shit. The last time he tried, he ended up with the fire department at his place due to the amount of smoke. But his biggest issue is that he can't keep a personal chef on his payroll to save his life. His most recent one threw the towel in a little before Christmas, leaving Handsy at risk of setting his entire building on fire in his attempt to roast a chicken.

"I think cooking lessons might be more useful than a vacation," I chip in.

"I will fucking end you if you put me in the middle of a class and expect me to wear an apron and sauté anything."

"I'm just impressed you know the word sauté."

"Bet he doesn't know what it means," Killer deadpans.

The friendly chirping continues as the time ticks by, but

no matter what's said or what game we play, thoughts of what Parker could be doing never leave me.

At some point, clouds roll in and rain begins pelting against the windows that usually give me a great view of the city.

"Is everything alright?" Marilyn asks when the game comes to an end. Handsy has disappeared to the bathroom and Killer is in the kitchen, grabbing more drinks.

I glance over at our rookie, hating that he already knows me well enough to read my mood.

"Yeah, of course."

"What's with the flowers, Storm?" Killer asks.

My eyes shoot to the dining table, where the colorful bouquet I bought for Parker still sits.

"Umm..."

"Something you need to tell us?" Handsy asks as he rejoins us.

"Yeah, but I need you guys to keep this between us." I knew that I'd need to confess if I want them to keep coming around and hanging out here. But I also don't want the whole franchise to know. It became even more important to keep it quiet after what Parker confessed to earlier about the way certain members of staff see her. The last thing she needs is for everyone to know she's living with me. I don't want anyone thinking she got her job because of anything I did.

All of them lean a little closer, as if I'm about to tell them my biggest, darkest secret.

"I've got a roommate."

Killer barks a laugh. "Who the fuck wants to live with you?"

As if on cue, there's movement on the other side of the apartment, and when I look up, I find Parker standing there. She's utterly soaked. Rainwater drips off her, leaving her standing in her own little puddle.

"I can assure you, it wasn't by choice," she states.

Her expression is blank as she says the words. There is

none of her usual joy when we spar together. There's... nothing.

I launch from my seat on the coach.

"Parker, what—ow, fuck," I bark as pain shoots up my leg.

Parker instantly drops her purse, a tote bag she didn't have earlier, and her shoes that are once again in her hand, and surges forward.

"What's wrong?" she asks.

I stand a little taller and stretch out my leg.

"It's fine. Just a bit of cramp."

"Lincoln," she warns.

"Honestly, it's fine. Overreaction." I force a smile on my face, but from the way her eyes narrow, she's aware that I'm lying.

The guys sit silently, looking back and forth between us like they're watching a tennis match.

"You two..." Handsy starts.

"Are you living together?" Killer finishes, like an old married couple.

"It's a temporary thing," Parker explains. "There was a fire in my building, and I didn't have much of a choice."

"And I love it so when she makes me feel appreciated," I deadpan.

She rolls her eyes but watches me closely as I sit back down on the couch.

I'd be lying if I said the pain had subsided. But it will.

I'm playing our next game. There is no question about that.

"I'll get you some ice, then I'm going to bed. Continue as if I'm not here."

My eyes track her as she moves to the kitchen and bends over a little to open the freezer.

Fuck, she has a spectacular ass.

"How was the date?" Marilyn asks when she turns around and walks back toward us.

Parker sighs before pulling on a smile. It's all I need to know that it didn't go well.

"Yeah, you know. About as good as any date you find on Tinder."

"That good?" Handsy asks.

"Yep," she says before turning her eyes on me. "Massive disappointment."

I open my mouth to say something, although I'm not entirely sure what, but she beats me to it.

"If you have any more issues, you know where to find me. If not, enjoy the rest of your night."

"You're welcome to join us," Killer calls as she walks away.

"Maybe another time. You guys have already lost once this week. I'd hate to see you do it again. And to a girl."

The guys all chuckle before Marilyn announces, "I like her."

"Excuse me?" I blurt before I can think better of it.

"Whoa, not like that. I just mean I'm glad she's a part of the team. She's better than Mitchell, and she's fun to talk to."

I raise a brow, and he holds his hands up in defense. "I'm not interested, I promise."

I look at each of them and find a whole range of questions in each of their eyes. None of them voices them, though. Instead, Killer slaps his thighs and says, "We should probably head out. Let you rest that leg."

Only a few minutes later, they've gathered up all their stuff, and they're heading toward the elevator.

"Please don't say anything about her being here," I say quietly.

I don't want to be a reason her life is harder at work than necessary.

"Your secret is safe with us, Storm. Any secret, for that matter."

"Get the hell out of here," I bark before the elevator doors close on them, leaving me standing in the middle of my silent apartment.

Turning around, I start toward my bedroom when another door opens and Parker pokes her head out.

"They didn't need to leave because of me."

My eyes drop to the Bandits zip-up hoodie and sleep shorts she's wearing that expose her legs.

"They didn't. They were heading out anyway."

"Right."

"I told them to keep you staying here to themselves."

She nods in appreciation. "Not sure how I feel about being your dirty little secret, Storm," she muses as she slips past me and into the kitchen for a bottle of water.

"Most women would pay good money to be in that position."

"Good thing I'm not most women, then, isn't it?" she asks before twisting the lid off and drinking almost half the bottle.

"What happened tonight, Parker?"

She shrugs one shoulder as she lowers the bottle to the counter.

"He wasn't worthy," she says, as if it explains everything.

"And he abandoned you in the middle of a downpour?" I ask, gesturing to the puddle that's still in the entryway.

She laughs. "No. I needed some air, so I walked."

"Back from The Carlton."

"Hmm," she mumbles. She's lying. "Did you want me to look at your leg before I go to bed?"

28

PARKER

inc stares at me. A small frown pinches his brows as he weighs his options.

For a moment, a little rejection trickles through my veins, but then I remember where we are and what we're doing and it shifts to disappointment that for once in his life, he's going to do the right thing.

He's trying—in more ways than one—and I really appreciate what he's doing.

"It'll be okay. We should probably just head to bed."

He's right, but worry tugs at me.

"Let me just look quickly. I'll worry all night otherwise."

"You really don't—'

"Please."

He sighs.

"Okay," he concedes before taking a step back.

"Strip down to your boxers and go lie on your bed."

"Who says I'm wearing any?" he teases.

Images I shouldn't have fill my eyes, and the second a smirk curls at the side of his mouth, I realize he can read my mind.

Goddamn him.

"I'm not coming near you if your balls are hanging free, Storm."

"Aw, I love it when you talk dirty to me," he mocks as he tucks his thumbs into his sweats and shoves them down his legs, revealing his tight black boxer briefs beneath.

"You're a nightmare," I mutter under my breath.

"Nah, I'm pretty sure I spend more time in women's dreams."

"Christ."

Grabbing my water bottle from the counter, I follow him toward his bedroom.

Linc's house, especially his bedroom, is so different to what I was expecting when he first brought me here.

In my head, it was going to be a bachelor pad with clothes and takeout containers strewn everywhere. Posters of naked girls on the walls and pairs of panties hanging from lamps. But the reality is far from that.

This place is homey. From the moment I walked through the front door, I felt relaxed. It doesn't scream sex den or party pad. I could actually live here, which is a thought I really don't need to have. I also don't need to get used to it, because the kind of place I'm going to be able to afford is going to feel like a cardboard box after this.

I may have been in his bedroom already, but today, the second I step over the threshold, it feels completely different.

The air is thick with tension, and I can only assume that's because there is a half-naked Adonis of a man lying on the bed.

I run my eyes up his solid, muscular legs, pausing when I get to the bulge in the front of his boxers.

Walk away, Parker.

Go to your room and lock the door.

"Little P?" Linc questions, and the second I realize I'm standing here staring at his dick, my eyes dart to his and my face burns bright red.

"Sorry, I—"

"It's okay. You look all you like."

"Linc," I warn as I move closer.

Despite knowing it's the worst thing I can do, I'm drawn to him like a magnet.

"Tell me about your date," he demands.

A laugh erupts. "You really don't want to hear about that."

"I do," he argues.

What he means is he wants to know why I walked home in the rain, and probably why I looked so miserable when he found me dripping all over his expensive wooden floor.

"It...it wasn't right," I say as I trace up his adductor muscle, watching his reaction for any sign of pain.

"In what way?"

I sigh as I begin massaging the area he's been struggling with.

In a way that I couldn't put myself in a position of being with another man when I can't get thoughts and memories of you out of my head.

"I don't know," I lie. "Seemed like a good idea through a screen. The reality wasn't what I thought it would be."

"He that unattractive, huh?"

"Not at all. In fact, he's probably one of the most attractive men I've ever seen."

"Other than me, of course."

"Good to see your ego hasn't taken a hit," I tease.

"You'd miss it."

"Mmm."

"So, are you seeing this guy again?"

"I don't know. Maybe. He isn't in town often."

"You've met him before."

"Uh huh," I agree, keeping my eyes focused on the task at hand, afraid that if I look up, he might read too much.

"Ah, it was that kind of date," he surmises.

"It was dinner," I counter.

"You know, you're a really bad liar, Parker." My eyes dart to his. "Your neck goes all red and blotchy when you lie."

"I'm not—"

"Sure. So this guy you went out with. He's a regular hookup of yours, is he?"

"Linc, can we not?"

"What? We're just two friends talking about our nights."

"We're not friends."

His hand shifts to cover his heart as he gasps.

"Ouch."

"Oh, come on. You know it's true."

"I'm not sure. There was a time when I considered you one of my best friends."

My heart races, and I keep my eyes locked on my fingers.

"That was a long time ago. We're...we're different people now. Want different things."

"Is that right? Because some days, I can't help but wish I could turn back time and have a do-over."

"Stop, please," I beg.

"You think about it, don't you?"

"No," I snap, refusing to go down this road with him. "I forgot about it years ago, put it into the correct box, and moved on with my life."

"Yeah," he muses. "I watched."

I stand tall, my hand slipping away from his skin.

"You don't get to say things like that."

"It's true, though."

"Fuck's sake, Linc."

"I'm sorry, can you just keep going? It feels better."

I hesitate, questioning everything.

"Please. I need to play our next day."

"Blackmail isn't going to get you anywhere."

"I just want to get back on the ice," he pleads.

"Fine. Fine. Can you just...I don't know, not talk?"

"Never been one of my talents."

"Trust me, I know."

"Just so you know," he starts, and I squeeze my eyes closed because I know I'm not going to like whatever comes next. "I never put anything about you in a box and forgot about it. I never will, either."

"Fuck," I breathe, and when I open my eyes, I regret not putting an end to this sooner.

The bulge in his boxers is bigger than before. He's...fuck.

I stumble back.

"I can't do this, Linc," I say, keeping my eyes downcast. "I'm your roommate and your trainer. I can't...we can't go back in time. We can't be those kids again. What happened...it—"

"No, we can't. But we can be us now."

A laugh bubbles out of me, and I finally look up. He's sitting on the edge of his bed with his hair a mess, strands hanging over his face as he looks up at me through his lashes.

"You're delusional."

"Am I?"

"Yeah," I insist as he pushes to his feet and stalks closer, although not before he sinks his hand into his boxers to adjust himself.

Fuck.

Heat descends through my body like an out-of-control inferno.

I went out tonight to get laid, and instead I ended up walking home in the rain.

And for what?

To end up even more frustrated by the man I'm currently living with.

Moving in here was a bad idea.

"Little P," he says, closing the space between us.

My hand darts out, and I press my palm against his chest. It looks tiny compared to his huge frame.

But despite my lack of strength and small stature, he instantly freezes.

"Look at me," he demands.

I don't.

"Parker, I said look at me." His voice is deep and commanding, leaving me powerless but to follow his orders.

Our eyes collide, and the air crackles between us.

Mimicking his move from earlier, he lifts his hand and tucks a lock of loose hair behind my ear. My tumbling curls are no more; instead, it's a frizzy mess. My makeup isn't faring much better, either. The outside of me looks as bedraggled as my insides feel.

"Whatever you need, all you need to do is ask. I told you once before, and I'll tell you again, I'll do anything for you, Parker. Anything."

A sob erupts, and I squeeze my eyes closed to try to ward off the threatening tears.

These aren't the words I need to hear. Not from a man who spends his life collecting puck bunnies like they're going out of fashion.

He's a player in every sense of the word, and in one way or another, they always break your heart.

I stopped it from happening six years ago. I protected myself and got out before I fell in too deep. I doubt I'll be strong enough to do the same thing twice.

The heat from his body burns down my front, and his warm breath tickles over my skin, making my nipples pebble behind the soft fabric of my tank.

It would be so easy to fall into something stupid here.

So fucking easy.

When he steps forward, his body bumping mine, my eyes fly open and I jump back. Only I don't get very far because I hit the wall.

"You're so fucking beautiful, Parker. Always have been," he whispers, his voice floating around me like a prayer.

"Linc, please." The words fall from my lips without instruction from my brain. It's my pussy talking, my desperation to get off and ride that high for a few blissful seconds.

His hips press against mine, allowing me to feel his

hardness. Heat floods my core as my clit pounds in time with my racing heart.

"God, Parker. I fucking dream about hearing you beg me."

He leans closer, and my fingers twist in his T-shirt.

Pull him closer.

Push him away.

Take what you need.

Protect your heart.

Your job.

You're—

"No," I cry a beat before his lips brush mine.

I dart from my position pinned between him and the wall and run toward the exit.

"Shit. Parker. I'm sorry. Fuck. I'm sorry, alright?"

"I know, Linc. I know," I cry as I race toward my door and swing it closed. The slam echoes around the bedroom.

My chest heaves as my heart continues to race. His scent still floods my nose, and my core continues to beg for what could have been.

I stare at the door, fear trickling through my veins. But it's not strong enough. I need a barrier between us.

You did the right thing.

You did the right thing.

But no matter how many times I tell myself this, I struggle to believe it.

"Fuck's sake," I hiss as I surge forward and grab the tote bag I carried home earlier.

After I gave up on my date, I asked the driver to take me to a street with one of my favorite stores. No sooner was I out of the car, I was walking through the front door. I ignored all the pretty lingerie that I'd usually wander through, and I walked straight to the back of the store.

I might need new underwear, but it's obvious that I don't have any need for anything that sexy. I can't even show up for dinner with a man, let alone anything else.

I went straight for what I want like a woman on a mission, just like I do now as I tug at the packaging.

There's a little voice in my head that warns me that it won't have enough charge, but I push it aside. Something has to go my way tonight.

"Goddamn it," I mutter as I battle with the almost impossible-to-open plastic. I need scissors, but I am not going back out there to find some.

Thankfully, I locate some nail clippers in the bathroom, and it's enough to make a hole so I can rip into the packaging.

In seconds, I'm shoving my sleep shorts down my legs and climbing onto my bed.

Please, please, last long enough to get me there.

I press the little button, and the toy in my hand buzzes to life.

Breathing a sigh of relief, I spread my legs and touch the tip of it to my clit.

I swear my gasp sucks all the air from the room.

Pushing it lower, I groan before pushing the tip inside.

My muscles clamp down, sucking it deeper as images of what could have happened in the room next door only moments ago fill my mind.

29

LINCOLN

"Fuck," I breathe as I drop my forehead to my arm that's resting against the wall I just had Parker backed up against.

I fucked up.

I know that.

I should have insisted my leg was fine and sent her to bed.

It was obvious when she turned up soaking wet that she hadn't had a good night, and yet I went and pushed. My need to know that her date went badly, that she didn't want the guy she was meeting, was all-consuming.

And when I discovered it was a hookup, things only got worse.

Images of her rolling around in bed with another man were the only thing I could see.

Jealousy shot through me faster than I could control.

It fucking terrified me.

I know that Parker dates. I know that she sleeps with guys and moves on in the way I do with women. But it's always been from a distance. She hasn't been with anyone I know since high school. Hockey aside, she's kept her life as separate from mine as possible.

If I'd have been signed to another team, we probably

wouldn't be a part of each other's lives at all, and that thought is fucking horrifying.

Parker, despite being completely unaware, has always been one of my favorite people. The thought of going through life without her being there, even if it is at a distance, doesn't sit right with me.

But suddenly, she's closer. Closer than she's ever been, and it's reminding me of how everything used to be. How much I like hanging out with her. How much fun bickering with her is. How fucking hot she is even when she's not trying.

Just like tonight.

Get it together, Storm.

She's right.

We can't do this.

She's just starting a new job. The last thing she needs is to be tangled up with you.

Dragging in a couple of deep, ragged breaths, I will my body to cool down before pushing from the wall.

Not ready to crawl into bed, I walk out into the hallway, and the second I cross the threshold, my eyes dart to her door.

It's closed.

Parker never closes her door, thanks to a prank Rett pulled on her years ago. The fact she's done it now to put a barrier between us has a fresh wave of self-hatred racing through my veins.

My legs move me forward, and in only seconds, I'm standing before her closed door.

Reaching out, I wrap my fingers around the handle and silently crack it open.

I hate the idea of her waking up in the night, seeing it closed and freaking out. I've already fucked up enough tonight.

I only push it open an inch. I don't want to be caught—I just...

"Oh god."

Panic sends my heart lurching into my chest the second her voice hits my ear, but when nothing else follows, I relax.

But then...

Holy shit.

Is she...?

Buzzing fills the air, and when another soft moan hits my ears, I know exactly what's happening on the other side of the door.

Knowing that I got her so worked up earlier when I barely even touched her sends a fire shooting through my veins.

Desire descends and my cock swells again.

As much as I hate that she ran away from me, knowing that she immediately started getting herself off sure takes the sting out of it.

She whimpers, and I squeeze my eyes closed, picturing her lying on my guest bed with her sleep shorts kicked off and her legs spread.

It takes every ounce of willpower I possess not to let out a groan of my own.

I bet she looks so fucking beautiful right now.

Did she leave her top on, keeping her perfect tits covered, or has she stripped that off too, so she can tease her nipples?

Fuck. I bet they're hard and begging for attention.

My tongue sweeps across my bottom lip as I imagine lowering myself over her body and sucking one into my mouth.

God, she'd taste so fucking sinful.

So fucking perfect.

"Yesss," she hisses, and I can't help myself. Pushing my hand beneath the waistband of my boxers, I wrap my fist around my shaft, slowly dragging it to the end.

The fabric is already wet with precum, and I use it as lubricant as I begin fucking myself as her moans and whimpers begin to get louder.

She's getting close, but goddamn, so am I.

I've barely touched myself and I'm on the verge of blowing.

I guess that's what happens when you've wanted something for so fucking long, only to get the briefest of tastes. Not that I got a taste. Not really. But feeling her soft body pinned between mine and the wall was enough.

Okay, no. It was nowhere near enough.

I fear that when it comes to Parker, nothing will ever be enough.

"Oh god. Yes."

I fall back against the wall beside her door, my face tipped to the ceiling and my eyes closed as I let my imagination run away with itself.

She isn't in there alone; instead, she's holding her legs open for me while I feast on her.

My cock jerks as my release surges ever closer.

Fuck, yeah.

I'm fucking her with two fingers, working her G-spot and making her wild with the need to fall over the edge as I suck on her clit.

Her body trembles violently as she chants my name over and over like a prayer.

She's so fucking sweet. The best thing I've ever tasted.

"God, yes."

I groan but keep my mouth on her, letting her use the vibrations to get her even closer.

"Right there. Right fucking there."

"Come all over my face, babe. Show me what a good girl you are."

"Oh, fuuuuck. Yessss."

My own release slams into me as her cries fill the air between us, and I come in my boxers like a horny teenage boy sneaking around in the shadows, secretly getting his kicks.

"Oh my god," she gasps before a loud thump makes me jump.

I'm ready to run, but when no movement follows, I relax

back against the wall, assuming it was her vibrator hitting the floor.

I picture her spreadeagled on the bed, one arm thrown over her eyes as she fights to catch her breath.

The temptation to look is so strong. If I'm right, she won't be able to see. I could do it unnoticed.

I shake my head.

Don't be ridiculous, Storm.

My body begins to cool, as does the cum that's now covering me. But it doesn't make me move. Instead, I stay exactly where I am, craving more of Parker.

Time seems to stand still as I wait for something, anything.

But the second she groans and begins moving around her room, I realize it was nowhere near long enough.

With my boxers now sticking to me, I force myself to move and retreat to my own room, pushing the door closed. I might not be scared of being locked in a room, but I do like the idea of leaving it open. I'm confident that it's an invitation she'd never take me up on, but the offer is there if she felt the need.

The thought of her sneaking in, in the middle of the night and crawling into bed with me, letting me roll over and tuck her into my body, makes my chest tighten.

Fuck. What I wouldn't I give to find out what that's like.

I've never spent the whole night with a woman before.

There's only ever been one that's made me even consider it as an option.

I'm more than happy when all the others get up and leave when we're done.

They all know the deal before we get down to business, and they're happy to agree to my terms.

But there is always an exception to the rules.

Stripping out of my boxers, I dump them in the laundry basket before marching toward my shower and turning it on.

I step inside, ready to shut myself away from everything and relax.

But it doesn't happen. The solace I usually find under the powerful jets of water is nowhere to be found.

Irritated, I clean up and get out.

With a towel wrapped around my waist, I stop in front of the sink and stare at myself in the mirror, but the man staring back at me doesn't have any good advice.

With a sigh, I tip my head back and blow out a breath.

Just play the game, Storm.

Trust that if the win is meant to be yours, then it will happen.

With a clean pair of boxers on, I grab my cell from the side and fall into bed.

I've got a whole stream of notifications, but there's only one that really catches my eye, and seeing it makes my heart drop into the pit of my stomach.

My father has always been my hero. I looked up to him all my life. Even with him gone, nothing has changed.

But there is another man who has watched every single move I've made in my career.

He was there at all my important games, looking proud the day I got drafted, and when he can, he still comes and supports me, despite his son being on a different team.

Clark Donnelly is an incredible man, father, coach, and back in the day, player.

I have the utmost respect for him, so knowing what I just did with his daughter sends a rush of shame through me.

When it comes to Parker, no man will ever be good enough in his eyes. And there is no doubt in my mind that I'd be at the bottom of his list of ideal suitors for his daughter.

> Superman: How's the injury? Gutted you didn't get to play the last two games. You were missed in that last one. Painful loss.

Linc: Hey, yeah, it sucks. So did watching my boys lose that badly. All part of the fun, though, huh? Injury is good, got this new kickass trainer who's putting us all in our place.

Superman: Glad to hear it. So proud of our girl.

Linc: Me too. She's a fantastic addition to the team.

Pride for what Parker has managed to achieve fills me. When she first announced her ambition to be a trainer in the NHL, Clark, Rett, and I all looked at each other in concern. Not because we didn't think she had it in her. We all knew, without a doubt, she did. But back then, there really were no women in the NHL. I'm so fucking relieved to say that in the past few years, things have started to change for the better.

We now have a handful of female staff in all departments, and it's steadily growing.

I know, like Parker said, that not everyone supports the change. But they're wrong.

Women bring so much to our sport, and long may it continue. I want Parker and all the others to inspire the next generation, girls like Sutton and her team. Girls with a dream of playing a sport they love and making a difference in the world.

Superman: How's she really doing? She was putting on a brave face when we spoke to her the other day, but we're worried.

"Christ," I mutter, dragging my hand down my face.

Linc: She's okay. Parker is strong. She won't let this bring her down.

Superman: She refused to let us help her get a new place. She said she's staying with a colleague, but is she really okay with that?

"Fucking hell."

Parker and I haven't had the conversation about where she told her parents she was living, and I really fucking hate lying to Clark, even if it is by omission.

Linc: She's really okay. She's welcome to stay as long as she needs. Once the season's over, she'll have more time to secure a place and get moved.

My stomach knots at the thought.

She's only been here a few days, but I already can't imagine her not being here.

I love this apartment; it's my safe haven from the crazy world on the outside. But with her here, it's turned into a real home. There's now life inside this place, and I love it.

30

PARKER

"No," I groan. "Go away."

But no matter how much I complain, my cell keeps ringing.

Rolling onto my side, I blindly reach toward my nightstand and grab it.

I hold it in front of my face and crack one eye to see who it is.

I groan again when I find my big brother's smug face filling the screen. And it only gets worse when I notice the time.

"This had better be an emergency," I mutter sleepily the second I accept the call and press my cell to my ear.

"Ah, good morning to you too. I do love hearing my little sister's happy voice first thing."

"Morning? It's practically still nighttime."

He tsks on the other end. "The Vipers are letting you off early if they don't already have you at the arena trying to fix up their wannabes."

"Hey now, one of those wannabes is your best f-friend," I stutter as a memory of the night before slams into me.

Fuck. I almost let Linc kiss me.

"Is everything okay?" he asks, sounding more concerned than I'd like him to.

The world thinks they know my big brother. They all think he's this powerful ice hockey player with serious anger issues. But that is far from the truth. Underneath all the bravado is nothing but a teddy bear. He loves with all his heart and cares so much more than he allows people to see. I see, though. Even if he was a jerk when we were growing up, I never doubted his love for me. We might argue and bicker, but we're a team, and we always have been. We spent years training together, trying to make the other a better player, and when I decided to go down the trainer route, he did everything he could to help me.

We're not as close as we once were now that he's playing in Seattle, but we try to catch up every week, and we do our best to squeeze in visits. But with me now following the Vipers around the country on road games, it's exponentially harder to make that happen. At least we'll have games against each other to look forward to.

Bandits and Vipers games are always fun with Rett and Linc going head-to-head with each other. The fans eat that shit up, and it always makes for an electric game.

They've already had a couple of matchups this season, but we have more to look forward to.

Shuffling, so I'm sitting against the headboard, I comb my fingers through my messy hair. I didn't do anything with it after getting caught in the rain last night; I can only imagine what a disaster it is after tossing and turning all night.

"Yeah," I force out. "Everything is fine, why?"

A beat of silence passes, and I panic that Linc has already told him I'm here.

My heart rate picks up and my lips part to say something when he beats me to it.

"Don't fucking lie to me, PK."

I swallow thickly and stare down at the sheets covering my legs, wishing that I could sink under them and put an end to all of this.

"Mom called me, asked me if I knew about your apartment," Rett continues.

"I'm sorry," I squeak.

"Why the fuck didn't you call me?" he asks. The hurt in his voice makes my chest ache.

I fucking hate disappointing Rett. He's always been my number-one supporter.

"You've got enough going on right now; you didn't need my drama."

"Fuck that, Parker. Your fucking home burned down. You could have been inside and—"

"But I wasn't," I quickly interrupt.

It's something I've refused to allow myself to think about. It's bad enough knowing that my neighbors were at home and had to escape. I'm just grateful that I had plans that meant I was away from it all. I'm also really fucking grateful for Linc. If I had taken that Uber home, what would I have done?

I know for a fact that I wouldn't be here right now. Which, let's be honest, probably wouldn't be a bad thing.

It sure would have been better for my sanity.

"I've probably lost all my stuff, but I'll get over that. It's just stuff."

"I know," he says sadly. "But it still sucks, and you still should have called me."

"I'm sorry. I was trying to be independent and—"

"You were too ashamed to confess about your insurance?"

"Goddamn it. Can't Mom and Dad keep any secrets?" I curse.

"They're worried about you. I am too."

"I'm fine. I promise. I'm…" I look around the room, debating whether to tell Rett the truth or not.

No. It's better for him not to know.

"I'm staying with a colleague. A friend," I add quickly, which is possibly a lie. I have no idea what Linc and I are after last night. Colleagues might be more accurate now.

"Do you need anything? I can wire you money. I can organize a lease—"

"No, Rett. Thank you. I really appreciate the offer, but I'm really okay. I have some savings, and I'm just going to replace things as I need them."

Pain lashes at my insides as I think of some of the sentimental things I'm probably never going to see again. But what I said before is true. It's just stuff. I'm okay. Everyone who was in the building got out safely. That's what really matters.

"I wish you weren't so stubborn," he mutters down the line.

"Nah, it would be boring if I was," I tease. "Someone has got to keep you on your toes."

"Have you met my coach?" he deadpans.

Yeah, I have. And for some reason, he fucking hates Rett. He loves what he can achieve on the ice, of course. But personality-wise, they clash big time.

"Ah, you love him."

"He's the reason I'm calling you so early. He's dragging us in early for extra conditioning sessions."

"Well, looking at your performance recently, I can understand why," I deadpan.

"Hey now, we can't all be top of the league."

A proud smile pulls at my lips. "You never know, maybe one day you'll land yourself a spot on a winning team."

"Harsh, PK. Harsh. Listen, I gotta run before Coach has me doing even more fucking drills."

I chuckle.

"Call me if you need anything."

"I won't, but thanks."

"Pain in the ass," he mutters.

"Love you, bro," I tease.

"Love you too. Be good."

He hangs up before I get a chance to point out that he's the one who needs that warning.

Letting my cell drop to the bed, I sink back into the warm sheets and close my eyes.

I regret it the second I do because all I can see is Linc looming over me last night, his eyes darting between mine and my mouth.

"Fucking hell," I mutter, opening my eyes and staring at the ceiling.

I'm achingly aware that I could accept help from Mom and Dad, or Rett, get myself a place and get the hell away from Linc. But...I don't want to.

I don't want to be bailed out because I screwed up. I want to figure this out on my own, even if it means I have to dance around Linc for the foreseeable future.

As I lie there staring at nothing, images I don't need on a constant loop in my head, the sun begins to rise, making the edges of the curtains glow, and not long later, the sound of someone moving around floats through the air.

If I were being a grown-up about it, I'd roll out of bed and go and talk to him. But the thought of facing him after how close we were last night makes me want to vomit.

So instead of dealing with my issues head-on, I continue to lie in bed and pray that he leaves before my alarm goes off and I need to step out of the safety of my bedroom.

LUCK IS on my side today.

By the time I needed to leave for the arena for my first session, Linc had shut himself in his home gym and I was able to slip out unnoticed.

I wanted to believe that he was hiding from me too, but this is Linc we're talking about. He hasn't hidden from a single thing in his entire life. I meet a few people I recognize as I walk toward the trainers' room, all of whom greet me with a smile, giving me some hope that my luck today might continue.

That all comes to an end when I push our office door open

and I find Dillion Mitchell standing right there with a scowl on his face.

"Watch it," he snaps, as if I could see through the wooden door to know he was there.

"Sorry," I mutter, moving to the side so I'm not in his way.

Why I do it, I don't know. I have just as much right to be standing in this office as he does.

My chin drops, but it's too late; he's already gone. Plus, there are other voices in the training room I just walked through to get in here, and the last thing I want to do is make a scene.

Instead, I silently fume as I put my things in my drawer and wake up my iPad to check over today's schedule.

As I stare at the first name on the list, I'm taken back to last night, when I stumbled into the penthouse looking like a bedraggled cat.

I trust Linc, and despite not knowing the rest of the team as well, I trust his judgment. If he says the guys can keep my secret, then I trust that they will.

I'm distracted reading an article about new research in muscle recovery when there's a rap on the door that scares the shit out of me.

"Shit. I'm sorry, I didn't mean to scare you," Cole Hansley says with regret in his features as I fight to catch my breath.

"It's okay. For someone so huge, you'd think I'd have heard you coming."

He chuckles as he leans his shoulder against the doorframe.

"You ready, Donnelly?"

"As ready as I'll ever be, Hansley," I counter, hopping to my feet, ready to get to work.

But as I step closer to him, he doesn't move like I was expecting him to. Instead, he ducks his head and whispers, "We meant what we said last night. Where you're currently sleeping is none of our business. We respect you, Parker. More than that, we trust you, and we want to prove that you can do the same with us."

As I stare into his dark green eyes, my own begin to sting with emotion.

Holy shit. Do not cry in front of a player.

"T-thank you, Cole. I really appreciate that."

He smiles softly at me.

"We hang out at Linc's place often, but if you ever don't want us there, all you have to do is say."

"I don't want to intrude on Linc's life any more than I already am. I'll be out of there as fast as possible so he can go back to entertaining bunnies every night of the week."

Cole's brow wrinkles and his lips part as if he's about to say something, but he thinks better of it.

Instead, he pushes back to his full height, which, even without skates, is ridiculous at six foot four. I have to tip my head all the way back just to keep eye contact with him.

"He's a good guy," Cole finally says. "You're lucky to have him in your corner."

"I know. He might drive me crazy, but deep down, he's got a heart of gold."

Cole smiles at me again before spinning around and marching toward the empty trainer's table. On the other side of the room, Mitchell is working with Isaac Hammond, our second-line goalie.

"So, what are we focusing on today? Where are you feeling it?"

"Hips," Cole says with a wince. "It's always the fucking hips."

I spend just over an hour working with Cole, but as our time together starts coming to an end, dread begins to drip through my veins. The next person on my table is going to be Linc.

I'm not ready to see him, let alone have to touch him.

"You okay?" Cole asks as we finish up.

I hate that he can read something on my face.

"Yeah, I haven't been sleeping great. The last week has been a lot."

"I can imagine," he says as he swings his legs over the side of the table. "Don't put pressure on yourself to feel okay. New home, new job, putting up with us assholes. It's a lot."

I smile at him, grateful for his words and support. "Thank you."

"Anytime. I'm much better with advice than the others."

"I won't mention you said that."

"Probably best not to." He laughs.

I turn my back to the room as I type up some notes, listening as Cole sorts himself out and Mitchell slips into the office.

"Are you going to be okay?" Cole asks, and I startle when I realize he's closer than I was expecting.

"Yeah, of course. Why?" I spin around, confused by the question, but the second my eyes land on the man standing in the doorway, it clicks.

I might not have said anything to Cole, but it seems he might be a little more perceptive than I was expecting.

"Oh," I breathe as Linc's eyes hold mine.

My heart pounds and my hands begin to tremble.

But I refuse to cower to any man, even one I'd happily crawl to if the situation were different, so I straighten my spine and plaster a smile on my face.

"We're all done here. I'll see you tomorrow?" I say to Cole as I grab the antibacterial spray and begin wiping down the table.

"You got it."

Out of the corner of my eye, I see Cole step up to Linc. He murmurs something I can't hear before he walks away, leaving us alone.

"On the table. Let's get you cleared for tomorrow's game."

31

PARKER

"This is even more depressing than the last place, and that's really saying something," I muse as Casey, Freya and I stand in the living room of yet another awful apartment.

We've seen three this afternoon, and they've gotten increasingly worse.

I swear that the damp scent has permeated my skin already.

"We're not looking at the rest of it. I refuse to allow either of you to live in any of the places we've seen today," Casey states before marching toward the beaten-up front door. "Let's go and get day drunk."

Freya and I look at each other before racing after her.

Cocktails are essential at this point.

It's been a week since the incident in Linc's room, and I'm doing my best to put it behind me and focus on my future.

Things between us have been...awkward and strained.

If he hasn't already left for the arena before I emerge from my room, then he's in his room or his home gym. If he's back when I get home at night, I mumble some kind of excuse and hide in my bedroom.

The only time we properly spend together is when he's in

the trainers' room. Thankfully, his groin has healed up nicely and I was able to remove his name from the injury report that next morning. It's meant fewer one-on-one sessions, which is a relief. I'm not sure I could cope with another hour like we had the morning after the night before.

It was awkward as hell. The air between us was charged, and there were many questions we wanted to ask, but as the session came to an end, everything went unsaid. It still does now, and I'm happy to leave it that way. He said more than enough that night. I don't need to hear anything else. It'll only make it all worse. The memories are more than enough.

He took to the ice on his first game back with vigor, and as well as ensuring Handsy had another shutout game, he added two goals to our score, helping us win the game three to zero.

Our winning streak has continued since, increasing our lead and clinching a playoff spot almost inevitable at this point.

The guys are on fire. They're healthy, and everything is looking fantastic.

I wish I could say the same for Rett and the Bandits, but they're still struggling, and Rett is getting increasingly frustrated.

With each day that passes, I love my job even more. The guys on my treatment list are incredible; they treat me with respect, they listen, and they embrace everything I throw at them.

When we're at the arena, Brooke and I almost always meet for lunch, whether that's in the on-site restaurant or heading out to get a breather. Our friendship is growing, and I couldn't be more grateful to have another fierce woman in my corner.

"I'm destined to live with my parents for the rest of my life now, aren't I?" Freya complains after we've had a round of strawberry daiquiris delivered to our table at a bar a little down from the building we just ran from.

"Absolutely not," Casey assures her.

She groans and takes a large sip of her drink.

Freya grew up in the house next door to Casey. She used to babysit for Casey, and me, if I was hanging out, when we were younger. She moved to Las Vegas after graduating from college and worked in a cocktail bar for a while before falling head over heels in love with a musician. He swept her off her feet and she followed him everywhere—until a couple of months ago, when he decided that he was done with her and she was forced to return home with a broken heart.

She's been back at her parents' ever since, trying to figure out what to do with her life now.

I feel for her. She gave up everything to be with that asshole and he just discarded her like a piece of trash. It's just more proof that men can't be trusted. And apparently, it's not just professional athletes who are happy to rip out our hearts and stomp on them until they're unrecognizable.

Freya continues talking about job interviews she's had, all of which have been a bust. The problem seems to be that she doesn't have a direction. She's lost at sea without a map, and I fear that until she figures out which way she wants to go, nothing is going to change.

My cell buzzes on the table, and my eyes drop to find a Tinder notification.

"I thought you'd sworn off men," Casey pipes up.

I confessed to her about my failed attempt to meet Henry last week and told her I was done.

While I might have been happy to tell her about ditching my hookup at the last minute, I kept what happened back at the apartment to myself. No one needs to know about that. Hell, I wish I didn't.

Every time I allow myself to remember, I get all hot and this fluttery feeling starts up in my stomach. The same thing happens when I see him. But much like everything else I don't want to think about, I keep trying to shove it all into a box and close the lid.

I did it all those years ago; I should be able to do it again, right?

"I have. But it's fun seeing all the disappointments I'm not going to waste my time on."

Picking up my cell, I open the app and stare at the profile picture of the guy I've been matched with.

"He's hot," Freya says, leaning over the table to look.

"If you're interested, I'm sure I can hook you up."

"Absolutely not," she states. "I'm with you. Happy to window shop, but I'm not buying anything. Hell, I'm not even trying anything on."

"I'd love to try something on," I complain, slumping in my seat.

"So go and do it. Women can have one-night stands too," Freya says innocently.

Casey turns to look at me, but I don't return her attention.

"I know. Trust me, I've had my fair share. I just...I don't know. It's not as appealing as it once was."

"I guess when you can get a battery-operated dick to do the job just as well, what's the point?"

"Oh no," Casey pipes up. "I know neither of you wants to hear this, but the right man blows any toy out of the water."

"Really?" I groan. "Are you really going to rub it in our noses like that?"

Casey shrugs. "I'm just saying. It's worth kissing a few frogs to find Prince Charming."

I can't help but giggle.

"What?" Casey asks.

"I'm sorry. It's just...the image of Kodie as Prince Charming that popped into my head. Please, can you buy him a crown and get him to wear it to work one day?"

Casey rolls her eyes. "As if he'd ever play along with something like that."

"Bet he would if you asked. He'd stop the world spinning if you wanted him to."

She gets this faraway look as she thinks about him.

"Ugh, you're so lovesick. It's disgusting."

"Jealousy isn't a good look on you, Donnelly."

"I just want the regular orgasms. I'm not interested in the rest."

"Shame. It's fun."

The conversation turns to the Vipers' upcoming games. We've got a travel day tomorrow and then two home games at the end of this week.

I knew going into this role that it was going to be full on, but I don't think I fully comprehended just how exhausting it was all going to be.

Worth it, though. So worth it.

Watching the guys excel and knowing that I had a hand in it...it blows my mind.

I'm so fucking proud of myself, I could cry every time I step up to the ice and watch them.

"Is it everything you hoped it would be?" Freya asks, dragging me from my thoughts.

"Mostly, yeah. I love being at the arena and around the guys."

"All of them?" Casey teases.

"Most of them," I quip back. "They're awesome. They've formed this little family. They look after each other, pick each other up when one is struggling. It's...it's a privilege getting to experience it."

"You're more than that now. You're a part of it. They'd go to war for you, too, from what I'm hearing," Casey explains.

"And what are you hearing?"

"That they love you. Those who aren't on your list are pissed that they're stuck with Dillion."

I can't help but laugh. "What?"

"Keep this between us, but Dillion is an asshole."

"That's not a secret. The guys don't like him either. Is he giving you a hard time?"

"Nothing I can't handle," I muse. I expected some kickback from starting this role, and if Dillion Mitchell is the worst I have to deal with, then I'll take that.

"Proud of you, P," Casey says, lifting her almost-empty

glass in the air for a toast. "To badass women who don't take shit from any man."

We spend over an hour catching each other up on our lives and laughing until our stomachs hurt.

When Casey announces that she needs to get back, we all call cars and head outside.

The sun has begun to descend, and it casts a beautiful golden light over the city I love so much.

As much as I want to travel and experience a bit of the world, I have no doubt that I'll always end up back here. LA is where my heart lies, and it always will.

With a nice buzz from the cocktails, I confirm Linc's address with my Uber driver and sit back and relax.

I'm feeling lighter after my afternoon. I love the guys, but there is nothing like setting the world to rights with my girls.

I make a note to try to organize a night out with Brooke and Leah, too, when we have a few days at home, and then climb out of the car once we get to Linc's building.

The car disappears the second I close the door, leaving me standing on the sidewalk and gazing up at the impressive building.

I've barely seen him this week; he's been keeping his distance as much as I have. He probably won't even be up there, instead using his night off to enjoy a bunny or two.

Something bitter bubbles up within me. But as fast as I try to shove it down, images of what he might be doing with someone else continue to pop up.

There might not have been any evidence of him hooking up with a woman since I moved in, but I know Linc better than that. He'll have just been doing it discreetly. I should be grateful that he's being considerate and not banging his headboard against the wall we share every night. But I'm not sure I am. Maybe evidence of him putting that night behind him is what I need to be able to do the same.

My cell pings as I wait for the elevator, and when I pull it free, I find another Tinder match.

The guy is more my type than the previous one, which immediately makes me uninterested. My type of men might be hot, but previous experience has taught me that they're only goal in life is to fuck and break hearts.

No, thank you very much.

I swipe right as I step into the elevator and close the app down as fast.

Any hopes I'd had of Linc being out and me having a quiet evening to myself are squashed long before the elevator doors open, because I can hear them already.

And when I step out, the shouting and laughing only get louder.

As I walk toward the living room to see what's going on, my eyes almost bug out of my head.

"What on Earth..."

32

LINCOLN

"You have got to be joking," I balk when Monroe upends the bag he carried into my apartment.

"What? It'll be fun. Or are you too much of a pussy to give it a go?"

A fire burns through me. I have never once in my life turned down a challenge, and tonight is no different.

The elevator dings behind us, announcing the arrival of a few more victims to Monroe's torture evening.

"What the fuck is—" Fletch starts, but he quickly gets interrupted by Handsy, who barks, "There is no way in hell I'm doing that."

"Aw, come on. It's great for balance and coordination."

"I think we can all agree that I'm fine with both of those. Any of you fuckers counting how many shutouts I've had this season?"

"You're killing it, man," Fletch says, clapping our goalie on the shoulder.

But despite his praise, Handsy marches past us, grabs a bottle of water from my fridge, and flops onto my couch.

"Who pissed on his fries?" I mutter.

"He just needs to feel the rhythm. It'll fix him right now," Monroe says confidently.

"Have you met Handsy before?" Fletch asks. "That man doesn't do anything he doesn't want to do."

Fletch's words don't deter Monroe. Our lovable puppy just smiles and states, "You mark my words, by the end of the night, he'll be up battling with us."

"You say that like any of us want to be a part of this," Fletch mutters.

"Storm's in, aren't you?" Monroe says, looking directly at me.

"Uh…"

"See. He's excited."

Fletch snorts a laugh as Killer and Brit emerge from the elevator.

"Oh, fuck, yeah," Killer shouts. "I used to fucking love doing this at the arcade when I was a kid."

We all gawk at him.

"What?" he asks as he begins dragging my coffee table aside to leave us with a big space in front of the TV.

"My little sisters will tell you that they were the best, but little do they know, I used to let them win."

"Dude, we've seen you in a club. You can't dance for shit."

"You wanna fucking bet, motherfucker?" Killer challenges as I set the TV on and give the remote to Monroe, assuming he knows where to find the game we need to get this disaster started.

He finds it and syncs the mats to it, making them light up and play an annoying tune.

"Marilyn, you in?" Killer asks, his eyes glittering with the same kind of excitement as when he scores a goal.

"Hell, yeah. I promised Harper that I'd film it so she can watch," he says, referring to his sister.

"Pulling out the big guns tonight, huh, Marilyn?" Fletch mocks. "Handsy doesn't stand a chance."

Our goalie glares at Fletch, but we already know he's lost this round. Give it thirty minutes and he's going to be on his feet and showing us his moves.

"I hate you all," Handsy sulks.

"Okay, I need to get in the zone," Killer says, dragging his hoodie off and tossing it to the end of the couch before ripping his shoes and socks off.

"Whoa...you can put them the fuck away," I bark. "They smell like rotting animals."

"I've showered since practice."

"I don't give a fuck."

"We can't do it in socks; we'll all be on our asses. You're just gonna have to get over your aversion to feet."

"We don't have to do this," Handsy mutters, but everyone ignores him.

"If you leave any trace of rotting corpse behind, you're paying to have this place deep-cleaned."

Killer rolls his eyes before he begins a series of warm-ups.

"Fuck me, he's taking this seriously," Brit mutters as he takes a seat beside me to watch the show.

"And to think, you nearly bailed on tonight," I mock.

"This is way better than having an early night."

Fletch takes a seat on the couch with Handsy, and we all wait for Marilyn to set up his cell to capture the action before they both take their places.

"I can't believe we're about to watch this," Fletch muses.

"I can't believe we're expected to join in."

"Take your position, Monroe. Everyone else, watch and learn."

"Christ, he isn't this serious before a game," Brit points out.

"Maybe ice hockey wasn't his calling in life after all. Maybe he was always meant to be USA's dance mat champion."

"There aren't actually championships. There are competitive events, though."

"Which you've been to?" Handsy asks, getting a little more invested in this whole thing.

"Nah, we used to watch footage, though."

"Of course you did," Fletch mutters with a laugh.

"Are you done chirping? Can we get this competition underway?"

"You got it. Although I think we already know who's going to win," Brit points out.

"I'm not so sure about that," Monroe states with a determined look on his face.

"Linc, you've got a little sister; you must have experience, too."

"Hell no. Nova wasn't really a gamer. Thankfully, I escaped this torture."

I think back to the things she used to get me to do as kids and an ache settles in my chest.

I'm not the only one who's suffering with Dad's loss. My little sister is too.

Nova was such a happy-go-lucky child. But I haven't seen that version of her in a long time. She's...she's changed and her behavior is getting wilder and wilder.

Mom pulled her out of her high school and put her into a prep school in the hope it would help rein her in, but I'm not sure it's really helping. She may have pulled the wool over Mom's eyes, but everything is not okay in Nova's world. I just can't put my finger on what's really going on. I just have to hope that, one day, she'll feel like she trusts me enough to confide in me. But I understand that despite my job and celebrity status, Nova is just as embarrassed by me as every little sister is of their big brother.

"Until now," Handsy points out dragging me back to the present.

"I've put the setting on medium," Monroe tells Killer, who scoffs. "Call it a warm-up round."

"Whatever. Just hit play."

Monroe does as he's told, and a countdown appears on screen.

Brit, Fletch, Handsy and I all wait with bated breath for the car crash that's about to play out before us.

The music starts, and Killer and Monroe start jumping around. Their eyes are locked on the screen, watching the instructions, but their legs...fuck. It's like they've got a lift of their own.

"Holy shit, they weren't lying," Fletch barks, pulling his cell from his pocket. "Reese has to see this."

The four of us sit there watching in awe as both Killer and Monroe hit move after move. Their scores rise on either side of the TV screen, but neither takes the lead.

They're neck and neck, and neither shows any sign of slowing down as the timer begins to run out.

"Holy shit, this is tense," Handsy says, now fully invested in the proceedings.

Neither Monroe nor Killer says anything; they're too focused.

And then it's over.

"Yes, yes, motherfucking yes," Monroe cheers, his hands in the air as if he's expecting to accept praise from the crowd. "That was for you, Harps," he says, blowing a kiss toward his cell before he slugs Killer in the arm and then walks over to stop the recording.

"Nah, fuck that. I did not just lose to a rookie."

"The scores don't lie, loser," Monroe mocks.

"We need a rematch," Killer insists.

"Oh, don't worry, we will," Monroe says smugly. "But I think we need to see the others in action first."

They look at each of us, waiting for volunteers.

"Fine, if you're gonna be pussies, we'll pick."

"Linc and Fletch, let's go," Killer says, clapping his hands to build up the excitement.

"Fucking hell," I mutter as I shift to the edge of the couch.

I look at Fletch on the opposite couch, and his eyes narrow.

Oh, it's on.

"What level do you want?" Monroe asks.

"Is there anything lower than beginner?" Fletch asks.

"Nope. But if little girls can do it, I'm sure you'll be able to handle it." Monroe laughs.

Monroe lowers the setting before he and Killer take a seat and press start.

"Ready for this?" Fletch asks as the countdown appears.

"Absolutely fucking not. You?"

"Nope. Go," he cries.

The first step lights up on the screen before us, but despite it being in front of me, I don't know where it is, and I have to look. But by the time my eyes drop and my head tells my leg to move, the light has already gone out, and it's time for the next move.

"Holy fuck, this is hard."

"We always knew you were uncoordinated, Storm, but come on, at least try." Killer laughs.

"Fuck you. I've got this."

Taking a moment to gather myself, I look at all the points I need to hit around me before focusing on the screen.

My next attempt is better; I actually manage to score a few points. I even get into some kind of flow, but it all comes crashing down—literally—when Fletch loses his footing and collides with me, sending me tumbling toward Handsy on the couch.

"Ugh, you assholes," he grunts, shoving us both from his lap, letting us fall to the floor.

Laughter bounces off my walls, and as I roll onto my back, I can't help but join in.

Fuck, this feels good.

This past week has been awful. The only relief I've had from regretting what I did in my bedroom that night has been when I'm on the ice and focused on the task at hand. The second I've stepped off, it all comes flooding back.

Parker is ignoring me, and in turn, I've been giving her as much space as possible.

I was the one who fucked up.

She was just trying to help me.

I was the one who took it a step too far.

I wish she'd at least give me a chance to apologize, but other than spending time together at work, where we can't talk about it, she hasn't given me the opportunity.

She's either out or hiding in her bedroom.

"This was the best idea ever," Killer announces a beat before he holds his hand out for me so he can haul me up.

"Handsy and Brit, you're next."

"Fuck off. I'm not doing that," Handsy barks as Brit gets to his feet and pulls his socks off.

He rolls his shoulders back and does a couple of hamstring curls to loosen up his muscles.

"Oh, but you are," Killer muses.

The two of them glare at each other until Handsy finally relents and gets to his feet to a round of applause from us.

"I'm requesting a transfer. This is fucking bullshit," he sulks as he takes the center spot on the mat.

"Ready?" Monroe asks.

"No."

"Shame, because we're going in...three...two...one..."

Brit is fucking awful. If it's possible, I think he might be worse than me. But the biggest surprise of the duel is that Handsy can move.

Obviously, we all know his hand-eye coordination is insane, but apparently it extends to dancing.

"How the fuck are you doing that?" Brit shouts as he glances at Handsy's score and balks.

He's getting slaughtered by our grumpy goalie.

This could be the best thing I've ever seen.

"Come on, Handsy. Move those hips," Killer shouts, cheering him on. "Oh yeah, left, right. Left, left, right. And two feet."

"Man, I fucking love you guys," Monroe says. When I glance over, he's got a soft smile playing on his lips and I swear a little moisture in his eyes. "I'm so fucking glad I ended up here with you. You're the brothers I never had."

"Aw, we love you too, Rookie," Fletch says, roughing up his hair like he's a little kid.

Handsy is easily declared the winner, but seeing as Fletch and I both crashed out, they insist we go again so the winners from each round can dance off against each other.

"Okay," I say, shaking out my body as I take my position.

"We've got this, man," Fletch says, holding his fist out for me to bump.

"May the best man win," I say, flashing him a grin before the timer runs out and we jump into action.

Now I've got a feel for it, it comes a little easier, and I smile when I see my score slowly increasing.

We're almost at the end of our song, and I'm about to claim victory, when a voice cuts through the room.

"What the hell are you doing?"

"What does it look like, Doc? We're dancing," Monroe replies proudly.

33

PARKER

I blink. Surely there aren't a bunch of hockey players in front of me playing on a dance mat.

I have to be dreaming.

"Oh, yes, motherfucker. Get in," Linc roars, and when I rip my eyes from where he and Fletch stand side by side on matching mats, I find that the TV screen is declaring him the winner.

"Fuck's sake," Fletch mutters as he collapses on the couch, his chest heaving and his face flushed while Linc cracks out the robot as a celebration dance. But when he spins around and his eyes land on me, he pauses, letting his arms drop to the side.

"Hey, are you coming to join us?"

"Do I want to watch the six of you battle on dance mats? Hell yes. I'm gonna film the fuck out of it and send it to Brooke. It'll be viral in seconds."

Linc's face lights up at my agreement, but Handsy doesn't sound so thrilled as he barks, "Oh no, you can't do that."

"Yesss, they'll all know that I wiped the floor with Calvin Keller," Monroe announces happily.

"It was just a warm-up round," Killer mutters, crossing his

arms over his chest and doing a very good job of mimicking a sulking toddler.

"Sure it was," Monroe says, patting Killer's head patronizingly and making me snort a laugh.

"Grab a drink, Parker. The fun is only just getting started."

Noting that they all have bottles of water, I do the same after dropping my purse on the kitchen island, abandoning my coat and tugging off my boots.

Curling my legs beneath me, I get settled at the opposite end of the couch to where Fletch is now sitting and assess the setup.

"So is this something you guys do regularly or—"

"First time," Fletch explains.

"My sister shipped these to me. Dared me to play with the guys and send her a video," Monroe adds.

"She needs an extra big Christmas present for that," I tell him happily.

"Have you got a league going or—"

"Handsy and Storm have won the first round against Brit and Fletch."

"Only just," Fletch mutters.

"Can't say the same for Brit. Handsy has rhythm," Killer tells me.

"And I missed it?" I laugh, my eyes finding our grumpy goalie.

"Don't worry, there is going to be a second round. Handsy vs Storm."

I bounce in my seat. "Oh, this is going to be so much fun. Maybe living here isn't so bad after all." My eyes find Linc's across the room. For a moment, he looks sad, but as he registers the teasing in my tone, the corners of his lips twitch into a smile.

"Hey," he mouths, while the others are distracted with bickering over who's the best dancer. It's not something I thought I'd ever get to experience.

"You okay?"

He nods. "I am now."

Warmth floods through my chest, and the muscles that have been pulled tight for the past week begin to loosen. A genuine smile spreads across my mouth, and I duck my head as my cheeks burn, breaking the contact between us.

"Let's go then, Rook," Killer taunts, making me wonder what I missed. "You're not going to beat me for a second time."

"We've created monsters," Fletch muses.

"Medium again, or are we upping the ante?" Monroe asks, setting up the next round.

"I can't believe you're even asking that." Killer snorts, stretching out his shoulders as if he's about to go into a strength and conditioning session.

"Your funeral, man," Monroe mutters as he changes the level to expert and gets into position.

"There's going to be bloodshed tonight," Fletch mutters. "And I'm not bailing any of you out when you turn up tomorrow with busted faces."

Killer and Monroe ignore him as they get into the zone.

I'm ready to watch this battle, excited to see if their ability matches their confidence.

Just before Monroe starts the game, Linc decides to drop onto the couch between me and Fletch.

The second his ass hits the cushion, a rush of his scent hits me, and I'm instantly thrown back to that night a week ago.

My eyes lock on the side of his face as he gets settled, and despite knowing that I should look away, I can't.

He's shaved in the last couple of days; his jaw now covered in short scruff instead of what was turning into a full beard, and his hair could do with a cut, but I can't help but think what a great length it is to grab onto.

Stop it, Parker.

You're putting this behind you, remember?

Sensing my attention, he turns to look at me.

"I hope you're ready to be impressed," he muses, his smile from earlier still firmly in place as he watches me.

"They can't really be that good. Are they?"

The music starts, and we both turn to watch and...holy shit, do I have to eat my words?

"What the fuck am I watching?"

"Fuck if I know," Linc mutters as Killer and Monroe battle it out.

Their eyes are locked on the screen, and their legs. Fuck, they're a blur.

The points climb higher and higher, but there is never more than a few hundred in it at a time.

"How are they so good?"

"Because they have sisters, apparently."

"Then why are you so shitty?" I deadpan.

Linc turns back to me while Fletch mutters, "Burn, bro," behind him.

"It was my first go. Nova isn't really a dancer."

"Sounds like an excuse to me," I tease, turning back to watch the guys in awe. "Have you ever seen *The Kissing Booth*?"

"Sounds like a chick movie."

"Well, yeah."

"Then no, I haven't."

"I bet they have," I muse, picturing younger versions of Monroe and Killer with bowls of popcorn, cushions, and blankets, having a movie date with their little sisters. "You missed out."

"Maybe it's something we need to fix."

"Better message Nova then, see if she's interested in a movie date."

"Not what I was thinking."

"Nooooo," Killer screams before he collapses to the ground, kicking out in frustration. Meanwhile, Monroe silently celebrates another win by holding up his index fingers, proclaiming himself as number one.

"Woot woot. Let's see your celly dance, Marilyn," Brit hollers, setting Hayden off on a whole new dance routine.

"I'm never going to live this down," Killer complains. "My sisters will disown me."

Hayden stands over him, watching with a smirk.

"Aw, Killer. It's okay, nothing a little practice won't fix."

"Fuck you, Rookie. We're meant to be better than you at everything."

"Hate to break it to you, Kill," Fletch starts, "but Monro—"

"Don't even start, Cap. He's second line for a reason."

"Ohhhh...it's getting ugly in here," Linc teases.

"Right, who's next?" Brit asks, clearly confident it's not going to be him, seeing as he lost in the first round already.

I shrink back into the couch when all eyes turn on me.

Shit.

Maybe I shouldn't have been so excited to watch this play out.

"Doc, you gonna show us what you got?" Monroe asks.

I look at him before moving to each guy currently looking at me.

"Fine. But I'm not going up against either of you," I say, pointing between Hayden and Calvin. "And," I start as I hop to my feet, "I need to go put on a sports bra."

"Aw, that's not fun," Killer complains. "Ow, what was that for?" he grunts, and when I turn around, I find that Handsy has gotten to his feet and smacked him around the head.

"Don't talk about Parker like that. She's one of us. You should want to see her tits bouncing around as much as you want to watch my balls."

"Ew, bro. That isn't a visual I need."

"Exactly. Get it together."

As I turn away to dash to my room, my eyes meet Linc's.

He holds them for a beat before they drop down my body.

I'm not wearing anything special, just a casual dress over a pair of leggings. But even still, his attention burns a trail from my head to my toes.

I rip myself away before I can think too much more about it and focus on changing into something more sensible for the task at hand.

I pull my dress and leggings off before replacing them with a work pair and one of my most supportive sports bras.

I almost walk out there in just that, but at the last minute, I pull a wide-armed tank from my drawer and throw it over my head as well. I'd hate for Killer to end up with a concussion and be unable to play in our next game.

"Socks off, Donnelly," Linc states as I return.

"Oh, so it's just our feet you have an issue with," Killer sulks.

"There is not a single chance on this Earth that Parker's feet have ever smelled as bad as yours," Linc mutters.

"Told you he was a foot man," Handsy mutters.

"Have you caught him sucking your toes in the middle of the night yet, Parker?" Brit asks with a laugh.

"Fuck off. I don't do that."

"Not yet, anyway," Fletch counters.

"You can stay the hell away from my feet, Storm," I instruct as I tug my socks off.

"I kinda get your point," Hayden says, his eyes on my feet. "Parker's are a hell of a lot prettier than yours."

"And you all think I'm the foot guy."

"Okay, enough about feet. Who am I dancing against?"

"Me," Linc says without missing a beat.

"Bring it on, Storm. I hope you're ready to lose to a girl, though."

"Pfft, as if that'll ever happen. You remember when we used to go up against each other as kids?"

"That was usually on ice or a basketball court. This is different."

The others look between the two of us as we bicker, probably reminding them that we've known each other for a lot longer than we've known any of them.

"Are you two done? You'll run out of energy before you get on the mats if you carry on," Monroe says.

"We're good. This is how we communicate," I say with a smile. I'd be lying if I said that bickering with Linc hasn't always been one of my favorite things to do.

"Intermediate?" Monroe asks, setting us up.

"Sure," I agree, although secretly I'd be happier with beginner. Not a chance I'm telling any of these guys that, though.

I might have had some practice, but it's been years.

Linc and I take our places, and I shoot him a look.

"You're going down, Storm."

"I can't wait, Donnelly." He winks, and heat surges up my neck, making my face burn red hot.

The countdown begins in front of us, and I forget about our audience and focus.

I have to beat him.

I have to.

The next three minutes are the longest of my life. My chest heaves and sweat trickles down my back, but as the time runs out, it becomes clear that it was worth it.

"Yesss," I squeal when the screen announces the winner.

"Fuck," Linc grunts, bending over and resting his hands on his thighs.

"All these years, and I finally beat you at something," I state smugly.

He glances over, but there's no annoyance on his face, only pride.

"Well done, Donnelly," he says, holding his hand out to shake mine. "Best man won." The second my palm slides against his, an electric current shoots up my arm. His eyes widen at the same time, and I can't help but wonder if he felt it too. Thankfully, no one around us recognizes it, and they quickly begin planning the next round.

With a tug, Linc pulls me toward the couch and we fall onto it side by side.

"That was fun," he says through his increased breathing. "I like hanging out with you, Donnelly."

"Hmm...you're not too bad either, I guess."

"Friends?" he asks, turning to look at me.

I smile at him, my heart racing and that fluttering I'm becoming used to taking over my stomach.

"Friends," I agree.

34

LINCOLN

"Fuck," I breathe as I fall back onto my couch.

"Yeah," Parker agrees as she copies my move on the one opposite.

The coffee table is still against the wall, and the dance mats are still in place.

I told Monroe that he should take them home so he could get some practice in. He proudly stated that he didn't need any and that they should stay here for next time.

Next time...

I'm not sure I've got it in me to do that all over again.

"I know hockey players are competitive, but that was something else."

"I can't believe Handsy. For a guy who was adamant he didn't want to play, he was shockingly good."

Parker giggles, and the sound warms me all the way down to my toes.

I've missed that sound this past week.

Hell, I've missed her.

I might have been with her at the arena almost every day, but it wasn't the same as hanging out with her. Not like tonight.

I'm not quite sure how she became such a vital piece of my

everyday life in only a few days, but it happened, and losing her again hurt.

It was like six years ago all over again.

No, it wasn't that bad. Nothing could be that bad—or at least, I hope not.

"Cole Hansley has got the moves," Parker sings, and when I twist my head to look over, I find her wiggling her hips and waving her arms in front of her. "Next time we all go out, I'm dragging him to the dance floor."

"I'd love to see you try," I deadpan. The thought of her trying to drag his six-foot-two body anywhere is laughable.

"I'll make it happen," she says confidently.

"If anyone can, it's you, little P."

She lets out an exhausted sigh.

"I should probably get to bed. But..." She lifts her head from the armrest and makes a show of glancing in the direction of our bedrooms. "They're just so far away."

I can't help but laugh. "Do you need me to carry you to bed?"

The second the offer leaves my lips, Parker's body tenses.

"I'm sorry," I blurt before really thinking about what I want to say. "About that comment. About what happened last week, the things I did, the things I said. It was out of line, and I—"

"It's okay," she says softly.

"No, it's not. I took it too far and pushed you away. That's the last thing I want to do. You're a part of us now, little P. We've got to work together, and the best way to do that is to be friends."

The word fucking stings. I've never wanted to be just friends with Parker, but that's where she's always drawn the line. Hell, most of the time she doesn't even call us that.

"Yeah," she muses. "It is. I'm sorry for avoiding you this week."

"Oh, have you? I hadn't noticed."

"You're not funny, Storm."

"Ah, but I am sometimes."

"Annoying, more like."

"I love it when you give me shit. It means everything is alright in our world."

"Yep, you being an asshole is very normal."

I chuckle and shift onto my side on the couch.

"Parker?"

"Yeah," she responds before turning onto her side and staring across the dance mats at me.

"I like having you here. It's less...lonely."

She shakes her head. "You're such a little liar, Lincoln Storm."

I rear back. "I am not. I've never lied to you, Parker Donnelly."

"Whatever you say," she mutters.

"I'm serious."

"Okay," she mumbles, but it's clear that she doesn't believe a word of it.

"Ready for another travel day tomorrow?"

"Yep. I've never been to New York."

"Are you serious?" I balk.

"It's somewhere I've always wanted to go. Just never had the chance."

"What do you want to see?" I ask.

"Are you kidding? It's New York; I want to see everything."

"I'm not sure we're staying long enough to see everything. But I guess we can see what we can do."

"We're there for one night," I point out.

"There are a lot of hours in one night."

She narrows her eyes at me, silently demanding to know what I'm thinking, but I keep my mouth shut as plans begin to play out in my mind.

"We should go to bed," I say.

"Talk about abrupt change of subject." She laughs.

"We've got a long day tomorrow. We should get some rest."

She mumbles her agreement and throws her legs off the couch. "This is going to hurt tomorrow."

"At least you don't have to train."

"True."

"Did you want a lift in the morning? Save taking two cars."

She hasn't wanted to even consider car sharing before. She doesn't want anyone to see us together and jump to conclusions. But it's stupid to keep driving separately when we're going to the same place. And if someone has anything to say about it, then they can come and fucking talk to me so I can put them straight.

I've got morning skate first thing, which she needs to be there for, then we're heading to the airport.

"Okay," she agrees.

"Really?"

"Yeah, really," she says, shooting her pretty smile my way.

"Okay then. My alarm is set for—"

"I know what time you get up, Linc," she interrupts.

"Yeah. I'll be ready."

"I'll see you in the morning then."

She pushes to her feet with a wince before lifting her arms over her head and giving me the pleasure of watching her do a full body stretch.

My mouth waters as her muscles ripple beneath the tight fabric of her leggings, and it only gets worse when her tank rides up enough to give me a shot at the sliver of skin between her waistband and her sports bra.

God, I bet her skin tastes so sweet.

"Goodnight, Storm," she says on a yawn as she spins and begins walking away.

I tell myself to be good, but I can't. My willpower just isn't good enough, and my eyes drop to her ass, giving me enough of a fix to get me through the night.

"Fucking hell," I groan, rubbing my hand over my semi. "Friends," I muse to myself. "Just friends."

I BARELY GET ANY SLEEP. After jerking off in the shower to the thought of peeling those leggings from her body and feasting on her until she could no longer scream my name—very friendly thoughts—I spent a few hours researching for our whirlwind visit of NYC. By the time I slipped under the sheets, my body was exhausted, and my brain was spinning.

I got a few hours, but when my alarm goes off the next morning, it's nowhere near enough.

With swollen eyes, I drag my ass out of bed, freshen up, get dressed, and throw some clean underwear into my permanently packed suitcase then head out in need of coffee.

I make two shots for Parker's iced coffee first before putting it in the freezer to cool down as fast as possible, then I make mine.

By the time she emerges from her room twenty minutes later, her coffee is chilled and ready for her. So is a bacon and cheese bagel.

"What's all this?" she asks, looking at it with wide eyes.

It's a far cry from the other mornings we've had since she moved in. But this is so much nicer than hiding from each other.

"Breakfast."

"Y-yeah, I can see that."

"So why are you asking? Iced coffee and a bagel. Is that everything?" I ask, nodding to the suitcase and bag sitting on top of it.

"Yep. Managed to drop a size from the last trip."

"You're learning," I tease. "Now grab your breakfast, and let's move."

"What about you?"

"I've already eaten mine. You can enjoy yours as my passenger princess."

"Princess, you say?" she asks as she lifts the travel mug from the side, quickly followed by the wrapped bagel.

"Come on, Donnelly, before I change my mind."

"You wouldn't."

"Want to test the theory?"

Apparently, she doesn't, because she hurries after me as I maneuver all our luggage into the elevator.

"I could get used to this," she muses as I struggle with everything and she sips her coffee.

"You always have been a bit of a princess," I deadpan, making her roll her eyes at me.

The ride to the arena is relaxed. The awkwardness that surrounded us whenever we were in close proximity last week has been banished. Instead, it's easy, relaxed, with just a little crackle of chemistry. It's something I've become completely addicted to over the years. If it ever disappeared, I'm not sure what I'd do.

"Shut up," she snaps, but there's no real bite behind it.

I have the best morning I've had all week. Thanks to Parker, I'm practically pain-free and back to being at the top of my game, hence our last few wins.

As we move around the rink, I'm achingly aware of her standing at the boards, watching us closely with her iPad in hand. I know she's working. She's studying our bodies and movements for signs of injuries and weaknesses, but that doesn't stop my blood from simmering just beneath boiling point.

"What's with the smile?" Fletch asks when he comes to a stop beside me when we pause for a drink.

"Nothing. Just happy."

"Why do I get the impression it's not because you beat both me and Handsy last night?"

"Fuck, that was good."

"Not as good as Monroe."

"That's because no one's as good as me," the man in question says, appearing behind us. "What am I the best at today?"

"Having the biggest ego," Fletch mutters.

"Dude, that's a lie. We all know Storm here owns that."

"True that," Kodie pipes up. "Nice moves last night, Marilyn. Who knew your hips moved like that? They certainly don't out here."

"My hips work just fine, Rivers. My young body can get down in the splits faster than you can, old man."

"Watch it," Kodie warns.

"What's that about your old hips?" Parker shouts over.

"Nothing. They're as limber as an eighteen-year-old's," Kodie barks back.

"Casey might buy that, but I'm not."

"Oh, burn, bro." I laugh.

"Whatever. Get back to work, ladies."

"You can tell he didn't dance last night; he'd be in a much better mood if he had," Fletch points out as he gets back on the ice.

"I'll figure out a way to get him to join. That man will do anything Casey says," Parker says, having made her way over.

"Lovesick fool," Killer mutters.

"Not a bad sickness to have," Fletch agrees.

"We all good here?" Parker asks.

"You tell us, Doc. You seem to know our bodies better than we do these days."

"Looking great out there. Just don't push it too hard."

"You got it," Marilyn says with a salute before throwing his bottle to the bench and hitting the ice.

"You good, Doc?" I ask. "Not aching too much?"

"I'm great. I can handle more than a dance-off with a bunch of hockey players."

"Good to know," I muse, walking backward and away from her. "We'll up the intensity of our workout next time."

"Bring it on, Storm. I can't wait to show you what I've got."

We all hit the ice, but before we skate off, Fletch's gloved hand wraps around my forearm.

"I hope you know what you're doing."

"What are you talking about?" I swallow thickly the second he looks over his shoulder at Parker. "Just make sure

HR knows and keep it above board, yeah? I'd hate for either of you to fuck up your futures here."

"Nothing is going on. We're friends."

"Yeah, and I remember being friends with Reese once upon a time. It was fun, until it got even funner." He winks before he takes off. Before I know what I'm doing, I've spun around and I'm studying her again.

She's wearing her Vipers' issued jacket, her polo beneath, and a pair of leggings that make her ass look insane.

Being friends with Parker has always been fun, but I've had a taste of how much better it can be, and it isn't something I'm ever going to forget.

35

PARKER

"Oh my god, Linc. This is incredible," I breathe as I walk close to the windows, taking in the most incredible view before me. "How did you manage to do this?"

He moves closer until the heat of his arm burns down mine when he stops beside me.

"Pulled a few favors," he says, like getting a private viewing on the one-hundred and second floor of the Empire State Building at the last minute is nothing.

"Linc," I breathe, my eyes darting to all the twinkling lights that are stretched out before us. "Thank you." The words don't feel anywhere near enough for what he's done since dragging me out of our hotel with the promise of the best night of my life.

He's...he's really thought of everything.

We've only had a few hours, but he's managed to take me to all the main tourist spots, and I've loved every single one of them. And I think I've loved it more because I've discovered them with him.

He turns to the side, and my face burns with his attention.

Reaching out, he tucks a stray lock of hair behind my ear, and it sends an electric current straight through me.

I twist around, my breath catching when my eyes find his. They're burning with an intensity that makes the ground shake beneath me.

"Anything, Parker," he muses, his voice raspy and sexy as hell.

Our eye contact holds, the air crackling between us.

"We've only got ten minutes," he reminds me, forcing me to rip my attention from him and to the incredible city before us.

With my hands pressed against the cool glass, I slowly move around the observation deck, making the most of every second.

I think of what I've achieved this year, securing my dream job and travelling around the country with some of the most incredible people I've ever met. And then there's the guy whose stare is still burning into me. He hasn't taken his eyes off me, despite the insane view, since the moment I turned around. It ensures my body continues to burn just as hot as when his fingers brushed my ear. He's everything I've convinced myself I don't want. He's the same as the other two men of my past who shattered my heart without a single care in the world.

I close my eyes for a beat. Over the years, I've done my utmost to keep my distance despite the chemistry that's always been there.

If I were to allow myself to be swept up by it, I have no doubt that I'd end up even more broken than the last two times.

When Seth went off with someone else, I was crushed. But we were still kids and didn't know better. I might still be bitter about the betrayal, but I've forgiven him.

Then there was my college boyfriend. Another ice hockey player. As much as I try not to have a type, it seems that I might just. Those bad boys who shoot a puck around are my kryptonite.

We were planning our future. He was entering the draft

after junior year and I was going to follow him once I graduated. We had it all planned; the only thing we didn't know was the location. But as long as I had him and hockey, I knew I'd be okay.

But then, he got drafted to his dream team, and he changed his mind. He wanted to go alone and have the full NHL experience.

I was devastated, and from that day on, I swore off all ice hockey players. They can't be trusted with anything more than a stick and a puck.

But despite knowing that, Linc has always been there.

Sure, he's got a puck bunny or five in every state to keep him entertained. But he's...

Fuck.

I don't know what he is.

He's just...always been there. Always looking at me like I'm something special. Even when we were kids, he'd always take time to check in on me. When Rett was being a jerk, Linc always tried to make it better.

And now...he's offered up his home to me. He makes my iced coffee and breakfast. He bought me flowers, for fuck's sake. And he's brought me here. With only a few hours' notice, he's worked his magic and helped me tick off a few items on my bucket list.

I sniffle in an attempt to stop my nose from itching as emotion builds up within me.

"Are you okay?" Linc asks, his heavy footsteps moving closer.

"Yeah, of course," I lie.

I open my eyes, but the view before me is now blurry with tears.

Tipping my head back slightly, I will them to subside, but it's pointless.

"Shit, Parker. What's wrong?" Linc asks the second he steps up beside me and finds the tears clinging to my lashes.

I turn to look at him, there's no point hiding now, and the second I look into his eyes, I shatter.

"Fuck," he grunts as I step into his body.

Without hesitation, he wraps his arms around me and holds me tight while I sob into his chest.

All the worry and the stress from the last couple of weeks spill free. I'm powerless to stop it.

His hand slowly rubs up and down my back as I fall apart, and it only gets worse when his hot breath rushes over the top of my head, and he presses his lips against me.

"It's okay, little P. I've got you."

Why does he have to say the most perfect things?

Why does he have to smell so good?

And why does his embrace make me feel so safe?

"I'm sorry," I whimper as my sobs begins to lessen.

"Take your time."

A broken laugh erupts. "We only have a few minutes."

"Fuck that. You're more important."

I suck in a ragged breath as his words wrap around my heart.

"You can't say things like that," I murmur.

"Why not? It's true," he confesses softly into my hair. "You've always been more important than anything."

Another sob bubbles up, and I allow myself another three seconds enjoying his embrace before I force myself to take a step back.

With my head lowered, I wipe my cheeks with the back of my hand, trying to clear away my tears.

"Hey," he says, reaching out and tucking his fingers under my chin. "Let me see those pretty eyes."

He tips my head up, but I keep my eyes lowered, terrified of what he'll see when he looks into them.

"Parker," he growls when I refuse to comply.

The second his commanding tone hits my ears, my eyes jump.

Fuck.

I'm pretty sure I'd do anything he asked of me if he used that voice.

"There she is," he says. His eyes bounce between mine, searching for...something.

Concern is etched into his features, and I hate it. He's usually so confident and sure of himself. To see him questioning this is unsettling.

"What's going on in that head of yours?"

I shake my head. "Nothing. Everything. I don't know."

"Spending time with me is that bad, huh?"

I can't help but laugh as another unwanted tear slips free.

"No, Linc. It's not. All of this...everything you've done. It's been more than I ever could have asked for."

Something wicked flashes in his eyes. "Everything?" he asks as he reaches up and wipes the tear from my cheek with his thumb.

I roll my eyes. "Almost."

Someone behind us clears their throat, making us both startle and jump back from each other.

"I'm sorry to interrupt, but you're going to need to finish up."

"No problem," Linc says as I focus back on the view once more. "Good to go?" he asks.

I want to say no and demand that we stay in this little bubble for the rest of our time. But I can't, so instead, I let out a sad sigh and turn toward the man waiting for us.

I only make it a step before Linc catches up to me and his fingers brush against mine.

I don't think anything of it for a moment, but then it happens again before his fingers twist with mine, squeezing gently in support.

"Thank you," Linc says, holding his free hand out to shake the man's who's holding the elevator doors open for us.

"A pleasure, Mr. Storm. Ma'am."

I smile at him, too dumbfounded by the hand holding to muster any words.

We stand side by side, hands still intertwined as the doors slide closed, locking us inside the enclosed space.

A million questions dance on my tongue, but none of them break free.

As the elevator slows to a stop, so we can switch to another that will take us back to the ground, Linc reaches for his back pocket and pulls his cap free.

I watch as he places it on his head, my heart still beating a little too fast.

"See something you like, little P?" he asks with a smirk.

"No, not really," I deadpan. He rolls his eyes, one side of his mouth kicking up in a smirk.

As the doors open, he pulls the bill of his cap lower, and still hand in hand we switch to a second elevator, but this one isn't private.

By the time the doors close, it's packed with people.

Linc is tucked into the corner behind me, trying to keep a low profile, but the second he tugs on my hand, I gasp in shock and turn multiple sets of eyes our way.

I step back, just like he intended, and he wraps our joined arms around my waist, pinning my back to his front.

My pulse jumps as his heat only makes my temperature climb.

He drops his head to my neck. I tell myself that he's hiding, keeping his identity hidden just in case any of the people around us are hardcore hockey fans in town for tomorrow's matchup. But the second he takes a deep breath and whispers, "Why do you always smell so fucking good?" I know differently.

"Because I'm not a sweaty hockey player."

"Are you trying to say I smell?" he asks, attempting to sound offended.

"You have your moments," I giggle. "That equipment you have in the hallway closet needs burning."

"Can't argue with that," he muses as the doors finally open and people begin spilling out.

"Where next?" I ask once we're on the street.

We've already done all the main sights, but this is New York—there is always more.

"We're heading to the most important place in this city. And if you're lucky, I might just buy you a donut on the way."

"I can get on board with that."

Without releasing my hand, we take off, Linc seeming to know exactly where he's going. While he might not have said a location, I can guess from his vague comment.

After stopping at a Dunkin' and ordering more donuts than the two of us could eat in a week, we approach Madison Square Garden.

"When I was a kid, it was always my ultimate dream to play here," Linc confesses. "The first matchup we had here was the moment I knew I'd made it. The atmosphere is always insane. It doesn't matter that most of the crowd are booing us. It's electric."

"I can't wait to experience it," I muse, looking up at the iconic arena. It's lit up with multicolored lights and LED screens showing their beloved teams and players.

"I always knew you'd do it. You're one hell of a player."

He tugs me toward a bench on the opposite side of the street, and we sit side by side.

"Donut?" he asks, opening the box he's been carrying for the last ten minutes.

"Thought you'd never ask," I tease. I quickly make my selection and pull it from the box.

I take a bite before Linc has chosen his flavor.

"Oh my god. So good."

He looks over, his eyes dropping to my mouth as my tongue sneaks out to lick the icing from my lips.

"Try some?" I ask, lifting it between us.

He looks between me and the donut for a few seconds before he wraps his hand around my wrist, brings the donut to his mouth, and takes a huge bite.

"Hey," I complain as he chews.

Goddamn, how does he even look good doing that?

"That is good," he admits once he's swallowed and licked his lips, which I absolutely did not watch while squeezing my thighs together. "Can think of something I'd rather eat, though."

36

LINCOLN

There's only one thing on my mind as Parker and I ride the elevator to her floor just after midnight.

We've had the best night, and every time she's smiled because of something I've done, it's made my heart beat a little faster. And what I've done has been so small and insignificant really. I've taken her on a whistle-stop tour of New York. It's nothing in the grand scheme of things, but she's acted as if I've shown her the world, not just a little bit of a busy city that never sleeps.

My fingers itch to reach out for hers again just so I can have some contact with her. But I hold back.

When she was upset earlier, it was easy to forget all the reasons why I shouldn't have done it. She needed...fuck, I really want to say that she needed me, but that's far from the truth. She just needed comfort and I was lucky enough to be there at that moment.

Watching her break down hurt. All I wanted to do was fix it, but I didn't even know what was wrong. I still don't, really, but fuck if I don't want to do whatever I can to stop it from happening again.

"This is me," she says, coming to stop at her hotel room as

if I didn't pick her up from here a few hours ago. "Thank you for tonight, it was amazing."

"You're welcome. It was fun," I say as I pull my cap from my head and comb my wild curls back before putting it back on, only backward this time.

She watches my every move, her eyes wide and curious.

"I guess I should let you get some sleep. Busy day tomorrow."

"Yeah. I don't need Coach on my ass because his star player is lagging."

I can't help myself. I take a step closer to her.

"Star player, huh?"

She rolls her eyes, her smile growing. "I'm sure some people would call you that. Can't say I've ever met them, though."

"You're such a brat," I state.

Her pupils dilate, and she swallows thickly.

Fuck.

Get the hell out of dodge before you do something to ruin all of this again.

"You'd be bored if I were anything else."

"I guess so." When my eyes drop to her lips, I spot a bit of frosting she missed from her latest donut.

She gasps when my thumb drags across her full bottom lip.

"So sweet," I muse as I suck it off my skin.

"Linc," she breathes. As much as I want to imagine it's an invitation to continue, I know it's not.

"I know, Parker. I'm going. I promise." But before I do that, I reach out and pull her in for a hug. "Thanks for tonight. I had fun hanging out with you."

"Me too," she mumbles against my chest.

I duck lower as I release her and drop a kiss on her cheek.

"Linc." She giggles, quickly covering the spot with her fingers as a blush creeps up her neck. She turns away to hide her reaction and busies herself with finding her key card and opening her door.

"Good night, little P. Sleep well."

"Sweet dreams," she calls after me as I take off down the hallway toward the elevator.

Yeah, they will be. They'll be full of you.

JUST AS I knew it would be, the crowd at Madison Square Garden is fucking electric, and the boos of the home fans only push us to play harder.

We end up finishing regulation with a tie, but then Kodie hits a world-class slap shot only a minute into overtime, securing us the win.

The celebration is wild, but despite our jubilation, we aren't able to go out and party the night away, because no sooner is the game over than we are heading to the airport to travel back home. We can't really complain because once we're home, we've got a day off.

Still riding high from our win, I tug my duffle bag higher on my shoulder and step onto the airplane. Most of the others are already on board, and apparently, they've brought the party. But as excited as they all are, it's got nothing on the moment Kodie steps on behind me.

The entire plane erupts in cheers. Anyone would think we hadn't celebrated the second the buzzer sounded.

"Fuck, yeah. Kodie Rivers is the man," I bellow, spinning around and bowing to him, much to his irritation.

"Go and get in your fucking seat, Storm," he barks, making those around us laugh.

He gives me a shove and I stumble forward. Unfortunately, I trip over my own foot and go flying forward.

"Linc," a familiar voice squeals as I catch myself on an armrest.

"Holy shit," I gasp, having seen my life flash before my

eyes. But the moment I look up, I forget about almost dying because Parker's wide, golden eyes are staring right at me. "Hey," I say, my lips curling into a smile. "Fancy seeing you here."

"Shocking," she deadpans.

Time seems to stand still as we stare at each other.

There's a little voice in my head screaming at me to celebrate tonight's win the only way I really want to.

I try to ignore it, but with Parker's lips only inches from mine and her sweet scent in my nose, it's really fucking hard.

"I think you're meant to be finding your seat," Brooke says from beside Parker.

"Shit, yeah. I'm going. I just...I needed—"

"Get moving, Storm," Fletch barks from somewhere behind me.

When I stand, I find that I've got the eyes of almost the entire team on me.

Fuck.

"Watch yourself, Storm. We won't ever forgive you if you squash our favorite trainer," Monroe says loudly enough for Dillion Mitchell to hear.

I cringe but don't bother glancing his way. It's true. The guy is a douche who thinks he knows everything.

"Donnelly is safe with me. If I hurt a single hair on her head, her big brother would get to me long before you guys would."

"I knew there was a reason I liked Rett."

"Shame he doesn't even know your name," Killer snarks from behind me.

"One day he will," Monroe says confidently. "Every motherfucker in this country will."

The guys continue chirping with Monroe as I finally make my way to my seat.

"You can thank me later," Kodie says when he drops into his seat beside me.

"For what, exactly?"

"Oh, come off it. As if you haven't been fantasizing about getting that close to Parker."

"Hmm," I mumble. "I think I'd prefer if she sits in my lap, though."

"You're so fucked, man."

"Things are good right now," I say, as I stretch my legs out before more, more than ready to lose the suit and pull on a pair of sweats.

He mumbles something in response but gets distracted by his cell. I don't need to look over to know that he's messaging Casey; the guy radiates fucking happiness when he so much as thinks about her.

Pulling my own cell free, I find my conversation with Parker.

> Storm: Sorry about that. Wouldn't mind spending the flight on your lap, though.

> Little P: I can think of better ways to spend a flight than under two hundred pounds of muscle.

> Storm: I do have a lot of muscle, don't I?

> Little P: I swear to God, if you say anything about me needing to rub them down later…

> Storm: Now you're talking. I do have this one that needs some attention.

> Little P: Turning my cell off now. There's a bathroom behind you if you need some private time with your muscle.

I snort, earning me a scowl from Kodie.

> Storm: Not sure it's a one-man job…

> Little P: Good thing I'm a woman then. Sounds like it's above my pay grade. Speak to Monroe, he's keen to impress.

I can't help it, I bark out a laugh, and when I push from my seat and look toward the front of the plane, I find that she's doing the same and glancing back to look at me.

My smile grows so wide, I'm sure it's about to split my face in half.

"Brat," I mouth.

"Player," she counters.

> Storm: Trust me when I say, there is only one person on this airplane whose hands I want on my body.

> Little P: See you on the other side, Storm.

"Fucked," Kodie repeats as the flight attendants begin to prepare the aircraft for takeoff.

"You don't know what you're talking about," I mutter, hating how well he can read me.

"Don't I?"

> Storm: If you want to watch me undress, now is the time.

> Little P: I'd never sleep again.

> Storm: That is the risk when you see a body as good as mine.

> Little P: Are you compensating for something with an ego that big?

> Storm: You know full well that I'm not. Feel free to check anytime…

> Little P: Menace

> Storm: Brat. Turn around and watch. I dare you.

Putting my cell to sleep, I climb from my seat and begin stripping out of my suit, my eyes locked on the back of Parker's chair. But at no point does she turn around. She must have stronger will power than me because I know for a fact that if she was stripping to her underwear only a few feet away, I'd be watching her every move.

***

"I THINK I'm going to sleep for a week," Parker groans as she drops into my passenger seat a few minutes after we've touched down back in LA.

"That's what the off-season is for," I tease.

"I don't know how you do it. I'm exhausted and all I did this evening was stand and watch you all."

"You did a hell of a lot more than that. Don't sell yourself short."

"I did use about a mile of athletic tape on Handsy's ass before the game."

My grip on the wheel tightens. "You've been touching Handsy's ass?"

She chuckles, and it does nothing for my jealousy.

"Yeah. It's a nice ass. Solid. Could bounce plenty of quarters off it," she deadpans.

"The fuck, Donnelly?"

She barks out a laugh.

"It's just an ass, Linc. Calm down."

"But you think it's hot."

"I never said that."

I huff out an irritated breath.

"I don't look at any of you like that when I'm working. You're a body, a machine. Muscles, tendons, joints, and bones."

"I know that, Parker. You're nothing but professional. I'm sorry. I just—shit, I'm an asshole."

She shakes her head and glances out at the illuminated buildings passing us by.

"You've got a good ass," she finally says.

"Best on the team?" I ask, my ego needing a little boost, even if she is bullshitting me.

She laughs. "Yep, best on the team."

"I'm going to ignore the sarcasm in your tone and take that."

"Whatever you need. So what's the plan? Are you dropping me off and heading out to celebrate with the guys?"

"What?" I ask, glancing over at her.

She rolls her eyes. "Are you going out to hook up?"

37

LINCOLN

Yeah, I think to myself, *that is exactly what I used to do after a win.*

With post-game adrenaline surging through my body, I would go out and find a woman who was willing to spend just one night with me to lose myself in.

But I've lost the need to distract myself with an unknown, willing woman.

I glance back at Parker sitting in my passenger seat.

Her hair is piled on top of her head in a messy bun; the makeup she put on before we left the hotel for the arena earlier has mostly rubbed off, and she's got black circles under her eyes from her exhaustion. She's beautiful. Always has been and always will be. And as I look away and focus back on the road, it's even more obvious than before that the only woman I want to spend the night with is her. Even if we are just lounging on the couch watching TV. That's what I want.

Okay, so deep down, I may want a little more, but right now, I'll take whatever she'll give me.

Aware that she's waiting for an answer, I swallow down my unease and be as honest with her as I can be.

"No, not tonight."

"Why? Isn't that your MO after a game? Go and lose

yourself in a willing woman for an hour or so and then wait to see if she's sold the story the next morning?"

I groan. Why does it sound so sleezy coming from her lips?

"It's been known to happen," I mutter, cringing over all the things that are probably floating around about me on the internet. In the early days, I would search it out. But now, I actively avoid that and all the other bullshit troll comments about my performance. Nothing good can come from reading that shit about yourself.

"So why not tonight?"

"What's with all the questions? Did you want me to go out and hook up?"

I glance over just in time to see Parker freeze, and I can't help but smirk.

The thought of her being jealous of me with someone else lights something up inside me. I really shouldn't like it as much as I do.

"You can do what you want, Linc. You've never needed permission from me before."

A smirk pulls at my lips.

"If it's okay with you, I think I'll just stay in with my roommate tonight."

Her chest expands as she sucks in a deep breath at my words.

"I've been looking at apartments," she confesses. The thought of her leaving has my grip on the wheel tightening again.

"There's no rush. You're welcome to stay with me as long as you like."

"I know. But I don't want to cramp your style. We both know you can't live life the way you used to with me there."

"Do we?" I mutter.

She wants to say something, but she changes her mind and slumps back into the passenger seat again.

"Are you going straight to bed?" I ask as we ride the elevator up to my apartment.

Parker yawns again, but to my surprise, she shakes her head. "No. I'm exhausted, but I'm not ready to switch off yet."

"What do you usually do to relax?" I ask, realizing that there is a hell of a lot about my best friend's little sister that I don't know."

She shrugs one shoulder before saying, "Read, watch TV, doom scroll, anything really."

"If you were to put Netflix on, what would be your go-to?"

I swear her cheeks heat a little as I wait for her response.

"Cheesy rom-com," she admits quietly.

"Interesting," I muse as the elevator's doors open and I take both of our suitcases in hand and walk out with them before she can reach for hers.

"I'm going to shower, then we can Netflix and chill if you want."

She spins on my heels and glares at me.

"I know I'm a little younger than you, Storm. But I'm not stupid. I know what that means."

Her nose is screwed up in the cutest way, and I can't help but laugh.

"First one back to the couch gets to choose what we watch."

"Jerk," she mutters as she takes her suitcase from me and stomps the few feet to her room.

"Are you hungry? I can order in."

She stills. "I could eat," she admits, glancing over her shoulder.

"Any requests?"

She thinks for a moment before saying, "Surprise me," and disappearing into her room.

The second I'm inside mine, I abandon my suitcase against the wall and drop my duffle bag on top of it. Falling onto my bed, I pull my cell from my pocket and scroll through a delivery app, trying to figure out what she might want.

I place our order, shower, shave, pull on a fresh pair of sweats and a T-shirt, and I'm lounging on the couch with drinks for both of us long before she emerges from her room.

She walks toward me in an oversized hoodie. It's obvious it's a man's, and it sends a shot of red-hot jealousy through me.

"Whose is that?" I demand, unable to stop myself.

She blinks at me, confused. "Whose is what?" she asks hesitantly.

"The hoodie. Whose is it?"

It takes her a moment, but I know the second a smile appears on her lips, she understands my issue.

"Why does it matter whose it is?"

My fists curl on my lap and my teeth grind hard enough to crack one.

"Because it does. Whose is it?"

She chuckles as if this is the funniest thing she's ever heard as she sits on the edge of the couch and points toward one of the sodas on the coffee table. "Is that for me?"

"Don't try to be cute and distract me. Whose hoodie is that?"

"Christ, Linc. Possessive much?" She rolls her eyes at me, and I can't stop myself. I jump to my feet and storm across the room. "Where are you going?" she calls, but I don't stop. I can't.

After finding my favorite hoodie, I march back into the room with it locked in my hand.

"Take it off," I demand, my voice hard and leaving no room for argument. Although this is Parker, she always manages to be a brat and drive me to the brink of insanity.

"I'm sorry, what?"

"Take. It. Off."

"Linc, you're being ridic—"

"Take it the fuck off, Parker. Before I do it for you." My entire body trembles with my need to rip the fabric from her.

It's irrational, fucking insane, but I can't fucking stop it.

"What if I don't have anything underneath?" she asks, fanning the flames that are raging.

"Then it really will be my lucky day," I state, taking a step closer to where she's still sitting.

I loom over her, waiting, silently praying that she'll defy me and force me to deal with this situation myself.

My fucking pleasure.

I'll have that hoodie in shreds before she knows what's happening. I might even watch it go up in flames for good measure.

Her eyes hold mine, defiance flashing in their golden depths.

Bring it, Donnelly. Let's see who really holds the power here.

After a couple of agonizing seconds, she shifts forward before pushing to her feet.

She stands to her full height, but I still tower over her small frame.

"You really are an asshole, you know that?" she taunts.

"I don't give a fuck. The only thing I give a shit about right now is getting some other guy's clothing away from your body."

"You're fucking deranged. I'm not yours, Linc. You have no say over what I do or what I wear."

I know that. I do fucking know that. But fuck...

Dragging in a ragged breath, I try to soften my expression and relax my muscles.

"Please, Parker. Please, will you replace that hoodie with one of mine?"

Her eyes crinkle with amusement, and her lips twitch, once, twice, before her beautiful smile breaks free.

"Sure. You only had to ask nicely," she says, her voice sickly sweet as she reaches for the bottom of the hoodie that hangs down on her thighs.

Please be naked underneath, please be—

My words die on my tongue as she reveals what really is beneath that hoodie.

"Oh fuck," I grunt, taking a step back so I can take it in properly.

She's wearing a sexy green lace bralette paired with matching silk sleep shorts. The lace of the top is just sheer enough to allow me to see the rosy pink of her nipples, and it's cropped at her ribs, showing off the dip of her waist before the satin covers her rounded hips, short enough to show off her muscular thighs.

I've just died and gone to heaven.

"P-Parker," I stutter.

I don't—

I can't—

"Did you want me to wear your hoodie or not, Storm?" she snaps, holding her hand out for the fabric I'm still clutching.

"I...umm...if this is the other option, then I think you should stay like—hey," I complain when she reaches out and snatches the hoodie from me before tugging it over her head and covering herself up.

Without a word, she drops back onto the couch, grabs her cell, opens up Instagram, and begins scrolling as if I'm not standing right here.

It's long, agonizing seconds before she finally speaks.

"Just so you know, that hoodie didn't belong to either of them," she states, her voice void of emotion.

"E-either of them?" I question, my brain still clouded with lust.

"Yeah, Seth and—"

"Don't," I warn darkly. "Don't say their fucking names."

Her eyes jump to mine. "What the fuck has gotten into you tonight?" she asks as if she has no idea about the way I feel about her.

"They hurt you," I say as if she's forgotten.

"Right. And they're in my past. Forgotten."

"Are they?" I ask, unable to let this go the way I probably should.

I hold her eyes captive as my chest heaves, my heart racing beneath.

"Is that why you think all hockey players can't be trusted? Is that why you turn and run at the sight of anything serious? Because you're over them and what they did?"

"What the fuck, Linc?" she demands, surging to her feet again and standing toe to toe with me. "Who the fuck do you think you are to criticize me and the way I live my life? You've never been serious about anyone, ever. You go through women faster than I go through athletic tape."

"Yes, I have," I correct.

"What?" she asks, a cute frown forming between her brows as she tries to remember what she just said.

I move closer again, letting her sweet scent fill my nose.

It's not enough. It's never e-fucking-nough.

"You said that I've never been serious about anyone in my entire life. But you're wrong. I have."

She rolls her eyes and lets out a patronizing laugh. "A hockey puck doesn't count."

"No, but *you* do."

Her frown returns, only deeper this time.

"What? No. That's—"

I step closer still, her body heat burning down my front and my fingers twitching at my sides to pull her to me, to prove to her that she's wrong.

"I meant what I said that night, Parker. I told you that—"

"No," she argues before stepping back. But I reach out before she gets too far and tug her back, this time making sure that she's pressed up against me.

Ducking low, I let my eyes drop to her lips before rising again.

"I meant every single word I said to you that night."

Tears pool in her eyes, making me feel like an asshole for

bringing this up when things have been so good between us. But fuck it, she needs to know.

I allowed her to walk away after that night without proving to her that I was serious.

I've never been more serious about anything in my life.

Hockey will come and go. My playing career will eventually come to an end, and I'll be forced to decide whether I still want to dedicate my life to the sport.

But Parker...she'll always be there.

She's my endgame. Always has been, always will be.

38

PARKER

Six years ago...

"Are you sure you're okay if we go?" Casey asks, her date behind her, holding her hand with a vice grip as if he's worried she's going to bail on him before the night is out.

"Of course. Seth's probably just gone to the bathroom or something," I say with butterflies fluttering wildly in my chest.

Tonight is the night.

I know it's cliché to lose your virginity on prom night, but it seemed like a good idea when we started talking about it.

Both of us have been ready for a while but agreed that we wanted it to be special.

And what's better than prom night?

The night we close one door on our lives and hopefully open a new one.

High school is done. Everyone we've grown up with is heading in all directions across the country, and who knows when we're going to see each other again.

Well, Seth and I know exactly when we'll see each other because we're going to the same college.

Okay, so it's not my dream college. But it's a good one, and he'll be there, so I figure the compromise will be worth it.

The last year together has been incredible. He's everything I want in a boyfriend. Sweet, funny, thoughtful, patient.

I hear the stories the other girls have of what it can be like, and I'm so grateful to have a boy in my corner who cares enough. Of course, there's always the threat of Rett and Linc ending him if he steps a foot out of line, but now that they're both at college, the danger level is a little lower.

I miss them like hell, and I can't wait to spend a little more time with them this summer—not that they're going to be home for long. But I'll take whatever I can get.

Seth is also going to be heading to training camp soon, and we have many plans before then.

Those excited butterflies flutter again, but right behind them is nerves.

We're taking a big step tonight. I know it's the right thing to do, but I'm still scared.

Will I do it right? Will he enjoy it? Will it hurt so much that I hate it?

Casey hugs me before making me promise to call her tomorrow for a debrief.

She's heading to one of the after parties, but Seth and I decided that our night with our friends ends here.

We've got a hotel room booked upstairs so that we have some privacy to take the next step of our relationship together.

I watch her walk out and then scan the room.

Almost everyone has left, but I still can't see Seth.

Pulling my cell from my clutch, I check it, but there's nothing from him.

"Where are you?" I muse before taking off in search of him.

After a few minutes of searching, I still can't find him.

The hotel key card in my purse taunts me, and I decide that he must have already gone up to set the mood. He told me earlier that he'd bought candles and my favorite bubble bath for after.

My heart tightens at his thoughtfulness, and I make my way to the elevators.

As the car climbs to our floor, my nerves begin to get the better of me. My hands are trembling and I'm fidgeting like an idiot.

I watch the numbers climb, and by the time I stop on our floor, I'm sure I'm only seconds from vomiting.

It'll be fine when I see him. When he pulls me into his arms and reassures me that everything is going to be okay. Hell, if I said I'd changed my mind, he wouldn't mind. Not that I'm going to. I've been preparing for this night for months.

I want to do this.

I need to do this.

Finding our room, I pull the keycard out and tap it to the panel beside the door before pushing it open.

I barely get it open an inch before I hear him.

My lips part to say something, but before I can, he grunts loudly. "Oh yeah, fuck. Right there."

My eyes jump up and as I push the door wider, my entire world crashes around my feet.

My perfect boyfriend of over a year is standing with his back against that wall, his head tipped back, his eyes closed, and his cock is in some other girl's mouth.

Tears burn my eyes as my hand lifts to catch the sob that wants to erupt.

Neither of them sees me standing there. They're both too lost in the moment.

His moment with someone else.

I stand there for another two seconds in complete shock before I force myself to step back.

With my hand pressed against the door, I slowly let it close in an attempt to sneak away without being caught. The last thing I need is Seth realizing and coming after me.

I don't want to see him right now.

Hell, I'm not sure I want to see him ever again.

He booked that hotel room for us.

For us to—

A sob erupts as I run toward the elevator and jab my finger against the button over and over in the hope it'll make it here faster.

Please be empty.

Please be empty.

I breathe a huge sigh of relief when the doors part and there isn't anyone inside.

My hands tremble even harder as I descend back through the building, and I'm even closer to being sick now.

The image of him with his fingers twisted in her hair, the expression on his face, her on her knees with her lips wrapped around his dick, all play on repeat in my head like a nightmare that never ends.

I thought he was the one.

I thought that despite all the odds, we were going to make it.

I accepted my place at his college, for fuck's sake. And what has he done for me?

He couldn't even wait for me.

My vision is blurry as I race through the hotel foyer. I don't know if I pass anyone from school; the only thing I can focus on is getting away.

With my floor-length dress tugged up so I don't trip over it and break my neck, I run around the side of the hotel in search of somewhere to hide.

I spot a bench surrounded by tall bushes on the other side of the parking lot, and I make a beeline for it.

The second my ass touches the seat, I shatter.

Loud, ugly sobs erupt. My shoulders shake, and I fight to drag in the air I need as devastation threatens to drag me under.

How could he?

On our fucking prom night.

It was meant to be our night—a celebration of the past and a step into the future.

I don't know how much time passes. All I know is that my throat is raw and my eyes are swollen and sore.

I'm a mess, physically and emotionally, and I have no idea what to do.

Seth picked me up.

I don't have my car. I don't have anything other than my cell phone and that key card.

Pulling the offending item from my purse, I lob it as far away from me as possible.

A self-deprecating laugh erupts when it lands only a few feet away, taunting me.

I wake my cell up and stare down at the notifications.

Messages from friends sharing photos from tonight. One from Mom wishing me a good night. Another from Rett reminding me to be safe and to kick Seth if he deserves it. And there is one from Linc.

> Linc: Enjoy prom, little P. Don't do anything I
> wouldn't do.

I pull up the Uber app to call a ride home. But before I can confirm the ride, I hesitate.

If I go home, Mom is going to ask questions.

She knows that I'm planning on staying out all night, although she doesn't know the details. If I turn up, she's going to know something is wrong.

I'm going to have to explain somehow, but not tonight.

I can't relive that. Not yet.

"Shit," I hiss, letting my head fall back as a fresh wave of tears hits me.

I could call Rett, but something tells me that he'll take one look at me and demand to know where he is. He won't rest until he rips Seth limb from limb. And while I might agree that he deserves it, Rett doesn't need an assault charge hanging over his head. He's going to the NHL. I'd put my life on it, and the last thing he needs is a record. His reputation for aggressive play is already making waves in the NCAA.

Closing Uber, I return to my messages. Or, one specific message.

Before I can overthink it, I'm typing.

> Little P: Hey, I need a huge favor.

Thoughts of him being with Rett and letting him read that message has me typing a follow up.

> Little P: One that needs to be a secret.

The messages show as read almost as soon as they've been delivered, and my heart jumps into my throat.

Please don't say no.

> Linc: Of course. Anything. What do you need?

> Little P: Can you come and pick me up? Alone.

> Linc: Where are you?

> Little P: At the hotel.

> Linc: On my way.

> Little P: I can't go home, though. I don't know where I'm going, but I'm not going home.

> Linc: Are you okay?

"Shit," I hiss.

> Little P: No. Please, can you be quick?

> Linc: Getting in the car right now. I'll be ten minutes, tops.

I have no idea where Linc is right now, but something tells me that it's farther than ten minutes away, seeing as there isn't much around here. But I'm not going to argue. I need him too much for that.

Time seems to slow to a stop the second his messages cease.

I want to reply, but I know he's driving.

So instead, I rest my cell in my lap and will my heart to stop hurting.

Every time I blink, even for a second, the image of them returns.

Where are they now?

Are they still up there?

Has he wondered where I am?

Silent tears continue as reality hits me over and over.

He gave me a key to that room. Did he...did he want me to find them?

I startle when my cell rings in my hands.

My first instinct is to reject it, but then I see the name.

Storm.

"Hello?" I rasp the second I press it to my ear.

"I'm here. Where are you?"

I swallow thickly.

"Can you see a row of bushes at the end of the lot, to the left of the hotel?"

"Uhh..." I squeeze my eyes closed, picturing him looking around. "Yeah."

"I'm behind them."

"I'm coming."

A beat before the line dies, I swear I hear him running to me.

I push from the bench, attempt to dry my cheeks, and wipe inevitable stray makeup from my eyes before taking a couple of steps forward.

Hearing movement, I look up.

And there he is, running toward me with his standard backward cap, a hoodie, sweats, and a look on his face I don't think I've ever seen before.

"Parker?" he pants, not slowing his pace at all.

"Linc," I sob, emotion slamming into me all over again, although not as hard as he does a second later when he gathers me in his arms and holds me tight.

"It's okay, little P. I've got you. I've always got you."

His words make me cry harder, louder.

He doesn't release his hold on me. He doesn't care that my tears are soaking his hoodie, or that my makeup is rubbing off on him.

He just holds me like I'm the most precious thing in the world, and the only place he wants to be right now is holding me together.

Pulling my face from his chest, I look up into his dark eyes. "Thank you for coming," I whimper when my sobs have subsided.

His hands move to my cheeks, holding me so tenderly, my eyes burn all over again. "You're my girl, Parker. I'll always come when you need me. Always."

39

PARKER

My heart is like a runaway train in my chest as Linc's eyes hold mine.

Memories of that night have emotions roaring within me.

Devastation, grief, sadness. But it didn't end there.

Linc turned up and proved to me that there's more to life than cheating, lying assholes.

But as good as things might have been, my heart was still shattered into a million pieces.

"Linc." His name falls from my lips like a plea.

His words. The way he's looking at me. The way his hands are twitching at his sides like he's desperately trying to stop himself from reaching for me. It's everything. The thing dreams are made of.

But I can't.

My heart has been ripped to pieces and stomped on one too many times by ice hockey players. And Linc...he's the biggest player of all.

What he just said...

Fuck, it makes my heart flutter in a way I'm not sure I've ever experienced before. But it would be naïve of me to allow myself to run away with them.

What I just said was true. Linc doesn't do serious. He does hook-ups. And if we were to do that…

Well, there would be no coming back from it.

He holds more power than those two forgotten men of my past combined. He always has.

If I were to hand myself over to him…

I can't. I have to stay strong, retain the power, and not let myself be swept away by his pretty words and sexy body.

He finally gives in to his need to touch me, and his hand lifts to my cheek. I startle as if struck by electricity as his warmth seeps through me.

Unable to stop myself, I lean into his touch.

"All you have to do is say the word, babe." My eyes close as the deep rasp of his voice flows through me.

It would be so easy to agree.

But it would also be reckless.

I'd be asking to get hurt.

I managed to do the right thing and protect my heart once.

I'm not sure I'll be strong enough to do the same thing twice.

The silence between us stretches on. The atmosphere is thick with anticipation and desire. But it doesn't matter how strong it is. I can't do it.

Forcing my eyes open, I stare into his. They're a darker blue than usual, and the sight of his own desire hits me like a truck.

He wants you.

Out of every willing woman out there, tonight, he wants you.

Fire courses through my veins, colliding between my thighs, causing a delicious ache that nothing but the man himself will be able to sate.

But he can't have me tonight. Because tomorrow, it'll be over, and he'll want someone else.

"Anything," he says softly, leaning forward and resting his forehead against mine.

I didn't think it was possible, but his scent gets stronger.

"Tonight. Tomorrow. Next week. Next month. Whatever you—"

I reach up and press my fingers against his lips.

I can't hear this.

My lips part to say something, although I'm terrified of what it might be. My resolve is cracking. The way he's looking at me with his big puppy dog eyes. Fuck.

Lincoln Storm is my kryptonite.

But before I get a word out, his cell chimes loudly.

Closing his eyes, he exhales a long breath that tickles over my face and down my neck. My nipples pebble, and thank fuck for the hoodie, because I have no doubt he'd be able to see just how he's affecting me without it.

"Dinner's here," he rasps.

"Then you should probably go and get it," I say, taking that as my cue to step back and finally put some space between us.

"Fuck," he breathes, his eyes dropping to his hand that was previously cupping my cheek. He hesitates for a moment before lifting it to drag through his hair.

The movement causes his shirt to ride up, giving me an uninterrupted view of the V-lines and trail of hair that disappears into his sweats. And when I get lower, I discover that I'm not the only one affected by our proximity. He isn't fully hard. But he isn't soft, either.

My thighs clench at the sight, but with the distance between us now, it's easier to brush aside.

"Parker, I—" His cell chimes again. "I'm going to get that."

With one final longing look, he takes off toward the elevator.

"Fucking hell," I mutter to myself as I tuck the loose strands of hair behind my ear and drop back onto the couch.

Despite needing a moment to myself to get my head straight, Linc seems to be back faster than humanly possible.

"Are you choosing something to watch?" he asks as he lowers the bag to the coffee table.

I keep my eyes locked on where the food is hiding as the scent of melted cheese and spices fills the room.

"You got out here first. You get to select what we watch. That was the rule."

His eyes shoot to me, but despite his attention making my skin tingle, I don't look up. I can't risk it.

"I don't have a problem with breaking the rules, babe."

I know he's smirking. I don't need to look up to see it.

"Well, unfortunately, I'm a rule follower. It's your choice."

He chuckles as he opens a container and passes it over.

The second my eyes land on the burger before me, my stomach growls obnoxiously loud.

Linc chuckles.

"Thank you," I mumble, taking the container from him.

Needing the distraction, I keep my eyes focused on my food instead of the man on the opposite couch, thanking my lucky stars that he decided against sitting next to me within touching distance.

He turns the TV on and loads up Netflix, but no sooner has the home screen come on than he clicks on something.

"What was that?" I ask.

"No idea. It's number one, so it can't be too shit."

"Interesting concept."

"Netflix roulette. You never played it?"

I shake my head. "Can't say I have. I like to know what I'm about to watch."

"Sometimes, you've got to live on the wild side," he muses before taking a massive bite of his burger.

"If you say so," I mutter, trying to figure out how to eat mine. It's freaking huge.

The movie he selected turns out to be some kind of gangster thing. It's full of fist fights, gun fights, and high-speed car chases. Not my thing at all. And that, along with the lingering tension between us, finally pushes me toward calling it a night.

"I can change it if you want to watch something else," Linc says in a rush after I've announced my intentions.

"No, it's okay. I'm tired. I'm gonna crash," I say, depositing my trash in the kitchen.

"What are your plans for tomorrow?"

A sigh escapes me as I think about the Pilates class I'd intended to go to in the morning. As much as I want to, right now, I'm too exhausted to even think about it.

"Sleeping," I say with a laugh. If only I could. I still barely have any possessions, and there's been no news about my apartment building. They're still trying to make it safe and waiting for the inspector's confirmation that others can enter. Nothing I've heard so far gives me any kind of hope for my belongings. I just need to know now. Then, I can attempt to put it all behind me and move on.

"Are you coming to Fletch's house for team dinner?"

"Uh...I'm, uh...not a part of the team," I point out.

Linc barks a laugh. "You're a bigger part of the team than some of the players."

"That's not true and you know it."

"We'd be nothing without you," he counters.

"It's been two weeks," I argue.

"Feels like longer. You're one of us, babe."

"Does anyone else go?" I ask. The thought of having to spend the evening with Mitchell scowling at me isn't appealing in the slightest.

"Nah, just the team. Reese will be there, of course, seeing as it's her house and all."

"No other staff go?"

"Uh...no. We don't like any of them enough. We once had an assistant equipment manager who used to attend, but he got a promotion elsewhere and left us."

I shake my head. "I don't think it's a good idea," I mutter. Dejection burns through me as I pad toward my bedroom.

As much as I love the idea of hanging out with the guys and being one of the team, it's not a place I can be.

"I'll speak to Kodie, make sure Casey and Sutton are there as well," he calls, stopping me in my tracks.

"Why?" I ask, spinning to look at him.

He chuckles like I'm the most adorable idiot in the world, and I frown, clearly missing the point.

"Because you belong there. Because *I* want you there."

I roll my eyes. "And the great Lincoln Storm always gets what he wants."

"What? That's not—"

"I'm not a part of the team, Linc. I never will be. I'm just an assistant trainer."

"You're not just an anything, Parker."

His words threaten to wrap me in a huge, warm hug, but I refuse to accept them. Refuse to be swept away by pretty words and a hot-as-hell man.

"I'll see you tomorrow," I say, continuing to my room again.

"I'm still going to speak to Kodie," he warns.

Not having the energy to argue with him, I slip into my room and push the door closed.

Exhaustion sweeps over me as the sound of the movie restarting fills my ears.

I should shut the door, block it out so I can sleep. But while I may have escaped to do so, it's not going to be happening just yet.

My blood is still simmering from our interaction earlier; my clit still aching.

There won't be any sleeping until I get some relief.

Dragging Linc's hoodie off, I throw it into the corner of the room as if this whole night, that interaction is its fault.

Tugging my nightstand drawer open, I pull out my vibrator and drop it onto the bed. Shimmying my shorts and panties over my hips, I let them fall to my ankles before climbing in.

The soft, high thread count sheets feel exquisite against

my sensitive skin, the sensation only making my need for a release more urgent.

Tugging the covers over me in the hope of muffling the sound of the buzzing, I switch my little friend on.

Despite there being a ton of options in the store, I went for the same one I had before. I trust it to do the job. It's more than I can say about most of the men I've spent time with.

My gasp rips through the air as I touch the end of the vibrating toy to my needy clit.

"Fuck," I groan. I'm so close already, it's embarrassing.

At least no one will know just how fast it's going to be. That Linc got me worked up enough out there with just his words and hand on my cheek to go off in mere seconds.

Okay, it's not just those things. It's the memories, too.

Memories of a night I've refused to allow myself to think about for six years. But he's bringing it all back. Forcing me to deal with everything I stuffed in a box. It's the safest place for it. If it's out in the open, if we acknowledge it, it's going to lead to pain. Pain neither of us needs.

"Oh god," I moan as I shift the toy lower, pushing it inside me as my fingers from my other hand work my clit.

I groan, circling my hips to hit the best spot inside me, and a loud moan spills from my lips as I fall over the edge.

And as I do, there's only one man in my mind...

40

LINCOLN

I sit in the living room with my knee bouncing. I've been awake hours despite having the day off. I've hit the gym, although I took it slow, in the hope of burning off some of the adrenaline that was pumping through my veins when I woke up. But it wasn't nearly enough.

I check the time again.

Forty-five minutes to her class, but still, no movement from her room.

I get it. She's exhausted from traveling and her two orgasms last night.

God.

I drag my hand down my face as the sounds she makes as she comes play back in my mind.

So fucking sexy.

Did I plant my ass on the couch and force myself to watch whatever movie was playing on the screen after she left?

I tried. I really did.

But the possibility of listening to her again was too much to ignore.

I was turned the hell on after our little exchange earlier, and from the darkness in her eyes as she stared up at me, I was tempted to say she was, too.

I wanted to kiss her so fucking badly. I wanted to run my hands all over her. Bury my face between her thighs and prove that the words I said to her were true.

She's the only one for me.

The only girl I've ever wanted more from.

The only woman I picture my life with.

But she's also the only one who's turned me away.

For a few years, I figured that was the reason I wanted her.

I wanted something I couldn't have.

But that's not true. It has nothing to do with what happened six years ago and everything to do with having her in my life.

I knew it before, but with her off doing her thing and me doing mine, it was easy to put it all to one side. But now she's here, living under my roof, working at the arena, traveling with us...it's all coming back to me.

And I want it.

I really fucking want her.

And not just for the night.

Forever.

When the clock hits thirty minutes, I can't stop myself any longer. I push from the couch and stalk toward her room.

It's completely silent, and when I press my palm against the ajar door, I find it's completely dark, too.

She's overslept

"Parker," I whisper.

Nothing.

"Parker," I say a little louder.

Still nothing.

Pushing the door wider, I poke my head around and smile when I find her curled up under the sheets.

A few years have passed since I got to watch her curled up in my bed, and this might technically only be my guest bed, but the sight of her still affects me in the same way.

"Parker." My voice cuts through the room, and she finally stirs. Although she doesn't wake up.

Walking toward the bed, I focus on the mass of red hair that covers the stark white pillow.

"Parker."

She groans and tugs the sheets up higher, making me chuckle.

She's never really been a morning person. Rett and I would regularly get up early to skate before school started. She used to say that she'd join us, but if she did, she was still half asleep.

A laugh bursts out of me as I think about the pillow crease that used to be on her cheeks, her bleary eyes and her messy hair. She was unashamedly Parker on those mornings, and I loved it. She was also grumpy as hell, which I found cute as fuck. I could never tell Rett that when he was moaning about her making us late.

"Don't laugh at me," she mutters.

"Sorry. You're just too cute," I confess, feeling lighter having said the words all these years on.

"I am not. I'm sleeping."

"Not for much longer. You're late."

"For what?" she asks, stretching out her legs under the sheets.

"Pilates."

She freezes. "I'm not going."

"But I'm ready."

Finally, she cracks an eye open and looks at me.

"You're...you're going to Pilates?"

"Yeah. You invited me, remember?"

She blinks, her head fogged with sleep.

"Okay. Let me know how you get on."

She attempts to turn her back on me so she can go back to sleep, but like hell is that happening.

"Lincoln, what the fuck are you doing?" she shrieks when I flip the covers back.

I smirk, but the second my eyes land on her body, it falls.

Holy fuck, I forgot about her outfit.

She flips over and gets to her knees, her hands defiantly on her hips. Her lace bralette is twisted from her sleep, showing even more than it was last night. Although it's still not quite enough.

"What the hell?" she seethes, her chest heaving.

"We're...uh...we're going to your class," I say, my eyes fighting to stay locked on hers.

"I'm not going," she repeats.

"Yes. You are. We're going together."

Finally, I lose my fight, and my eyes drop to her tits.

Christ, she's got good tits.

The perfect size. Not too big, not too small. Just right to slide my dick—

"Storm," she growls, quickly adjusting the fabric. "My eyes are up here."

"I know. But your tits are down here, and they're looking fine this morning."

"Fuck's sake," she complains as she climbs from the bed, giving me a shot of her ass in the tiny silk shorts she's wearing.

I bite down on my bottom lip and curl my fists as she stomps toward the bathroom.

The need to punish her for being a brat burns through me.

God, how I want to tie her to her bed and tease her until she's begging for relief.

"Get dressed, Donnelly. Your class starts in twenty minutes."

"I said, I'm not going," she repeats.

"No, *we* are. You have ten minutes. Your coffee will be ready," I state before forcing myself to walk out of her room to allow her to get ready.

"And what if I'm not ready?"

"Then I'll throw you over my shoulder dressed exactly as you are and enjoy every second of watching you work out."

"OH MY GOD," I pant, my legs trembling as our instructor brings the class to an end.

I'm sweating, my heart is racing, and my muscles are quivering.

That shit was hard.

I cringe, knowing exactly what Parker is going to say when we get out of here. I'm already regretting saying anything about how easy Pilates is; she really doesn't need to rub it in.

Risking a glance over, I balk when I find she's barely broken a sweat.

She looks...fuck, she looks really fucking hot.

Her leggings showcase her firm ass and muscular thighs. The sliver of skin between the waistband of her pants and the bottom of her sports bra is the ultimate tease. So is her cleavage. That top she's wearing is a thing of wonders. What I wouldn't give to lick—

"Everything okay?" she taunts, breaking through my filthy thoughts.

Her eyes crinkle with amusement, her lips twitching.

I sigh, unable to deny the truth.

"It was harder than I was expecting."

"So...not just a bunch of weird sex positions?" she deadpans.

My own smirk grows. "I mean...there was a little of that," I reason. For the last hour, I've cursed the fact that she was on a reformer to the side of me and not in front of me. I bet she looked fucking insane, bent over on that thing. I had to settle for her reflection in the mirrors, which was still a damn sight to behold.

My teeth grind as desire rushes through my veins.

"You're a nightmare," she tosses over her shoulder as she walks toward the instructor to thank her.

After wiping down my equipment, I follow. The second I approach, the instructor turns to me, her eyes wide, her smile calculated.

When I first walked in here behind Parker, she gave me a

double take. And since then, she's spent most of the hour eye-fucking me.

Previously, I'd have been all over it. Right now, I'd probably be asking what time she gets off work later. But I have zero interest in doing so. My focus is solely on Parker and what her plans are for the rest of the day.

"It was so great of you to bring a friend today," the instructor tells Parker without bothering to look at her. "And an athlete, too." She steps a little closer, making her intentions more than clear. "I do hope the class was challenging enough for you."

"More than enough, thank you," I state dryly.

"I'm fascinated by athletes and their bodies. I'd love to—" Parker snorts beside me before attempting to cover it with a cough. "Talk to you more about your body. I-I mean, your muscles and strength."

"Oh, Linc loves talking about muscles, don't you?" Parker taunts.

"Fantastic," the instructor sings. "I get off after this class. I'd love to grab a coffee or—"

"I'm sorry, I'm busy today. Maybe another time."

The instructor instantly deflates. "Oh, of course. It was silly of me to assume...can I give you my number? Maybe we can find a time when we're both free."

"Maybe," I mumble.

She spins around to pull something from a duffle bag behind her, and Parker shifts forward slightly.

Glancing over, I find her brow raised and a smirk playing at her lips.

Rolling my eyes, I politely take the business card offered to me.

"Thank you." I let my eyes drop. "Clare."

"Call me anytime."

"I'll see what I can do." I turn to Parker. "Ready to head out, babe?"

Clare startles as the final word leaves my lips.

"Yeah, I'm good."

"Oh, I know," I drawl as I throw my arm around Parker's shoulders. "I saw. Shall we go and shower off?"

Tightening my grip on her, I tug her toward the exit, refusing to let up when she attempts to twist out of my hold.

"What the hell are you doing?" she hisses. "She was interested. And she's hot."

"Was she?" I ask, finally letting my arm drop as we approach the main exit. "Didn't notice."

"You're such a liar," she accuses as she playfully shoves me through the door.

The second I'm outside, I stop dead on the spot and spin around.

Parker doesn't react fast enough and crashes right into me.

"The fuck?"

"I'm not lying," I tell her, staring down into her golden eyes. They're even brighter than usual with the sun reflecting in them. "I have no interest in her. And I didn't notice if she was hot or not." Reaching out, I tuck a stray lock of hair behind Parker's ear. "I only saw one woman in that room, and she was mesmerizing."

"Storm," Parker warns, taking a step back.

"Just being honest," I muse before taking my place at her side, ready to head to the parking lot. "Are you hungry?" I ask as we begin walking.

"Uh..."

"I know a great sandwich place a couple of blocks over, if you fancy it."

I glance over and find a conflicted expression on her face. She wants to say yes, but she's desperate to put some space between us.

I both love and hate that she feels that way.

"Come on, it's a sandwich, not a marriage proposal," I tease, playfully elbowing her.

"Fine," she sighs. "But you're buying."

"I wouldn't have it any other way."

41

PARKER

"We're going grocery shopping," Linc states after we've returned to his car, stomach full of arguably the best sandwich I've ever consumed.

Damn him for being right.

I didn't intend on spending my day off with Linc, but that seems to be what's happening.

"I'm sorry, we're what?"

"Going grocery shopping," he says slowly.

I stare at him as he waits for a reaction with his hands on the wheel.

There's a dimple in his right cheek, and my hand twitches in my lap to reach out and poke it.

It only appears when he's really trying to hold in a laugh. I can only hope that means he's joking.

Hell, when my alarm went off earlier this morning so I wouldn't be late for Pilates, I turned it off, intending to stay in bed all day.

I'm exhausted, but...I'm glad I allowed him to drag me out.

Pilates always makes me feel good. But watching him struggle beside me made it all the more entertaining.

He's an incredibly fit athlete, but even those at the top of their game struggle when things are different. And today was different. I have no doubt that I'm going to have him on my table tomorrow, complaining. A smirk twitches at my lips as I debate whether to go easy on him or not.

Of course I won't. Where would be the fun in that?

But I wasn't expecting a lunch date—it wasn't a date—and then a domesticated trip to the store.

"Can't we just order it? You'll be recognized and it'll be awful."

"We could. But there's no fun in that. I like choosing, experiencing things."

"Really?" I deadpan, not believing him for a second.

Finally, his smile breaks through. "If you're a good girl, I'll buy you a sweet treat."

I playfully smack him in the chest. "You're a nightmare."

"You wouldn't have me any other way," he states confidently as he puts the car in drive and pulls into traffic.

He turns the music up, stopping any further conversation before he begins singing along. It's infectious, and one song later, I'm joining in.

"Didn't have you down as a Taylor fan," I say when he's finished a god-awful rendition of "Cruel Summer."

"I like all kinds of music," he says, killing the engine and staring out at the store in front of us. "And she's a legend. How could I not like her music? That's like saying someone doesn't like watching me play hockey."

I laugh. "Conceited much?"

"Meh," he mutters with a shrug as he leans over me to pull a baseball cap from the glove compartment. "Ready?"

I sigh. "As I'll ever be. If you get swarmed, I'm calling a rideshare and leaving you here."

"You mean you won't rescue me from my devoted fans?" he asks as we round the trunk of the car. He pulls his cap on and tugs it low, doing the best he can to hide his face.

I've been out with both him and Rett loads of times where they haven't been recognized, or where fans are able to keep their distance, but something tells me today isn't going to be the day.

"I really don't need to watch you get molested by the female population of LA."

"I knew it," he says enthusiastically. "You're jealous."

"I am not jealous," I state firmly. "It's just...ugh."

"You sound jealous," he teases as I battle to find the right words.

"Women are strong and independent beings. We are capable of doing everything men can, and yet, they take one look at you, or any other member of the team, and go all weak at the knees."

Linc beams. "It's a special kind of skill to possess."

I shake my head as he grabs a cart.

"Come on, then, roomie. What are we getting?"

"Out of here?"

He laughs and links his arm through mine, tugging me into his side and pushing the cart one-handed.

"You're cute," he muses before diving into a conversation about meal planning for the days we're home this week.

I silently walk beside him, wondering who the hell he is and what he's done with Linc. Linc doesn't worry about meal planning. He just orders in after spending an hour banging a different girl. Or at least, that's what I assumed.

I'm starting to wonder if I've got it all wrong.

We're about halfway around and I've barely said a word when he pauses at the bread. I frown, wondering what he's doing before he turns to me with a wide smile on his face. "What would you prefer this week? White or seeded, sweetheart?"

I practically choke on my own saliva. "I'm sorry, what?"

He smirks at me as another couple walks past.

Narrowing my eyes in warning, I reach for a loaf of bread, not caring to look what type it is before throwing it into the cart.

"Watch it, Storm," I warn before taking off.

"Wait, love," he calls behind me, making me cringe. "You missed the soda aisle."

"I am going to hurt you," I quietly seethe as he steps up beside me.

"Aw, it's fun. You should play along," he suggests.

"You're not meant to be drawing attention to yourself," I remind him.

"You'd like Fanta. That's a fantastic suggestion, sweetie pie."

I inhale a deep breath, trying to find some patience.

We continue up and down the aisles until we get to the fresh bakery section.

"You've been such a good girl for me, you should get some donuts, baby."

A young guy walking behind us snorts, unable to contain himself.

Curling my fists at my sides, I just about refrain from punching the asshole.

"I'm done. I'll meet you back at home," I state, storming off, or trying to, at least.

I barely make it five steps before Linc's fingers wrap around my wrist. He tugs and I'm powerless but to go where he wants me, and not a second later, I find myself pressed up against the shelves with him crowding me.

He's so much bigger than me in all aspects that he's the only thing I can see. His scent rushes through my nose, and without permission, my thighs clench.

The air turns thick as my chest heaves and my body burns.

Time slows to a stop as I wait for what comes next.

Linc's eyes are dark with a fire roaring within them.

My tongue sneaks out on instinct, swiping across my bottom lip as if I'm preparing for a kiss.

"Parker," he breathes, closing what little space there is between us.

Panic roars within me. And for the first time, it's not

because he's about to kiss me but because he's about to do so in such a public place. The last thing either of us needs is a photo being leaked to the press.

"Oh shit, you're right," someone to the right of us cries. "It is him."

"Shit," Linc hisses before jumping back and smoothing his hands down his shirt.

"I'm so sorry, I know you're in the middle of...something," the guy says, looking between the two of us.

My cheeks instantly burn with embarrassment, regret surging through my veins.

I can already picture the headlines. *"Vipers' new female assistant athletic trainer only got the job because she's in a relationship with Lincoln Storm."*

"Is there any chance you could sign something for my son? He'll lose his mind when he hears that I've bumped into you."

"Yeah, sure," Linc replies, sounding completely unfazed. I wish I could say the same.

"I...um...I'm not sure..." the guy mumbles, patting down his pockets for something for Linc to sign before he turns to his cart. "Here," he finally says, pulling a packet of Ramen from the pile and thrusting it at Linc.

Linc laughs. "I think this might be a first," he admits, accepting the pen from the guy and scrawling his name across the packet.

"Thanks so much, man. I really appreciate this. My son is going to be so pissed he missed out. We'll see you at the game tomorrow, though. We're going all the way this year."

Linc agrees before the guy carefully puts his special Ramen back in his cart and continues down the aisle.

"Well, the price of those noodles just increased," Linc quips, making me shake my head as I trail behind him.

I pause in the toiletries aisle to grab a couple of feminine products—not because I need them, just because there is no surer way to make a man more uncomfortable.

I grab a few things before continuing forward.

An idea hits me, and I glance over my shoulder to ensure no one is going to overhear when I say, "We need to get some more lube, seeing as you struggle to get me wet."

Linc freezes, his grip on the cart he's pushing tightens, and an accomplished smirk pulls at my lips.

But the second he spins around and stares down at me, I realize my mistake.

Abandoning the cart, he prowls toward me, but despite needing to get away, my feet are rooted to the floor.

"Let's just get one thing straight, little P. You give me the chance, and you will never, ever struggle to get wet."

I stare up at him, my breathing labored, heat surging south, proving his words true.

I'm standing in the middle of a grocery store, and he's got me more revved up from a look and a wicked promise than any other guy I've ever been with.

"I doubt it," I mutter, forcing myself to look away. If I don't, there's a chance he'll be able to read the lie in my eyes.

He chuckles to himself as if he knows something I don't before grabbing a packet of condoms, extra-large, of course, and throwing them in the cart as I pass.

He follows me toward the cashiers, but his voice stops me before I can get in line. "Shit, we need to get something for tonight."

"What's tonight?" I ask, feeling like I'm missing something.

"Team night at Fletch's. It's a bring-a-plate situation."

"Okay, well, grab whatever you want."

"What do you want?" he challenges.

"Linc," I warn, guessing where this is going.

"You know you're coming. You may as well take something you want to eat."

"I'm not going," I argue.

"Casey is expecting you." He smirks like he's just won.

"You're an asshole," I seethe.

"I know. Now, what do you want to take tonight?"

FIVE HOURS later and I'm walking into Fletch and Reese's house with a huge bowl of salad in my hands. Just ahead of me, Linc holds their front door open with a homemade lasagne balanced in one hand, a bag full of drinks hanging from the other.

Noise echoes down the hall to us, and I grimace as I think about the attention that's going to be turned on me the second I step inside.

The guys are all great, but I'm not one of them. This is their evening, their time to bond. Like Linc said, no other staff members are invited unless they're involved with players. And I am not. I might be living with Linc, but that's where it ends.

"Come on, the guys are going to be stoked that you're here," Linc says, watching me hesitate.

"I'm not so sure about that. I'm the one who makes them hurt and forces them into ice baths."

"It's for our own good."

As I follow him down the hallway, the noise gets louder and louder. And just as I predicted, the second we appear in the doorway to Reese and Fletch's huge, open-plan living area, all eyes turn my way.

I swallow nervously. But I soon realize there's no need to be nervous. Despite a few lingering stares and glances between Linc and me as if they're expecting some kind of announcement, they accept me into the fold, just like they have at the arena.

42

LINCOLN

"The doc looks banging tonight," Monroe says as I join him and the guys in Fletch's kitchen.

"Shut the fuck up, man," Kodie barks on my behalf when I give our rookie a death stare.

"Seriously, though," Killer starts.

"Don't," I warn, grabbing a bottle of water from the fridge.

"What? I'm just saying, you two looked cozy as hell, walking in here together."

"You wouldn't know cozy if it bit you on the ass," I counter. "There is nothing going on," I assure them, although, even as the words pass my lips, I question their truth.

Sure, nothing has actually happened. But there have been moments...

Fucking hell.

I drag my hand down my face, wondering when the fuck I started caring about innocent moments more than I did hooking up with a different woman every night.

Those moments, though...the memories...

Fuck. They're all-consuming.

"Yeah, but it would be cool if there were," Killer adds. "We all know you guys have history." I look up so fast I don't know how I don't strain my neck.

"What?"

"You grew up together. You, Rett, Parker, and Casey. Your connection was built long before she started working with the team."

My mouth opens and closes. I want to argue and insist that we don't have a connection, but then they really would know that we were lying.

In the end, I settle on a pathetic, "yeah," and pray the conversation moves on to safer ground.

Thankfully, it does, and before long, Reese pulls something from the oven that smells incredible. After double-checking everything, she calls Casey, Sutton, and Parker in to grab some food first.

The second Parker walks in with a wide smile on her face and Sutton holding her hand, gazing up at her like she just hung the moon, I swear I stop breathing.

Having her here, in a place that feels like a second home to me, with my boys...fuck.

I lift my hand to my chest and rub the spot above my heart. Is the air thick in here, or is it just me?

"Everything okay, Storm?" Parker asks when she notices me watching her.

"O-of course. Just starving, so if you could hurry up about grabbing food, that would be awesome."

"Typical man. Always thinking with his stomach," she says, making Sutton laugh.

"Daddy is the same," Sutton confirms.

We stand back patiently while they fill plates and disappear with Reese behind them before we all descend on the food everyone brought.

"God, I miss homemade food," Killer complains around a mouthful of the moussaka Reese made.

"Dude, can't you even wait until you sit down?" Brit complains.

"It's just so good."

"You need a new chef," Fletch points out.

"You think I don't fucking know that?" Killer snaps, filling his plate with as much food as he can fit on it.

Thankfully, the promise of full stomachs means the guys don't stop long enough to get into an argument and instead head out to find a seat the second their plates are full.

"Is this seat taken?" I ask when I emerge into the dining room to find the chair beside Parker suspiciously empty.

"Sadly not," she mutters.

I chuckle as I sit down, aware that I've got both Casey and Reese's eyes on me.

"Are you having a good time?" I ask quietly so no one else can hear.

"That was never in doubt," Parker says with a smile.

"See, told you," I say with a smug grin.

"Linc, look at this picture I drew," Sutton pipes up before sliding a drawing toward me.

"Oh wow, that's incredible, Lil Rivers."

Sutton blushes at the praise as I take the piece of paper from her and stare down at the illustration of myself on the ice in full uniform.

"I've done one for everyone," she announces proudly.

"Sutton," I sigh, clutching my chest. "I thought I was special."

She laughs at my dramatics before finding the drawing she's done for Monroe and racing toward him with it.

"How the fuck did you make such a cute kid?" I ask Kodie once she's out of earshot.

He shrugs one shoulder. "Fucked if I know. You're aware that that needs to be pride of place somewhere before her next visit, right?" he asks, nodding toward the drawing beside me.

"Goes without saying."

The next couple of hours pass as a blur of laughter and happiness. While my own family might now be a little fractured, all the people around me remind me that it still exists. And that family isn't about blood. It's about so much more than that.

"I'm gonna head out," Parker says from behind me, where I'm playing Xbox with Killer.

"What?" I ask, unsure if I heard her correctly.

"I'm leaving. Casey is going to—"

"No," I bark, dropping the controller and surging to my feet.

"The fuck, man?"

"Marilyn, take over," I demand before storming around the couch to where Parker is standing.

"We came together," I point out.

"Right? And we can leave separately. It's not a big deal."

Silence passes between us as we stare at each other.

She's right. It shouldn't be a big deal, but it fucking is.

"Guys, I'll see you in the morning. We're heading out."

Those who already know we're currently living together turn our way with smug looks on their faces. Those who are still here who don't mostly look shocked.

I'm aware that I probably shouldn't have done that. That I promised I'd keep Parker's living arrangements under wraps so it doesn't undermine her role. But fuck...she isn't going home with anyone else, even if it is Casey.

"You're unbelievable," she mutters once we're out of the house.

"What?"

"Just because I was ready to leave, it doesn't mean you have to."

"It doesn't matter to me. We've got an early skate in the morning; it's better that I head to bed."

"Sure," she mutters as she drops into the passenger seat of my car. "And thanks for basically announcing that we live together. Real smooth."

"The guys don't care," I counter.

"It's not the guys I'm worried about," she mutters under her breath.

"Oh?" My hand falls from where it was about to press the start button, and I turn to her instead.

"It's nothing," she says, staring out the window as if she hasn't got a care in the world.

"You're lying."

She tenses, her shoulders bunching up around her ears.

"What's wrong? Is someone giving you grief about living with me?"

"No, because the idea was that no one knew about it."

"It was never going to stay a secret all that long. Not when you're hanging out with the guys at my place."

"They're your closest friends," she argues, and I know she's right.

"Who are you worried about, Parker?" I ask, my voice firmer than before.

"It's nothing. Can we just go home, please?"

I continue to stare at her profile, irritation bubbling up within me that she's hiding something.

"Fine," I concede, finally starting the engine. "But just know, all you need to do is give me a name, and I can sort it."

"That's exactly why I won't. My battles aren't yours to face, Linc. They're mine."

I fucking hate that she's right.

With my fingers tightly wrapped around the wheel, I pull away from Fletch and Reese's house, silently fuming. Whoever is giving her shit, I'll find out.

"Did you want to watch TV, or..." I ask as we walk into my apartment and she makes a beeline for her room.

"I'm having an early night," she announces over her shoulder.

"Oh, okay." Disappointment sits heavily in my gut. I'm not sure at what point I started enjoying having a roommate, or at what point I forgot how to hang out alone, but both seem to have happened.

"I'll see you at the arena tomorrow," she says before disappearing and pushing the door behind her.

That inch of gap between the door and the frame is the ultimate tease.

With my teeth clenched, I march into the kitchen, annoyed with myself. I grab a bottle of water and fall onto the couch with a groan.

I'm not going to lie, that Pilates class this morning was a bitch. I'm already aching. Tomorrow is gonna hurt.

Pulling my cell from my pocket, I ignore the notifications waiting for me and find a contact I've been meaning to touch base with for a while.

It rings three times before the call connects, and the second it does, I'm reminded of what a shitty brother I am.

"I'm sorry, who is this?" Nova asks.

"You're funny."

"I really am, compared to you," she deadpans.

I groan again, dragging my hand down my face.

I love my little sister dearly. But I don't have the patience for teenage girl sass.

"How's everything?" I ask.

"Yeah, you know."

"No, I don't. If I did, I wouldn't be asking."

"Jeez. Who pissed in your coffee this morning?"

"Have you seen Mom much?" I ask, ignoring her previous comment.

"Thankfully, no."

"Nova," I warn.

"What? Whenever I see her, all she does is tell me everything I'm doing wrong. It's exhausting."

I want to argue with her, say something positive about Mom. But she's right. Since we lost Dad, their relationship has changed, and not for the better.

"How's school?" I ask with a wince. The answer to that question is usually about as positive as the previous one.

"Yeah, it's okay."

Her upbeat response throws me for a loop.

"Uh...really?" I ask, hating my skeptical tone.

"Yeah. It's...better."

"That's amazing. I'm so happy you're finding your footing there."

"Yeah, it could be worse. So, what about you? What's new in your high-profile celebrity life?"

I laugh her comment off.

"Not much. My agent has a couple of possible new endorsement opportunities in the pipeline."

"And you're top of the division?" she adds.

"Yeah, there is that too," I say, unable to keep the proud smile from spreading across my lips. "Have you been watching?"

"Of course."

We fall into easy conversation about hockey, but it still drifts off to other places. And as always, Nova quickly reminds me that the teenage sass she gave me at the beginning of the call is just a cover. If I'm honest, she's probably already more mature than I am.

Before I know it, an hour has passed and I'm still lying on the couch, gossiping with my little sister.

"I should let you go," I say, realizing the time. "It's a school night."

"It's barely ten," she points out. "I've still got homework to do."

"Why didn't you say?" I ask, feeling guilty that I've stopped her from working.

"Because it's nice to hear your voice."

Christ.

"I'm sorry I haven't been in touch enough."

"It's okay. I'm just as much to blame. I have your number, too. Life just gets busy, doesn't it?"

I glance toward my guest bedroom, wondering what Parker is doing. Did she go and have a long soak in the bath, or did she curl up in bed? If I'd stood at her door, would I have heard that familiar buzz of her vibrator and the soft moans she lets out as she comes?

"Yeah," I muse, dragging my thoughts from the gutter. "It does. You need to come to a game."

"I do. It's been forever."

"Let me know what game you can make and how many tickets you need."

"Aw, you're the best."

"I do try. Wanna lift the cup this year."

"It's going to happen. You're all killing it. Especially your new rookie. He's hot."

"Nova," I warn. "Stay the fuck away from my teammates."

The second the words pass my lips, I understand the irony.

Here I am warning my little sister away from my teammates, while I've got my best friend's little sister living rent-free in both my guest room and my dirty fantasies.

43

PARKER

The next week passes in a blur of traveling, games, and exhaustion. But despite that, every day I love my job and the direction my career is going even more. This job might have turned my world upside down, but as I expected, it's in the best way possible.

The guys are incredible. They're midway through the season, and their bodies are beginning to show the signs of exertion. With every game, there is more athletic tape used to keep them together, and the postgame sessions on my table get longer, as do the ice baths.

It's late afternoon when my final athlete of the day rolls off my table, dresses, and slips out of the room.

With my own exhaustion and need for a quiet, early night setting in, I take my iPad to our connecting office and fall into my chair to get some notes written up.

The sound of Mitchell and the athlete he's working with filters through the air, but I easily block them out and focus on my own job.

It's not until his shadow darkens the doorway to the office a while later that I finally look up from what I'm doing.

"I'm late," he tells me as he grabs his bag and throws it over his shoulder, ready to leave.

Suspicion rolls through me, and I push to my feet and look out into the training room.

The table he abandoned is still covered in his athlete's sweat, and there is tape littering the floor, equipment everywhere.

"You can clean up for me, can't you?" he sneers as he pushes past me.

My chin drops as fury shoots through my veins.

I'm so stunned that he's long gone before my brain can conjure up any words.

"Fucking asshole," I seethe. But it's too late.

I stare at the mess he's left behind. There's a huge part of me that wants to ignore it. To turn my back and walk away.

But I can't.

I refuse to allow Jarad, or any other member of staff, to walk in here tomorrow and think I was okay to leave it this way.

With trembling hands, I set to work, and not fifteen minutes later, the room is sorted and ready for another day of treatment.

Tiredness pulls at my muscles as I gather up my own things, turn the lights out, and head for the exit.

As I'm walking toward my car, I pull my cell from my pocket and find a notification waiting for me, confirming my appointment for tonight.

"Fuck," I hiss.

I hadn't forgotten. This morning, I was fully aware of what my evening consisted of. But today has been so busy, and my desire for a relaxing night happily wiped the thoughts out.

Dread sits heavy in my stomach as I drop into my car and rest my head back. My eyes close automatically, which is dangerous, and I sit there for a few minutes, trying to gather my thoughts and courage to do what needs to be done.

I need to know the full reality of the situation, but also, I really don't want to.

My cell taunts me from the center console as I drive. The

need to call Casey and have her come with me burns through me. But I fight it.

She's got a life now, a family, a man who's spent most of this week away traveling; she doesn't need me to be constantly calling on her for support. Things have changed, and I need to accept that.

Hoping that I'm going to need it, I stop by Linc's apartment for the suitcase I bought to travel with and a couple of tote bags. It might be wishful thinking, but a girl can hope. What's that saying about planning for the outcome you want?

With my head held high, my shoulders thrown back, and hope in my head, I tug my empty suitcase from my room and toward the elevator.

It was empty when I passed through a couple of minutes ago, but I suspected Linc wasn't far away, considering I just parked beside his car. But I soon discover that is no longer the case when his voice booms around me.

"What are you doing?" There's something in his tone that instantly makes me spin around.

Panic, maybe?

"W-what?" I stutter, finding him standing in the middle of his kitchen, wearing only a pair of sweatpants and a deep frown.

He rubs the back of his neck as his eyes bounce from my face to the suitcase.

"Are you moving out?"

I continue to stare at him in surprise. He looks... devastated.

It has to be his own exhaustion peeking through, because there is no way that can be true.

"I'm...uh... going to my old apartment. They've said that the building has been secured and that we can—"

"Alone?"

"Y-yeah." Do I want to do this alone? No, not really. But I'm also aware that I need to pull up my big-girl panties and just get it done.

"No, you're fucking not," he states, surging forward. "Let me get dressed. I'll take you."

He marches away, leaving me watching the muscles of his back pulling as he moves.

"You don't need to do that," I call after him.

He shakes his head but doesn't say anything before he slips into his room.

Not two minutes later, he's back, wearing a hoodie and a pair of sneakers, asking, "Do you need another suitcase?"

"I'm not sure I'm even going to need this one," I say sadly. The truth of it is that everything could be destroyed. Being able to bring anything back here is wishful thinking.

Taking the suitcase from where it's sitting at my feet, he shocks the shit out of me by grabbing my hand and then towing me toward the elevator.

The heat of his skin sears mine and burns all the way up my arm. I stare down at where we're connected as we wait for the doors to open.

Is he...is he really holding my hand?

"Come on, we need to get this over with," he says, pulling me inside at the first possible opportunity.

The second the doors close, I swear all the air is sucked from the enclosed space, and it only gets worse when he continues speaking.

"Why didn't you say?"

I shrug my shoulder not connected to the hand he's holding.

"Why would I?" I mutter, already knowing it's the wrong thing to say.

"So I could do it with you. It's a shitty thing to have to do alone, little P."

I shrug again as I stare ahead, not able to find any words.

"What have they said?"

"Just that it's safe for a short visit. They gave a couple of dates to get in, but tonight is the final one. We were traveling for the others."

Linc exhales heavily but doesn't comment.

"How long do we have?"

"By the time we get there, an hour, maybe less."

He nods and strides out of the elevator like a man on a mission. With my hand still locked in his, I have no choice but to run along behind him.

The second we're at his car, he opens his passenger door for me and waits while I climb inside before closing me in. After putting my suitcase in the trunk, he marches to the driver's side and drops in beside me.

Silently, he pulls out of his space, and moments later we're on the road, heading for my building. Or what was my building.

It's taken quite some time to come to terms with the fact I've lost my apartment, even weeks on, the whole situation feels surreal, but I'm getting there.

Or at least, I think I am.

The second Linc pulls up outside the black and singed building, I realize that maybe I haven't come to terms with anything.

A huge ball of dread sits heavily in my stomach as I stare up at the blown-out windows.

It's worse than I remember.

My mouth waters as if I'm about to vomit, and I throw the passenger door open as I suck in a deep breath through my nose.

I startle as a large hand lands on my shoulder, and even more so when he speaks.

"You don't have to do this if you don't want to," he assures me as he lowers to his haunches.

Our eyes meet, mine watery and emotional, his set with determination.

"All you have to do is say the word, and I'll go in and pull out everything I can."

As nice as that option sounds, I can't. It's my apartment. My stuff. I need to do this.

"Thank you," I say weakly. "But I have to do this."

"Okay," he agrees, before pushing to his feet and reaching for my hand again.

I should say no. I should be brave enough to do this without his touch and support, but I don't think I am.

With a nod, I slip my hand into his and allow him to pull me to my feet.

Side by side, and with dread sitting heavy within me, we greet the security guy guarding the entrance and step inside.

The second I breathe in, the need to vomit returns.

The air is full of death and destruction. Deep down, I know that thankfully, no one lost their life here, but it's hard to believe with the smell.

Linc's grip on my hand tightens as I lead him toward the stairwell.

"Which floor were you on?" he asks hesitantly.

"Fifteen," I confess, staring at the stairwell as if it's a mountain I'd been told I've got to climb.

"Could be worse," Linc mutters as we begin our ascent.

Despite us both being fit, we're panting by the time we get to our floor. I'm pretty sure it's the air that's full of smoke and ash that does it.

"Did you used to take the stairs often?" Linc asks as I walk past the doors of what used to be my neighbors' homes.

"No, I can't say I've ever done that before. Here," I say, reaching out with a shaky hand to push the twisted door open.

I close my eyes for a beat before opening them and walking in. But it turns out that no amount of time to prepare would have been enough.

While my windows might still be intact, and my things not burned to a crisp, everything is black. And I mean everything.

"Oh my god," I gasp, my hand lifting to cover my mouth as the tears I'm barely keeping at bay finally spill over.

I had an image in my head of what this moment might be like, how my apartment might look, but it was nothing like this.

Everything about my life is here in this apartment, and it's ruined. All of it.

My entire body trembles as I take a few steps forward, attempting to see through the tears flooding my eyes.

The second my gaze lands on a shelf that's full of photos of those I love, covered in black soot, I lose it.

An ugly sob rips up my throat as the stress and grief I've been battling with since New Year's finally comes to a head.

But I only have to endure it alone for a brief moment because, not a second later, a pair of strong arms wrap around me and I'm nestled into his hard body. The scent of destruction takes a back seat, and I bury my nose into his chest, breathing in deeply and allowing myself to drown in him.

He ducks his head, pressing his mouth to the top of my head, and a contented sigh erupts.

"It's okay, little P. I've got you. I've always got you."

44

LINCOLN

er sweet, floral scent fills my nose as I hold her, her body trembling in my arms.

I fucking get it. This place...her home...

It may not have burned, but the damage is devastating. I'm sure there are things that we can salvage, but she's lost so much.

I soothe her the best I can, whispering words of support and rubbing my hand up and down her back, but I have no idea how much it helps. This isn't my area of expertise. If she really wanted support, she should have done this with Casey. She'd have known exactly what to say and do.

She was going to do this alone, a little voice points out.

Fuck, I'm so glad I didn't allow her to do that.

The minutes stretch on as she sobs in my arms, and I stand there helplessly, trying to be the man she needs in this moment.

As time goes on, the self-doubt begins to set in hard.

If you were helping, she'd have stopped crying by now, right?

You have no idea how to support someone else.

Why haven't you said anything? She needs you.

"P-Parker?" I stutter, needing to banish the voices in my head.

She sucks in a ragged breath, her grip on me tightening for a beat before she finally pulls her head from my chest.

My breath catches as she stares up at me with big, beautiful, teary eyes.

That look...it's like being hit by a truck.

Suddenly, I'm a teenager again, staring at the girl I've wanted for as long as I can remember, breaking down because her asshole of a boyfriend shredded her heart.

Pain rockets through me.

All I wanted to do that night was help. And just like now, I did everything wrong.

But it's Parker. I'm powerless to resist.

My heart begins to race as memories from that night collide with this moment.

She continues gazing at me. Her eyes are red, her makeup smeared everywhere, and her cheeks are wet.

She's still the most beautiful girl I've ever seen. And watching her in pain is the worst thing in the world.

Her hands shift, and I startle at the movement as they slide around my front and then up my chest. Her brows pinch as if she's deep in concentration, learning the lines of my body. It's not necessary; after only a few weeks, I feel like she knows my body better than I do.

But then, my brain short-circuits when she wraps her arms around my neck and lifts up slightly on her toes.

The air between us crackles like a live wire, and I swear, I have to be dreaming. Sure, we've become close over the last few weeks. But this...

It's never felt like this.

My head drops, closing the space between us.

Desperation, grief, and the need for an escape roll off her. She's using me. Just like she did that night.

But I don't care.

Parker Donnelly can use me for the rest of my days, and I'd die a very happy man.

"Parker," I whisper, both terrified to do something to stop her, but also needing to give her the option.

Her lips part, and I swear the quietest, softest, "please," I've ever heard in my life slips past them.

Fuck it.

In a heartbeat, my lips are on hers and my grip on her body has tightened again, pinning her up against mine.

I kiss her sweetly, once, twice, testing to make sure she's really into this before I begin to deepen it.

The second she feels my tongue sneak out and trace her bottom lip, she groans.

Her mouth opens, giving me the access I crave, and that's it. I'm done for.

One hand lifts to cup the back of her head, my fingers twisting in her hair as the other drops to her ass. Her ass that's been taunting me in these fucking leggings every day for weeks now.

Her own arms tighten around my neck, and she stretches up on her toes to meet my height.

Our tongues slide against each other, and I swear it's the best thing I've felt in years.

Kissing has never really been my thing. A means to an end.

Unless it's Parker.

But then, everything is different with Parker.

I lose myself in her taste, sweet but slightly salty from her tears, the soft yet desperate way she kisses, the soothing yet slightly painful way her fingers twist in the hair at the nape of my neck.

I swear the fire that rages through my body is far hotter than the one that ripped through this building not so long ago.

Everything surrounding us falls away; the only thing that is important is her.

I don't know how long it goes on for. It could be just a few minutes, or we could be standing there an hour. Time no longer exists.

But I do know that when she pulls back, it's nowhere near long enough.

"I'm sorry, I—"

"Never apologize for that," I rasp, my voice thick with desire.

Parker shakes her head. "That wasn't..."

Predicting what she's trying to say, I make the decision for her.

"Let's get out of here," I say, taking a step back and giving her little choice but to come with me.

She hesitates, but only for a second.

"My things," she whispers.

"I'll sort it," I promise.

"But tonight is my last chance to get in here."

"I'll sort it," I repeat.

There's no way on Earth I'm letting this place be cleared out before she has a chance to go through it and see what she can save.

"Linc," she warns.

"Shush, babe," I whisper in her ear, loving the way she shudders the second my breath hits her skin. "Trust me to take care of you."

She swallows thickly, and I know instantly that she's thinking about that night. It does nothing for the tent I've pitched in my sweats. Thankfully, with everything going on, she's too distracted to notice.

Silently, we make our way back down the stairs, my arm locked around her shoulders.

Her body continues to tremble, and every now and then, she lifts her hand to wipe a tear.

I fucking hate it. But aside from taking her away and removing the stress, I don't know what to do to fix it.

The second we both step outside, we both inhale a deep, clean breath of air. I swear, it's never felt so good.

"I'm sorry for—"

"Whoa," I say, turning toward her and taking her cheeks in my hands.

Her eyes are dark, sadness etched into every single one of her features. My thumbs wipe her cheeks, clearing away the silent tears that continue to fall.

"You have nothing to apologize for. You didn't ask for any of this."

Her eyes search mine. I don't know if she finds what she's looking for, but after a few seconds, she sighs.

"I know, but if I weren't so tired then—"

"This week has been a lot," I assure her. She's not the only one who's feeling a little broken. "But as much as I want to tell you that it's going to get easier, the season is speeding past, and things are only going to get wilder as we hit the playoffs." She raises a brow at my confidence. Sure, there's still a chance we could fuck it all up, but with our current position and determination, I have every belief that we're going to make it. How far we get is another question entirely. "We've just got to make the most of the downtime while we have it and know that summer is coming."

She hums in agreement.

Stepping closer, I press a kiss on her forehead before promising, "Everything will work out, little P."

She nods, her fingers twisting in the sides of my hoodie.

There's a huge part of me that wants her to demand we continue what we started upstairs, but I'm aware that we're now standing on a sidewalk, and that I really need to get her home.

"Come on," I say, reluctantly taking a step back and leading her toward my car.

Just before she climbs in, she looks back up at her building with tears in her eyes again.

"I loved my place here. It was my home, you know?"

Pain cuts through my chest. She hasn't just lost a place

where she slept. She's lost her safe place, her home. And I can only imagine how hard that must be.

"I know, babe. I know," I say, pulling her in for one more hug before I allow her to drop into my car.

We drive with the music on low and her ragged breaths filling the air. She's trying to be strong, but all she wants to do is break down. I'm torn between letting her fight it because listening to it will be heartbreaking, and growing a pair and allowing her to get it all out.

In the end, the only words out of my mouth are, "Are you hungry?"

"Umm...a little, I guess."

"Did you have lunch?" I ask, aware of how busy she's been with everyone today.

"I grabbed a cereal bar at some point."

"That would be a no, then. Any preference?"

"Whatever you'd like."

When I'm sad, there's only one option.

Taking the next right, I head toward a place that I hope will bring her the kind of joy I got when I was a kid.

"McDonald's?" Parker asks in surprise as I pull into the drive-thru line.

"Yep," I agree, my heart beating out of my chest.

Will she remember?

"Your happy place," she whispers to herself, and I can't fight my smile.

"What would you like?"

"Your choice."

Leaning on the door, I give the lady behind the window an XL version request of what I always used to enjoy before tapping my card and moving forward.

Parker doesn't say anything, but when I glance over, she's got a soft smile playing on her lips that I can't help but mimic.

"Now what?" Parker asks once I've loaded her lap up with food.

"Now we eat, obviously."

"In here?" she asks, looking around my spotless car.

"Hell yeah," I agree as I pull into a space as far from everyone else as possible.

"But your car...it—"

"It'll be detailed at the arena tomorrow."

Parker laughs, but she doesn't hesitate in moving her seat farther back as I do the same to give us more space.

We divide up the feast between us and dive in.

"I can't remember the last time I did this," Parker confesses, her voice lighter than it was only a few minutes ago.

"Me either. I didn't realize how much I needed it," I say, dipping another nugget into some BBQ sauce and throwing the entire thing into my mouth as Parker slurps on a milkshake.

"Thank you for tonight."

"Nothing to thank me for," I muse, going for a handful of fries. "And it's not over yet. There's still time for a few more surprises."

When I look up, her cheeks are glowing, and I can't help but wonder what she thinks I might have up my sleeve.

Was our kiss only the beginning?

45

PARKER

"You don't need to escort me in. I'm not going to shatter," I say over my shoulder as Linc follows me into my bedroom, only seconds after we arrive home. But even as I say the words, I know they're a lie. I'm barely holding it together, and if I'm being honest with myself, he's the only thing stopping me from falling apart.

His touch.

That kiss.

Do not think about it, Parker.

"I know," he says as he disappears into my bathroom.

Curious, I follow him.

My breath catches when I stop in the doorway and find him leaning over the bathtub, turning the faucet on before reaching for a bottle of bubbles and pouring some in.

Instantly, the floral scent hits my nose, and with the steam rising from the water, it takes every ounce of my self-control not to strip my clothes off right there and then and sink into it.

"Linc," I breathe as he stands to his full height and turns to look at me.

His expression is soft, and all it does is remind me of the man he can be under all the fame and bullshit.

The man from prom night.

The man who picked me up, listened to me, gave me a shoulder to cry on.

The man who made me feel more beautiful and sexier than I ever had in my life.

The man who worshipped me and showed me how I deserve to be treated.

And then I ruined it all.

"Go and relax, Parker," he says as he moves closer.

"What? You're not going to try to convince me to let you join me?" I quip, trying to pull this conversation into safe territory.

I know where we're at when we're giving each other shit.

This right now...I have no idea how to deal with this.

I kissed him.

I caved, and I kissed him, and it was everything.

And now I want more.

Amusement crinkles his eyes. "Babe, I would love nothing more than to sink behind your naked body in that water. But I think we both know that that is the last thing you need right now. Take your time," he instructs as he reaches out. "Try and get everything that's happening up here to slow down." His finger lightly taps my temple, and just that simple touch sends fireworks shooting through me.

This isn't good.

This really isn't good.

"O-Okay," I croak although, right now, I feel like it's an impossible task.

How am I meant to figure all this shit out in one bath?

"I'll be right out there if you need anything," he says before leaning forward and kissing my forehead.

My eyes flutter closed as the warmth from his kiss flows through me.

The need to lift up and claim those lips again is almost impossible to ignore, and my hands clench at my sides as I fight to stop myself from twisting my fingers in his hoodie and pulling him to me.

But before I get to decide if I want him more than I want the bath waiting for me, he's gone, leaving me alone with nothing but my thoughts.

He doesn't close the door; instead, he leaves it open an inch.

Because he knows.

A sob erupts, and I slap my hand over my mouth before a sound escapes.

As much as I might want him to come back and wrap me in his arms, I know it's not the answer.

With my thoughts spinning around my head at a million miles an hour, I slowly strip out of my clothes. The scent from my building floods my nose, and it makes my eyes burn again.

Naked, I pull the door open and throw the items into my bedroom in the hope it banishes the smell.

"Oh my god," I moan as I step into the water. It's a little too hot, just the way I like it.

My skin prickles and burns as I sink lower, submerging myself and disappearing beneath the bubbles.

No sooner have I stretched out and rested my head back do images of my blackened apartment return.

On some level, I think it might be easier to deal with if it had burned to the ground. At least then I'd know that everything was gone. But now...

It's all too much.

The thought of going through everything, of sitting surrounded by that bitter scent while sorting through everything I own to see if it's salvageable, is just too much.

I lie there lost in my own head until long after the water has gone cold. I just don't have the energy to move.

After the traveling, the long hours with the guys, Mitchell and his constant belittling comments and irritated glances, and my life going up in smoke, I'm wrung out.

I've been given the most incredible opportunity, the job I've always dreamed of, and I'm falling apart.

I want to give it my all. The guys deserve for me to be at

my best so they can do the same in return. But I'm a fucking mess, and no amount of athletic tape is going to hold me together.

Climbing from the tub is like trudging through mud. All I want to do is fall face first into my bed, close my eyes, and hope for relief.

With a towel wrapped around my body, I wash my face and brush my teeth before pulling the door open.

A gasp rips from my throat as I take in the room before me, and like the emotional mess that I am, I immediately break down.

The clothes I threw out, God knows how long ago, have gone. My sheets have been pulled back ready for me to slide in, my cell is charging on my nightstand, and there is a fresh mug of hot chocolate, fully loaded with cream and marshmallows beside it.

A laugh bubbles out of me when I step closer to the bed because there are a couple of chocolates on my pillow. But it's not those that really steal my attention; it's the note beneath them.

Little P
I'm right here if you need me.
For anything.
L x

Why can't he just be the asshole that I know and love? Why does he have to show me this side of him again?

It's not fair.

He can't be that hot and this thoughtful and kind.

I don't stand a chance.

I survived him once. I built my walls up and held my head high as I put what happened between us behind me, convincing myself that he was a player who would break my heart just like Seth did.

But I won't be able to do it again.

I pull on a tank and some sleep shorts before climbing into bed and lifting the mug to my lips.

It's hot, really hot. He's only just been in here to deliver this.

He must have been waiting, listening for me to release the water, so he could slip in unnoticed.

The sugar hits the spot, and I swallow it all down, chewing the gooey marshmallows.

With it warming me from the inside out, I sink down, pulling the sheets up to my neck.

The apartment is silent, and I hate it. I want to hear him moving around so that I know I'm not alone. Even if I could just hear his TV, I'd know someone was there.

He is, I know he is. I believe his note. But...

A tear slips free, soaking into my pillowcase.

It's ridiculous to feel lonely. All I have to do is pick up my cell, and I could talk to someone in seconds. Mom and Dad, I'm not exactly sure where they are right now, but they'd drop anything to talk to me. Casey would, too. And Rett. Hell, I could probably call some of the guys and they would answer.

But I don't want to interrupt any of their lives with my bullshit.

Sure, I lost my apartment and my things. In the grand scheme of things, it's nothing. Everyone I love is happy and healthy, and they're all living their best lives. I've got my dream job, and I'm traveling around the country, discovering new things every week. I shouldn't be wallowing, but I can't pull myself out of the slump I've fallen into.

The tears fall harder, the sobs that accompany them gradually growing louder, but I lose the ability to care. I figure that if I get it all out, I'll feel better afterward, so I fully allow myself to drown.

I have no awareness of the time, only that my eyes are sore, my throat burns, and my pillow is soaked.

I pray for sleep to claim me and take me off to somewhere else, but it doesn't come.

A miracle doesn't happen until...

The mattress dips beside me and I gasp, opening my

bleary eyes to find Linc crawling into my bed, wearing only a pair of boxers.

"Come here," he says softly, settling on his back and slipping his arm under my shoulders to pull me to him.

Multiple questions dance on the tip of my tongue as I settle with my head on his bare chest, my arm around his waist, and my leg hooked over his.

It's so easy. So natural. And he holds me with the kind of confidence of someone who's been doing this for years.

His lips press against the top of my head, and he breathes me in as my own ragged breath evens out.

He doesn't say a word. He doesn't press me to know why I'm crying. He just...holds me. Supports me. Gives me the relief and the comfort that I was craving but too stubborn to ask for.

Time ticks on. I have no idea if it's still night or if we're creeping into morning. But it doesn't matter. Nothing does in that moment.

Only us and the connection I thought I'd managed to sever all those years ago.

"I think about it, you know," he whispers, letting me know that he's still with me, and apparently that his thoughts are in a very similar place.

"Think about what?" I ask, my voice hoarse from crying.

He chuckles.

"And I don't just think about that night. I think about all of it."

"All of what?" I ask, intrigued enough to be led down this road.

"You. Any part of my life that involves you."

My brain misfires, and I drag my bottom lip into my mouth as I consider his words.

"B-but...you hate me."

His body shakes with a laugh again. "I've never hated you, Parker. And I don't think you ever hated me, either. You just convinced yourself you did to protect yourself."

I push from his chest and stare down at him.

Fuck, is it a mistake.

His eyes are hooded with exhaustion. He's got a good couple of days' stubble on his jaw, and his hair is messy. And his lips...damn, his lips are so full and kissable.

"What did you just say?" I ask, struggling to focus on the words I just heard.

"It's not a conversation we need to have tonight," he says softly, coaxing me back to his chest.

"Then why did you bring it up?"

"Because when I'm with you, I struggle to hold anything back."

My mouth opens and closes more times than I can count with different responses to that comment. But in the end, I never decide on one.

It takes me so long, in fact, that Linc's breathing evens out, letting me know that he's drifted off.

I lie there listening to him, thinking about what he just said and how true it is.

So painfully true.

I walked away from what happened that night, put the biggest barrier up between us because I knew I'd end up broken. I took every annoying trait he has and turned myself against him. He saw it all and made it worse, seemingly enjoying the banter between us. But I never once suspected that he knew exactly what I was doing. That the hate I was throwing his way was nothing more than a coping mechanism because if I spent long enough convincing myself that I hated him, that everything about him was abhorrent, then maybe, just maybe, the other feeling would go away.

46

LINCOLN

Six years ago...

Her body trembles in my arms as I hold her tight. But while she's devastated, anger and the need to hurt someone rips through me.

I don't need her words to confirm who's hurt her. It's obvious. And I'm going to fucking ruin him for it.

He assured Rett that he could be trusted with his little sister.

Well...

Just look how that turned out.

She continues to cry, and I swear, each sob rips another piece of my heart away.

I hate it.

I've always hated it when she cried. But this time is so much worse.

This time, she is really hurting.

Eventually, she pulls back, although she doesn't look up at me. Instead, she keeps her gaze locked on the stones beneath us.

"He...he..."

"Shush, babe. It's okay. You don't have to explain."

She nods, but she either doesn't agree or just needs to get the words out regardless.

"He's upstairs in the hotel room he booked for us with…" My jaw tightens as disbelief flows through me. I squeeze my eyes closed for a beat, wishing her sentence ends another way, but I know what's coming.

I'm going to fucking kill him.

"Someone else."

Pure, unfiltered rage takes hold.

"Motherfucker," I hiss, desperately trying to get myself under control.

She needs me present and with her right now, not storming off to find the cheating fuck and teach him a lesson.

"It was meant to be our night."

I close my eyes and tip my head to the sky as I drag in a deep, calming breath.

She needs you, Linc. Don't fuck this up.

When I look down, she's still staring at the floor.

"Parker?" I whisper, but she doesn't move.

"Little P," I say a little louder as I tuck my fingers under her chin and force her to look up at me.

My chest tightens painfully the second her red, watery eyes meet mine.

She's heartbroken. And yet, she's still hands down the most beautiful girl I've ever laid eyes on.

I'm pretty sure Parker Donnelly was made for me.

There isn't a single thing about her I don't like.

In fact, I like everything about her a little too much.

Rett would kill me if he ever found out. But I haven't been able to stop myself. Falling for his little sister has been the easiest thing I've ever done. It's been as natural as breathing.

But as easy as it might have been, it's also one of the hardest parts of my life.

Holding myself back has become almost a full-time job. Sure, it helps that we're at college now and I'm not around her as much as I once was. But still, she's a permanent fixture in my everyday life, even if it is from a distance.

She's the first thing I think about when I wake up in the morning, and the thing I fantasize about before going to sleep.

The other girls don't mean a thing. They're just some fun. A distraction from the fact that I'm never going to be able to have the one I really want.

"I-I'm sorry I called you," she whispers, regret dancing in her eyes. "I didn't know what else to do."

Sorry? She's sorry?

She never needs to be sorry about a single thing.

I'm not going to say it because she doesn't need to hear it right now, but Seth fucking up tonight is probably the best thing that could have happened.

If she'd have gone through with it...my stomach rolls over as images of what they could have been doing right now play out in my mind...she'd have regretted it. Sure, tonight might have been great, but this would have still happened. And it would have hurt even more.

I force a smile on my face.

"I'm glad you called me," I tell her honestly.

"Thank you for coming."

She falls into me once again, and I happily accept her embrace.

Dropping my lips to the top of her head, I press a kiss there before breathing her in.

My eyes flutter closed as I allow myself a moment to indulge in the feel of her in my arms.

You're fucked, a little voice pipes up, but like usual, I shove it back down.

"Come on, let's get you home," I say, adjusting her so she's at my side.

She stills. "I can't. I can't go home. Mom will—"

"Whoa, calm down," I soothe. "I'm taking you to mine. Mom and Nova are out. We'll have the place to ourselves."

My idea of heaven.

"O-okay," she stutters before we begin walking again.

As we move, something to my side flashes in the overhead light and catches my eye.

Without thinking, I release her for a beat and pick it up.

A hotel key card.

My fingers curl around the piece of plastic as my instincts tell me just what room it is.

"Linc?" she questions.

As fast as I can, I tuck the card into my back pocket and pull her back into my side.

She doesn't say anything as we make our way to my car, and I can only hope that's because she didn't see.

Pulling my passenger door open, I wait for her to drop into the seat, but she lingers.

"Parker, what's—"

Her lips cut off my words as she reaches up and presses them to mine in the briefest, sweetest kiss of my life.

"Thank you, Linc. I—"

Unable to stop myself, I wrap my hand around the back of her neck and duck, resting my forehead against hers.

The need to kiss her properly burns through me. My cock jerks and my pants get too tight at just the thought of tasting her. I just know that she'll be so much sweeter than I've imagined.

Her big, golden eyes gaze up at me, almost begging, and I swallow thickly.

She needs you to do the right thing here, Linc. She's hurting. Do not take advantage.

"Just so you know, Seth has made the biggest mistake of his life tonight. There won't be a day that goes by where he won't regret this."

Her breath catches, her eyes filling with tears again.

"I don't care who he has up there with him. She'll never be you."

Parker shuffles forward, bringing our lips almost within touching distance.

I close my eyes, needing a moment to remind myself to do the right thing.

"In you go, little P. We've got a full night ahead of us."

It's not true, it's already speeding toward midnight, but I have every intention of at least attempting to turn her night around.

Finally, she drops into the car, taking temptation away.

I deserve a medal for holding out.

My reprieve only lasts a few moments because, before I know it, I'm in the driver's seat with her sweet scent surrounding me.

"You look beautiful, by the way," I tell her honestly as I back out of the space.

The emerald-green dress she's wearing fits her like a glove, and I'm not sure what it's doing to her tits, but fuck me gently.

Forcing my eyes to stay on the road, I cringe when she lets out a self-deprecating laugh.

"Maybe that was true earlier. Pretty sure I've ruined it now."

"Not even close, Parker. Even on your worst days, you're still the most beautiful girl in the world."

The second the words leave my lips, the air around us turns thick.

"You...um...you don't need to try and make me feel better."

I bite down on the inside of my cheek, stopping myself from assuring her that I'm telling the truth.

We drive in silence for a few minutes before I take a turn she wasn't expecting.

"Where are we going?" she asks, although it soon becomes obvious when I pull into a McDonald's.

"When I was a kid and something had gone wrong, my dad would always bring me on a trip to McDonald's as a treat to try and cheer me up."

"He was a good man," she says quietly, making my heart constrict.

"Yeah," I say, forcing the word past the lump of emotion now clogging my throat. "He was the best."

I lose myself in memories of the man who taught me everything he knew, the man I try to live up to every single day of my life.

Before I know it, we're at the window to order and I have no idea what Parker wants.

"Uh...what do you—"

"Whatever used to be your happy food," she responds.

I smile, unsure that what I used to eat with Dad back then would cut it now.

I glance over at her sad face before placing a ridiculous order for the two of us.

With her lap loaded with food plus two huge sodas sitting in the drink holders, I continue toward my family home.

Parker sits silently beside me, chewing on one of her pretty gold nails, her eyes locked on the world passing us by. I desperately want to ask if she's okay, but I already know she's not.

She's just had her heart broken by a jerk who didn't deserve to have access to it. Of course she's not okay.

Lifting the hand I have resting in my lap, I hesitantly reach over the center console.

She might not want my touch or support, but right now, all I can think about is keeping her close.

She startles the second my fingers brush her palm. Her head twists toward me, her eyes wide with surprise. But she doesn't pull her hand away or break our connection; instead, she shifts slightly and twists her fingers with mine.

Heat rushes up my arm and shoots straight down to my dick.

Get it together, Storm.

That is not what this is.

Just be the guy she needs.

My teeth grind as I force myself to keep my eyes on the road.

The closer we get to my childhood home, the more my mind starts to spin.

Images I shouldn't be having of her standing in my room, crawling onto my bed, fill my head.

She's been in the room before. Countless times. But Rett is usually there, too.

We've never been there together.

With an empty house.

Fuck. This was a really bad idea.

I shake my head.

What am I even thinking? She isn't going to want to come to my room. She'll most likely lock herself in the guest room and try to figure out how to deal with the heartbreak she's suffered tonight.

Thankfully, by the time we pull into the driveway, her tears have ceased and she's breathing more steadily.

We sit there as the music plays softly from the speakers, just staring at the dark house before us.

It feels like a big moment, but I know that I'm the only one thinking it.

Be the friend she needs, Storm.

"I don't think I can wait any longer for a burger," I confess before killing the engine and pushing the door open.

"Do you ever not think about food?"

All the time...when I'm thinking about you.

"Every now and then. It's my fuel. A machine this powerful needs every bit it can get."

She snorts as I take the box from her lap.

"I'm pretty sure you should be eating healthier 'fuel' than McDonald's."

"Yeah, but tonight can be an exception. We all need food that makes us smile every now and then."

"Yeah," she muses as she climbs out.

I meet her at the hood, and side by side we walk to the front door. "Are you sure they're going to be gone all night?" she whispers as I find my key and push it into the lock.

"Yep. You don't need to worry about being caught."

"Who says I'm doing anything I shouldn't be?"

Lifting my hand to my neck, I rub the tense muscles, regretting my choice of words.

"N-no, you're not doing anything wrong. I just meant—"

"It's okay, Linc. I know what you meant. I've heard the rumors about you having girls in your room before."

"Girls in my—you want to go to my room?"

Get it together, you fucking moron.

"Sorry, I just assumed that we'd hang out up there."

I stare at her, taking in her red-rimmed eyes and tear-stained cheeks.

"We can do whatever you want to do. I won't be offended if you want to just disappear into the guest room."

She shakes her head and takes a step closer.

"I want to hang out. With you. Show me that not everything about tonight is fucked up."

I nod.

I can do that.

Taking her hand, I lead her up to my room, praying that she can't feel mine trembling.

47

LINCOLN

I've woken up at the same time every morning since I was a kid.

But this morning, there is one significant difference.

Parker.

She's curled up beside me with her ass resting against my morning wood and her back pinned to my front.

I'm pretty sure it's the best morning I've ever had.

I stay still, not wanting to wake her but needing a moment to enjoy this.

I didn't plan on slipping into her bed last night, but the second I heard her crying, I didn't know what else to do.

She needed me. Okay, so maybe she didn't need me exactly, but I was the only one here who could support her, and there was no way I was turning my back and letting her sob alone.

Honestly, I expected her to turn me away the second my knee pressed against the mattress. But to my surprise, she relaxed into me. And even better than that: her sobs subsided.

I helped.

Pride flows through me.

But what is this morning going to bring?

If she were to wake up, would she freak out that I'm here?

Or would she be happy?

Will she even remember it?

That question causes pain to cut through my chest.

I close my eyes and hold her a little tighter, committing all of this to memory.

With a heavy sigh, I prepare to slip away from her. As much as I'd love to stay here until she wakes up, I need to get to the arena.

I'll see her in a couple of hours. She'll be at the bench during our morning skate. She'll have her eyes on me. Okay, for a whole other reason than why I really want her looking at me, but I'll take anything I can get right now.

My heart jumps into my throat as I go to slide my arm from around her waist. "No," she mumbles sleepily before she grips onto me tightly.

She wants you here.

Suddenly, I feel like I'm being ripped in two. I want to be here with her. I want it so fucking badly. But I have a meeting with Coach. He'll rip me a new one if I miss it.

But Parker...

She wriggles against me, her ass putting the most perfect pressure against my aching cock, and I have to bite down on my cheeks to stop me from moaning.

She's asleep. She has no idea she's doing this. But damn, I'm not likely to forget.

I count to thirty in my head, and then I try again. This time, my arm slips free, and I'm able to carefully roll away.

I swear I don't breathe until I'm standing beside her bed, gazing down at the sleeping beauty before me.

She's shoved the sheets down so they're only covering her calves, leaving the rest of her exposed. My eyes run up her muscular thighs, pert ass, and over the dip of her waist. The sight does nothing for my boner.

Swallowing thickly, I continue up. Her tank is bunched up and resting just beneath her tits, allowing me to slide my eyes up her toned stomach before I get to the swells of her breasts.

The fabric covering her is all twisted up, but not enough for me to see anything. It's for the best; I'd feel like even more of a perv if I could really see anything. It's bad enough I'm standing here and getting my fill like this.

Silently, I stalk around the bed, my erection straining against my boxers. I should leave and remove the risk of her waking up and looking directly at it, but I'm not ready for this to be over yet.

When I get to her side of the bed, I drop to my haunches and just look at her.

Her eyes are closed, her pale lashes resting on her slightly pink cheekbones. I can't help but wonder if even unconsciously she's a little turned on from our snuggling. Damn, I hope so. What I wouldn't give to stay in bed with her and see if she needs some kind of relief...

My attention drops to her lips. Her full, parted lips. I can't help but to drag my tongue across my bottom one as memories of our kiss last night slam into me.

The second her mouth pressed against mine, I was powerless but to fall into it with her. I've craved it for so long. Nothing could have convinced me to pull back, even though I knew I should have done so.

I keep saying it, but I really don't think Parker understands that when I say that I'll give her anything, I really fucking mean it.

Unable to stop myself, I reach out and tuck a loose lock of hair behind her ear.

It's a risk, and I'm pretty sure I stop breathing as I do it, but the temptation to touch her is just too much.

Finally, I glance at the clock on her nightstand and find exactly what I was expecting.

Hanging my head, I force myself to stand, and after allowing myself one more look at her, I walk out of her bedroom. The second I'm in mine, I drop my boxers, kick them toward the laundry basket, and march toward my shower, naked, with my hand already wrapped around my cock and images of how this morning could have played out clear as day in my mind.

COACH TRIES to catch up with all of us once a month to check in. It's become normal over my time with the Vipers, but that doesn't mean sitting in the chair before him in his office doesn't send nerves rattling through me every time.

Deep down, I know he's just checking in. But there's always a risk I could be told I'm about to be traded to the other side of the country.

I was unbelievably lucky to be called up to play for my dream team from college. But it would be unrealistic of me to think that I'll be here forever. I'd fucking love it if I could, but I need to keep my feet on the ground and prepare for the day this meeting isn't just a catchup.

Thankfully, today isn't the day. Instead, we've chatted about our current performance, our upcoming games, and predictions on how the rest of our season is going to go. It's nice. Really fucking nice. Because it reminds me of times gone by with my dad.

I've never told Coach just how important he is to me, or how much I respect him. Not only was he an unbelievable player, but he's a fantastic coach who puts all his players and the staff around him first, and of course, he's an incredible father. Everything he's built here, he's done as a single father after he lost his wife, and Casey, her mom, when she was young. Really, he's a fucking legend, and I'm proud to be a part of his roster—I'm also incredibly relieved that he saw enough in me to want to have me as part of his Vipers' family.

As our conversation draws to a close, I prepare to head back downstairs to hit the gym before our morning skate session starts. I scoot to the edge of the chair, ready to stand, when he hits me with a question I wasn't expecting.

"How's Parker doing?"

I hold his eyes as a soft smile pulls at my lips.

"She's...she's doing okay. Really loving her job, but the stress over her apartment and everything is bringing her down a little."

"I can imagine," he says, clearly aware of the situation. "Has she said anything to you about other members of staff causing her issues?"

I narrow my eyes. I was already suspicious that something had happened. She's made a few comments, but she hasn't even wanted to name anyone.

"I'll take from your silence that she has."

"She's alluded to some things, but I don't know anything more than that."

Coach nods. "It's twenty-twenty-five. Women have a huge part to play in professional sports, and I refuse to entertain anyone who doesn't have the same opinion. Parker has been a great addition to our medical team, and—"

"She's incredible. And I'm not just saying that as her friend. The guys all love her, and if they had their pick, they'd all have her working on them over Mitchell."

Coach raises one brow, and it's all I need to know.

"Thank you, Coach. This has been a very informative meeting."

"Don't do anything stupid, Storm."

"Protecting my girl is never stupid," I shoot over my shoulder.

When Coach doesn't respond, I spin around to look at him. I find a wide grin on his face, excitement glittering in his eyes. "Parker's good for you, Storm. Don't let her get away."

My heart slams against my chest as silent understanding passes between us.

"Fuck," I breathe, dragging my hand down my face. "She's not...she's not there yet," I confess.

I haven't breathed a word about what's developing with Parker to anyone, and I can't lie, it feels good to have someone to confide in.

"These things take time and patience." He gives me a hard stare, well aware that the latter isn't something I'm particularly good at.

"Thanks, Coach. I really appreciate it."

"Any time. My door is always open."

Emotion burns behind my eyes as I nod and slip out of his room.

Time...

If it means I'll eventually be able to call her mine, then I'll give her all the time in the world.

The temptation to go straight to the training room the second I know she'll be in is strong.

After what Coach said—or didn't say—about Mitchell, all I want to do is sit in there with her and protect her.

She doesn't need it. I know that. She's more than capable of fighting her own battles. But fuck...she shouldn't have to.

My internal battle over how to handle my newfound knowledge is written across my face as I march into the locker room. Fletch and Killer take one look at me and retreat, as if I am about to go at them.

Thankfully, they leave me to myself so I can get dressed and head out, although I don't miss their questioning glances or those of the rest of the team.

Kodie is the first one brave enough. "Everything alright, man?" he asks as we step out onto the ice.

"Yeah, no. I don't know," I mumble like an idiot.

"Parker giving you hell, huh?" He chuckles.

"It's not—" I cut myself off from lying.

Yeah, it's Parker. It's always fucking Parker.

Kodie smirks at me knowingly.

"Has something happened?" he asks.

I shake my head as I run through the events of last night and this morning.

Yes, something has happened, but I'll be fucked if I'm sharing the details with anyone.

Dragging my attention from Kodie, I scan the rink.

She should be here. But she's not—

My thoughts vanish as I spot her walking toward the ice with her iPad tucked under her arm.

She looks beautiful with her hair pulled back into a high ponytail, her makeup so light she might as well not be wearing any, and her sinful leggings and Vipers-issued vest to keep her warm while we train.

The sight of her has my pulse racing and my muscles aching with the need to rush over there and pull her into my arms.

Does she remember?

Not a second later, her eyes meet mine, and I get my answer.

Her smile is shy, totally un-Parker-like, and her eyes dance with secrets that only the two of us know.

48

PARKER

Nerves rattle through me as our eye contact holds across the ice.

When I first woke up this morning, I thought it was all a dream. But then I rolled onto the other side of the bed, and there he was. Not in person, of course; he'd already slipped away. But his scent was there.

I kept my eyes closed and just breathed him in.

It was ridiculous, and I felt so pathetic, but I couldn't stop myself.

Since the moment we drove around that corner and saw my building burning, Linc has been incredible. He's had no obligation to do any of the things he's done for me in the last few weeks, and last night was just another example.

He was there for me, his support unwavering as he did exactly what he said he would and gave me everything I needed.

That kiss.

My hand twitches at my side with the need to touch my lips. They tingle with the memory alone.

I focus on Linc as he shoots around the back of the goal, puck gliding across the ice in front of him. He's a vision to watch. It's easy to forget about the more brutal side of the game when he's like this. It's like watching a dancer. He moves so effortlessly, so fluidly. It's intoxicating.

The way he moves his hips…

"Donnelly."

I gasp loudly as something—or someone—taps me on the shoulder.

"Earth to Donnelly," Mitchell mutters. "Christ, don't you have a job to do instead of standing here checking out the players."

I blink, staring at Mitchell without really seeing him as the image I just had in my head of Linc melds with embarrassment and anger.

Heat races through my body, and I pray that he can't see the flush that is no doubt spreading across my cheeks and down my neck.

"I'm focused on my job," I seethe.

"Is that why you didn't hear me calling your name a million times?" He quirks a brow, and my fist curls with the need to punch it off his face.

I hate this guy.

Suddenly, there's a loud bang in front of me, and I shriek as I take a step back. But when I look up, I find Linc glaring at Mitchell beside me.

It takes a couple of seconds, but everything about his expression changes when he turns his eyes on me.

"My quads are tight," he shouts through the plexiglass. "Can you check me over after?"

I frown. He doesn't look like he's struggling, but I guess he knows his body better than I do.

"Yeah, of course," I agree as his eyes continue to hold mine. They're darker than usual, and the thought of him thinking about our kiss, about our night in my bed, has my thighs clenching.

Nothing happened, but from the way he's looking at me, you'd think so much more was going on here.

And Mitchell is observing every second.

"Thanks, Donnelly. You're the best." He winks before shooting Mitchell a glare and skating off.

Mitchell scoffs at the blatant insult and saunters off with his shoulders tensed.

When I look back at the ice, Linc isn't paying his surroundings any attention; instead, it's all focused on me.

My chest tightens, and my heart rate increases. Looking at him through plastic gives me some kind of protection, but in an hour or so, he's going to be lying on my table, and I'm going to have my hands on him.

I'm not sure how I'm going to handle that after everything.

MUCH TO MY RELIEF, Mitchell disappears after morning skate, leaving Jarad and I to work on players in the trainers' room, not that any of them seem to mind having us instead.

Linc doesn't appear, and I hate that I spend more time worrying about where he is than I do focusing on Kodie, who's lying before me while I work on his shoulder.

Thankfully, he doesn't say much, but then, Kodie never does. The only time I see him truly smile is when he's with Casey and Sutton. Here at work, he's nothing but focused.

I'm almost done when his deep voice suddenly rumbles through the room.

"You and Casey have a table booked at seven tonight."

"W-what?" I stutter, convinced I just misheard him.

"I've booked you a table."

I frown. "Why?"

"Because I feel like you need a girls' night."

I shake my head, a smile playing on my lips.

"And what makes you say that?"

"Storm. He's in a weird mood, and I'm guessing it's got everything to do with you. He's got something he needs to say but won't, and I figure you might need to get something off your chest as well."

"Nothing's happened," I say quietly, aware that my boss is standing only a few feet away. He might be deep in conversation with another member of the team, but that doesn't mean he doesn't have one ear on what we're saying.

"I didn't say it did. But he's stressed, and selfishly, I need him focused on the rest of this season."

"So do I. I want you guys to go all the way this year."

"And we can. But not without Linc.

"Go out with Casey tonight and—"

"You just want the gossip," I tease. Whatever I tell her will undoubtedly get back to him.

"I can assure you, I don't."

I can't help but chuckle as the thought of Kodie sitting on his couch, crossed-legged, waiting for Casey to get home to spill the beans pops into my head.

I bet he loves the gossip, really.

"And while we're out, what are you doing to be doing?"

"Seeing if I can talk some sense into your boy."

"He's not mine," I counter quickly.

Despite me still having my hands on his shoulder, Kodie pushes from the table and twists to look at me.

"Parker," he says, his eyes bouncing between mine as if he's looking for a secret. "I hate to tell you this, but Linc has it bad for you."

I swear to God, my heart stops. But while hope and all my teenage dreams might threaten to bubble up at his words, I force it all back down.

Instead of jumping up and down like an excited little girl, I keep my eyes locked on Kodie's.

I sigh. "Linc isn't made for a life like you have with Casey. He's a player—he loves the game, the limelight, the celebrity status, and the puck bunnies who come along with that."

"When was the last time you saw or heard about him being with a bunny?" Kodie asks, his brows lifted.

"Since you moved in, what has he been doing with his evenings?"

"Uh..." Images of him chilling on the couch watching TV or gaming fill my head. Him hanging out with friends, their dance mat battle. Nights on the road where he might go for a drink with the guys, but then head to the room not long after Kodie.

That isn't the Linc we all used to know and...tolerate.

He's...he's different.

"Exactly," Kodie says with a smug grin.

"It's so easy to get swept up by the glamor of this life. We've all done it. I know it might be hard to believe, but back in the day, I was out every chance I got and making the most of the benefits." Now it's my turn to lift a brow. I'm teasing, though—thanks to Casey's lifelong obsession with the man sitting before me, I'm aware of what his life was like before Sutton came along. He was no different to all the others. To Linc.

But now, he's a family man who'd choose spending time with Casey and his daughter over anything.

"It gets old, Parker, and guys start looking for other things. For a quieter life. Maybe that time has come for Linc."

My mouth opens and closes like a fish.

"And maybe you're the reason."

Christ.

Kodie and I finish up in silence. Even if I wanted to continue a conversation, I'm not sure I could form the words.

It's not until he's dressed and about to walk out that I speak.

"Where is he?" I question, my concern for his lack of presence only getting worse.

"He stayed out on the ice with Killer and Brit; they're working with the rookie."

A smile appears as I think of Hayden. On the outside, he seems overly confident, and it looks like he fits right into life on the team, but as a rookie, I find it hard to believe that's the case.

"I'm sure they'll all be in to hound you soon. Enjoy the rest of your day, and your dinner."

"Wait," I call as he ducks around the door. "Where are we going?" I ask quietly.

AS I CLEAN UP, Jarad finishes with his player, and as soon as he's done, he disappears into the office, leaving me waiting anxiously.

It'll be fine.

It's not like he's going to come barreling in here telling everyone who will listen how he slept in my bed last night because I was crying like a baby.

Grabbing my iPad, I sit at the small desk and attempt to write some notes into Kodie's file, but I soon discover that I have the attention span of a gnat. And it'll remain the same until I see him.

Before me, the screen goes blank, and my mind drifts back to all the things Kodie said.

Is he right?

Does Linc actually like me?

Something akin to hope flutters in my stomach as I think back over our time together recently, and before long, I drift even further back.

He sure said and did all the right things that night to make me believe he thought of me as more than just his best friend's little sister.

I remember the way he touched me. The soft words he whispered in my ear.

My cheeks burn all over again.

It doesn't matter how much time has passed; the memory still affects me as if it happened yesterday.

I hear them long before I see them. Their deep voices and laughter echo down the hallway that houses both my training room and office, and their locker room.

My stomach knots as my eyes lock on the door.

The sound of their skate guards on the concrete floor acts like a countdown to them approaching the door, and by the time I spot a shadow, my hands are trembling.

As predicted, Linc leads the group, and the second he appears in the doorway, his eyes scan the room.

Disappointment floods me that I wasn't his first thought, but that's all forgotten when he finds me.

His eyes darken, and his lips pull up into a smirk as he holds my gaze.

"I'm gonna shower, then I'm all yours, Donnelly," he says, his voice a deep rasp that hits me in places it shouldn't.

"What gives you first dibs on her?" Killer complains behind him.

"Roommates' rights," he states before marching off.

The others linger, looking between the two of us before they eventually follow him to clean up.

The minutes seem to turn into hours as the room remains quiet. It's unusual, and I can't decide if it's a welcome silence or not. At least if there were some guys in here stretching or even complaining from the ice bath, I'd have a distraction.

But eventually, heavy footsteps draw closer, and suddenly those long minutes seem like no time at all, because he's standing in my doorway, wearing nothing but a pair of athletic shorts, his T-shirt thrown over his arm and his chest still dotted with water droplets from his shower.

"Were you in a rush to get in here or something?" I muse as I push to my feet.

"Babe, you have no idea."

49

PARKER

The second I read his message, my heart drops into my stomach.

Linc. On a date.

I'm not sure that's happened since he started playing for the Vipers. Or if it has, he's kept it very well under wraps.

"Are you okay?" Casey asks as she retakes her seat in front of me.

The restaurant Kodie booked for us has been incredible. The food is mind-blowing, and the cocktails are exquisite.

"Um..." I hesitate, unsure how to explain how I'm feeling right now.

Angry. Dejected. Rejected. Hurt. Jealous.

I could go on, and none of them are good.

I didn't see Linc again after our session earlier. I messaged him about going out with Casey, and that message received a thumbs-up. Not exactly the kind of response I was expecting after last night. But then, I guess he was busy.

Suddenly, dots start bouncing on my screen, and my eyes zero in on them, waiting as questions begin filling my head.

If he's on a date, why is he messaging me?

Where did he meet her?

Is she a bunny? No, bunnies don't date. They just fuck.

Is he on dating sites? Is Kodie right and he's actively looking for someone to settle down with?

When his message comes through, I quickly discover it isn't a written reply, but a photo. And the second I register who's in it, I relax.

"Oh my god." I laugh.

"What?"

Making the image larger, I hold my cell up so Casey can see.

"Aw, they're the cutest," Casey whispers, her face getting all sappy as she looks at them together.

By the time I spin my cell around again, I find another message.

Storm: Me and my bestie 😸

A smile pulls at my lips as I stare at him sitting on Kodie's couch with Sutton next to him, her arms around his neck as she kisses his cheek.

My heart thumps harder as I take in the state of his hair. He has a million small ponytails with multicolored bands everywhere.

"He's so good with her. He's gonna be a great dad one day."

It takes a few seconds for Casey's words to register, but the second they do, my eyes jump to hers.

"Do you think he wants that? A family?"

"I don't know; he's never said. Maybe he doesn't even know. It's not like he's ever been serious with anyone to consider the next steps."

"I guess," I mumble, my attention dropping back to the photo.

I stare at Linc. A man who's almost as familiar to me as my own brother. He's been a part of my life, my family, for almost as long as I can remember. So why is it that I'm suddenly looking at him so differently? And it's not just because of my stupid teenage crush that likes to poke its head up every now and then. That's just because he's hot. This is...

I close my eyes as I remember how his embrace felt last night.

"Are you okay?" Casey asks softly.

When I look up, I find her brows pinched in concern.

I've told her about last night, about the state of my apartment and how overwhelmed I felt in the moment. I've told her that Linc was there for me when she chastised me about doing it alone.

But I haven't delved into what really happened.

I haven't told her about the kiss or how he slipped into my bed and held me all night.

It doesn't feel right sharing that. It's been us.

Our little secret.

"Yeah, I'm fine," I lie.

She glares at me across the table.

"I know this year isn't what you expected"—I can't help but scoff at that—"but everything happens for a reason. You need to remember that."

"And what's the reason for my apartment? That I needed to rebuy everything and start over?"

She shrugs. "Maybe. I never said it has to make sense. Have you seen anything worth checking out?"

I shake my head. Honestly, I've stopped looking at apartments; it's too depressing.

"Freya is struggling too."

"How is she?" I ask, a little guilt trickling through my veins that I haven't reached out.

"She's so lost. I just wish she could find some kind of purpose. But cooking for her parents and my dad, and then locking herself in her childhood bedroom, isn't it."

"She'll figure it out," I mutter sadly.

"Yeah, she will. When the time is right."

We continue talking as we finish our drinks. We attempt to pay, but the second we ask our server for the check, she smiles at us and tells us that it's already been covered.

"Kodie Rivers," Casey muses.

"You're a lucky girl, Case," I tease as I pull my coat on and hook my purse over my shoulder.

"Yeah," she says, her eyes practically hearts as she thinks of the man waiting for her. "Did you want to come back? Linc is probably still at our house."

I almost say yes. The temptation to see him, to be close to him, is strong. But I don't. I've got things I need to sort out at home. We're heading out for another two road games at the end of the week; I have dull things like laundry to do.

"Maybe another time."

"Oh, we should totally go out on a double date."

"Linc and I aren't dating," I point out.

"Oh, yeah, I know that. But it would be fun."

I mumble a response because I'm not sure I agree. It would feel very coupley, and that's not what Linc and I are. We're temporary roommates. Friends, kind of.

By the time we get outside, our rideshare is waiting for us.

It drops me off at Linc's first before carrying on to deliver Casey back to Kodie. I stand on the sidewalk and wave her off, a foolish part of me hoping that she's wrong and Linc is back.

She isn't.

With a sigh, I make my way through to my bedroom and kick off my shoes.

My suitcase lies half-packed on the floor. It's pretty much how life is now. I just need to fill it with clean underwear and clothes, and it'll be ready to go again.

I make quick work of stripping out of my dress, take my makeup off, twist my hair up into a bun, and walk back to my bedroom to find some pajamas. But the second I pull the drawer open, I pause.

The new items I've bought are all perfect. Some comfy, some sexy. But none of them are what I want.

I glance at the door, wondering if I can chance it.

"Fuck it," I mutter before walking out of my bedroom wearing only my bra and panties.

The second I step into Linc's room, I question myself. But it's too late now; I'm here. And if he catches me, well...I'll just have to deal with the consequences.

I march toward his drawers and pull one open before rummaging for something that catches my attention.

"Bingo," I hiss when my fingers find one of his old college shirts.

I gather the fabric to my chest before I close the drawer and slip back out.

After removing my bra, I pull the old, soft fabric over my head.

Perfect.

As I walk toward my bed, I lift the neck so it covers the bottom of my face and breathe it in. His scent floods my nose, and instantly, I'm back in his arms again.

Ignoring the jobs that are calling my name, I crawl into my bed. That also smells like him.

I have a problem.

I lie there for a long time with a million and one thoughts running around my head. But eventually, I'm distracted by the sound of someone entering the apartment.

My heart rate picks up, and I begin to question my decision to steal a shirt from his room. What if he notices? What if he comes in here and sees me?

But despite those concerns, at no point do I roll out of bed and take it off.

I can't.

He crashes about in the kitchen for a bit before his footsteps get louder as he walks into his bathroom.

He turns the shower on, and my mind runs away with me as I think about him stepping under the water. I bet he looks insane with rivulets of water cascading along the sculpted lines of his abdomen.

My temperature rises right along with my heart rate. I rub my thighs together, but it does little to quell the desire that's getting more and more insistent between my thighs.

It's been a few days since I pulled out my vibrator. Maybe that's why I'm so tense. I just need a private moment to let go.

I'm about to reach into my top drawer when the water cuts off.

It shouldn't stop me—it doesn't matter that he's no longer in the shower—I've still got a very vivid imagination, but for some reason, I don't move. Instead, I continue lying there with my clit pulsating, torturing myself with what could be.

Linc continues moving around as I picture him in those tight boxer briefs he likes to wear that leave very little to the imagination. I bite down on my lip as I try to picture how they might look when he's hard. There's no way they'd contain him. Linc is packing; I already know that.

After a few minutes, everything goes silent, and I assume he's crawled into bed.

My heart continues to race, my body begging for relief. But I already know that whatever I give myself is going to be unsatisfying.

I need more.

I need—

I sit upright as my door opens, the bottom brushing against the thick carpet. My room is in darkness, but that doesn't mean I can't see his shadowed figure moving at the end of my bed.

I don't say a word for fear I might scare him off.

Fire shoots through my veins, making me burn from the inside out at just the thought of what he's doing, of what's going on in his head.

It's not until his knee hits the mattress that words finally spill free.

"What are you doing?" I whisper.

"Your bed is more comfortable," he explains as he stretches himself out beside me.

"O-oh," I breathe, unable to find any other words.

Slowly, I lower myself back down, leaving us side by side.

Seconds stretch to minutes. The only thing I can hear is my own heavy breathing as I wait to see what's going to happen next.

Surely he didn't come in here to just sleep...did he?

"You need to turn that brain off," he whispers. "Your thoughts are so loud."

"W-what? I'm not even—"

"Liar." I huff in irritation that he knows me so well. "Either tell me, or roll over and go to sleep."

My mouth opens and closes, but I quickly decide there's no way I can tell him where my head is at right now. It's still full of images of him walking around his room in those boxers. Shit. Is he wearing them now?

I bet he is.

My fingers twitch to reach out and find out if I'm right.

"Parker," he growls, dragging me from my thoughts, and I quickly roll over, giving him my back.

He chuckles knowingly as he shuffles closer.

I stop breathing as the front of his body lines up with my back, and his arm wraps around my waist, holding me tight.

"You need to relax, little P."

I release the breath I was holding on his command, but I can't say I relax all that much. Especially when I wriggle a little in his hold to get comfy and discover something.

"Linc," I warn, the steel rod suddenly pressing against my ass the only thing I can focus on.

He's hard.

Lincoln Storm is in my bed, snuggled up with me, and he's hard.

So much for relaxing.

"I know," he rasps. "Trust me, I know."

Desire shoots through me, and before I know it, I'm rubbing my thighs together again.

His warm breath races down my neck.

"Unless you want me to do something about it, I suggest you stop wiggling your ass like that, babe."

50

LINCOLN

She was wearing my T-shirt.

She snuck into my room, stole my T-shirt, and then proceeded to wear it to bed.

Those thoughts have been on constant circulation in my head since I woke up the other morning with enough light spilling in around the side of the curtains for me to see her.

She was wearing my T-shirt and the smallest, sexiest pair of panties.

Fuck, I'm getting hard now just thinking about it.

It's been three days since I made this discovery. Three freaking days, and I can't get it out of my head.

It's driving me insane.

No. She is driving me insane.

We've barely seen each other since, unless I've been in the trainers' room with her. Every morning I've been up before her, and every night I've been out later.

I hate it.

I'm not sure when everything started changing, but it has. I no longer want to be at VIP events, being photographed for someone else's gain. I don't want to be out in clubs or doing meet and greets—okay, okay, I do want to do those because I fucking love our fans, but that's not the point.

I want to be at home.

With her.

Every single night this week, once I've gotten in, I've showered and abandoned my bedroom, my bed, in favor of hers.

Does that mean she wants me there? I'm not entirely sure. But she isn't doing anything to stop me, so I'm taking that as an invitation.

Each time I crawl into her bed, I'm hard. It doesn't matter that I've jerked off in the shower to try to combat it. The thought of discovering what she's chosen to wear and pulling her hot body into mine is enough to have me ready and raring to go.

I'm pretty sure she's feeling equally as horny, the way she rubs her ass against my dick.

Lifting my hand, I bite down on my knuckles to stop me from groaning out loud.

She's taunting me.

Tempting me.

Making me lose my goddamn mind.

It's fucking working.

"Everything okay?" Fletch asks from across the table, his eyes dancing with amusement as he watches me fight my internal battle with my libido.

My hand drops like a rock into my lap.

"Yep, I'm good," I say, a little too enthusiastically. "Excited for the game tomorrow."

His brow quirks in question before Killer drags him into conversation about something he read online.

We're at a restaurant of Handsy's choosing. It's turned into a thing whenever we're on the road. He wants decent food that he hasn't attempted to cook himself, and we're all more than happy to tag along for the ride.

He's sitting at the head of the table with his hands on his stomach, looking very pleased with himself, while Monroe chats away about something Handsy is clearly not interested in.

Beside me, Kodie sits quietly, watching everything happening around him.

Meanwhile, somewhere else in the city, Parker is out with Brooke and Leah. My teeth grind at the thought of other guys having their eyes on her.

What if she's dancing with some asshole who has his hands all over her right now?

Jealousy and anger shoot through me; how I manage to stay seated is beyond me.

"You're on edge," Kodie observes.

A laugh tumbles free. "Yeah, I guess I am."

"Anything to do with someone I know?" he asks quietly so the others can't hear.

"No idea what you're talking about," I mutter.

He shakes his head, but there's a smirk playing on his lips. "Fun, isn't it?"

Handsy refuses to let us leave the restaurant until we've ordered one of every dessert on the menu for him to try. We oblige because...well, he's our goalie, and we owe him everything.

By the time we leave, we're all full, and everyone but me seems to be in high spirits.

"We should hit a bar," Monroe calls from the back of our group.

"Are you even old enough for that?" Kodie deadpans.

"My ID is legit, fuck you very much," Monroe quips back, making us all laugh.

"I'm in," Killer states. "Hands? Linc?"

I consider his question for two seconds tops. "Nah, I'm not feeling it tonight. I'm gonna just head back."

"We've got a game tomorrow," Fletch points out.

"I know, Cap. I'm not suggesting we stay out late. One drink and a little dance."

"Yeah, I'm out," Fletch muses. "And if I hear that any of

you came crawling back in sometime before dawn, you're gonna fucking regret it."

"Yes, Cap," Killer, Handsy, Brit, and Monroe sing as they salute him.

After a few minutes, they double back, heading to a club that Killer knows of, while Kodie, Fletch, and I head back to the hotel.

Fletch tells us about Reese's work on the upcoming Valentine's gala, while Kodie talks about Sutton's game that he's missing this weekend, but he's confident they'll get the W based on the other team's record this season.

Listening to them both talk about their families and their lives outside of hockey hits differently than it used to. I never used to understand it. Hockey was my life. Now, though, now I can see the appeal of having someone to go home to at night. Someone who understands and accepts you for exactly who you are.

Before long, we're walking through the entrance to the hotel. We stop to sign some things for fans before excusing ourselves to the elevators and riding up to our floors.

Fletch is one above us, so we leave him behind as we head to our room.

"At least I don't need to worry about making myself scarce so you can have phone sex with your girl. Not when she's right down the hall."

"We're not hooking up," I argue as the hotel room door falls closed behind me.

"Okay," he says, although his tone tells me that he doesn't believe it for a second.

"Are you calling Casey?" I ask, aware that'll mean I need to either lock myself in the bathroom for a bit or disappear back downstairs.

He chuckles. "You're safe tonight. If we win tomorrow, though..."

"I know, I know. I really need to speak to Coach about getting my own room."

"You'd miss me," Kodie deadpans as he toes his sneakers off and drags his shirt over his head.

"Yeah," I muse.

"But there's no point getting your own room when there is a perfectly good one down the hall with an empty side of the bed."

"Will you stop?"

"Oh, because you did when I was sneaking around with Casey?" he points out.

"That was different," I argue.

"Was it?" he asks, staring me dead in the eyes. "She's someone you think you can't have. You're freaking out about what you're feeling. You don't think you're good enough for her."

"Hey, any woman would be lucky to have me. I'm a catch."

He smirks, not needing to point out that I completely ignored the rest of his comments.

So what? He might just have a point, but still, Parker and me, and Casey and him are not the same.

Being with Kodie was never going to affect Casey's job. Sure, they had the added complication of her being Coach's daughter.

Kodie mutters something under his breath as he disappears into the bathroom.

Flopping onto my bed, I open Instagram and immediately find her account for clues about where she might be.

There's nothing. She hasn't posted in weeks. But that doesn't mean it's the end of the road because she's with Brooke, and Brooke posts every second of her life on social media.

I don't need to type her name in; she's right there beneath Parker's in my search history.

It may not be the first time I've done this…

I groan as my eyes land on the first image of the three of them from earlier this evening. Brooke and Leah blur into the background. The only woman I see is Parker.

She's wearing a navy fitted, short dress. Her hair is up, and her makeup is heavier than usual. She looks fucking hot. And she's out in public right now.

My grip on the screen tightens until I'm sure it's about to crack as I scroll through the images Brooke posted an hour ago.

Each one hits me harder. But it's one of Parker laughing with a drink in her hand that really catches me. She looks so happy and carefree. The opposite of how she's been recently.

I want to give that to her, but when we're back in LA, it's like the entire world is pressing down on her shoulders.

"Don't tell me you're stalking Parker," Kodie states as he emerges and falls into bed.

"Okay, I won't tell you."

"Is she back yet?"

I glance at the time. It's not late, but then we've all got to be at the arena early tomorrow, so there's every chance she will be.

"I don't know."

"Are you going to find out?"

"I-I—" I want to.

"Just go, Linc. She might need help getting out of her dress."

Kodie flips over, giving me his back and focusing on his own cell. I don't need to look to know he's chatting with Casey.

I ignore his comment and continue scrolling. Most of my feed is full of hockey news, both factual and fake, and I read it all with a grain of salt.

We're almost at the halfway point. All-Star games are next week, giving the rest of us some much-needed time off before we hit the rest of the season hard.

The playoffs are almost in touching distance. We're going to do it this year. Will we go all the way? That's yet to be seen, but we're in a better position than we have been in years.

Much more than I can say about Rett and his team, I

discover, when the score from his game tonight flashes up on my screen.

Closing the app, I find my message thread with him, ignoring the guilt that threatens. It's nothing new; I've been battling it for years. Six, to be precise.

> Linc: Unlucky tonight, man.

Donnelly: Did you see the highlights? We fucking sucked.

> Linc: I already knew that. When are you gonna get a trade to a real team?

Donnelly: Fuck you. At least I spent less time in the box tonight than you did in your last game.

> Linc: It was worth it. Hendrikson was asking for it. Did you see the way he was going after our rookie?

Donnelly: Never said I didn't agree.

Our messages continue for the next thirty minutes, all focused on hockey. At no point does he ask me about Parker, so I can only assume he still doesn't know where she's living. Fine by me. The last thing I need is the protective big brother speech

As Kodie's snores begin to fill the room, I lower my cell and tip my face toward the ceiling.

I'm exhausted. What I really need to do is sink down into the sheets and sleep. But something tells me that I'm not going to be able to. Not alone.

Lifting my cell back up, I open Brooke's profile again, and my eyes widen at the most recent post.

It's a bubble bath in her hotel room, with what I assume are her heels from tonight abandoned beside it.

If she's back, that means...

51

PARKER

"Yesss," I hiss as I kick my heels off and gingerly press my feet flat on the floor.

There was a time when partying all night in heels came as easily as breathing, but it seems those days are gone because...ouch.

Abandoning them, I walk across my hotel room toward my still-mostly-packed suitcase. Despite limiting myself to only two alcoholic drinks tonight, I've got a nice buzz going on. I'm not sure it's from the cocktails, though. I'm pretty sure it was the company and the dancing.

For a couple of hours, I left my worries and thoughts at the door of the bar and just let go.

Well, almost all my thoughts.

There was one that never left me.

Even as I was laughing with Brooke and Leah, in the back of my mind, I was wondering what Linc was doing.

Was he also out partying, or was he back at the hotel, being a good boy?

There was nothing on his social media—yes, I admit I checked when I locked myself in a restroom fairly early in the evening. But then, that's not unusual.

I also hadn't posted anything.

I was tempted. If he knew where I was, then would he come and find me?

Honestly, if the answer was no, then I really didn't want to be standing there looking over my shoulder all night.

It was girls' night. A player-free zone.

Even if, deep down, I really wanted him to step up to me on the dance floor, grip my hips, and tug me back into his body.

Heat rushes through me at just the thought.

Reaching behind me, I pull the zipper of my dress down.

It gets stuck at the waistband, and I curse as I try to force it over.

My eyes catch on my purse that I laid on the dresser, and I still.

I could message him to help me.

He would. I know he would.

My heart pounds harder, and I squeeze my eyes closed, making the image in my head as real as possible.

His breath would rush over my neck and shoulders. The heat of his body would burn into mine as he stood a little too close, ensuring his scent engulfed me.

The sound of the zipper being lowered would fill the room, along with our heavy breathing as he tugged it free, allowing my dress to fall to my waist, showing him exactly what I'm not wearing beneath.

"Parker," he'd growl in my ear as he stared at the reflection of my chest in the mirror, his eyes dark with arousal.

He'd step forward, pressing the steel rod of his erection against my ass, just like he has done every morning this week.

I thought that the second night he crawled into bed with me was a bonus. But it didn't stop there. Every single night after he's showered, he silently slips into my room, climbs into my bed, and pulls me back against him.

My eyes fly open, and I stare at the bed beside me.

It's stupid, and I hate it, but...I'm not sure I'm going to be able to sleep without him tonight.

A heavy sigh escapes me as I return to the task at hand without reaching for my cell to call in backup.

He's probably already asleep anyway. We've got an early start tomorrow.

Finally, I manage to free the zipper, and my dress falls from my hips, pooling around my ankles.

Stepping out of the fabric, I leave it where it is to deal with tomorrow before I pull the sleep shirt I hid at the bottom of my suitcase for this trip, knowing that I'd need a little bit of him surrounding me.

Despite sleeping in it the other night, when I bring the fabric of his shirt to my nose, I can still smell him. Comfort washes through me, but it doesn't come alone, because the desire that had me squeezing my thighs together with my little fantasy only moments ago is right on its tail.

I glance at my suitcase. I might not be able to see it, but what I need is hidden in there somewhere.

"Fuck it," I mutter as I sink my hand into my packed clothes, searching for my little friend. "Yesss," I hiss as my fingers brush the smooth silicone.

With my toy in hand, I walk to the bed and climb in with my heart racing and arousal pumping through my veins.

I'll get myself off, and then I'll be able to have a good night's sleep and wake up ready to face tomorrow.

The second I'm on my back, I shimmy my panties down my legs and kick them off.

Switching my vibrating friend on, I rest back and spread my legs, trying to clear my mind so I can really sink into this.

I take myself back to my earlier fantasy. What would happen next?

As I let my mind wander, I move my vibrator between my legs and gently touch it to my clit.

My entire body jolts with the sensation, and more heat pools in my core.

God, I need this.

In my head, Linc's hands cup my bare breasts as his lips

trail hot kisses up my neck. He pinches my nipples, making me cry out and rub my ass back against him. He groans, desperate for more.

Spinning me around, he tugs my dress from my hips, his eyes feasting on me standing before him in only my panties while he's still fully dressed.

"Fuck, I've waited so long for this," he'd confess quietly.

I press the vibrator harder against my clit as my release begins to build.

But it's not enough. I need more.

God, I need so much more.

Reaching down with my other hand, I tease my entrance before pushing two fingers inside.

I cry out at the sensation of being filled, although, again, it's not enough. But it'll do.

I ride my own hand, imagining Linc walking me back to the bed before giving me a gentle shove so I fall down onto it. Then he hooks his fingers in my panties and drags them down.

"Oh god," I whimper. I'm close. So freaking close.

His hands land on my knees and he spreads me open, his gaze taking a slow trek from my eyes all the way down to my pussy.

"Perfect," he'd muse, licking his lips like he hadn't eaten for a month.

Then he'd drop to his knees...

"Oh god."

Trail kisses up my thigh...

"Please, yes."

Until he got to my—

Bang, bang, bang.

"Noooo," I sob quietly as my almost release ebbs away.

There's another knock, ensuring I won't be continuing this.

"Parker," a deep voice hisses, although muffled by the heavy hotel door.

I sit bolt upright.

I'd know that voice anywhere. What the hell is he doing?

"Parker, open the door before I wake everyone up," he demands.

"For fuck's sake," I mutter, abandoning my toy and climbing from the bed.

The soft fabric of his T-shirt falls over my heated skin, and I shudder.

I was so fucking close.

I pause a beat before opening the door and glance down at myself.

I should change. But...

"Hurry up before I get caught out here."

"For fuck's sake," I mutter under my breath before I pull the door open a few inches. "What?"

My breath catches. Linc is shirtless and wearing only a pair of sweatpants. Even his feet are bare.

"What's wrong? What's happened?" I ask in a panic.

"I could ask you the same thing," he muses as his eyes take in my appearance.

I cringe. I didn't even look in the mirror.

"I just got in," I say in a rush, "I'm getting ready for bed."

"Perfect," he whispers before pressing his hand to the door.

A frown wrinkles his brow.

"Babe?" The way he looks at me with hurt, puppy-dog eyes makes my chest ache.

But it doesn't immediately make me follow orders.

"What are you doing at my door, half naked?"

"I..." His arm lifts so he can rub the back of his neck. "I... uh...couldn't sleep."

I raise a brow, amusement and a little relief hitting me.

But just as I open my mouth to say something, the ding of the elevator fills the silent hallway and we both panic.

He's right. We can't be caught like this.

Without thinking, I open the door and drag him in before anyone sees him.

The second the lock engages, he spins on me, backing me up against the door.

His minty breath rushes over me as he takes his time studying every inch of my face.

"W-what are you doing?" I stutter.

His eyes linger on my lips for a few seconds before they lift to find mine.

My breath catches at the hunger reflected back at me.

"I don't know," he confesses. "But whatever it is, I can't stop."

His forearms lift, caging me in as we stare at each other.

The air is electric, and all I can think about his having his lips on me.

That kiss in my old apartment has been haunting me for days. I want a repeat. I'm desperate for a repeat.

And if the way he lowers his head tells me anything, it's that he can't stop thinking about it either.

My chest heaves, my previous desire returning full force.

When I discovered that I needed more than my vibe and my fingers a few minutes ago, this wasn't entirely what I had in mind. Okay, okay, it was. I just...I didn't think it would happen.

His eyes continue to hold mine as he closes the final few inches between us. Silently, he's telling me to stop him.

But...but I don't think I can.

I don't—

The second his lips brush mine, every single thought in my head vanishes.

A moan rumbles between us, but I don't know if it came from me or him as I blindly reach for him.

My hands hit the hot, taut skin of his stomach, and I delight in the way his muscles dance as I slide them upwards until I've looped them around his neck.

He steps forward, pinning me against the door as I open for him.

Oh god, this is heaven.

Kissing Linc is like nothing I've ever experienced with anyone else.

It's all-consuming.

It's...it's everything.

"Parker," he groans, deepening the kiss even further. But as much as I want it, hearing that drags me kicking and screaming back to reality.

We can't do this.

One second, I'm right there at his mercy, and the next, I've ducked under his arm and I'm backing away from him.

"W-what?" he questions before leaning forward and pressing his forehead against the cool door.

I stand there a few feet away, watching his back and shoulders rise and fall with his increased breathing—mesmerized by the way his muscles ripple with the movement.

He takes a few seconds to get himself together before he turns around. And the moment he does and his eyes find mine, I question every single one of my life choices.

"Linc?" I whisper, hating the rejection I can see so clearly in his eyes.

"It's okay," he says softly as he walks deeper into my room. "It's—you did—"

His words falter as his eyes land on my bed.

I follow his attention and am instantly hit with the reminder of what I was in the middle of when he knocked on my door.

"Parker," he rasps, his voice suddenly a few octaves lower.

My face burns red hot. I can only imagine what colour my cheeks are.

"Oh my god," I mutter as my desire and embarrassment collide.

Lifting his arm, he combs his hair back as he rips his eyes from my bed and turns to me. "Parker, were you..."

He doesn't finish his sentence; he doesn't need to.

I nod, unable to find any words.

Even if I could find a lie, what would be the point? The evidence speaks for itself.

"While wearing my shirt?" he asks, his eyes dropping to the cotton covering me. His attention lingers on my chest, and I have no doubt it's because my nipples are hard and trying to bust through.

"Mmmhmm."

"Okay, wow. Fuck," he mumbles almost incoherently. "Did you...did you...finish?"

52

LINCOLN

My heart thumps against my ribs as I picture Parker lying on that very bed, wearing my T-shirt with that purple vibrator pressed against her clit.

Fuck.

When she abruptly ended our kiss, I thought it was over.

I expected her to send me back to my room with my tail between my legs and regret bubbling over. I never thought this was what I was going to experience next.

I keep my eyes on her as my mind spins out of control and my cock threatens to break through the fabric containing it.

Shyly, she bites down on her bottom lip before she shakes her head.

Fuck. Me. Gently.

"Get on the bed." My voice is rough, and my demand is intense in a way I hope it can't be ignored.

"L-Linc, we can't—"

"I said, Get. On. The. Bed, Parker."

She hesitates, but this time she doesn't argue and instead scrambles to the middle of the mattress.

"We can't do this," she whispers. There isn't much conviction in her tone. She's trying to do the right thing. Her head is screaming at her to keep her walls up, to keep that final bit of distance between us. But her body…

How the fuck I didn't see it when she first opened the door, I don't know.

Her hair is a mess, her cheeks are blazing, and her golden eyes are almost brown, they're so dark.

I'm hit with a bolt of lust so powerful, I don't know how I remain standing here.

I don't think I've ever wanted a woman as much in my life.

"I'm not going to touch you," I tell her.

It's going to fucking kill me, but I'm not.

"Then what—"

"But I'm going to get you off. I need to, Parker."

Her lips part, but she doesn't say anything as she squirms.

"Are you wet for me, babe?" I ask, imagining her already soaking the sheets beneath her.

She bites down teasingly on that bottom lip again.

Fuck. What I wouldn't give to make it mine.

It takes her a second, but eventually she gives me an almost imperceptible nod.

Christ. This woman is going to be the death of me.

"Lie back on the pillows," I order.

With my eyes locked on her, I stand unmoving at the end of the bed.

She does as she's told, and in seconds, she's laid out before me, wearing nothing but my T-shirt.

The sight does fucking good things to me.

"Do you have any idea how hot you are?" I ask absently.

"Linc," she whimpers, her chest heaving, her nipples hard and begging for attention through the fabric of my shirt.

What I wouldn't give to rip that shirt from her and suck them into my mouth.

One step at a time, Storm.

Taking a step closer, I reach for one of the two items she left on her bed.

Hooking my fingers into the lace, I lift her panties in front of me.

They're white and way too innocent for all the images I have playing out in my mind that involve this woman.

She watches me, her lips parted as she waits to see what I'm going to do next.

Lifting them higher, I bunch them in my palm in front of my face before inhaling.

"Holy shit," she breathes.

"Yeah," I agree as I stuff them into my pocket.

Mine.

Her eyes follow my movement, and the second she sees the size of the tent in my sweats, she gasps.

A cocky smirk kicks up the corner of my mouth.

I don't know why she's surprised. She knows exactly what I'm packing down there.

It's not like this is our first rodeo.

Although things are very, very different right now.

While she might be unsure of the situation, confidence rolls off her in waves.

She knows what she's doing now, and she knows the power she has over me and every other man walking the planet.

The idea of her learning all of this with other men threatens to put a damper on things, but I force the thought away.

Right now, she isn't with other men.

She isn't wet and desperate for them.

It's for me. Only me.

"Spread your legs. Show me what you're hiding, pretty girl."

Slowly, she pulls her feet up. She's teasing me, making me wait, and it's fucking working.

My boxers are already soaked with precum. Before long, it's going to start showing on my sweats, giving away just how on the edge I am already.

"Parker," I warn when she keeps her knees pinned together.

"What's the magic word?" she taunts.

"Parker, will you please show me your pretty pussy... please."

Fuck if the accomplished smirk doesn't make her even more irresistible.

I step closer, the magnetic pull I feel toward her at an all-time high.

Honestly, I'd give my left testicle right now to be able to touch her, taste her, make her mine.

But all those thoughts fall from my head when she finally does as she's told and spreads her thighs for me.

My eyes drop to her, and my mouth waters.

"Fuck, you're even more perfect than I remember," I breathe.

"Linc." I don't know if it's meant to come out as a warning, but all I hear is her begging for me.

It's everything I've wanted to hear for six long years.

"I've got you, babe. I've always got you."

Reaching out, I snag her abandoned vibrator and hold it up, inspecting it.

"I've listened to you, you know." I don't know where the confession comes from, but before I know it, it's out in the open.

Parker's eyes widen.

"The first time I heard you moan, I thought something was wrong, so I moved closer to your room to check. Then I discovered the truth."

"Oh my god, Lincoln," she cries, covering her face with her hands.

Too late to be embarrassed now, babe.

"Look at me," I command, and her hands fall away in a heartbeat.

"Do you know how fucking hot it is, standing on the other side of the door, listening? Do you know how fucking hard I get, hearing you enjoy yourself? Do you know how fucking hard I come after I've heard you get off?" Her thighs shift as if she's going to pull them back together. "Don't you dare move," I warn.

Her response is a roll of her hips.

"You're killing me in the best way here, pretty girl."

Her eyes shutter at my new nickname for her.

Well, it's not new. I've been thinking it for years, and I've only allowed myself to use it on one occasion.

Clearly, she remembers that occasion just as clearly as I do.

"Does hearing that I get off listening to you make you hot?"

"Yes," she answers honestly.

I reward her by pressing the button on the end of her vibrator, letting it come to life.

"Is this the one you use when I've been listening?"

She nods, her eyes locked on the toy as if she can summon it closer with a hungry look alone.

"You have no idea how fucking jealous of this thing I am."

Lifting it to my lips, I stick my tongue out and swirl it around the tip, letting her taste flood my mouth.

"Jesus Christ, Linc," she moans.

"You're so fucking sweet, babe."

I push almost the entire thing into my mouth and suck her from it, releasing it with a pop.

"You just..."

"I promised I wouldn't touch you," I remind her. "I never said I wouldn't taste you."

She rolls her hips again, and this time, her glistening, needy pussy lures me in.

I crawl on the end of her bed, between her spread thighs, and get comfortable. I don't have any intention of moving anytime soon.

Her breath catches as I press the vibrator to the inside of her knee and begin dragging it slowly down her thigh.

It's exactly what I'd do with my lips, if given the chance.

"Oh god. Please, Linc."

"Fucking love it when you beg me, pretty girl."

"Lincoln, I need it. Please. Please."

I close my eyes, absorbing those words.

If only she said *you*. I need *you*.

It's coming.

One day.

Just be patient.

"Yes," she cries the second I touch the point of the vibrator against her clit.

Her hands fist the sheets beneath her, and her hips jump from the bed.

"Feel good?"

"Yes. More. Please."

She squirms, her breathing fast and labored as I alternate between teasing her clit and pushing the vibrator inside her. It's the wrong shape to hit the spot that will really make her fly. But I'm not sad about that. I don't want a toy to give her that high. I want to do that myself.

It doesn't take long for her legs to start trembling.

"Look at you," I muse. "Wearing my shirt, dripping wet, and begging for me to get you off. It's the thing my wildest fantasies are made of."

I have no idea if she's hearing anything I say at this point. But honestly, I don't care. I'll tell her every single one of my secrets if it'll ensure I get to do this again.

I think about all the nights we have on the road in the next few months.

Maybe this could become a thing.

But then, what about at home?

How can I go from having this in other cities but not in my own home? In my own bed?

So far, I've only ever crawled into hers. But really, deep down, I want her in mine.

"Fuck. I'm right there. Yes. Yes. Linc. I'm gonna coooooooome," she cries as her body shatters into pleasure.

Her grip on the sheets tightens, her mouth forms a perfect O, and her body convulses as she rides the waves of her orgasm.

It. Is. Fucking. Beautiful.

It goes on and on, and I watch every second of it, committing it to memory.

"Oh my god," she gasps as she comes down from her high, sucking in deep lungfuls of air. "That was—"

"The hottest thing I've ever seen," I say, sitting a little higher and sinking my hand inside my boxers, squeezing my aching length.

My teeth clench as lust shoots up my spine.

Parker stares at me, waiting.

I really need to fucking come. But I'm aware that I've possibly already pushed her too far.

Closing my eyes, I take a moment to think rationally.

I shuffle back. "I'm just gonna use the—"

"Stay," she instructs, suddenly turning the tables on me. "I want to watch."

"You...you want to watch me get myself off?"

Her teeth sink into her bottom lip again before she nods.

"Do you think you'll be able to get off again while you watch me?"

Another nod.

Fuck me sideways.

"I'm not gonna last long. I'm probably gonna embarrass myself."

"I won't either."

I smirk. "Already getting revved up again thinking about me jerking off over you, pretty girl?"

Her cheeks get redder.

"I've never been able to say no to you."

With my free hand, I pass her the vibrator I dropped on the mattress before I shove my sweats over my ass, freeing my cock.

Her eyes drop to it immediately as I wipe my thumb across the tip, collecting the precum to use as lube.

"Christ," I groan as I stroke myself. I'm already embarrassingly close, and it only gets worse when the buzzing of her toy fills the room again.

She presses it against herself and shudders.

"Sensitive?"

"Yeah," she agrees.

"Show me, babe. Show me how you get yourself off while I'm standing on the other side of the door, listening."

53

PARKER

I swear my body is going to burst into flames at any moment.

I thought him having my vibrator and being in control of my orgasm was hot. But that had nothing on watching him slowly work himself.

His grip is tight, the muscles running down his corded forearm are taut, his abs are tense, and the V lines that cut down to his cock are deeper than ever.

He looks like my every dirty fantasy come to life.

With my vibrator pressed against my clit, my next release builds faster than I thought possible.

I can have multiples, but usually only when I'm alone. I've never had more than one with a man. They've never cared enough to bother. Linc, though, seems to care more about my pleasure than his own. Something tells me that if I'd agreed, he'd have disappeared into the bathroom to find his release without a fuss.

I hate the idea of that. Especially after what he just gave me.

"Fuck, Parker," he grunts as his pace begins to pick up.

"Oh god," I moan, my legs widening until my thighs rest against the mattress.

His eyes are locked on what I'm doing with my vibrator, as if he's learning what I like and how I touch myself.

"Are you going to come for me again, pretty girl?"

"Yes, yes," I cry as my pussy contracts around nothing.

I need more. I need him.

Another moan rumbles up my throat as I imagine how it would feel if he shuffled forward and pushed himself inside me.

I want it.

I want it so badly, but...

If we go there, we can't take it back.

I managed to put him behind me once. I'm not strong enough to do it again.

Just doing this is dangerous enough.

But more...

No.

I can't.

I won't survive it.

No matter what Kodie says, or the differences I see in Linc, it doesn't mean that anything has changed.

He's still Lincoln Storm, the ice hockey player who loves to party.

He's still my big brother's best friend.

He's still my colleague.

I've barely got my feet under the table at work; the last thing I need is everyone talking about me being in a relationship with a player.

It's one of the least professional things I could do.

I'd be a laughingstock.

Mitchell can't take me seriously as it is. No one would have any respect for me after that.

Parker Donnelly only got the job with the LA Vipers because she's in a secret relationship with star winger, Lincoln Storm.

"Fuck, are you there?" Linc rasps, his jaw tight as he holds himself on the edge.

I nod, although it's not entirely the truth.

Skating my free hand down my stomach, I push two fingers inside myself.

"Christ," he groans, his nostrils flaring as he watches me fuck myself. "Are you tight?"

"Uh-huh."

"Bet you'd fucking strangle my dick in the best kind of way. I'd stretch you out so good, pretty girl."

He fucking would, too.

I haven't been with anyone else the size of him. I can only imagine how it would feel being full of him. I bet it would hurt in the most delicious kind of way.

"Linc," I try, his words, the image they paint and the sensation of my fingers curling inside me enough to push me closer to the edge.

"Fuck, pretty girl. Can I...can I come on you?"

My heart slams against my ribs, and my orgasm crests.

"Yes, yes, yes," I chant as I fall.

"Fuck, Parker. Fuuuck," he groans as he finds his release.

Quickly, he shuffles forward as his cock jerks in his hand.

The moment his warm cum hits my stomach, another wave of my release crashes through me.

Holy shit, this is the hottest thing I've ever experienced.

Linc's body sags once his orgasm has subsided. His cum cools on my stomach, but I'm too exhausted to do anything about it.

"Fuck. That was—"

"Yeah," I agree. "It was."

He sits there with his chest heaving and his softening cock out. I'm no better; I don't so much as make a move to close my legs.

"That wasn't why I turned up at your hotel room door," he explains after a couple of silent seconds.

"Sure it wasn't." I laugh, finally pulling my thighs together and hiding myself from him.

He pouts like a child who's just had his favorite toy taken away, but he doesn't say anything.

"It wasn't," he assures me. "I mean, I'd be lying if I hadn't thought about it. But it wasn't my intention."

I nod, accepting his words as he climbs off the bed and tucks himself away.

I want to complain and beg him to strip down to nothing so I can ogle him, but I keep my mouth closed.

We've already done way more than we should tonight.

"I really couldn't sleep. I...I missed you."

"That's cr—"

"Crazy, I know. Trust me, I know."

Pushing up on my elbows, I glance down at the mess he left on my stomach.

"Wait. Don't move," he demands before he darts toward the bathroom.

The water runs for a minute or two, and then he's back with a washcloth in his hand.

"What are you doing?" I ask as he crawls back onto the bed.

"Cleaning up my mess," he explains.

I knew that. His intentions were obvious the second he emerged, but...

No guy has ever been like this after sex.

No. That's not true.

No *other* man has ever been like this after sex.

Over the years, I've forced myself to forget the details of that night.

It was safer to lock it all up in a box and shove it to the back of my mind. But over the past few weeks, the lid has been lifting, and everything I've tried so hard to forget is beginning to surface.

"It's the least I can do after..." He gestures between us.

"Is that your way of apologizing?" I ask lightly.

"Hell no. I'm not apologizing for something I'm not sorry about."

My brows lift.

"That was...that was everything, Parker. There's no fucking way I'm apologizing for getting to experience that."

He finishes cleaning me up before getting off the bed again.

"What happens now?" I ask his retreating back.

He pauses, his muscles tensing.

"Now, you need to go to the bathroom, and then we're sleeping."

"Sleeping?" I question.

"Yeah, that's what I came here for. I sleep better when you're beside me, pretty girl."

My eyes fall closed as warmth spreads through me at the use of that nickname I've only heard on one previous occasion.

He takes a couple of minutes in the bathroom, and when he returns, he jerks his chin in the direction he's just come from, silently commanding me to go and do the same.

I stand on weak, post-orgasm legs and wobble my way toward the smaller room.

The second I close the door and catch my reflection in the mirror, I gasp.

My hair is like a bird's nest on top of my head, my cheeks are still burning, and my bottom lip is swollen from biting on it.

I look...thoroughly satisfied.

It's a good look on me.

I make quick work of what I need to do before attempting to smooth down my hair—hopelessly—before walking back out.

This time, my legs are steady, but the nerves are stronger in my stomach.

It's just Linc, I tell myself.

Yeah, Linc, who just watched me get off twice.

And like he promised, he didn't touch me once.

I shouldn't be surprised; this is Linc we're talking about.

A man who knows what he's doing.

I turn the light off and immediately discover that he's done the same in the bedroom. The only light, glowing from a bedside lamp.

I walk around the corner with my heart in my throat and confusion warring within me.

I believe that he didn't turn up at my door hoping for a booty call. I'm completely to blame for what just went down in here. If I'd known, I'd have quickly put my vibrator away...or would I?

Deep down, did I leave it all there, knowing it was him and hoping something would happen? We both know it's been building over the past few weeks. Despite not wanting to acknowledge it, it was inevitable, wasn't it?

My head is spinning as I round the corner, but the second my eyes land on him, it stops. He's resting back against the headboard with the sheets pooled low on his stomach, so low in fact, I question whether he still has his underwear on or not.

I don't need to put much thought into which I'd prefer.

Lock it down, Donnelly.

Draw the line.

You've done enough.

Linc's eyes track me as I move across the room and to the other side of the bed.

The air is heavy between us, but neither of us speaks as I pull the covers back and slip into bed with him.

The second I settle, I become achingly aware that I'm still not wearing any underwear.

Damn it.

Would it be weird to get back up now and put some on?

"Hey," Linc says, interrupting my freak-out.

"H-hey," I stutter. "Are you really sleeping here?"

"If you'll let me."

As much as I might be spinning out over all this, I'm not sure I've got it in me to send him away.

The truth is, I'm not sure I'll be able to sleep without him, either.

I may not want to admit it, but his presence calms me, and I've slept better than I have in ages the last few nights.

As much as I might want to say it's the exhaustion that did it, I know that would be a lie.

"I'll think about it," I mumble as I sink lower and turn away from him.

As I expected, he shuffles closer in the blink of an eye. His arm wraps around my waist, tugging me against him until there's not an inch of space between us.

"Again?" I gasp when I feel the press of his erection against my ass.

"I'm in bed with the hottest woman on the planet. And correct me if I'm wrong, but said woman isn't wearing any underwear."

Seconds pass where my silence does nothing but confirm his suspicions.

"We shouldn't have done that," I blurt.

"Maybe not. It was fucking good, though."

I can't help but smile.

"Listening to you get off is hot as fuck. But watching too... fucking hell, babe. You've ruined porn for me forever."

Pride rushes through me, warming me from the inside out.

"You looked pretty hot, too," I admit.

"Is that right?"

"Mmm," I mumble, already feeling the first clutches of sleep on the horizon. I guess two powerful orgasms will do that to a girl.

"Just imagine what it could be like if I touched you."

Yeah, just imagine.

His grip on me tightens as his lips brush the few inches of my shoulder exposed by his shirt.

"Goodnight, pretty girl," he murmurs. "Sweet dreams. Make sure they're of me."

LINCOLN

I hate to do it, but I don't have a choice. I have to get back to my room before Kodie wakes up and discovers I slipped out.

Leaving Parker fucking kills me, though.

She's so warm and soft. She smells so sweet.

I drop a chaste kiss to her shoulder before forcing myself to release her and roll away.

Silently, I locate my sweats that I abandoned beside the bed and pull them up.

I can barely see her, it's so dark in here, but that doesn't mean I don't keep my eyes on her.

I need more. So much fucking more.

Shoving my hand into my boxers, I attempt to adjust my boner, but it does very little.

I'm painfully fucking hard again. It's as if last night never happened.

God, I want more.

"See you soon, pretty girl," I whisper before backing away and, hopefully, silently slipping from the room.

I glance each way before darting to the right in the direction of my room. The sun might not be up yet, but that doesn't mean some of my teammates won't be awake. Like me, many of them are up before dawn, their bodies conditioned from years of early workouts and skates.

My heart is racing as I tap my key card against the panel and push the door open, thankfully unnoticed. Or at least, I assume unnoticed.

As slowly and carefully as I can, I close our door and then tiptoe into the room.

When I find Kodie still in bed, I breathe a sigh of relief before stripping my sweats off again and slipping into bed.

I'm about to lie down when a voice hits my ears, scaring the ever-loving shit out of me.

"Nice try, Casanova."

"Fucking hell," I gasp as I collapse on the mattress, my heart pounding a million miles a minute. "Was that fucking necessary?"

Kodie chuckles.

"I could ask you the same thing. You know I don't care."

"Maybe I couldn't sleep and went to the gym," I counter.

"Your sneakers are beside your bed," he points out with more smugness in his voice than necessary.

"Fine, I went for some fresh air."

"We have a balcony," he counters.

"Motherfucker," I breathe, rolling onto my back and throwing one arm over my eyes.

"Admit it. You're gone for her."

I bite down on the inside of my cheeks to save me from replying.

"Scary, isn't it?" he muses when I remain quiet.

"We haven't slept together," I blurt.

"Wow." He laughs. "It really is serious."

My lips part, but no words appear.

"Your secret is safe with me, Storm."

I mumble some kind of response, but it's unintelligible at best. Thanking him properly means something is going on, that I do really feel that strongly about her, and I'm not ready to admit that to anyone yet.

KODIE and I make our way down to the hotel ten minutes before our call time. It was his idea; apparently, I was getting on his last nerve with my pacing back and forth.

I couldn't help it.

I'm on edge.

Restless.

I need to see her.

I need to know that I didn't fuck everything up last night.

If I have...fuck, I don't know how I'll cope.

If she walks away now like she did before, it's going to fucking wreck me.

"I am so ready for this game," Killer says as he joins us. "We're gonna fucking kill it. This man right here is going to have another shutout game," he says, backhanding Handsy across the chest. "And we're gonna continue our reign as division leaders."

"Amen to that," Fletch says with a wide smile, although it falters when his eyes find me and the lack of excitement on my face. "Everything okay, Storm?"

Beside me, Kodie chuckles knowingly. "He's frustrated and ready to burn off some energy."

Fletch quirks a brow.

"We're going out after our next game," Killer announces, as if they didn't do something after our meal last night.

"Aren't you tired?" Fletch asks, but before Killer can respond, someone stalks toward us who does look tired. "Oh, for the love of god."

"Who let the rookie get wasted?" I ask, taking in his pale face and red eyes.

"I'm not—" Monroe says, holding his hand up as he sucks in a deep breath. "I think I ate something I shouldn't have."

"Wonderful," Fletch muses. "You gonna be okay joining us?"

"Hopefully it'll subside."

"Coaches are here," Brit points out, and we all begin heading outside.

I turn back as I follow the guys toward the exit.

Where is she?

I look around at all the faces waiting to head to the arena.

Everyone else is here.

I drag my hand down my face before turning back to look at the elevator.

Should I go and get her?

But as I consider making my way up to find her, the doors open, revealing the woman I'm waiting for looking even more beautiful than ever.

Her red hair is pulled back into a sleek, high ponytail. Her large, golden eyes twinkle in the bright overhead lights, and her lips are glossy and full.

Shit. The way I want to worship this woman.

I spin around fully to face her, and her eyes land on mine.

Her breath catches, and I swear her cheeks brighten.

Is she thinking about last night?

It takes her a moment to move, and I revel in the thought that I rendered her useless.

"Come on, Donnelly," someone calls from behind me, snapping her out of her trance.

She rushes from the elevator and attempts to march straight past me to join the rest of the medical staff waiting to exit the building.

"Whoa, slow the fuck down," I hiss, reaching for her wrist as she attempts to race past me.

"What are you doing?" she snaps, turning to glare at me.

"Not ignoring you, which is what you seem to be attempting to do to me."

"Life isn't all about you, know you. I've got to go."

She tugs her wrist from my fingers and spins away, her ponytail swishing behind her.

Fuck.

She rolls her shoulders as she approaches the medical staff, and as she turns slightly, I catch the wide smile she gives them. The complete opposite of the reaction I got.

My heart aches as I study her, but that quickly changes when I watch Mitchell study her for a few seconds before lifting his gaze and immediately finding me.

Double fuck.

She's just protecting herself and her position, Storm.

She's right. This isn't about you.

It's about her.

Exactly as it should be.

"Come on, man. Now isn't the time. We've got a game to win," Kodie says as he practically drags me out of the hotel.

The second I'm seated on the bus, I pull my cell from my pocket.

> Linc: I'm sorry, that was selfish of me. I hope you have a good day.

> Linc: I missed you this morning.

I stare at my screen for a few minutes in the hope she'll read my words. I'm not expecting a reply; I'm not that fucking delusional. But knowing she's seen my apology would be nice.

But when nothing happens, I pull my AirPods out, pull up my game day playlist, and attempt to focus on what today will bring.

"WHERE THE FUCK ARE YOU GOING?" Fletch calls after me when I immediately turn in the opposite direction to everyone else as we get off the bus.

"I'll be ten minutes, tops," I call over my shoulder as I take off running.

The whole way here, all I could think about was my reaction to Parker's attempt at professionalism this morning.

I'm not going to be able to focus until I've put things right. I'm not an idiot; a message isn't going to cut it.

Actions.

Actions speak so much louder than words. And luckily for Parker, I can do actions.

Thankfully, there's a coffee shop right around the corner. My foot taps on the floor as I wait for the two customers in line to place their orders.

I keep my head down and just pray no one notices me. I didn't plan for this. I don't have a cap or even any sunglasses to hide behind.

Everything is fine until I look up at the barista waiting for my order.

The second our eyes connect, she squeals.

Literally fucking squeals.

"Oh my god, it's Lincoln Storm. Fuck. The actual Lincoln Storm."

Fuck. Maybe this was a mistake.

I should have just ordered it.

"Can you sign something for me?" she asks in a rush. "And can we have a photo?"

"Uh, yeah. Sure," I mutter as she searches for something for me to write on.

Unable to find much, she settles on a branded cup sleeve.

"This?" she asks as if it's the weirdest thing I've signed.

It isn't.

I take it, glad she didn't decide to ask me to sign a body part instead.

It wouldn't be the first time a girl has pulled their top up or down and asked me to sign their tits.

The first time was fun, the second too, but the buzz has more than worn off now. Especially as there is only one pair I'm interested in looking at and touching.

And it hasn't escaped my attention that I didn't even get a glimpse of them last night.

"It's Matilda," she says as I hover the pen over the card.

"Will you be coming to the game tonight?" I ask as I sign.

"Absolutely. I wouldn't miss it for the world. I'll be wearing your jersey as well."

"There you go," I say, happily ignoring that last comment. There is only one woman I want wearing my jersey, but I can't see that happening anytime soon, seeing as she works all our games.

"Will you all be going out after the game?" she asks, her eyes hopeful.

"Ah, I'm not sure yet," I lie.

We're travelling straight after leaving the arena, ready for another game tomorrow, but she doesn't need to know that.

"I'll keep an eye on socials, see if my friends and I can catch you anywhere."

"Sounds good, Matilda," I say, making her cheeks blaze.

Christ. Bunnies are so easy.

Once upon a time, I used to get off on their eagerness.

Now, though...now, the only thing that gets me going is the game that Parker and I are playing.

She wants me; I know she does. And hell knows I want her too. She's just...trying to do the right thing.

It's admirable.

But she can only hold out for so long.

I place my order, Matilda scrawls my name on the cup, and then I move to the other end of the counter where a guy is making the orders.

I get a few glances from others in the coffee shop, but thankfully, no one else asks me for anything. The barista in particular looks completely unfazed when he hands me Parker's iced coffee. With that, and a pastry in a bag, I make my way back to the arena before Fletch and Coach have a coronary that I'm missing.

Despite needing to be in the visitors' dressing room, getting ready for our time on the ice, I divert toward the training room.

The door is open, and voices filter down to me.

I come to a stop just shy of being seen as Parker's voice hits my ears.

I listen as she passionately talks about players and what injuries they're battling. She discusses their need to keep a particular eye on Monroe's defense partner due to a hip flexor injury during our previous home game. She explains how she's advised Jarad to put him on the IR for tonight.

"I assessed him yesterday. He'll be fine," Mitchell dismisses.

"That may be so, but is it a risk we're willing to take at this point in the season?"

"Typical woman, worrying too much about nothing."

Anger shoots through my veins. How dare he firstly dismiss her professional opinion like that, and secondly, it's her literal job to worry about players' health.

It is not nothing. It is everything.

Surging forward, I march into the room without knocking.

"Excuse me," I bark, interrupting the tense conversation. "Mitchell, don't you have some athletic tape to organize?" I snap as I move closer to Parker.

He mutters something under his breath, but thankfully, he shuffles away.

"What the fuck was that?" I hiss, aware that he's probably still in earshot.

"Nothing," Parker snaps. "Shouldn't you be getting dressed?"

"Yes, I should. Coach will probably rip me a new one for being late, but I had to do something first."

"What's more important than—" Her words falter as I lift the iced coffee in my hand.

PARKER

He brought me coffee.

No, not only a coffee. He brought me what looks like my favorite iced coffee with salted caramel foam and a drizzle of caramel sauce. It's my ultimate guilty pleasure.

He should be getting dressed for morning skate right now, but instead, he went out and got me coffee.

How does he even know my favorite?

The frustration I was feeling earlier begins to wash away.

It wasn't his fault that I missed my alarm and woke up late.

It wasn't his fault that I was running around like a headless chicken, thinking I was going to miss our call time and end up getting an Uber to the arena and facing the scrutiny of Mitchell—not that being on time or good at my job prevents that from happening anyway.

I was short with him. I was feeling vulnerable, even more so the second I looked into his eyes and remembered everything that happened last night.

In the harsh light of day, do I regret it?

Honestly, no, I don't think I do.

Am I worried about what happens next and the repercussions? Abso-fucking-lutely.

Mitchell has already shown me this morning that he doesn't respect my professional opinion. It'll only get worse if what's developing with Linc gets out.

What am I saying, if?

It'll be when, and the second it's out, my professionalism and ability to do my job are going to be under the spotlight.

"I also got you this," he says, holding up a bag, hopefully with something sweet in it.

"Thank you," I whisper.

His smile starts small and almost shy, but it quickly spreads to one I'm much more used to.

"Anytime, pretty girl," he says quietly so that I'm the only one who can hear.

My cheeks heat as desire pools between my thighs.

Nope, definitely don't regret it.

If I'm being honest, the only thing I'm regretting is not taking it further.

Having him get me off and not touch me was hot as hell.

But what if he had touched me? How good could it have been then?

The need to find out burns through me.

"You should go."

"I know. Coach is going to rip me a new one. But...I needed to see you smile before I head out there."

I can't help it, my lips twitch at the corners.

He brushes his knuckles along the line of my jaw.

My entire body jolts as if I just had an electric current run through me.

"I'll see you later."

I nod. "Uh-huh. Yep. Later."

Christ. I sound like a lovesick teenager.

With one final, longing look, Linc spins around and walks out of the visitors' training room, leaving nothing but his scent and the effect he has on my body behind.

Lifting the cup to my lips, I groan as the mix of rich coffee and sweet caramel hits my tongue.

He even got a double shot.

This is fucking book boyfriend material—and that is very, very dangerous.

No sooner have Linc's footsteps faded than another set makes itself known.

"Well, that was cozy," Mitchell starts up.

I groan and roll my eyes.

"Whatever, Mitchell. We've got jobs to do."

As I say that, Jarad and a couple of equipment managers come rushing into the room.

There's a flurry of activity around us as we get ready for the day, but it seems that Mitchell doesn't forget anything he witnessed this morning, because the second we're alone again, he makes his second hit of the day.

"You know, I'm pretty sure it isn't only Coach who'll have something to say about that this morning. I think HR will be very interested, considering the fraternization term in our contracts."

As my chin drops with that low blow, Mitchell walks out, leaving me standing alone in the middle of the room as somewhere in the arena, the guys take to the ice.

My head spins as reality settles into my veins.

"Shit," I hiss, standing there unmoving as panic over losing my job before it's barely begun gets the better of me.

I was worried about people's opinions; I never considered I could actually lose my job because of it.

I think back to the day I got my contract. I was so excited. It read it, sure. But I'm not sure how much actually went in. The adrenaline was pumping too hard.

Needing a moment to get myself together, I walk toward the counter where I abandoned my half-drunk coffee, but before I pick it up, something catches my eye.

On the side of the cup, there's writing.

Picking it up, I inspect it closer.

"The fuck," I balk, discovering a name and phone number staring back at me.

Clearly, Matilda has no shame.

In a rush, I pull my cell from my pocket, snap a photo, and send it on to Linc.

The irritation I felt this morning returns tenfold, and I walk out of the trainers' room with fire licking through my veins.

There is no fucking way I'm letting any man ruin this chance for me, whether it be Mitchell trying to take me down, or Linc who reminds me too much of the girl I used to be.

I'm not her anymore.

I'm stronger.

I'm...fuck.

I'm still desperately in love with him.

MUCH LIKE EVERY GAME DAY, I'm discovering, the hours pass by in a flash.

I might have Linc on my table for a few minutes after morning skate, but at no point are we alone, and at no point does he bring up last night or say anything untoward.

I'm grateful, but at the same time, standing beside him, let alone touching him, hurts.

I focus on my job, laughing and joking with the guys as if nothing is wrong. But deep down, all I can think about is if Linc messaged Matilda.

We've got a couple of hours after the game tonight before we need to be at the airport. Will he make the most of the opportunity and hook up with her?

Jealousy twists up my insides just thinking about him being close to another woman.

I hate it.

I shouldn't care.

I've managed to push his antics with women over the years to the back of my mind. Why can't I do it now?

As we tape up the last few players, readying for the game tonight, I can feel the excitement and anticipation already in the air.

I glance at the time. The stands will already be filling up with eager fans, and honestly, I don't blame them.

Hockey runs through my blood just as much as everyone else's here. I love it, and the fact I now get to work here means everything to me. Too much to throw it all away by allowing Linc to drag me into whatever game he's playing. I should have forgotten him years ago. Hell, I did. I put all of it behind me. I just can't make it stay there, apparently.

The crowd is already buzzing with energy as I walk toward the rink, where our guys are out on their final warm-up session.

I scan the sea of our white and green road jerseys until I find him.

Christ.

He's on his hands and knees, thrusting his hips at the ice.

That is the literal last thing I need to be thinking about right now.

Images of last night as he towered over me, stroking his cock fill my head.

What if I'd let him do more? Would he have rolled his hips like that as he filled me up?

I startle when an arm drapes around my shoulders.

"Hey, how's it going?" Brooke asks without a care in the world.

The second I look over, she must be able to read the torment in my eyes, because her face falls.

"Shit, what's wrong?"

"Nothing," I lie. "Everything is fine. It's just been a long day. What are you doing down here?"

"Just getting some footage. Gonna try and speak to a couple of the guys before the puck drop, if they let me." I smirk, more than aware of how superstitious hockey players can be. She might just be out of luck there.

"Awesome. Don't let me stop you," I say, stepping back to allow her to pass.

"Are you sure you're okay?"

"Absolutely." I force a smile on my face, hoping that she doesn't know me well enough yet to be aware that it's fake.

Before long, our first line guys are out on the ice, and Fletch is facing off against our opponents' forward, waiting for the puck to drop.

We've already beaten the Blackhawks this season, and they're floundering toward the bottom of the division. They're going to be coming out fighting.

We can take them, though. I might have a lot of questions spinning around my head right now, but I don't doubt that the Vipers are going to come out on top tonight.

And just to prove me right, less than three minutes into the first period, Linc manages to get a breakaway and shoots the puck right between their goalie's legs, earning his first goal of the evening.

Pride shoots through me as his teammates surround him on the ice.

I shout and scream along with everyone else, completely swept up in the moment as I celebrate my team.

I forget about everything troubling me—or at least, I do until the guys let him up and he immediately looks at the bench, searching, almost in a panic. But the second he finds me, he relaxes.

His smile hits me like a truck, and I take a step back as he moves closer.

As he taps his glove against his teammates' on the bench, his eyes never leave mine.

My heart pounds and my hands tremble.

This is bad.

Really fucking bad.

And it only gets worse.

By the time the buzzer sounds, Linc has managed his first hat trick of the year, and the Vipers' fans are going wild, chanting his name, while the Blackhawks fans have already mostly left after a painful three-to-zero loss.

While the guys continue their victory laps, I disappear to the trainers' room to hide.

I already know I won't see Linc for a while; he'll be heading off to do press with Fletch and Coach after that incredible performance. But I have plenty of other players who are going to be needing massages, ice baths, and a whole lot of other things before I'm able to leave.

Not that I'll get much relief because we'll be on an airplane and heading to our next city before I have a chance to blink.

Maybe everything will be simpler in Texas.

Maybe I'll find some clarity and answers to all my problems.

I might have my back to the door when Linc finally emerges, but I know he's there the second a round of cheers erupts across the room.

Glancing over my shoulder, I watch as he accepts the praise like the showman I know him to be, bowing to the crowd.

Rolling my eyes, I throw a couple of towels in the laundry before reaching for the antibacterial spray to wipe down my table.

The excitement in the room continues as I work, but everything falls away when the warmth of a body—his body—presses in behind me.

"What? No congratulations?"

"Linc," I warn.

"Ah, I get it. You're waiting until later."

"Are you getting on the table or not?" I snap, unwilling to play this game with him.

"Oh yeah, I need your hands all over me tonight."

A rush of air whips past me as he pulls his T-shirt from his body.

"Shoulders first, then my legs. My hammies and quads are really giving me some grief."

I grit my teeth.

This is your job, Parker.

You are a professional.

Give him what he needs and then send him on his way.

My little pep talk works while Linc has his back to me. I work on his shoulders and then move down to his back. The room is still buzzing with life, but slowly, everyone begins to filter out. Jarad disappears, and Mitchell excuses himself to the office, which surprises me. I thought he'd stay and watch to see if he could get any dirt to use against me.

And the second Linc flips over so I can get to his quads, everything changes.

I'm as hard as a fucking rock. And there is no way in hell I'm able to hide it.

Not that I want to hide from Parker.

It's just that we're in the visiting team's training room in the Blackhawks' arena, and anyone could walk in at any moment and discover me pitching a tent in my athletic shorts.

So much for keeping it professional.

Fucking kill me now.

I close my eyes as Parker runs her fingers up my right thigh. A groan rumbles deep in my chest as pain shoots up my leg, but it does very little to relieve my situation. If anything, it makes it worse.

The only thing that's making this bearable is that I don't think she's noticed.

How that's possible, I'm not fucking sure. But her movements and focus haven't faltered, and surely, surely, they would if she knew I was achingly hard for her.

Honestly, I'm not struggling that much. My tight muscles aren't anything that an ice pack couldn't solve, but the temptation to be closer to her was too much.

"Ah, shit. Right there," I gasp, and she digs her thumb in a little more. "Fuck, Parker."

The second the groan is out of my mouth, I panic.

I sense her attention on me, and my temperature spikes a couple more degrees, but when I open my eyes to look at her, her gaze isn't locked on my face. It's on my crotch.

"I-I think we should probably call it a day," she says, her voice deep and raspy. It hits me right in the balls, but despite my need to reach out and drag her back, she steps away, putting way too much space between us.

"Parker, I didn't mean—"

She looks around, her eyes darting to each corner of the room as if we're being watched.

"You should go."

"W-what?" I stutter like an idiot. I can't help it; all the blood in my body has ventured south, and my brain is hanging on by a thread.

"You need to go. We can't...I can't..." Her hand gestures to my crotch. "If someone saw...if Mitchell—"

"Fuck that motherfucker. I don't give a fuck what he thinks."

Something I don't like flickers in her eyes. I think it's fear. But that can't be right.

There's no way on Earth my girl is scared of that pussy.

"What's going on?"

"Nothing is going on. That's the whole fucking point. And yet you're sitting there like that as if it's the best day of your life."

"Maybe it is. I woke up with a pretty girl in my arms, and I just scored a hatty. Who knows where this day could take me next?"

"To Texas," Parker deadpans.

"Where the possibilities are endless."

Her expression is blank, her excitement for what might come non-existent. Her walls are up so high right now, I'm not sure even I can scale them.

"You're wasting time," she tells me.

I frown, confused as fuck.

"For what?"

"Matilda."

My frown deepens.

"The fuck are you talking about?"

"She'll fix your little issue right up, I bet." Her eyes dart to my crotch again, and I smirk.

"Little? I think we both know that—"

A bang sounds from somewhere behind us, and when I glance over, I see a shadow move in the office doorway.

"You need to go, Linc. Now."

Her hard, determined eyes hold mine, and I quickly find myself sliding from the table.

"You can finish this off later, though, right?"

I mean my legs.

I totally mean my legs.

"Leave, Storm."

Her use of my surname gives me pause. It seems like a long time since we only spoke to each other using them. In reality, it's only been a few weeks, but so much has happened. So much has changed.

"Okay," I concede, because I can see her beginning to freak out. "But this isn't over, Donnelly. Whatever is going on here, we're going to talk about it."

She exhales heavily and rolls her eyes.

My brows shoot up and my fingers curl. The image of her bent over my knee with her bare ass in the air fills my head.

"Fucking hell," I groan to myself as my cock jerks in excitement.

"We're done here. There is nothing to talk about," she insists before turning her back on me and walking away.

I stare after her, watching her ass and hips sway in her leggings, feeling like I just got punched in the face.

What happened? And where is my pretty girl from last night?

I leave with my tail between my legs and head back to the dressing room, where the guys are still goofing around, high on our win.

Fletch takes one look at me and sobers instantly.

"Storm, what's—"

I grab his forearm and drag him away from the others.

"How much do you know about Dillion Mitchell?"

He blinks, taking a moment to register my question.

"Not much, considering how long he's been with the organization. Why?"

"None of the guys want him as their trainer. Is it just because Parker is better, or is there more?"

"I mean, he can be an opinionated asshole when he wants to be. He mostly keeps it locked down, but I've overheard some things."

"Like what?"

Fletch scratches his chin. "Er...well, you remember when Lars Henrikson came out as gay?" Fletch asks, referring to a player who was traded to the Wildcats when I was a rookie.

"Yeah."

"Mitchell wasn't impressed."

"So he's homophobic?" I ask.

"Yeah, amongst other things. Why? What's going on?"

"I think...I think he's giving Parker a hard time."

His lips part as if he's going to ask why, and then it hits him. "Because she's a woman. Motherfucker."

"I need him gone," I state.

"We can't just—"

"We can, with the right evidence. I want to know anything that anyone overhears. The second we have something concrete, we're taking it to Marsh," I state—our GM. "And as much as we can, I don't want her alone with him."

"Storm, we can't exactly..." His words trail off as my glare gets harder. "I'll speak to the guys. If he's fucking about, we'll find out and do what we have to do. In the meantime, you really should convince Parker to put in a complaint."

"She's barely talking to me."

"You were just in there," he argues. "I walked past and—what did you do?"

"I didn't do anything, fuck you very much." Although, as I say the words, I figure that I must have. I can't think what, though.

"I'm sure you'll figure it out," he says, clapping me on the shoulder.

I wish I had even an ounce of his confidence.

I stand there for a moment with my head spinning as the guys pull on their game day suits, ready to head out.

A couple of hours and we'll be on a flight to Texas, then the real challenge begins: finding her hotel room number and doing whatever it takes to make her agree to let me sleep in her bed again.

I spend the bus ride back to the hotel gazing out the window, trying to figure out what the fuck I did wrong and ignoring everyone around me.

Killer and Monroe try to drag me into conversation, but they soon give up when I don't even turn around.

I don't doubt that I'll get a grilling for it later, but for now, they're content with celebrating.

I should be doing the same.

I won the fucking game.

So why does it feel like I've lost?

The second we get into the hotel, we all disappear to our rooms to shed our suits before dinner.

But no sooner have I stepped into the room than my cell starts ringing.

Hope blooms that it could be Parker.

It's ridiculous. I'm not sure she's ever called me in her life.

We've only ever messaged.

But today might be the day.

I feel like a grade-A asshole when disappointment hits at the sight of my sister's name.

Get a fucking grip, Storm.

"I gotta get this," I tell Kodie as he changes. "I'll meet you down there."

He agrees, and I pull the sliding door to our balcony open and step out into the bone-chilling cold.

I've spent my life in LA. I'm not used to windchills like this. But right now, I need something to help me focus, or I fear I'll drown in my own dark thoughts.

"Hey, sis, how's it going?"

"Hey, superstar. You killed it tonight."

"Aw, you watched," I tease.

"You know I watch all your games."

"Only when you're not partying."

"Once or twice that's happened."

"Suuure."

"Well, whatever you did before tonight's game, you need to do it again." My mind goes straight to Parker. "We want that cup this year."

"Tell me about it."

"Dad would be so proud of you, you know that, right?" Nova says, sounding so much older than she really is.

A lump climbs up my throat as I think of him. The pain and loss never leave me. Sure, it's gotten easier to deal with as the years have gone on, but post-game is always the worst. I'd love to know his thoughts on my performance, on things I could improve, and ways the team could work together better.

"I like to think so," I muse, my voice thick with emotion.

"So, Dallas tomorrow? Feeling good about that one?"

"Obviously," I deadpan.

They beat us in our last match-up, so the pressure is on. They made it all the way to game seven in the last round of the playoffs last year, and they're going to want to improve on that this year.

"Cocky as always," Nova taunts.

"How are things with you?" I ask.

"Yeah, you know. School is school. Life is...well...life."

"Wow, you really painted the picture for me there."

"Not much to say, really. I'm just ready to be done with it all."

"Seen Mom?"

"Nope. You?"

"No," I confess, feeling guilty for not reaching out.

After Dad died, I made sure I called and messaged her every day. I hated the idea of her being alone. I mean, I still do. She and Dad had been together all their lives. Inseparable. And then all of a sudden, he's gone, and she's been left behind.

But as the time passed, I discovered that I was the only one making any effort. At no point did she check in on me and see how I was coping. Once that reality hit, I took a step back.

Was it the right thing to do? Fuck knows. But I couldn't keep holding myself in the past because she was refusing to grieve and deal with what had happened. I had a life to live, and I fully intended to live it—both for me and for my dad.

Nova and I chat for a little longer before our call comes to an end.

As I lower my cell from my ear, a strong gust of wind whips past me, and I shiver.

"Fucking hell," I mutter as I let myself back into the warm hotel room.

I need to get changed and go and get food, but the thought of being around everyone so soon doesn't appeal. Instead, I sit on the end of my bed and unlock my cell.

I have messages, emails, and notifications from all my social media apps. But really, there is only one person I want to hear from.

Sadly, I doubt she's reached out.

But just in case I'm wrong, I open my messages.

My heart jumps into my throat when I find an unread one from her.

Opening it, I frown when I find a photo of the coffee I got for her this morning staring back at me.

It takes me a moment to figure out what I'm looking at it, but then I notice the writing.

And beneath the photo...

Little P: Wouldn't want you to miss an opportunity.

Suddenly, everything starts making a little more sense.

57

PARKER

"What's wrong?" Brooke asks the second I drop into the seat next to her just a few minutes before we're due to take off for Texas.

"Nothing," I mutter, not really in the mood to talk.

The team appears at the entrance to the plane, and one by one they walk down the aisle to their seats.

I keep myself busy, pulling my iPad from my bag along with my headphones.

I don't want to shut Brooke out, but also, I just need quiet. Some time to think, if that's even possible on a plane full of hockey players and staff.

As the guys continue moving, my skin begins to prickle with awareness.

I know why, and I refuse to give him the satisfaction of knowing I'm aware of his presence.

My grip on my iPad tightens, and my shoulders tense.

I don't want to talk to him right now.

I don't even want to think about him, but that seems to be a challenge too much, because every time my mind drifts, I see him kneeling at the bottom of my bed with his dick in his hand and nothing but unfiltered pleasure on his face. If it isn't that image, it's one from earlier: hard on the trainer's table.

My mouth waters, and I curse myself for being so weak.

I'm stronger than this.

I'm not the kind of woman who falls under the likes of Lincoln Storm's spell.

My heart rate picks up as he gets closer, and by the time he stops beside me, it's practically beating out of my chest.

"Parker?" His deep, raspy voice rocks through me like a shockwave, but I don't look up.

Despite not earning my attention, he continues anyway.

"Parker, I didn't— I wouldn't—I...I didn't even know it was there. Not that it would have made a difference if I had."

The silence that follows his words is probably the loudest of my life.

"Just go, Storm. You're holding everyone up."

Beside me, Brooke gasps at my cold dismissal. But it needs to happen.

I can't do this right now, and we certainly can't do this here.

He hesitates, but after a couple of seconds, he must realize that I'm right, and he continues shuffling down the aisle.

Others follow him, but I don't dare look up. I don't need to know who heard that.

I startle when a giant hand reaches out and squeezes my shoulder.

My heart launches into my throat, but when I look up, it's into Kodie's understanding eyes.

He gives me the briefest smile and doesn't say a word as he continues toward the back of the plane. Out of the corner of my eye, I can see Mitchell glancing over, probably trying to figure out his next move and how he can make it hurt.

Ignoring him, I sit there with my head spinning as the rest of the team files on.

Once they're all on board, the flight crew prepares us for take-off, and boisterous chatter fills the air. While I'm losing myself in thoughts and regrets, it's easy to forget the magic that Linc produced on the ice tonight.

"Sooo," Brooke starts once we're in the air.

"Men are jerks," I mutter, loud enough for at least Mitchell to hear me.

"I can't say that I don't disagree." She laughs. "But given our current situation, you might want to keep your voice down."

She's right. We are literally surrounded by men.

"Urgh," I complain, resting my head back and closing my eyes.

"I went on a date the other week," Brooke says quietly. "He was hot as hell. I should have known it was too good to be true the second I saw his profile picture. But we matched, so I thought fuck it. Let's go and see who he really is. Amazingly, he actually was the guy in the picture, and if anything, he was even hotter in real life.

"So we have a few drinks, and then he invites me back to his place."

I'm already cringing over this story and I have literally no idea what is coming next.

"We're kissing, and it's all great. We're vibing, the air is crackling. I'm thinking, yes, this is it. Until..."

"Oh god," I groan.

"He didn't want me to take my clothes off."

I frown, staring at her and waiting for what comes next.

"He only wanted my shoes off."

"What?" I laugh.

"He was only interested in my feet. MY FEET, Parker." The horrified look on her face has laughter erupting out of me.

"Do you have nice feet?" Monroe asks, poking his head between the seats, obviously eavesdropping.

Unfazed that he's joined our conversation, she turns to him.

"I mean, I think they're okay. I've certainly seen worse. It just...well, it wasn't my toes where I was expecting the sucking action to be happening."

I gag.

"I'd freshened up for the date, of course, but that didn't include a pedicure, and I'd been on my feet all day at work and—"

"Did he look like he cared?" Hayden asks.

"Not in the slightest. It was so disappointing."

"What did you do?" I ask, intrigued.

"Well, I tugged my foot from his mouth and asked if he was interested in using his tongue on any other part of my body. Honest to God, he looked horrified at the thought alone. At that point, I grabbed my heels and walked out, alone and unsatisfied."

Laughter peals out of me.

"I'm not a foot man, myself. I mean, I can appreciate a pretty set of toes and all, but my mouth much prefers to be elsewhere. More than willing to share my services, if the need ever arises," Hayden offers, while the rookie sitting beside him groans in mortification.

"That's very sweet of you," Brooke says. "But I've got to be honest, I'm pretty sure I'd eat you alive in the bedroom, Marilyn. We need you on the ice too much for that."

"Well, damn," Hayden breathes before falling back into his seat with his hand over his chest. "You're missing out, Brooke baby. I'll have you know that I'm a real freak in the sheets."

The other rookie snorts a laugh.

"Dude, you can't pull a chick for shit. When the hell do you ever get a chance to be a freak?"

"I get by," Hayden states.

I can't help myself, the thought of him sitting there pouting has me fully turning around to look at him, but the second I twist around in my seat, Monroe's puppy-dog eyes aren't the first ones I find.

Linc is sitting in his seat beside Kodie with a tight expression and his arms folded over his chest.

He should be celebrating, but instead, he's shooting daggers at me for having a laugh with his rookie.

Well, fuck him.

If he can go swanning around town picking up Matilda's number, then I can enjoy myself with his friends.

Ripping my eyes away from his hard ones, I find exactly what I was expecting: Hayden sitting with his bottom lip pushed out.

"Aw, next time we all go out, you can practice your lines on me," I offer. "Don't get your hopes up, though. I won't be going anywhere near your hotel room."

"Damn, Donnelly. Way to get a guy excited," he teases.

"You wouldn't want me. I come hand in hand with my brother's wrath."

"Yeah...I quite like my face as it is."

"Then you probably chose the wrong sport," Brooke points out. "Give it a couple of years, and you'll be just as ugly as the rest of them."

"Hey," Killer shouts. "We heard that."

"You were meant to," Brooke calls before dropping back into her seat.

"Man, I love my job and these guys. I might give them shit, but I wouldn't change them for the world."

As much as I hate to admit it, I feel the same. But mostly about one of them.

***

IT'S late by the time we get to our hotel, and even later by the time all the key cards have been handed out.

With another game tomorrow, everyone heads for the elevators, ready to get some rest.

"So, Donnelly," Hayden says, throwing his arm around my shoulders and plucking my key card from my hand. "What room do I need to visit for my hookup lessons?"

"Whoa," I say, snatching it back, hoping he hasn't already clocked the number scrawled across the front of the little card wallet. "I never said anything about lessons."

"Come on, I'm on the tenth floor too. We can discuss details on the way up."

"You know, if you weren't so cute, you'd be annoying," I say as I wave to Brooke and head for the elevator.

"I knew you liked me." He laughs.

We chat away, thankfully not about any kind of hookup lessons, or about Linc, as we climb through the building.

"Looks like I'm heading this way," he says after studying the sign when we exit the car. "Sleep well, Donnelly. See you in the morning."

I turn in the opposite direction, tugging my small suitcase behind me until I find my room number.

The second I'm inside, I kick off my sneakers and unzip my suitcase to find my toiletries and pajamas. But I pause the second my fingers brush over the soft fabric of Linc's T-shirt.

I can't wear that tonight.

Digging deeper, I find my actual pajamas and pull them free.

With everything in hand, I shut myself in the bathroom, turn the shower on hot, and strip down.

I stand under the burning, powerful jets of water for the longest time, hoping it does something for my tight muscles.

It's only once my skin is wrinkled and my body begs for sleep that I finally cut the water and step out.

I take my time doing my skincare, blow-drying my hair and brushing my teeth.

I tell myself that I'm not putting off going to bed, but I know I am.

The thought of sleeping alone shouldn't bother me. I've done it all my life; it should be normal.

But just a handful of nights with Linc wrapped around me and everything has changed.

Turning the light out, I abandon the mess I've made across the counter. That's tomorrow's problem.

I head straight for my purse to grab my cell, but the second I round the corner into the bedroom, a blood-curdling scream rips from my throat because someone is sitting in the chair by the window.

Okay, not someone.

Linc is sitting in the chair by the window, waiting for me.

"What the fuck are you doing?" I screech. "And how the hell did you get in here?" His smirk grows as my heart slams against my ribs.

"We need to talk," he states as he pushes from the chair.

"No. Right now, you need to leave, and I need to sleep."

"I'm not leaving this room until you hear me out."

"I'm not interested," I mutter, turning my back on him and moving closer to the bed.

"Why aren't you wearing my T-shirt?" he growls.

"Really?" I snap, turning back to look at him. "Of all the things, that is the most pressing issue on your mind?"

"I swear to you, Parker, I didn't know that number was there."

"It's not about the number or the woman who wrote it, Linc. She's not important."

"Glad we agree on something," he mutters.

"It's more than her. It's...all the women, the life you live, who you are, all the reasons why whatever this is," I say, gesturing between us, "can't be anything. It's fucking crazy, and we're even crazier for allowing it to get this far."

He takes a step forward, and I immediately take one back.

"I can't argue with the crazy. Or who I am and the life I lead. But the reasons that whatever this is *can* be something...I can talk about that all night long. Although, honestly, I'd prefer just to show you."

"Fuck's sake," I mutter. "This isn't a joke, Linc. This is our lives. Our futures."

"I know that," he argues. "But I don't see a future for me. Not unless you're in it."

58

LINCOLN

My words hang in the air between us.

She says nothing, and I begin to panic that I said too much.

Today has been...fuck, it's been everything.

The highs have been incredible. But the lows...yeah, they're best forgotten about.

"I know you're scared. Worried about your job. But I swear to you, I won't let anything happen."

"How can you say that? You're just a player."

Okay, ouch.

She's right, though. I am just a player. But I'll lay down everything to ensure she doesn't lose her position.

I'm not going to let her get this far to have it all taken away from her. She's already lost too much.

"Parker, I just—"

"Enough," she says, holding up her hand to stop me. "I'm too tired for this," she explains, her eyes glassy with tears.

You asshole, you're making her cry.

"I'm sorry, I just—" I take a step forward, but my leg gives way and I stumble, cursing as my muscles pull.

"For fuck's sake, Linc," Parker complains. "Take your sweats off and get on the bed."

Excitement flashes through me.

Not needing to be asked twice, I tuck my thumbs into my waistband and shove them down my legs before crawling onto the mattress and flopping onto my back.

Resting my hands behind my head, I wiggle my body.

"I'm all yours, pretty girl. Have your way with me."

"I should send you back to your room with an ice pack."

"Yeah, you probably should. But you won't."

She stands at the side of the bed with her hands on her hips. I desperately try to keep my eyes on her face and not allow them to drop to the way her nipples press against the thin white fabric of her tank. Honestly, the fact that it's a little see-through is the only thing stopping me from demanding she strip it all off and pull my T-shirt on again.

"I'm going to sleep after I've done this," she explains.

"Fine by me." I smile up at her as she glares at me. But as she crawls onto the bed, she loses her fight, and her eyes trail down my body.

Shamelessly, I clench my abs, making the lines that disappear into my boxers even more defined.

"I know what you're doing," she warns.

"And I know that you like it," I counter.

She shakes her head as she gets settled between my legs.

It's dangerous, and my cock jerks in excitement. But as much as I try to talk him down, he doesn't listen, and the second her fingers connect with my thigh, he swells.

She doesn't comment. Instead, she focuses on the job she started back at the arena hours ago.

I groan as she digs her thumbs into my muscles in the most dizzying way.

She's so fucking good at this. But then, she always has been.

I was fifteen when she first talked about her desire to become an athletic trainer. Clark was the first to let her test out her skills, then Rett. And once she was confident with what she was doing, she asked me if I would allow her to work on me.

Fuck, that first time was hard. Pun most definitely intended.

I was a horny, almost-fifteen-year-old with zero control over when I got a boner.

But as painful as that part of my body was, where she was touching felt so fucking amazing, I couldn't stop her.

Before long, after training and game massages from Parker became a thing.

With her confidence growing, and thanks to Clark's connections, she found herself shadowing the doctor and PT who worked with our youth teams, and that continued into college.

Sure, it might have been Clark's legacy that helped her get into the position she was in, but it was her skill and determination that kept her there. By the time she graduated, she was a huge part of our old college team. Of course, she still had years of training to get the qualifications she needed, but no one had any doubt that she'd end up exactly where she is now.

She works with focus and precision, loosening up my muscles, all the while ensuring nothing short of an inferno is happening beneath the surface.

"I missed having your hands on me," I confess.

"Please, don't," she begs.

"I'm talking professionally, Donnelly. You're the best I've ever had."

She blushes so hard her ears turn red.

"I appreciate that."

"It kills me that I'm going to have to move to another trainer."

Her head lifts, her eyes locking on mine.

"Why?"

"Because while your job might be safe, treating me would be a conflict of interest."

"I'm not letting you switch to Mitchell," she snaps.

If I have my way, none of us will be switching to that asshole.

"Let's just take it one day at a time," I say softly.

She continues working, the air charged and crackling between us.

Eventually, though, like all good things, it comes to an end.

Parker sits back on her haunches and looks down at her hands resting in her lap.

She looks utterly defeated, her shoulders slumped and her pretty, red hair hanging around her like a curtain.

"Babe," I whisper, hating that she's hurting and that it's because of me.

I want to be making her feel better, not worse.

"Look at me, please," I beg.

It takes her a few seconds, but eventually, she lifts her head.

Once again, her eyes are full of unshed tears.

"I'm sorry. I never meant to make your life harder. I just...I want..." Fuck. "You."

Her chest heaves as she stares at me, her eyes wide and circled with exhaustion.

Her walls are down. Crumbled around her feet.

I hate it.

I want her fight, her sass, her witty comebacks and insistence that she hates me.

I know how to handle that.

This...this I have no fucking clue how to navigate.

A sob erupts, and I act on instinct, sitting up and pulling her into me.

"Please don't cry," I whisper as I hold her tight.

Her body trembles against mine, her tears soaking my chest.

I don't move. I won't.

If she needs me, I'll stay like this all fucking night.

Eventually, her sobs subside and her hands slide up my chest before her arms wrap around my neck.

She pulls back and hesitantly looks up at me through her wet lashes.

"You can go, if you want. You don't need to stay and—"

"I'm not going anywhere," I assure her softly. "I'm sorry about today. I was trying to do something nice. It backfired."

"It was nice. I really appreciated the coffee. And I'm sorry too. I'm trying to do the right thing, and yet, all I want to do is the wrong thing."

At her confession, my lips twitch into a smile.

"Tell me more about this wrong thing. Sounds fun."

She smiles too, the twinkle I love so much coming back into her eyes.

"You're a nightmare."

"Maybe so, but I'm your nightmare, if you'll have me."

"This is crazy, Linc."

"I know," I agree. "But don't you think we've waited long enough to find out if this could actually be something?"

"What if it goes wrong? What if I can't—"

"What if it goes right?" I counter, lifting my hand to cup her cheek, my thumb dragging over her tempting bottom lip.

Her eyes shutter at my touch, and when they open again, they're blazing with fire.

Fuck, I want her.

I want her in a way I've never wanted anyone or anything before.

"Parker," I breathe.

"Please," she begs.

Fuck if I'm able to deny her of anything.

Leaning forward, I brush my lips against hers in a soft, almost innocent kiss.

Her arms tighten around me, her fingers twisting in the too-long hair at the nape of my neck, urging me to take it further.

My cock aches, desperate to do so, but I know it would be the wrong thing to do.

It takes every ounce of self-control I possess, but I pull back and rest my forehead against hers as our breaths mingle.

"W-what are you doing?"

"For once in my life, I'm doing the right thing. We need to sleep."

"Yeah," she agrees softly.

Still holding her tightly, I drag her with me as I fall back onto the bed. Together, we get under the sheets, and no sooner have I flicked off the light than I gather her up in my arms again, breathing in her sweet scent.

"Just give me a chance, Parker. I promise, I'll be so fucking good to you."

She whimpers in the darkness, but she doesn't say anything as I press a kiss to her forehead and hold her even tighter.

———

I DON'T SLIP out of bed before sunrise the next morning.

Kodie already knows where I am, so there's no need for sneaking through the hotel to attempt to look like I've been in my own bed all night.

Instead, I stay exactly where I am, entwined with Parker, and just watch her sleep.

The sight of her with her hair splayed across the white pillow, her full lips parted and her eyelashes fluttering as she dreams is mesmerizing.

Time ceases to exist as I lie there with the sun brightening the room, improving my view of my girl.

Eventually, her cell begins blaring with her alarm, and she stirs to life.

The second she realizes I haven't left, she tenses, her eyes opening.

"Y-you're still here," she rasps, her throat dry with sleep.

My smile grows. "Couldn't drag myself away."

"But shouldn't you be..." Her words trail off.

"Shouldn't I be doing what?" I ask, curious to know what she thinks we do in a hotel room the morning of a game.

"Umm..."

"There isn't anywhere else in the world I'd rather be right now than watching you wake up."

Heat blooms on her cheeks and spreads down onto her chest.

"How do you look so good?" she asks, making me laugh.

"Babe, I'm a mess compared to you."

She shakes her head. "My hair will be a matted mess, and my—"

"You're beautiful," I say, leaning forward and stealing a quick kiss.

She gasps as our lips connect, but she doesn't pull away.

"How long do we have?"

My eyes bounce between hers.

"Nowhere near long enough for all the things I want to do to you."

Her blush deepens.

"We'll be home tonight," she muses.

"We will," I confirm.

"What happens then?"

"If you're asking if I'll still be sleeping in your bed, then the answer is yes. If you're asking if I want you to go back to wearing my clothes to sleep in, then the answer is also yes. If you're asking what happens next with us, then that's up to you. I've already waited for what feels like a lifetime for this, pretty girl. I can wait a little longer as long as I know you're mine."

"So...no more online dating?" she asks with a wicked glint in her eye.

"And no more bunnies," I confirm.

My words give her pause, and I allow her the time to process her thoughts.

"When was the last time you were with someone?"

I think back, but it's all a blur. That's all women were to me. A means to an end, a bit of fun for an hour or two before I turned my back on them and forgot they existed.

"Before Thanksgiving. Possibly even before Halloween. I can't really remember."

"That's a long time for the infamous Lincoln Storm."

I shrug. "The whole thing lost its appeal."

"Why?"

I exhale, trying to figure out how to put how I feel about that way of life into words.

"Because it was fake. Empty. Unfulfilling. The complete opposite of everything I feel when I'm with you."

"Why now?"

"Because as scary as this is, at some point, you will meet someone else, and I might lose you for good. And that prospect is utterly terrifying."

59

———

PARKER

Exhausted and desperate for bed, I stand curled into Linc's side, my head resting on his chest as the elevator rises through his building.

Today has been a lot. But as tired as I am, I'm glad to be home rather than in a hotel.

Linc's arm is banded around me, holding me in place tightly as if he never wants to let go.

My heart flutters in my chest. Everything he's done or said since turning up in my hotel room last night has been what dreams are made of.

It makes me think that maybe the wistful teenage girl inside me will get her happily ever after with the only guy she's truly cared about. But that's too good to be true, right? It can't be that easy.

"Come on, pretty girl. Let's get you to bed," he says softly as the number finally hits the top floor.

With both of our suitcases in one hand and me still tucked into his other side, we make our way toward the bedrooms. Only, he doesn't so much as pause at his. Instead, he leads us straight to mine.

"Don't you want to sleep in your bed?"

"I want to sleep with you."

A million and one reasons why we shouldn't be doing this crash around in my head, but the second he turns to me and presses a kiss to the top of my head, they all fall away.

How can something that feels so right be wrong?

We continue forward, and I sigh with relief when I finally lay eyes on my bed. Well, his bed. Whatever.

Finally, he releases me, and I walk forward in a daze.

"Do you need anything? A drink? Something to eat?"

I shake my head as I toe my sneakers off and tug my Vipers jacket from my shoulders.

"I'm going to have a quick shower, and then I'll—"

"Can you get me a T-shirt?" I blurt.

When Linc doesn't reply, I glance back over my shoulder.

What I find makes my heart skip a beat.

I'm not sure I've ever seen such a wide, happy smile on his face.

"Yeah, of course. I'll get it right now."

He darts from the room like the hounds of hell are snapping at his ass.

Unable to wait, I continue undressing. I peel my leggings from my legs, drag my polo from my body, and drop it all to the floor, leaving me in just my bra and panties.

I have my hands behind my back, about to unhook my bra, when his footsteps get louder.

Despite having my back to him, my lips twitch into a smirk when I hear his gasp of surprise.

"Don't stop on my account," he rumbles, so I don't.

I pull the garment away from my body with a sigh of relief.

My skin prickles and my nipples pebble, knowing he has his eyes on me.

He may have seen me naked before, but that was a long time ago. I was just a girl then. I'm a woman now. Things have changed.

"Keep going," he demands. "I want you in nothing but my T-shirt."

Desire sits heavily between my thighs, and before I can think better of it, I tuck my thumbs into my panties and push them over my hips and down my thighs, bending a little as I do so.

Behind me, Linc groans as if he's in physical pain.

"Better?" I ask, glancing over my shoulder.

My heart is racing, my temperature is soaring, but at no point do I turn around. And from the look of awe on his face, I don't think he minds one bit.

"Y-yeah," he stutters, finally stepping forward. "Fucking perfect."

I wait with my breath caught in my throat for him to touch me. I'm standing here naked; surely, he—

My thought is eradicated when fabric covers my head and then falls down over my body. His scent engulfs me, and I breathe it in as if it's the air I need to survive.

"There," he soothes.

Glancing down, I find myself covered in a gray and green Vipers shirt.

"Why this one?" I ask as I push my arms through the holes and turn to face him.

His pupils are blown with desire, making me even more curious about this T-shirt choice.

"Because of this," he says, gently directing me to stand in front of the mirror.

I frown, not seeing a reason for his reaction. But then he turns me around and it all starts to make sense.

I find "Storm" printed across my shoulders and a large seven down my back.

"One day, there will be a game you're not working, and you're going to be right behind the plexiglass, wearing my jersey and cheering my name."

I nod, swept away by the images he paints.

"Okay," I breathe.

"Get ready for bed, babe. I'll be right back."

I stand there in the middle of the room and watch him

leave. It's ridiculous, because he's only on the other side of the wall, but I miss him.

Shaking my head at how pathetic I am, I shuffle toward my bathroom.

Less than ten minutes later, Linc is fresh from the shower, wearing only a pair of boxer briefs, and he's slipping into my bed.

The second he wraps his arms around me and hauls me against him, I relax, and only moments later, sleep claims me.

I WAKE the next day to the scent of bacon filling the apartment and my stomach growling loudly.

I guess if I can't wake up with him next to me, having him cook me breakfast is the next best thing. Assuming that's what he's doing, of course.

Needing to know, I roll out of bed and stumble into the bathroom to freshen up.

Still dressed in nothing but his T-shirt, I make my way to the kitchen.

I pause in the entryway, finding Linc moving effortlessly around his kitchen with a tea towel thrown over his bare shoulder.

My eyes drop, taking in his exposed chest and abs before I get to the waistband of his boxers and sweats.

Hottest chef I've ever seen.

The bacon sizzles in the pan while a waffle maker sits on the counter.

It beeps, and he lifts the top, revealing two perfectly made waffles.

I'm impressed.

Next come the eggs. He pours the already-beaten mixture into another pan and stirs.

I already knew Linc could cook, but eating what he's made and watching him create it are two very different things.

"I know you're watching," he suddenly says, scaring the shit out of me.

Busted.

"I...uh...yeah. I guess I am," I confess.

"See anything you like?" he teases, combing his hair back from his brow, making his abs tighten.

My eyes freeze on the dark bruise that covers his right shoulder from a rough hit he took at last night's game.

"We need to stretch that out today," I tell him, ignoring his question.

He shrugs it but winces in pain.

"It's fine. I've been icing it."

"Please, let me look at it," I beg, hating the idea of him being in pain and even more terrified that he'll go into our next game carrying an injury.

"Okay," he agrees before lifting the pan from the stove and carrying it toward two plates that are waiting. "You didn't answer my question," he teases, shooting me a wicked smirk.

"The waffles. I love the look of the waffles," I tease.

He shakes his head as he continues plating our food.

"Go and take a seat. Your coffee is waiting."

"Wow," I say, looking around. "What did I do to deserve this?"

He shrugs again.

The table is set as if he's waiting for a date. There's even a fresh bunch of flowers.

"Did you go out and get all of this?"

"It's not a big deal, babe."

My heart clenches. It is to me.

No man has ever done anything like this for me.

With a plate in each hand, he walks over.

"This looks incredible," I breathe as he places it before me, my stomach growling embarrassingly loudly.

"Eat up."

"Why? What do you have planned?"

His smirk makes everything south of my waist clench.

Oh my god.

Oh my god. Oh my god. Oh my god.

Are we going to...

While things might have been progressing with us, aside from the other night with my vibrator, we haven't messed around.

In that respect, he's been the perfect gentleman, giving me space and not pushing me for more when he so obviously wants it.

I do too. I'm desperate for it. But I know that once we cross that line, there will be no going back. Not for me, at least.

Any other man, I could walk away from.

"Aren't you hungry?" Linc asks when I don't immediately dive for my food.

I look up at him sitting across from me with an expectant look on his face.

He wants your approval, a little voice says.

"Yeah, I'm starving. Just...a little distracted by the half-naked chef who prepared it."

His smile grows. "Yeah?"

My cheeks burn as I grab my knife and fork and gather up my first mouthful.

I groan the second the salty bacon and sweet syrup covering the waffles hit my tongue.

That's all he needs to hear for his megawatt, panty-melting smile to appear.

"Not just a pretty face, I guess," I tease as he finally dives into his food.

"I've got so many talents, babe. I can't wait to show you all of them."

I squirm in the chair, excited to learn what they all are.

"WHAT ARE your plans for the rest of the day?" I ask as I help Linc clean up the kitchen, much to his annoyance.

I figure that, seeing as he cooked, I should clean. But he wasn't keen on that idea and wanted to do it all himself.

Not happening.

So now, we're standing at the sink, side by side, as he washes and I dry.

He's got a perfectly good dishwasher, but for some reason, we've found ourselves here. Not that I'm complaining. Somehow, Linc even manages to make cleaning fun.

"Oh, I have plans," he teases, wiggling his brows.

"Care to share?"

"I will, when the time is right."

"So cryptic," I muse. "Are you going out?"

"Not when I could spend the day here with you."

"Smooth," I tease.

Suddenly, he turns to me, abandoning his scrubbing duties.

His eyes hold an intensity that has me rubbing my thighs together.

"Why would I want to go anywhere when I have you right here with my name and number on your back and nothing else?"

Heat rises to my cheeks.

"I...uh..."

"I do have a meeting with my agent later, but that's not for a few hours," he confesses.

"Right." A little disappointment trickles through my veins. I liked the idea of spending the day with him a little too much.

"But I'm free as a bird until then."

I'm so lost in his eyes, I don't see his hand move at his side. Well, not until it's too late, anyway.

"Lincoln," I scream as he covers the side of my face in bubbles. "What the hell?"

Darting forward, I dip my hand into the water and splash it at him.

It hits him in the chest, and I get to watch as the rivulets roll down the lines of his stomach before soaking into his waistband.

"Look at that; you're all wet."

"Hmm," he hums as he closes in on me. "The question is, are you?"

I gasp as my lower back hits the counter.

I look left then right and quickly discover that he's pinned me into the corner.

"Linc," I warn, although I can admit that it comes out as more of a moan.

His eyes flash with desire as he steps closer, his body heat burning down my front.

"God, Parker. You're fucking killing me," he groans, leaning forward to press his forehead against mine. "Can I kiss you? Please, tell me that I can kiss you."

60

PARKER

It shouldn't be so hot that he's asking for permission, should it?

His eyes are dark and hungry, his chest heaving as he waits for my answer.

The whole thing blows my mind because I'm not sure Linc has ever waited for anything before in his life.

He's the kind of man who just takes.

Or at least, he is to the outside world. The version of him that I get is very, very different. And it doesn't escape my attention how freaking lucky I am to know this side of him.

"Linc," I whisper, barely able to catch my breath.

His hand slides up my arm, making me shudder with anticipation before he wraps it around the back of my neck, his fingers massaging my tight muscles as he patiently waits for my response.

"Oh god," I moan when he hits a bit that makes me want to purr like a cat. "Yes, please. Kiss m—" He cuts me off with his lips, brushing mine with the sweetest of kisses.

I reach for him, my hands sliding up his sculpted back. His muscles ripple at my touch, and knowing that I'm affecting him when I'm barely touching him lights me up inside.

"Can't get enough of you," he murmurs against my lips.

But what if he does?

The thought hits me from nowhere.

"Parker?" he questions, pulling back slightly when he feels me tense. "What's wrong?"

"What happens if..." I close my eyes, already regretting opening my mouth.

"What happens if what, pretty girl?"

"What happens if you do?"

I swallow thickly, feeling vulnerable, but I've come too far to turn back now. "Get enough of me."

My eyes fly open when Linc lets out a laugh. I frown at the smile on his face and the twinkle in his eyes.

"Are you joking?" he asks incredulously. "Don't you think that if that were going to happen, it would have by now? It's been years, Parker. Yeeears, and I'm still obsessed with you."

I fight my smile as my heart expands in my chest.

"You're obsessed with me?" I ask innocently.

"Yeah, babe."

"Since when?"

"I dunno exactly. Since I was like, fourteen."

I balk. "Fourteen? But that was ten years ago," I point out, in case he hasn't done the math.

"Trust me, I know how long it's been."

I blink as his words settle within me.

Obsessed with me.

For ten years.

How?

How didn't I know?

Why didn't I know?

"B-but—" My words are cut off when he presses two fingers to my lips.

"Can we talk about this later? I've got a more pressing issue I'd like to take care of."

I rear back. How can he go from telling me that he's been obsessed with me for ten years to telling me he's got something more important to be doing?

That doesn't make any sen—

His lips crash against mine, and he makes the most of my parted lips by sweeping his tongue past them.

"Oh god," I groan, wrapping my arms around his neck and dragging him closer.

This is what he meant.

This is more important.

Stretching up on my toes, I allow myself to be swept away by him.

His hands start at my waist, and I groan when he lifts them and drags his thumbs across the underside of my breasts. They're heavy and desperate for him. I arch, hoping for more, but he moves in the opposite direction, skimming over my hips.

"Yes," I cry into his kiss as he grabs my ass and pins me against his body. The length of his hard cock is more than obvious against my thigh.

Heat surges south, desire unfurling in my lower stomach.

"More." The plea falls from my lips without thought.

The second he hears it, his hands drop to my thighs, and he lifts me from the floor.

My grip on him tightens until he lowers my ass to the counter. I gasp at the coldness of the granite against my ass. But the second he spreads my thighs and steps between them, thoughts of anything but him vanish.

His hands are everywhere as our kiss turns wild.

God, I want this man unleashed so fucking badly.

Last time...last time he was so tender and gentle.

I needed it. Not only had my life just imploded, but it was my first time.

Now, though...now, he has no reason to hold back.

I want him both at his best and his worst, and everything in between.

Fuck. He isn't the only one with an unhealthy obsession.

My body burns red hot when his hands slip under the fabric of his T-shirt that's pooled around my thighs. He slides them up so slowly, taunting me, teasing me with everything I could have.

My head falls back, a wanton cry falling from my lips, as he takes my breasts in his calloused palms.

"Lincoln," I moan as he pinches my nipples, his lips kissing a trail down my throat.

"Fuck, I could listen to you moaning my name forever and it would never be enough," he groans, his deep voice vibrating through my body, adding to the sensations that are threatening to overwhelm me.

Dropping one hand, he presses it against the small of my back, scooting me closer to the edge. Closer to— "Fuck," I gasp as his fabric-covered erection presses against my greedy clit. "Oh god. Fuck. Linc."

"Can you feel how hard I am?" he rasps. "It's always the same when you're close. You fucking own me, Parker, and you have no idea."

He keeps rolling his hips, grinding himself against me. His lips find mine again, and his kiss, along with everything else he's doing, ignites something inside me.

Oh god, could he make me come like this?

Surely not. It's never that easy.

I claw at his back as my release builds.

"Don't stop," I mumble into his kiss.

"Couldn't even if I wanted to," he mutters.

Our kiss turns desperate, our touches and movements frantic as we chase a high I'm not sure would be possible with anyone else.

We're both half-dressed in his kitchen, for fuck's sake.

This shouldn't be—

"You're going to come all over me, aren't you, pretty girl?"

"Linc, please."

"I'm right here, babe. And I'm not going anywhere. Use me. Take what you need."

"That's it. Right there. Right—" My words die as my orgasm crashes over me.

I throw my head back, my eyes slamming closed as pleasure takes over, my body convulsing on the kitchen counter.

"So fucking sexy," Linc groans, his voice deeper than I'm sure I've ever heard. "Fuck. I can't. Fuuuuck."

My eyes fly open as my release begins to subside, and I get to watch as his face pulls tight with pleasure.

"Holy shit. Are you…"

My words trail off as his eyes blaze with heat, his grip on my hips tightening, pinning us together and allowing me to feel his cock pulsate.

"Coming in my pants? Yeah," he confesses. "Shit."

He drops is forehead to my shoulder and sucks in a ragged breath.

I can't help but giggle.

I've never done drugs, but I'm pretty sure this is how it feels to be high.

I'm high on Lincoln Storm, and I never want it to stop.

"Fucking hell, Parker." He chuckles, his voice now light with amusement. "You drive me fucking crazy."

The second he pulls back and looks into my eyes, I'm hit with aftershocks.

"The feeling is most definitely mutual."

His eyes hold mine as we remain where we are, our bodies cooling and reality setting in.

"I don't know how to do this," I admit quietly.

"And you think I do?" he teases.

"Linc, I—"

"We're just gonna take every day as it comes, yeah? No pressure, no expectations. Just…us. However we want that to look."

"What about work?"

"What about it?"

"I can't…I can't treat you. Not if we're…"

"Not if we're what?" he asks, his eyes twinkling with mischief.

I know what he wants to hear, but I'm not ready to admit anything out loud. This is all too unbelievable.

"Going to keep things professional and above board. There are already a ton of reasons why I could lose my job; I'm not adding to that list on purpose."

"I already told you, pretty girl. You don't need to worry about your job. I'll sort it."

My cell starts ringing down the hall before I manage to find a response to that.

I hate the idea of no longer being his trainer. But there is no other way around it.

If we're doing this, we have to go about it the right way.

Suddenly, I'm hit with thoughts of what others are going to say.

I know I shouldn't care. But this is my career, my reputation I'm toying with here.

"Parker, look at me," Linc demands as soon as I close my eyes and cut myself off from him.

My eyelashes flicker open to find his kind and compassionate eyes staring back at me.

"I'm not going to let anything bad happen. You have to trust me, babe."

My cell rings again as he holds my eyes, silently begging me to trust him.

I do.

I always have.

The problem here isn't him.

It's everyone else.

He knows as well as I do what the press can be like. The second they get a hold of this, all hell is going to break loose.

I'm not ready to be thrust into the spotlight with whatever spin they'll put on this.

Linc's hands frame my face.

"In case you didn't get it already, you're it for me, Parker. There has never been, and won't ever be, another girl for me." I quirk a brow. "They don't count. They were a distraction.

There's only been one I've ever cared about. Only one I've ever wanted more from."

"Are you sure that's not just because I'm the only one who walked away?"

He shakes his head. "Have I ever told you how much that fucking hurt that day?"

I bite down on the inside of my lip, hating that my actions might have caused him pain.

I thought I was doing the right thing to protect myself. I was convinced that he'd go back to college and return to having a different bunny in his bed every night. Was I wrong?

If I'd allowed my heart to rule back then and not my head, would things have turned out differently?

"Everything happened for a reason," he muses, as if he can read my thoughts.

"I'm sorry."

"It's okay. It might have hurt, but I understood why you did it. I also think it was the right thing to do. I wasn't ready back then. I needed a few years to get all that shit out of my system."

"What if I'm not ready now?" I ask, voicing one of my fears.

"One step at a time," he reminds me.

My cell starts ringing again.

"Someone really wants to get a hold of my girl, huh? Should I be worried?"

I shake my head. "There hasn't been anyone," I confess.

His brows lift. "No one ever?"

"Well, maybe there was this one guy, but it was a long time ago, and I'm pretty sure it was a rebound thing."

He chuckles. "It was never a rebound thing, and you know it."

'I know," I mouth.

When my cell starts ringing for a third time, he lets out a breath and finally steps back. The second he does, my eyes drop to the wet patch on his sweats.

"Shit," I gasp.

He follows my stare.

"Babe, look at what a mess you made." When he looks back at me again, his eyes are molten.

"I'm sorry." I cringe, my cheeks heating.

"Never, ever be sorry for that. And anyway, I guarantee the mess I've made inside is a hell of a lot worse."

61

PARKER

I race into my room with trembling legs, my cell ringing again.

Whoever it is, whatever it is, it can't be good.

Dread sits heavy in my stomach, eradicating any previous good feelings I had from my moment with Linc in the kitchen.

Fear floods through my veins the second I see Mom's name on my screen.

I snatch it from my nightstand, swipe to connect the call, and press it to my ear.

"Mom?" I all but cry.

"Hey, sweetie," she sings.

I frown.

"What's wrong?"

"Huh?" she asks in confusion. "Nothing's wrong."

"Then why are you blowing up my cell like someone has died?" I ask, collapsing on the bed in relief.

"I just wanted to talk to you. I know it's your day off, and you haven't responded to any of my messages or voice mails, so..." She trails off, hurt evident in her tone.

"I'm sorry," I whisper, feeling like a chastised child. "Life has just been chaotic."

"I know, sweetie. Between you and Rett, I can barely get a reply these days."

Sadness wraps around me. I don't want to distance myself from my parents, but unfortunately, I have a life now. A busy one that distracts me from touching base with them as often as possible. It also doesn't help that I never know what time zone or country they're in.

"I'm so incredibly proud of you both. And I can't wait to see you. Give you both a big squeeze."

A smile curls at my lips—not just at the thought of a hug from her, but also the image that pops into my head of my not-quite-five-foot mom hugging my giant of a big brother. It's like a kitten trying to hug a bear.

"I know. I miss you guys too."

I saw them briefly for the holidays, but no sooner had they arrived home than they set off again.

"Well, lucky for you, we arrived home a few hours ago."

"What?"

"Parker, do you not even read the messages or listen to the voice mails I leave you?"

Guilt descends.

"It's been a hectic few days, Mom."

"I'm sure it has," she deadpans. "So can I assume you know nothing of the table I have reserved for tonight?"

"Uh..."

She chuckles down the line.

"Seven at Papa's Steak House."

"O-okay," I agree, my head spinning with all this information. I know it's my own fault, but still.

"You can come?" Mom asks hopefully.

"Yeah, Mom. I can come," I agree, excitement already fluttering.

Tears burn my eyes at the thought of seeing both of them.

I feel like I've coped okay these past few weeks after my life went up in smoke. But now they're so close, I realize just how badly I need to see them.

"I've booked the table for four. Feel free to invite your new roommate." As Mom says that, heavy footsteps thump my way before Lincoln appears in my doorway. He's showered already and standing there with just a towel wrapped around his waist, the ink covering his torso still wet.

My chin drops as I stare at him.

Fuck, he's hot.

And...mine?

"Parker, sweetie, are you still there?"

"Y-yeah," I stutter.

"So, tonight..."

"Can I let you know about the fourth person?"

"Of course. I can't wait to see you later. I want all the details about your new job. We've been watching all the games, spotting you by the bench on the TV." I groan. "So proud, sweetie. You have no idea."

"Are you in town for our next game?" I ask, knowing full well who it's against.

"That's one of the reasons, yes. I wasn't going to miss a chance at seeing both of my babies down there, doing what they love," she coos.

A mixture of excitement and anxiety collides in my stomach as I think about Linc facing off against Rett in a couple of days.

It'll be the first time either of us has seen him since I moved in. Since we started dry-humping in his kitchen...

"It should be a good game."

"With Linc and Rett playing? It's guaranteed. I love watching my boys."

My heart squeezes as I think of how Mom treats Linc like one of her own. She always has. He's been a part of the family for as long as I can remember.

I lift my eyes from his abs and meet his curious gaze.

My stomach rolls. Are we going to ruin everything by doing what we're doing?

"Me too," I muse.

"So, seven tonight, yes?"

"Yes, I'll be there."

She squeals. "Oh, I can't wait. Wear something pretty."

I chuckle. "You got it, Mom. See you later."

As I hang up and lower my cell to my lap, Linc continues to hover, looking like a GQ model in my doorway.

"Your parents are in town?" he asks excitedly.

"Yeah. They've invited me to dinner tonight."

He pushes from the doorframe and moves closer.

"And you don't want to go?" he asks, reading my expression.

"No, of course I want to go. It's just...she invited my new roommate to join us."

His footsteps falter.

"They still don't know?" Something darkens his eyes. Hurt.

Fuck.

"I've barely spoken to them, as Mom was more than happy to point out. It just...it hasn't come up. And also, I didn't think it was a conversation to have over the phone. They'd tell Rett and—you haven't told Rett either," I point out.

Guilt flickers across his face, and he swallows thickly.

"Tomorrow night," Linc mutters.

"We have to tell him."

"Uh..."

I can't help but laugh at his hesitation. "Lincoln Storm, are you scared of my big brother?"

"Would you think differently of me if I said yeah, a little?"

I shake my head, pushing to my feet and moving closer to him.

"You stepped up and took care of me in his absence. He'll respect that."

"I'm not sure he'll respect what we did in that hotel room. Or what just happened in the kitchen," he deadpans.

"No, probably not. But we don't have to tell him everything."

"You ashamed of me, pretty girl?" He quirks a brow.

"Maybe, or maybe I'm stopping you from ending up with a broken nose, or worse."

"I can hold my own against Rett, babe," he counters.

"Are you sure?" Rett is a D man, and he's built. I swear, every time I see him, he's bigger. He's intimidating, even to his friends and family.

"I play with guys like him multiple times a week," Linc argues.

"That's different."

"Yeah," he confesses quietly, his eyes dropping down the length of my body before slowly moving all the way back up. "He's going to kill me."

"We don't have to tell him yet. Not everything, at least. We can tell everyone I'm living here, that you took me in in my hour of need, and then the rest can follow once we know what's happening."

He takes a step forward, closing the space between us.

"I know exactly what is happening," he states confidently before wrapping his hand around the back of my neck and drawing me in. "You can wait as long as you want to tell people, but I fear I might just give it away. Now I've started, I'm not going to be able to stop." He seals his words with a kiss that has my toes curling into the carpet beneath me.

I melt into him, my hand sliding down his still-damp back until I can grab his ass.

He groans, thrusting his hips into me, proving his previous words to be true.

With his tongue teasing mine, he walks us backward until my calves hit the bed. Then he lifts me effortlessly from the floor and climbs onto the bed with me in his arms.

He settles me on my back and then shuffles between my legs.

Fire licks at my insides as my heart races.

His kiss doesn't falter. It goes on and on as if he's making up for all the years we haven't been doing it.

But despite our position, he doesn't push for more.

His restraint and desire to take this slow only make me burn hotter for him.

"Linc," I moan, wrapping my legs around his waist in an attempt to get us closer.

"Pretty girl, you're drive me crazy," he groans, dropping to my side and pulling me into his body.

We make out like a couple of teenagers for the longest time. Our hands roam, learning each other's bodies, tracing the lines and ridges.

It's the thing my teenage dreams used to be made of.

And now it's happening.

Lincoln Storm is in my bed, wearing only a towel, and his hands and lips are all over me.

It's a heady feeling.

Throwing my leg over his hip, I pull us closer, gasping the second I feel him hard beneath the towel.

He pulls back from our kiss, his lips swollen, his eyes as black as the night, and his chest heaving.

Christ. I did that to him.

Tracing my finger over the intricate ink that covers his chest, I take in each piece that I've seen many times before.

I already know the reason behind many of them. But there are a few I'm yet to discover.

His breathing is labored as he watches me explore his body. His abs jump as I trace the lines of his six-pack.

I shift, allowing myself to continue down the design I'm working on, but as my leg moves over his, his towel becomes untucked. One side falls to the bed while I shamelessly continue pushing the other side away, leaving him exposed to me.

"Babe," he warns as his hard cock bobs between us.

I stare at him. Hard and beautiful with moisture pooling in his slit.

Shuffling closer, I fully hook my leg over his hip, lining us up.

His mouth attacks mine as his length grazes my pussy.

Without breaking our kiss, he rolls me onto my back and settles between my thighs.

Oh yes. Yes. Yes. Yes.

He pushes up, holding his weight on an arm planted on either side of my head.

His breath rushes over my skin as his eyes bounce between mine.

"I've dreamed about making you mine again every goddamn day for six years," he tells me quietly, honestly.

"Linc," I breathe, blown away by everything he's confessed today.

"I know you can't say the same, but that night was the best night of my life."

He shudders as I drag my nails gently down his back.

"I learned a lot that night," I tease.

"I shouldn't have done it," he counters, his conscience getting the better of him.

"I begged you."

"And I discovered just how powerless I am when you start doing that," he teases.

I roll my hips, letting the head of his cock drag over me. The thought of him painting me with precum has my inner muscles clenching around nothing.

I want him.

All of him.

No barriers or holding anything back.

Just him. And me.

"Linc," I repeat.

"Yeah, pretty girl. What is it you want?" he teases, his own hips moving now, driving me wild.

"I'm on birth control. I'm clean, I—"

"Me too. I haven't been with anyone since I was tested."

I swallow thickly, wanting this so badly I'm terrified.

"This wasn't how I planned it," he confesses.

"You...you planned it."

Biting down on his bottom lip, he nods almost shyly.

I smile, desperate to know what he was planning, but also on the brink of losing my ever-loving mind with the way he's teasing me.

"A do-over. The way it should have been."

I shake my head. Who is this man hovering above me, saying all these incredible things?

"Linc, I—"

His watch starts buzzing and he groans, dropping his head to my shoulder.

"What? What's wrong?"

"That's my alarm. I've got to go and meet my agent."

"Really?" I balk.

"Really. He's got some endorsement deals he wants to talk to me about. I've already put him off a few times."

He dips low to steal another kiss before sitting up between my thighs.

Holy cow, I need a camera, because wow...just wow.

His hair is a mess where I've run my hands through it, his lips are still swollen, his chest still moving rapidly, and then... those V lines and what they lead to just waiting between my thighs.

I will never ever forget this image for as long as I live.

When I find his eyes again, I discover he's just as distracted by my spread thighs.

"So...uh..." Ripping his gaze away from my pussy, he finds my eyes as his hand shifts to rub his neck. "About this dinner with your parents."

"Uh-huh," I mumble, unable to find any words.

"What time is it, and do I need to wear a suit?"

62

PARKER

I exhale slowly, letting a stream of air blow past my red-stained lips as I stare at myself in the mirror.

Feeling nervous is stupid. It's just dinner with my parents and a boy I've known all my life.

They see him as one of their own. They love him.

But we're going to turn up together.

They know we don't get on. They've spent years watching us bicker, just like Rett and Casey did.

We agreed to tell them that he's the colleague I've been living with. But we're keeping everything that's growing between us under wraps for now.

I'm not ready to hear others' opinions.

Okay, Rett's.

My parents will be happy for us, I'm sure. But Rett...he's going to be another story.

All my life, he's been fiercely protective. No guy I've spent time with has ever been good enough, and I know for a fact that, despite Linc being his best friend, he isn't going to live up to what Rett would want for me.

It's bullshit. But I guess it's his big brotherly right.

Linc is home. I heard him rush into the apartment a little over ten minutes ago after the meeting with his agent ran over.

He messaged me the second he got out and told me to be ready.

Well, I am.

I'm also terrified.

It's just Linc and your parents; you have nothing to be scared of.

I thought he was joking when he asked if he needed to wear a suit.

But it turns out that he was deadly serious. He wanted to be my plus-one tonight. Hell, he practically begged me.

It was...mind-blowing.

I was lying on his guest bed with my legs spread, everything on display, and he was asking to tag along to meet my parents. His hard dick was out the entire time, and we were talking about having basically a double date with my parents, as if it's freaking normal.

Spoiler alert, it is not fucking normal.

It's heart attack inducing.

I smooth my dress down with trembling hands before I force myself to move. If I stand here any longer, I'm going to convince myself that tonight isn't necessary and go and hide in the bathroom.

Grabbing my purse, I walk out of my bedroom with my head held high, hoping like hell I can cover up the nerves that are running rampant under the surface.

My classic little black dress tickles against my thighs as I walk, and I swallow nervously.

After telling me that he was coming tonight, Linc handed me his credit card and told me to go shopping.

I tried giving it back to him, point-blank refusing to spend his money, but he wouldn't have it.

He threatened to order something and have it delivered here, but I knew that he'd buy something ridiculously expensive. And while I know he's good for it, I'm not interested in his money.

As it is, my dress still cost more than I'd usually spend for a dinner out with my parents. I just hope he likes it. And the shoes that I chose with a very vivid image in my head that I'm sure he'll appreciate the fuck out of.

As I pass his room, I hear him moving around. I pause as the scent of his cologne hits my nose and I breathe him in. Just that small hit of him is enough to give me a little extra confidence.

Continuing forward, my heels begin to click against the kitchen floor.

I glance at the time. We need to leave.

Pulling my cell from my purse, I open Instagram as a distraction and scroll through Casey's. A smile pulls at my lips and warmth spreads through me as I take in her new little family. And it only increases when I find a photo that shows Kodie gazing at her. He is so in love with my girl; it's the cutest thing.

I'm still staring at the photo when a shadow falls over me.

My breath catches, and I look up to find Linc looking devastatingly handsome in a fitted black shirt and a pair of dark gray slacks that look like they've been sculpted around his thighs.

Oh, holy hell.

"Wow, you look—"

"Nowhere near as hot as you," he interrupts. "That dress. Those shoes," he drawls, his tongue practically hanging out.

The dress is fitted with a square neckline, exposing a teasing amount of cleavage, and it stops a good few inches above my knees. And the shoes...well, he's right. They're classic black peep-toe court shoes with a bow at my heels.

"Shit. What I want to do to you in those shoes."

My cheeks heat, probably giving away the innocent look I'm going for.

"Oh?"

He chuckles. "Nice try, pretty girl. But I know you're thinking the same things. I can see it in your eyes."

My smile grows.

"Are you ready?" I ask, changing the subject before we both have a reason not to leave the apartment.

"Yeah. Just one thing, though."

"Oh?" I ask as he steps forward.

"My meeting didn't run over. I actually stopped to get you something." I frown as he pulls a gift bag from behind his back.

Oh my god.

Lincoln Storm is buying me gifts.

My heart flutters and my hands tremble harder the moment he holds the bag out for me to take.

"What did you do?"

Our eye contact holds for a few seconds, the air crackling between us.

"Open it."

Turning, I rest the bag on the kitchen island and reach inside.

I swear my heart skips a beat when I pull out a black velvet jewelry box.

"Linc," I breathe as I flip it open. "Oh my god."

I blink a few times, unable to believe what I'm seeing.

"Do you like it?"

I look between his anxious expression and the beautiful tennis bracelet twinkling in the spotlights above us in awe.

"You...you bought me diamonds?"

"I didn't know what dress you'd choose, so I kept it simple."

"It's...it's...too much," I blurt.

I dread to think how much this cost him.

"Never," he states before stepping closer. "May I?"

The second I nod, he takes the box and places it on the counter before pulling the bracelet free. It's so delicate and pretty, I'm terrified I'm going to break it and lose it.

"I know I've done everything wrong," he says as he drapes the cool jewelry against my wrist. "But all I've tried to do is the right thing. When you walked away after that night, I convinced myself that you regretted it. That I'd ruined your night even more than he already had. So I tucked my hurt away and got on with life. You were always too good for me, anyway."

"Linc, no—" I start, but he continues, needing to get his point out.

"I never thought I'd get this chance. And as much as I hate what you had to go through to get here, I'm so fucking grateful for the time we've had together."

Tears pool in my eyes as he deftly secures the bracelet.

"This time, I want to do everything right. I don't want to rush. I don't want to give you a reason to run. I just...I want you to want to be here. I want you to want me as much as I have always wanted you."

A sob erupts as he cups my jaw, tenderly brushing his thumb across my cheek.

"Linc," I whimper.

"You don't need to say anything. Not now. I'll give you all the time and space you need." I quirk a brow in question. He smirks. "Apart from at night, when I'm sleeping right next to you. Have you noticed how well I play after you've spent the night in my arms?"

Maybe, but I didn't want to say anything.

Ice hockey players are superstitious as fuck, and as much as I'd love to become a part of Linc's, it's also terrifying. It's a lot of pressure to put on a person.

"I'm just...I'm all in, Parker. I need you to know that. We can keep it under wraps for as long as you want. We can take it as slow as you want. Anything. Just...be mine. Please."

The more he talks, the more bricks tumble from the walls I'd built around myself after prom night. I needed to keep him out; otherwise, I knew I'd never survive. But things are different now. He isn't the only one who's changed. I have, too. And maybe, just maybe, I am ready for this.

"We really need to go," Linc says when I stay quiet.

My heart is in my throat. He takes my hand and leads me toward the elevator.

The second the doors open and we step inside, my breath catches at the sight of us in the mirror.

"We look good, huh?" Linc muses.

Yeah. We do.

"You do know your parents love me, right?" Linc asks once we're in his car and heading toward my parents' side of town and my father's favorite steak restaurant.

"Of course. I've heard them bleat on about you enough over the years."

He lights up.

"Is that right?" he asks.

I chuckle as he takes the next turn.

"They'll be okay with this...when you're ready to tell them. Rett, too."

"Really?"

"I mean, maybe not initially, but he'll get used to the idea. He'll have to. There isn't really another option."

Nerves continue to rattle through me, but the moment he reaches for my hand, everything gets a little quieter.

I wish I could be as calm as he is about all of this.

He parks beside my father's truck and demands that I wait for him to open my door.

My need to tease him has my fingers twitching for the handle, but I hold myself back. There are times for playing games, and right now isn't one of them.

He holds his hand out, and I happily slide my palm against his, allowing him to help me from his low Porsche.

As we walk toward the entrance, his hand finds its home on the small of my back. Heat radiates through me as his scent fills my nose. His silent support wraps around me, and I use it to keep me moving forward.

"Mr. Storm," the maître d' sings as he steps up to his station. "Great games this week." The two men shake hands before he turns to me. "Miss Donnelly, you're looking ravishing tonight." Linc's fingers twitch against my back, and

I'm pretty sure I catch a low growl that rumbles in his chest. "Your parents are right over here. Please, come with me."

We follow as instructed, and the second there's a little space between us, I turn to Linc with a smile on my lips.

"Are you serious?" I whisper.

"What?"

"He's like, three decades too old."

His jaw tics, his fingers shifting again.

"He was looking at you. You're mine, Parker."

Warmth explodes from my head and seeps through the rest of my body.

Linc is hot even on his worst days, but jealous and possessive Linc? Whoa. I'm pretty sure my panties just melted.

The second we turn the corner, I spot my parents. It takes a moment, but both of their eyes widen in shock as they take in the man standing slightly behind me.

They look between the two of us, and their shocked faces morph into happy ones.

"See, everything is going to be fine," Linc whispers in my ear as they both stand to greet us.

"Parker," Mom breathes. "And Linc. This is a surprise."

She pulls me in for a hug, and I instantly relax.

Out of the corner of my eye, I watch as Dad and Linc shake hands before giving each other a man hug.

"PK," Dad cries the second Mom releases me and pulls me into a hug.

"Well," Mom starts as we take our seats. "When I suggested you bring a friend, this wasn't what I was expecting."

Mom studies us before turning to Dad. The pair share a look before turning back to us.

"So, to what do we owe this pleasure?" Dad asks, making me want to crawl under the table and hide.

63

LINCOLN

"Linc is my roommate," Parker blurts. "After the fire, he let me move in while I got everything sorted."

Alison and Clark's expressions don't change as they focus on their daughter.

"Why don't you look shocked?" Parker asks, almost sounding offended by their lack of reaction.

"We kinda figured, sweetie. We knew that Linc would look after you."

Parker's mouth opens and closes.

"Plus, you've been really quiet. You only do that when you're hiding something."

"No, I don't. And I don't have anything to hide. I've just been really busy with the new job and traveling and—"

"It's okay, Parker," Clark soothes.

"We are surprised that you brought him tonight, though."

"That's my fault," I interject. "I sort of invited myself. I heard she was meeting you two and that there was steak involved."

Clark chuckles, fully understanding my thought process as our server comes over to take our drinks order.

"So, what's been going on with you two then?" Alison asks innocently.

"What? Nothing. Nothing is going on with us," Parker blurts, sounding guilty as fuck.

The girl can't lie to save her life—no wonder she goes quiet when she's hiding something from her parents.

Clark chuckles fondly. "You've been playing incredibly well the last few games, son."

"Thank you. Things are clicking right now. We're all working well as a team, all focused on where we want the rest of the season to go."

"Well, it's fantastic to watch. Shame I can't say the same thing for the Bandits."

I can't help but laugh. "They've had better seasons."

"Rett is getting more and more frustrated." I nod in agreement. "Every time he's on the ice, I worry that he's going to do something stupid."

"Just on the ice?" Alison asks.

"Well, no. All I can say is, I'm glad I'm not head of PR at the Bandits."

"I've had to stop looking at social media. I just...I can't."

"It's probably all lies, Mom," Parker assures her, but even as the words roll off her tongue, I'm not sure she really believes them.

"I'm sure some are, yes. But we all know what your brother is like."

Alison looks up at me. "Whoa," I say, holding my hands up defensively. "I have nothing to do with his actions these days. Sure, you could have blamed me for a lot of it in the past, but things are different now. Rett is his own man, making his own bad decisions."

Alison groans. "I just hate seeing my boy getting bad press."

Clark leans over and squeezes her hand. "He'll sort himself out," he assures her.

"Enough about your brother. How are you enjoying your job, Parker? Is it everything you always hoped it would be?"

"It's a lot harder than I thought. Who knew hockey players

were such divas?" she teases. "But I love it. It's hard work, but it's so rewarding. Watching the guys overcome injuries and then seeing them out on the ice...it's incredible."

"We're so proud of you, PK," Clark says, his eyes full of love for his daughter. "I'd have killed to have a trainer as dedicated as you back in my day."

"She's the best there is," I say, earning soft smiles from both Parker's parents.

The conversation continues to flow easily from hockey and Parker's job to Alison and Clark's travels.

The food, as always, is incredible.

The evening is everything I expect it to be, and thankfully, nowhere near as anxiety-inducing as Parker was expecting.

After making plans to see them both again, we say our goodbyes and head for the car.

"See, that wasn't so bad, was it?" I say, starting the engine.

"I can't believe they knew." Parker laughs.

"Your parents know you well. Never forget that."

"Do you think that means Rett knows?"

I laugh. "No."

"But he might."

"Babe, trust me. He doesn't."

"How are we going to tell him?" she asks, chewing on one of her nails.

"Stop worrying. Even if he isn't impressed, what is he going to do about it? He's in Seattle. It's not like he's in LA and has to see us hanging out together. Or worse, catching us doing anything."

"He would kill you."

"He'd get over it. Like your mom pointed out, it's not like he hasn't got his own drama to deal with."

"My brother is a dog," she states.

"He's just living his best life. It'll hit him eventually."

"What will?" she asks.

"The need to settle down," I explain.

"Is that what happened to you?"

"I mean, nothing literally hit me. But I started to realize that nothing meant anything. The hookups, the girls...they were meaningless. Pointless.

"Honestly, I think watching Kodie and Casey fall in love helped. For the first time, I got a front-row seat to what life could be like if I went down a different path. Suddenly, it didn't seem so scary."

"What if you change your mind?"

"What?"

"What if you change your mind? What if settling down is boring, and you crave the excitement of having a different girl every night?"

"I won't," I assure her, twisting our fingers together and holding her tight.

"But how do you know?"

"Because being with you is a better high than being with any other girl has ever been," I answer honestly. "Every girl I've ever been with, I've wished it were you.

"You ruined me for anyone else years ago, pretty girl. It's just taken me a while to get my head out of my ass and do something about it. And anyway, how do I know that you're not going to miss the online dating scene and want to go off to meet some rando at a bar?"

She snorts.

"Have you ever heard me say anything good about online dating?"

"Thankfully, I've never heard you say much about it. If I knew when and where you were meeting these assholes, I'd have turned up and intercepted."

"You would not," she argues.

"Totally would. The thought of someone else getting close to you makes me murderous. I know it's hypocritical, but I want to end any motherfucker who has gotten to touch you since that first time."

I'm not sure what reaction I'm expecting to that comment,

but it's certainly not for Parker to smile wider than I'm sure I've seen all night.

"What?" I ask, happiness I don't think I've ever felt before buzzing under the surface.

"Nothing."

"Oh no, something definitely made you smile like that."

"You did," she states.

Pride swells in my chest.

"Parker," I warn.

"What?" she asks innocently.

"You liked it when I got all jealous, didn't you?"

A few seconds pass, my question hanging in the air between us.

"Maybe," she whispers.

"I'm not joking, Parker. You're mine. And I'm going to make sure every other man out there knows it."

The second we're out of the car, I take her hand and all but drag her to the elevator.

"Linc, what—" I cut off her words as I back her up against the wall and slam my lips down on hers.

She melts into me, her hands gripping my hips as I pin her to the wall, letting her feel how hard I am already.

God. I can't get enough.

Her taste, her scent, her everything.

I've known that I've been addicted for a long time, and while I thought I'd managed to keep the memories of our one and only time together alive in my head, being with her again proves just how little I truly remember.

The elevator climbs through the building, and all I can think about is her. She's all-consuming.

Hockey has been my life. It has been for as long as I can remember. My one focus in life. Nothing has ever come close to pushing it aside. But Parker...fuck.

When she's in my arms like this, nothing else in the world exists.

The chime announces that we've made it to the top floor, and the doors open, but neither of us even attempts to leave.

After a few minutes, the doors slide closed again.

"Linc," Parker gasps when I kiss along her jaw and down her neck.

"Yeah, babe. What do you need?"

"You," she confesses. "Always you."

"Fuck," I breathe, pressing my forehead against hers as I try to catch my breath.

When she says stuff like that, it makes me feel like a king.

Better than scoring in a game. Better than any trophy I could win. Better than any-fucking-thing.

"Come on," I say, grabbing her hand and jabbing my finger against the open-door button.

I don't bother stopping in the living area. It's late—okay, that's a lie. It's barely ten, but I've got to be at the arena first thing. We've got a game to prepare for, and there is no way in hell I'm letting the Bandits get the better of us—not with the way they're playing this season. Rett might be my best friend, but there is no way I'm letting him off easy on the ice. I already know he isn't going to offer me any reprieve when he finds out what I'm doing with his sister.

Instead, I head straight for Parker's bedroom. We both know it's where we're going to be sleeping tonight, after all.

The desire to detour to mine is strong, but doing so seems like a big deal.

I'm trying to take this at her pace, and until she asks, we'll stick to her room.

I kick the door gently, not wanting to shut it just in case it freaks her out, even with me in here, before I turn to face her.

Lifting our joined hands, I kiss down her wrist to where her bracelet lies.

Our eyes hold as I brush my lips over it.

The second I saw it, I knew it would look incredible on her.

My agent was pissed when I called our meeting to a

close before he was ready. But the moment the idea hit, I knew I had to follow through with it. Parker deserves to be treated like a queen, and I fully intend to ensure she knows it.

"One day," I whisper, "I'm going to fuck you in nothing but this and those heels."

Her breath catches, and she swallows thickly at my words.

"No one is stopping you."

Yes, they are.

I am.

I'm stopping me.

"Turn around," I command, my voice thick with desire from the image I just painted for her. "Good girl."

She whimpers as I drop her hand in favor of brushing her wavy, red hair over one shoulder, exposing the zip that runs down her back.

Pinching the small bit of metal, I slowly begin undressing her.

God, this is torture at its finest—unwrapping the best gift I've ever received, already knowing I'm not going to allow myself to fully enjoy it.

Not yet.

But soon.

Real fucking soon.

I kiss the skin I expose at the base of her neck. The second the zipper stops, I lift both my hands and push the fabric from her shoulders.

The dress falls to her feet, and I close my eyes for a beat, preparing myself for what I might see looking back at me in the mirror.

"Linc," Parker breathes. "Look at me."

Unable to deny her anything, my eyelids lift, and I look directly into the mirror she's standing in front of.

Oh, holy fuck.

The lingerie set she's wearing.

Fuck. My. Life.

The black lace is so delicate that I'm sure I could rip it apart with very little effort.

It's also very see-through, letting me see her rosy nipples hiding beneath, along with her hairless pussy behind the tiny triangle of fabric that disappears between her legs.

She's so beautiful. So perfect.

And I really don't fucking deserve her.

As I make my way back up her body, I find myself captured by her dark, golden eyes. "Why are you holding back?" she whispers, almost as if she's afraid she might scare me off if she asks the question too loudly.

I take a moment, dragging my bottom lip between my teeth as I try to find the right words.

"Because...the last time we took things too fast, I scared you off. I won't survive that again."

64

PARKER

With Linc and Kodie working late, Casey invited me back to their place for dinner.

The second I step through the front door, all I hear is giggling.

It's infectious, and I soon find myself smiling with them as I kick my sneakers off, abandon my purse, and head for the kitchen to find out what she and Sutton are up to.

I find both of them sitting at the kitchen island with face masks on, and more nail polish than I've ever seen scattered across the counter.

"You two look like you're having fun," I say as I move closer.

"Parker?" Sutton squeals, hopping off her stool and racing toward me.

"Watch you don't cover Parker in a face mask goo," Casey calls.

"We've got one for you and Freya, too," Sutton happily tells me as she wraps her small arms around my waist and squeezes tight.

"Is that right?"

"And Freya is bringing the food. She's got loads of desserts."

"Can't wait. I'm starving," I say, joining them at the island.

"Good day?" Casey asks.

"Busy," I say. "Those guys know how to keep me on my toes."

"I guess that's what happens when you're the best they have and they all want you."

I let out a sigh. "There are worse problems to have, right?"

"Absolutely. So, what are we doing here?"

"Girls' night," Sutton squeals excitedly.

Casey smiles at her before turning to me with a shrug.

"It's like you knew how much I needed some pampering. Your daddy and his team are exhausting."

Sutton giggles. "All boy hockey players are hard work. Girls are way better."

Casey laughs. "She's got a point there," she says confidently. "I'd definitely choose to coach Sutton's girls' team over the Vipers."

"Which one do you want, Parker?" Sutton says, offering me a selection of face masks.

I select a watermelon one that is meant to brighten my skin and offer it to Sutton to put on.

She rolls her eyes. "You need to take your makeup off first."

"Ah, yes. Silly me," I tease.

"Here. Face wipes. Then mask."

"Right. Got it. Good thing you're here."

Sutton is halfway through applying my face mask when the doorbell rings.

Casey hops up to let Freya in, leaving me with Sutton.

"There," she says once she's happy with her work. "You're going to look even prettier after."

"I hope so," I tease.

"Linc will think you're really pretty."

"Oh?" I ask on an exhale.

She smiles, and it makes my heart beat a little faster.

"Daddy says that when you're standing by the rink at training, all Linc does is stare at you."

Happiness explodes within me, sending tingles shooting through my body.

"I'm sure that's not true."

"It is. Daddy wouldn't say it otherwise. He said he's a lovesick fool and needs to do something about it."

Suspicion weaves its way through me. "Sutton, were you eavesdropping?"

She glances away, giving me all the answer I need. "They were talking really loudly."

"And where were you?"

"Sitting at the top of the stairs," she says quietly.

"Sutton, you know you shouldn't do that. Casey and your daddy were having a private conversation."

"I know. I just...I couldn't sleep, and I like listening to their voices. It's soothing."

My heart aches for this incredible little girl.

"Aw, come here, sweet pea," I say, holding my arms out to give her a cuddle. "I won't say anything. But you can always tell me everything they say about Linc." It's naughty of me, but I'm more than happy to hear more about how much I distract him at practice.

"What about what he said himself?" Sutton asks. "He was here the other night and—"

"Holy cow, how much did you make?" I blurt when Casey and Freya walk in with arms full of food.

"I may have gotten a little excited," Freya confesses, her cheeks burning red, as she lowers the trays stacked in her arms to the counter.

"It all looks incredible," Casey says.

"Freya, it's time for face masks," Sutton calls.

"I'm all ready for you."

"You took your makeup off already?" Sutton asks, shooting me a look that makes me roll my eyes.

Chastised by a child. What is my life coming to?

"Yep, good to go."

Freya takes a seat opposite me and allows Sutton to get to work. Her eyes meet mine, and she smiles by way of greeting.

"Sutton and I made virgin margaritas," Casey explains as she lowers four salted cocktail glasses in front of us before returning with a jug.

"Sounds perfect. Fill those babies up."

Once Freya is masked up, she begins talking us through our dinner.

She's made moussaka with a fresh Greek salad, and then, as Sutton said, she's made three desserts. A salted caramel cheesecake, brownies, and very British apple crumble.

The second she begins showing it all off, my stomach growls loudly.

"Am I okay to use your oven?" Freya asks.

"After bringing enough food to feed us for a week? Yes, knock yourself out."

We all sit around the island, sipping on our mocktails, listening to tales of Sutton's elementary school. As always, Freya's food is incredible, and we all eat way more than we should.

Eventually, Casey manages to convince Sutton that she needs to go to bed. Seeing as she's practically falling asleep in her second bowl of apple crumble, she doesn't argue and instead wraps herself around Casey when she lifts her into her arms and carries her from the room.

Freya and I make ourselves useful while she's off telling bedtime stories by cleaning up the kitchen.

Before long, Casey is back, and we move to the living room.

"I think I'm going to go back to school," Freya blurts.

"Oh, that's exciting," Casey says, giving Freya her full attention.

Freya has been back at her parents' for a few months now after going through a pretty awful breakup. When it first happened, she fled to England and spent some time hiding out with her cousin, but she came back at the end of last summer, not knowing what to do with her life.

She met him in Las Vegas, and he completely swept her off her feet, showed her the world, and dropped her as if none of it meant anything before continuing on his way.

She's doing better now, but she's still struggling to move on. She gave up her purpose in life, her dreams, to be with him, and she's been left with nothing, no direction.

"What for?" I ask, already guessing her response.

"I want to do something with food," she predictably explains. "Being in the kitchen, making things for people...it's becoming my happy place. I want to see if I can turn it into something."

"You don't need to go to school to learn how to cook," I point out.

"No, I know. I'm thinking more nutrition, dive into the science behind it all."

"Oh, you should do sports nutrition. It's huge and pays incredibly well. Diet is so important to pro athletes. We could hook you up with Jade Easton, the team's nutritionist. She's really lovely. I'm sure she'd be able to answer questions if you were interested in going down that route."

"Maybe," Freya muses. "It's a big commitment. I want to make sure it's the right decision."

"Anything that makes you happy will be the right decision," I assure her.

"You're coming to the game tomorrow, right?" Casey asks.

"Sure am. Dad is super excited about the tickets you secured."

"Aw, he's so welcome. It's going to be a good night."

"Possibly not for Rett and the Bandits."

"That's because our boys are far superior," Casey states. "Have you told him you're living with Linc yet?"

"No," I say on a groan. "And I don't intend to until after the game."

"YES, MONROE," Killer shouts, as he manages to steal the puck from Linc and dart around toward the goal, where Handsy is waiting for him.

He pulls his stick back, ready to make a slap shot, but Linc has already recovered and is faster.

The second Monroe leaves the puck unattended, Linc steals it back.

"Motherfucker," Monroe curses, taking off behind Linc again.

I've been sitting here watching them run drills with Hayden now for almost an hour.

The kid is exhausted, but at no point has he lost the smile on his face.

He was born to be here, there is no doubt about that. But he's a rookie, and the guys surrounding him have years of experience playing.

Linc skates closer, and the second his eyes lock with mine, he winks.

I feel like a schoolgirl all over again. Only now, he's giving me the attention I always craved.

I used to sit like this, watching him and Rett, always begging for him to look my way.

He suddenly turns, and I shriek when he hits the boards.

"You should join us," he shouts.

"What?" I ask, assuming I misheard him.

"Go and get some skates."

"That's crazy. I can't. You're practicing."

"We finished hours ago. We're just putting in extra time."

"Exactly. You're working."

Sure, I've been on the ice fairly recently. Casey and I brought Sutton here while the guys were away last year, but that's stopped now that I'm travelling with them. But despite all my years playing, there is no way I could hold my own against them.

"Aw, come on. We'll take it easy on you."

I want to stand my ground. But when he looks at me with those puppy-dog eyes, it's hard to remember what my point is, let alone why I'm arguing with it.

"Casey has full gear in the closet with the kids' stuff."

"Oh no, I'm not—"

"We wouldn't want to hurt you, babe."

"Then maybe I should stay right here."

He quirks a brow.

"It's been years since we were on the ice together."

"Yeah, and you're even better than you were back then. I don't stand a chance."

"Linc, you doing this or what?" Handsy barks.

He holds up a gloved hand.

"Trying to convince Donnelly to join us."

Kodie and Monroe head over.

"You play?" Monroe asks.

"She used to play with Casey," Kodie fills in.

"Then you should definitely join us. Casey is incredible."

Kodie beams at Monroe's words.

"Some might say she's better than you."

Monroe scoffs.

"Well, what are you waiting for. Go and grab some skates and let's goooo," Monroe says, pushing away from the boards and skating backward to join the others.

"So..." Linc prompts.

"Fine," I hiss, pushing to my feet. "But if I break anything, you're telling Jarad and Grady why their guys' favorite trainer is out of action."

"Not going to happen, babe. You know I've got your back."

Kodie glances between us with a knowing look in his eyes.

"I can't believe I'm doing this," I mutter before turning my back and walking away from them.

There are whoops and hollers on the ice as I head toward the storage closet, where I'll find everything I need.

It takes me longer than I ever remember getting dressed.

The protective equipment is heavy and uncomfortable, but in a weird, familiar kind of way.

Once I'm sorted, I stand on my skates and glance in the cracked mirror that hangs in the empty visitors' dressing room I've made my own. I give myself a double take.

It's been years since I saw myself dressed like this.

It feels like another lifetime.

As I walk toward the ice, nerves erupt in my stomach.

I'm not nervous about not being able to play, skating is like riding a bike; you never forget. But I'm about to step onto the ice with a bunch of NHL players. Is there anything more intimidating than that?

"Oh shit," Linc gasps the second he sees me.

He skates straight over, but the second his eyes drop to my shoulders, his expression tightens.

"Why are you wearing Rivers' jersey?" he demands.

"Because, as you know, I'm borrowing Casey's gear." I fight my smirk. I could have chosen Casey's Polar Bears jersey, but that seemed too easy.

This is a whole lot more fun.

"Nah, that's just fucking wrong. Take it off," he demands, his voice leaving very little space for argument.

"W-what?"

"Take it the fuck off. Monroe," he bellows. "Go and get my spare practice jersey."

"I'm kinda busy here," he dares to argue.

"I don't give a fuck. Go and get my spare practice jersey, or all extra training sessions are off."

"Linc," I soothe, reaching for his arm in the hope of calming him down.

"Take it off, Parker. I'm dead fucking serious right now."

"What if I'm not wearing anything beneath?"

65

LINCOLN

oly shit. I didn't think it was possible, but I've just fallen even harder for Parker Donnelly.

I stand on the ice, watching in awe, as she plays hockey with my teammates, thankfully now wearing my number.

She's still really fucking good. And she's so small and light that she flies across the ice to the point that Killer and Monroe are struggling to catch her.

"Shoot," I bellow, unable to move as she darts toward Handsy.

He's ready for her; his eyes locked on the puck.

Just like every goalie, he's competitive as fuck and hates to see the puck hit the back of the net, so I have no reason to believe he's going to take it easy on her.

Hell, if he was going to take it easy on anyone, it would be Sutton, but he doesn't.

It'll pay off in the long run—it'll make her an even better player—but it kind of sucks for her right now.

"Yes, yes, YES," I scream when Parker gets the better of Handsy. I'm flying toward her before I've even thought about moving. "That's my fucking girl," I shout before I collide with her. Together, we slide backward until she hits the boards.

I pin her in place, gazing down into her excited eyes.

"I scored." She laughs, a smile splitting her face.

"You did, babe. It was fucking incredible."

Reaching up, I rip my helmet from my head and drop it to the ice.

My hand lifts for the buckle on hers, too desperate to kiss her, to celebrate her success, to think about where we are and who could be watching.

I'm about to pull it free when Parker panics.

"No," she cries, reaching for the helmet she's borrowed and holding it tight. "Not here."

Anxiety is etched into every inch of her face. I push away from the boards, putting some space between us.

I feel like an asshole, but I was just so excited.

"I'm sorry; I didn't think."

"It's okay," she assures me, but it's not. I've made her promises, promises that I'm desperate to keep, and kissing her out here where anyone could see isn't doing that.

"I'll do better. I'll—"

"Stop, Linc. It's okay. That was..." Something wicked flashes in her eyes. "The most exhilarating thing I've done in quite some time."

I frown. "Is that right?"

"Yep," she says, popping the P.

"Well, I'd better up my game then, if scoring a goal is the biggest rush you've had recently."

"You said it, not me," she states before pushing from the boards and skating past me. "Uh...where did everyone go?"

I spin around and find the ice deserted, apart from her.

"Uh..." I shake my head, a smile ghosting across my lips.

I fucking love my teammates.

"I think maybe they were giving us some space," I explain.

"What were they expecting us to do? Start fucking like rabbits in the middle of the rink?"

"I mean...I can think of worse ways to spend my evening."

"I'd rather avoid freezer burn on my ass, thank you very much."

"I'm sure we could figure out a position."

Image after image of us entwined a few feet from where we're standing right now fill my mind. Hell, I could even take her over the goal.

"Lincoln Storm, stop it. Stop it right now."

"What?" I hold my hands up in surrender. "I'm not doing anything."

Parker shakes her head and skates toward the gate. "We should probably head out," she says over her shoulder.

"Is that your way of suggesting I sneak you into the locker room?"

"Are you kidding? I know how bad it smells in there. And you've been in that gear for hours."

"Aw, you know you want to. You can't tell me that you don't have a fantasy of being taken in the locker room."

"Maybe I do, maybe I don't," she teases.

"You totally do. And one day, I'll make it happen for you, babe."

The thought of us fooling around in there when anyone could walk in makes my temperature rise. Of course, considering she works for the team, it would be really reckless to do. But also, really fucking hot.

"Go and shower, you stink," she says, pausing when she gets to the visitors' dressing room. "I'll meet you out here in fifteen minutes."

"Make it five, and we'll shower at home."

Her brow lifts in question.

"Clock's ticking, pretty girl. Don't be late. I've got plans for you."

She darts into the dressing room before I have a chance to stop her. The temptation to storm in after her and take exactly what I need is beyond tempting. I remind myself that I'm being a good boy and continue toward our dressing room.

It looks totally different from the one she's in. In ours, we each have our own stalls with our names on. Sure, it smells like a bunch of sweaty dudes have died in it, but it's home, you know? It's also empty. Seems like the guys didn't just disappear from the ice.

I'm stripping long before I get to my stall. I haphazardly throw stuff onto the bench, and stuff others into my duffle, before pulling on a pair of athletic pants and a T-shirt. No sooner do I have my sneakers on than I'm marching toward the door with my bag thrown over my shoulder. I'll sort the rest of my shit out tomorrow. I've got more important things to worry about right now.

As I wait, I pull my cell out.

I find a series of messages waiting for me in the group chat I have with the guys.

> Killer: @Storm Enjoy the rest of your game
> *winky emoji*
>
> Handsy: @Storm Your girl has a better shot than you.
>
> Big D: @Storm Go and talk to HR.
>
> Marilyn: @Storm does she have a sister?
>
> Brit: @Marilyn just a big brother…a little rougher around the edges but some may say he's equally as hot
>
> Killer: @Brit did you just say Rett Donnelly is hot?
>
> Brit: No, I said some may think he is. I do not. I like my hookups with a little less dick, fuck you very much.

"Jesus," I mutter, shaking my head and dragging my hand down my face.

> Storm: @BigD don't worry, everything is in hand. You're not getting rid of either of us that easily.

Handsy: @Storm you are replaceable. Parker
isn't.

"Asshole," I hiss, but any reply I might have to that message is long forgotten when Parker emerges.

Her hair is sweaty and sticking to the sides of her face, and her cheeks are flushed red with exertion. To put it simply, she looks hot as hell.

"Just so you know, you're the hottest player I've ever hit the ice with," I tell her as she closes in on me.

"Oh really?" she teases. "Even hotter than Handsy and Killer?"

I snort a laugh as jealousy threatens.

"Too fucking right. You're in an entirely different universe from those ugly motherfuckers."

"Oh, I don't know," she says, biting on her bottom lip as if she's daydreaming about them.

"Watch it, pretty girl," I warn. "I might have let fucking you in the dressing room go once, but just so you know, the option is still fully on the table."

Her eyes widen in interest.

"Come on," I say, spinning around and heading toward the exit.

"What about my car?" she asks as I beeline for my Porsche.

"We really need to start riding in together."

"You get here before sunrise," she squeaks.

"Maybe you should give me a reason to stay in bed a little longer."

She shakes her head.

"I'll call us a rideshare in the morning, then we can bring yours home tomorrow night."

To my surprise, she doesn't argue and instead happily climbs into my car.

"You killed it out there tonight," I tell her once we're on our way.

She scoffs. "Oh, hardly. I was like a little kid scrambling after you all. I'm way too out of practice to be playing with you guys. I can barely keep up with Sutton, and that's on a good day."

"Trust me, you looked like you were coping just fine."

I don't need to look over to know that she's rolling her eyes.

"You were just too distracted to notice."

"Mmm...you on the ice in full uniform and wearing a jersey with my number on. Yeah, I was a little distracted."

"Don't forget about your center-ice fantasy."

"Almost as hot as your dressing room one."

'That's not...I don't..."

I laugh when she fails to finish each sentence she tries.

"Oh, you so do. Don't worry, babe. One day, we'll knock it off your bucket list."

Twisting my fingers with hers, I lift her hand so I can kiss her knuckles. It's the bare minimum of what I really want to do to her, but it's all I can get right now.

I press my foot harder to the gas to get us home a little faster.

I need her naked and wrapped around me about as much as I need my next breath.

The short journey seems to take forever. We have little choice but to stop at every stoplight, and for some reason, the traffic is worse than normal at this time of night. I can't help but think that the universe is fucking with me.

By the time we pull into my underground garage, my knee is bouncing with adrenaline that rivals the minutes before stepping out on the ice before a game.

The second I pull to a stop, I kill the engine and all but jump from the car.

Parker is still gathering her things when I open her door and drag her out.

"Jesus, what's the rush?" she asks.

I don't say anything. I can't. My mind is on one thing, and one thing only.

"Linc, what the hell is going—" Her back hits the back wall of the elevator, and I surround her.

"Can't wait any longer," I groan before my lips are on hers.

It takes her a couple of seconds to catch up, but the second she does, she melts into me.

With her arms wrapped around my neck, I hitch one of her legs over my hip, opening her up for me and allowing me to grind against her. I'm already hard. I have been since the moment she started walking toward me at the arena.

"I need you," I groan into our kiss.

"Then take me. I'm right here, Linc."

Dragging my lips away, I press my forehead against hers and keep my eyes shut for a few seconds as I attempt to get myself under control.

"Linc?"

I swallow thickly. "We need to get upstairs. Now."

"Then you should probably press the button," she teases.

When I spin around to do so, I discover that the doors aren't even shut.

After tapping my fob to the panel, I hit the button for my penthouse. I'm pretty sure all the air is sucked out of the car the second the doors close because when I turn to look at Parker, it's all I can do to suck in a breath.

"Linc," she breathes as she steps forward, her eyes locked on mine.

She gazes up at me with wide eyes and swollen lips.

God. She's everything.

My everything.

My loud gasp fills the air when she reaches out and cups my dick through my pants.

"Shit," I hiss, already too close to the fucking edge.

Do not come in your pants again.

"Mmm, is this for me?" she rasps, not helping the situation one bit.

"Uh-huh." I nod, and she slowly begins stroking me. "All yours. Every inch."

Her smile turns wicked, and she licks her lips. Visions of her on her knees for me fill my head, and precum leaks from the tip, soaking my boxers.

"I can't wait," she whispers.

66

PARKER

Linc drags me through the apartment as if our lives depend on it, and he doesn't stop until we're standing in my bathroom.

"What are you..." My words trail off as he leans into the shower cubicle and turns it on. The second he's back, standing in front of me, he begins stripping.

Oh. Now we're talking.

I lower my purse to the floor, my eyes focused on every bit of skin he reveals.

His T-shirt hits the floor as he toes off his sneakers, and then his thumbs are in his waistband and he's pushing both his pants and boxers down his thick thighs at the same time.

His hard cock springs free, and my mouth waters.

I want him.

I want him so much I could cry.

The game he's playing right now is driving me crazy. I understand his need to take this slow— hell, I agree and appreciate the fuck out of his thoughtfulness. But it's driving me to the brink.

He stands before me as naked as the day he was born, save for the ink that now stains his body.

"What are you waiting for?" he asks, confused.

"Uh…I said that we were showering when we got home."

"Y-yeah, I know. I just didn't…" Slowly, I drag down the zipper of my Vipers vest before letting it hit the floor.

Linc's eyes blaze with heat as I reach for the hem of my long-sleeved shirt.

He groans as I peel it up my body and reveal my pretty lace bra beneath. It definitely wasn't ideal for playing hockey in, but it's certainly doing its job now.

Linc swallows thickly as my hands drop to my leggings.

I drag them over my ass before pulling them from my feet along with my socks, leaving me in just my underwear.

"Jesus Christ," he mutters as I take two steps toward him.

The fire in his eyes is a massive confidence boost, and I stand with my shoulders back and my tits out.

"Did you want to help with the rest?" I ask coyly as I gaze up at him through my lashes.

"You have no fucking idea how much I want to help," he confesses before reaching out and grazing my hard nipple through the lace cup of my bra.

I whimper with need.

"Turn around," he demands. Slowly, I follow orders, giving him my back.

"Christ, this ass," he groans, palming my bare cheeks.

"Lincoln, please," I beg.

Dragging his knuckles up my spine, he pauses at the clasp of my bra.

"I've dreamed of seeing you naked again every fucking night for six years."

My breath catches at his honesty as a little regret stirs deep within me.

What would have happened if I hadn't walked away without looking back six years ago? Would we have figured this out earlier? Or was it too soon? Did we need this time, the distance, to allow us to come back stronger?

Fuck, I really hope it's the latter.

In a quick flick of his fingers, he undoes my bra, and the fabric falls forward.

I groan as my full breasts are freed.

Gently, he pushes the fabric from my shoulders, and it falls to the floor with a gentle thud.

Linc's lips kiss across my shoulder as his hand skates around my ribs. I arch for him, my ass grazing his cock as I silently beg for his touch.

The second his fingers graze the underside of my breasts, I groan and fully lean back into him, afraid that my legs will no longer hold me up once he fully gets his hands on me.

And I'm right. The second he cups my breasts with his huge, calloused palms, my knees buckle.

"Oh god," I moan, my head falling back against his shoulder as he gently squeezes me and pinches my nipples.

Heat surges to my core, and I wiggle my hips in the hope of some relief.

"Are you wet for me?" Linc whispers in my ear, making me shudder.

"Yes."

"Just wet, or soaked?"

"Find out."

He groans as his hands drop to my hips. I want to complain at the loss of his touch, but I know better things are coming.

He hooks his thumbs into the side of my panties before dragging them down.

Glancing over my shoulder, I discover he's dropping with them. As the lace hits my ankles, he's resting on his haunches, my ass right in his face.

Leaning forward, he presses a kiss to my ass cheek as he taps one ankle and then the other to get me to lift up to free my panties.

He moans the second he wraps his fingers around them.

"Soaked," he groans as he lifts them to his face and inhales. "And so fucking sweet."

I cringe, remembering just how sweaty and disgusting I was while chasing him and the others around the ice earlier, but he doesn't seem to care.

He discards them the second I turn around, and his eyes drop to my body.

His jaw tics as his teeth clench and his throat ripples with a heavy swallow.

"You're a fucking goddess, Parker." He steps forward, splaying his hands on my stomach and then sliding them around my back, pinning our bodies together. "And all mine."

"Linc."

"Say it," he demands.

I hold his eyes so he can see the truth in the next word that falls from my lips.

"Yours."

One minute, I'm standing there with the heat of him against my back, and the next, I'm in the shower with water raining down on me.

Linc wraps one hand around the back of my neck and bands his other arm around my back, pinning us together before kissing the life out of me.

I cling to him just as tightly as he does me as he completely consumes me.

When our lips finally part, I'm panting, my chest heaving with my need for air.

"Parker," he whispers, stepping into me and giving me no choice but to move back.

I gasp when my back hits the cold tiles, but the second his body presses against me, I forget all about it.

"Can I touch you?" he asks, his eyes bouncing between mine.

"I think you already are," I point out, covering his hand that's resting on my waist with my own.

"Y-yeah, I am. But that's not what I mean."

"I know," I whisper, taking his hand and sliding it across my stomach, and then down.

I swear he stops breathing.

"I'm yours, Linc," I tell him. "Tease me, touch me, take me. Do whatever you want to me, just...just don't let me fall."

"Never, babe. I'll always catch you. Always."

I swear my heart grows a couple of sizes with those words.

I push his hand lower until his fingers graze right over the spot I really need them.

"Please, Linc. I *need* you to touch me."

We stand there frozen for a long second. His fingers twitch against me, but it's nowhere near enough to give me what I need.

"Stop holding back," I whisper. "You won't scare me off. The only place I'm running is into your arms."

He smirks.

"That was too cheesy, wasn't it?"

He shakes his head. "It was perfect. You are perfect." And with those words, he presses two thick fingers against my clit, and I cry out.

My fingers curl around his shoulders as I fight to stay upright.

He teases me, circling my clit before he pushes back and easily slides two fingers inside me.

"Fuck," he grunts, discovering just how wet I am. "Perfect."

He curls his fingers, finding my G-spot almost instantly, and I can't help but think the same thing.

"N-no, w-what?" I stutter when he pulls his hand away, leaving me cold and my pussy clenching around nothing.

"Need a taste, babe. Gonna die without it."

I watch as he sucks those two fingers that were just inside me into his mouth. His eyes shutter as my taste covers his tongue, and the corners of his lips curl up in a smile.

"Delicious," he muses before dropping his hand back down at the same time his lips collide with mine.

It's everything.

Every-fucking-thing.

He works me as if he's been doing it all his life. His pressure is perfect, speed is exquisite, and long before I'm ready, my release is tightening inside me, ready to explode.

Ripping my lips from his, I rest my head back against the wall and breathe as pleasure edges closer.

"Keep those eyes on me, pretty girl. I want to watch every second of you coming apart on my fingers."

I nod, my lips parted but unable to respond as my orgasm hits.

I cry out, my knees buckling as pleasure hits me so hard I no longer know who I am. The only thing I'm aware of is Linc and mind-numbing pleasure.

His movements slow as I ride out wave after wave of my release, and it's not until I've fully come down from my high that he pulls his fingers away.

I whimper at the loss, but he makes up for it by sucking them clean again.

"Incredible," he muses. "Fucking incredible."

His cock bobs between us, and I act on instinct.

"W-what?" He gasps as I slam my palms against his chest, giving him little choice but to step back. "Parker, w-what are you doing? You said you wouldn't—" His words and his panic both die as I slowly sink to my knees before him. "Oh fuck," he breathes. "You don't...babe. I didn't do that so you could—"

"I know," I assure him, leaning forward and kissing his hip.

His cock jerks in excitement.

"I don't expect—"

"I know."

"You don't have to—"

"Lincoln Storm," I chastise, sitting back on my heels. "Are you trying to stop me from sucking your dick?"

"What? No, no. Never. I fucking dream about you sucking me—oh holy fuck. Parker," he barks as I wrap my hand around him and suck on the tip.

His fingers sink into my hair as his head falls back.

"Oh Christ," he groans when he looks back down and finds me with his cock in my mouth. "Fuck. I'm not gonna last, babe. Too good. Too fucking good."

"At least you get to come in my mouth not your pants this time," I quip, pulling off him for a beat.

His fingers tighten in my hair, giving me little choice but to take him back into my mouth, only deeper this time.

I relax my throat and hollow my cheeks, fully intending to give him the best blow job of his life.

I never got to do this before, and I've regretted not knowing how he tastes ever since.

The saltiness of his precum covers my tongue, and I groan, desperate for more.

I give him all my best moves, and from the way he moans, I think it's hitting the spot.

"Yes, babe. Fuck. Are you going to swallow me down like a good girl?"

I nod the best I can while he's filling my mouth.

"Fuck, yeah."

Reaching up, I cup his balls, squeezing gently, and he barks out, "Fuck, I'm...fuuuuck."

His dick gets harder, bigger, before it jerks violently in my mouth, ropes of hot cum hitting the back of my throat.

I swallow it all down, savoring every drop as he gazes down at me like I'm the most precious thing in the world.

The second he's done, he lifts me from the floor, gathers me in his arms, and kisses me breathless, not giving a single shit that I taste of him or that the remnants of his release are still on my tongue.

"You are hands down the most incredible person I've ever met," he tells me softly as he pulls back from our kiss.

"You're not too bad yourself," I confess.

"Let me take care of you," he whispers.

"I'm pretty sure you already have," I tease.

He smirks. "Not just like that. Can I wash your hair?"

Christ, how can a girl say no to that?

67

LINCOLN

"You know, it's just not fair that you're good at everything," Parker sulks.

I snort a laugh. "I promise you, I'm not. Have you ever seen me draw?"

Parker giggles. "Remember that piece of art you did in middle school that was meant to be a family portrait? I thought your mom was going to end you right then and there."

"I must admit, it wasn't the most flattering of paintings, but I worked really hard on that."

"I'm sure you did, baby," she soothes, gently rubbing her arm down my bare back.

Her touch has goose bumps erupting instantly.

"Okay, so art aside. You're a pro hockey player who can cook like a chef, and look at you," she says, waving her hand up and down my body. I smirk. I spend hours working out; I can't help that I'm cut and look great on billboards advertising underwear, or anything really.

"Can't say I'm complaining about the view either, pretty girl."

Despite everything we did in the shower, this is what makes her cheeks burn red.

She's standing in my kitchen, wearing one of my T-shirts

and nothing else. She has a knife in her hand and an onion on the chopping board before her. Prior to this conversation, she was looking at it like it might jump up and bite her.

"What did you want me to do with this again?" she asks with a groan.

"Dice it."

"Right. Yep. Dice," she mutters, rolling it around and holding the knife as if she's about to stab it.

"You know how to do that, right?"

"Of course, I'm just...you know...warming up."

"Warming up?"

"Uh-huh."

Making a decision, she grabs it and moves to cut it through the center.

"Why don't you try it this way?" I say gently before turning the onion so she'll cut through the root. "It'll help keep it all together."

She nods and does as she's told as I move in behind her. Being close to her is too tempting.

Her fresh-from-the-shower scent hits my nose and I sigh, my breath making her drying hair flutter over her shoulder.

A groan rumbles in her throat as I press in behind her, and her eyes fall closed.

"Watch, Parker. You have a sharp knife if your hand."

"Then maybe you shouldn't distract me," she warns, sticking her ass out and wiggling it against my cock.

"Pretty girl," I groan.

"What do I do next, Chef?" she teases.

Unmoving from her back, I talk her through how to dice an onion while having an arm wrapped around her stomach, pinning her against me.

"Peppers next," I tell her, reaching out and placing one on her board.

"And what jobs are you doing?"

"Teaching, babe."

She shakes her head but doesn't complain as she chops the pepper.

"Anything else?"

I happily talk her through chopping up everything else we need for our ragu before passing her a garlic press.

"You know what that is, right?"

"Duh, of course."

"Perfect," I say as I tip the onions into the pan. "You can crush two cloves into her."

She blinks. "Cloves?"

"Yeah." I fight the smirk that wants to appear.

"Aren't they a holiday thing that go in mulled wine and candles?"

"Can't say I've ever had garlic in my mulled wine or candles before, but to each their own."

Parker purses her lips, her face burning as she reaches out and smacks my shoulder.

"You're a jerk."

"And you're cute."

"Incompetent, more like. I feel like an idiot."

"It's never too late to learn how to cook, babe."

"Who taught you?" she asks.

"Myself. I didn't want to live on takeout or have a personal chef like some of the guys do. But I needed to be eating healthily. So I learned."

"And there I was thinking you were partying every spare second."

"I had my moments. But partying was always at the end of my list. My career always comes first."

"I'm learning that."

"The press likes to blow shit up," I mutter as I break into a bulb of garlic and hand her a clove.

"Just like this?" she asks, hesitating.

"Yep, flip that over and then pop it in."

Her eyes darken as the innuendo floats between us.

"Is that right?"

I chuckle and watch as she completes her next task.

JUST OVER AN HOUR LATER, we're sitting at the dining table with our homemade ragu in front of us and a fresh green salad in a bowl.

Parker's stomach growls loudly as she stares down at it. "This looks amazing."

"You did a good job, babe," I praise, smiling at her across the table.

"Pretty sure the only credit I can take is for not cutting a finger off."

"I wouldn't have allowed that to happen; I need those fingers too much."

Her face drops at my words. "What's wrong?"

"I need to go to HR and get you moved off my treatment list."

Reaching across the table, I take her hand. "It's all going to be okay, Parker." She looks into my eyes. "We'll just turn the third bedroom into a personal trainer's room and—"

"Whoa, I don't remember agreeing to being your personal servant."

"It was in the fine print of this agreement," I tease.

"And what is this agreement, exactly?"

"That you're mine."

She pauses and looks down at her dinner.

"And what does that entail exactly? I don't want to be the woman asking what this is and where it's going, but—"

"It's okay, Parker. You can ask anything."

She nods, but no words come.

"I want this. Us. I always have. Am I scared? Absolutely. Am I terrified of fucking this up and hurting you? One hundred percent. But I've waited so long for this chance. I can't do it any longer.

"Having you here...you've turned this apartment into a

home. I love my job, it's everything I've ever wanted, but for the first time ever, I'm excited to finish for the day. I want to come home to you. When I'm at the arena, it's all I can think about."

"Linc," she whispers.

"I can't promise you that I'm going to be perfect. I think we both know that I'm not. I've never had a relationship before, and I have no idea what I'm meant to do. But I want to...with you."

Tears fill her eyes as she stares back at me, absorbing my words.

"I said I'd never have a relationship with a hockey player ever again."

"I'm not just a hockey player, though, am I?"

She shakes her head. "No, you're so much more than that, Linc. So much more."

"So is that it? Are you my girlfriend now?" I ask. The word feels weird rolling off my tongue, and not just because I've never called anyone it before, but also because it doesn't feel serious enough.

Previously, that thought would have terrified me. But not now.

Parker was always destined to be mine. And now I have her, I never want to let her go.

A nervous laugh erupts. "Lincoln Storm's girlfriend," she muses.

"Ah, come on. You can't tell me you haven't dreamed of having the position," I tease.

She thinks for a moment. "You know, I'm not sure I have."

"You're such a little liar." I laugh.

Picking up my fork, I stab a piece of pasta on my plate.

"It was all I ever dreamed of when I was a teenager, Linc."

"And yet you walked away that night," I mutter.

"I had to. It wasn't our time."

"I know. Our time is now," I state confidently.

"I'm still scared," she confesses as she also picks up her fork.

"I'd be worried if you weren't."

"Oh my god," she moans as she tastes our dinner. "This is incredible."

I beam with pride. "Of course it is. We made it."

She smiles at me across the table, and my brain fast forwards us a few years with her pregnant and me chasing a little hockey-obsessed terror around.

Suddenly, that kind of image sends a rush of excitement through me instead of fear.

"I'VE GOT A SURPRISE FOR YOU," I confess after we've loaded the dishwasher and tidied up the kitchen.

"Oh?"

Taking her hand, I tug her from the room and lead her in the opposite direction to our bedrooms.

"Linc," she warns from behind me. "There is no way I can work out after all that pasta."

Twisting the handle, I throw the door open to my home gym and pull her inside.

"Holy shit, you weren't joking." She gawps, her eyes falling on the trainer's table in the corner.

"That's not actually your surprise; that one is all for me."

"Unbelievable."

"You want me at my best, don't you, babe?"

She rolls her eyes. "So what is my..." Her words trail off as I spin her by her shoulders and show her what I really brought her in here for.

"O-o-oh." She laughs, staring at the two brand new reformers I had delivered while we were at work. "Now I get it. I get the job of breaking you on one of those before I have to fix you over there."

"I thought you'd like it."

"I am going to have so much fun with this," she exclaims as she spins in my arms and stares up at me, her eyes glittering with mischief. "And this way, you don't have to embarrass yourself in a class with other people."

"I didn't embarrass myself." I totally did.

She quirks a brow. "Uh-huh, sure."

"Did you want to test it out?"

"The reformers? Not a chance. But if that's your way of asking for a massage, then I guess I could be convinced to get my hands on you."

I smirk, desire heading straight for my dick.

We are going to have so much fun with that table.

"Go on then," she says, gently shoving me toward the table. "What do you need?"

"My groin area. It's feeling all kinds of hard."

"You're funny."

"Trust me, there is nothing funny about having to hide a semi all day and night because you're everywhere I turn."

"You're a nightmare."

"Your nightmare."

She mutters something under her breath as I climb onto the table and lie on my front, much to her surprise.

"My shoulder," I confess.

"I knew you were lying," she chastises.

"I didn't want you worrying."

"Linc, that is literally my job. That hit was brutal. Never hide how much pain you're in from me again," she says fiercely.

"Okay," I mutter, feeling like a little kid getting told off for missing curfew.

"I'm serious. I don't care about your macho bullshit. I want you healthy and in top form. We'll spend all night every night in here if we have to because you've been lumbered with fucking Mitchell as your trainer."

"He's on borrowed time," I blurt.

"What? Why would you say that?" she asks as she picks up the oil I left on the side for her and warms it between her palms.

"Because he's an asshole who treats you like a piece of shit. We're a team, Parker. We don't stand for someone belittling one of our own. Ow, fuck," I cry when she digs her thumbs into a sore spot.

"I don't need anyone fighting my battles for me."

"Is that why you haven't told me how bad it is?"

"His bullshit opinions aren't anything I can't handle."

"But you shouldn't have to. He's a jerk, Parker. And his time as a Viper is coming to an end."

She wants to argue, but knowing it won't get her anywhere, she falls quiet as she works.

"Oh god," I groan as she digs into a knot.

"Just because we're at home, that doesn't mean you can make sex noises while I do this."

"But I've been holding them in for years. Do you have any idea how hard it was when we were teenagers and you used to do this? Fuck, Parker. The other night wasn't the only time I've come in my pants from your touch."

"You're lying." She laughs as she comes to stand at my head.

Her bare, toned legs appear before me, and I can't stop myself from reaching out and running my palms up her thighs.

"I'm trying to focus."

"And I'm enjoying the experience," I shoot back.

I relax into it, loving having her hands on me.

We're both so distracted by each other's bodies that we don't hear someone entering the apartment.

Nor do we hear footsteps moving closer.

But we both jump apart the second a deep voice booms through the room.

"What the fuck are you two doing?"

Turning to my side, I find my gigantic best friend filling my doorway with a murderous expression on his face.

His eyes move between mine and his little sister behind me.

"I asked you two a question."

68

PARKER

y heart races, my hands tremble, and dread like I've never felt before in my life sits heavy in my stomach as my big brother stands in the doorway to Linc's home gym with his hands on his hips and a terrifying expression on his face.

Grown-ass men are scared of my big brother, and despite knowing him better than almost anyone, right now, I'm totally intimidated too.

Because you've been lying to him.

I banish that unhelpful thought and try to remember what question he just bellowed at us.

Linc shifts in front of me so he's sitting on the table, but he also doesn't say anything.

Is he waiting for me?

In the end, it's Rett who speaks first.

"So I guess this explains why Mom told me to warn you that I was coming first." He steps forward with his fists curled at his sides, and I panic.

I cannot bear to watch him wail on Linc.

We've done nothing wrong, not really.

Okay, yeah. We should have told him that we were living

together. And we probably should have mentioned that things had progressed beyond that.

But also...he shouldn't have just let himself into Linc's apartment unannounced.

Linc could have been doing anything up here...

A shudder rips through me as I think about all the things he could have been doing.

I force that thought away. It's not helpful, right?

I believed everything he said to me earlier about wanting this for years, about being serious about a future together. Hell, he called me his girlfriend.

Lincoln Storm's girlfriend.

It's a title I could only ever dream of. And now it's mine.

My heart flutters wildly.

I am his, and he is mine.

I dart around the front of the table, getting between the two of them before Rett loses his shit.

He's always had a short fuse, but thankfully, most of the time, I'm able to defuse the situation; hopefully, now is one of those times.

"I was just working out Linc's shoulder. He took a hard hit the other night and—"

"The fuck are you wearing?" Rett balks, staring at Linc's old college T-shirt.

"Uh..." I hesitate. I don't have any answer that's going to make any of this better. I only have the truth, and I'm not willing to go there yet. Not until I can talk Rett down from the edge.

Rett's eyes shift from mine to the man on the table behind me. "You're the colleague," he accuses. "You're the one who took her in." Silence. "Fucking hell," Rett barks, his fingers twisting in his hair and pulling until it looks like it hurts. "You fucking asshole."

"Rett, no," I scream as he surges forward.

Linc gently moves me to the side as he stands to full height, ready for my brother's assault.

"What would you rather I did? Drop her at a hotel? That's what she wanted. We'd just found her apartment going up in flames, and she wanted me to take her to a hotel and leave her alone. It was New Year's Eve, for fuck's sake. I'd never do that. I have no doubt you'd have had something to say about it if I did."

A deep growl rumbles in Rett's throat as he snarls at Linc.

I've seen the two of them go at it more times than I can count over the years. But it never had anything to do with me. They were always fighting over some other girl or some boy bullshit I didn't understand.

I refuse to let them hurt each other because of me.

I love them both too much for that.

"Please," I cry, attempting to get between them again.

Linc's arm darts out, stopping me before he wraps his fingers around my wrist and drags me behind him.

"Stop it," I complain, attempting to free my arm, but it's pointless.

"What were the last words you said to me before you left for Seattle?" Linc demands, standing toe to toe with Rett and glaring right into his eyes.

"You motherfucker," Rett mutters under his breath.

"What were they, Rett? Parker wasn't there; she doesn't know."

"Will you two just stop?"

His nostrils flare as he inhales a deep breath, and his jaw tics in irritation.

"I told you to look after my little sister," Rett confesses.

"And what do you think I'm doing, asshole?"

Their words are like a bat to the chest, and I stumble back. Thankfully, Linc lets me go.

He only did all of this because of a promise to Rett?

I shake my head.

That can't be right.

He wanted me here. Not because of some fucked-up

promise to protect me like I'm some helpless little woman, but because he wanted me here.

Didn't he?

"You'd do the same for Nova," Linc adds.

"Yeah, and you wouldn't expect to find us half-dressed with her hands all over me."

"Perk of living with an athletic trainer," Linc says, popping one shoulder as if I'm not standing a foot away, losing my goddamn mind. "Look, I'm just giving her a place to stay. She's been looking at other places, but they're all expensive as fuck and complete shitholes. And as you well know, we're hardly ever at home."

I feel like I'm floating above my own body, listening to them talk about me as if I'm not even here.

Linc and I haven't talked about me getting my own place since things changed between us. At no point did I assume I'd just stay here. He might have called me his girlfriend, but I'm not running before I can walk here. There is a big difference between embarking on a relationship and living together.

Is there, though? a little voice asks.

You've been living together for weeks. Why not just...keep going?

A growl rips through the room, and it's not until they both turn and stare at me that I realize it came from me.

"You two are unbelievable," I shout, anger bubbling up inside me faster than I can control. "I'm standing right here, you know. I'm not some pathetic little girl you don't want to hang out with anymore. I'm a fully grown woman with a career and a life.

"I'm so fucking sick of men thinking they're better than me, that they can make decisions for me, and that I'll just follow along like a good little girl."

They both stare at me with open mouths.

"Yes, Linc took me in when I had nowhere else to go. And yes, I've been living here ever since. We should have told you, but as Linc just said, as soon as I can find another place to live, I'll be gone. You never needed to know.

"Excuse me," I bark before darting forward and out of the room as fast as my legs will carry me.

"Parker?" Linc calls.

My heart aches as I ignore his plea and rush into my room. The loud bang as the door slams startles me, but for once, I don't stop to open it again. Right now, I'll happily hide behind a closed door, away from their macho bullshit.

Fearing they'll hear me, I race into my bathroom, also closing that door, before I allow my sob to rip free.

I'm angry. I'm frustrated. I'm hurt. And it all collides into loud sobs and ugly tears.

I hate it. I wish I was the kind of woman who could punch a wall and move on. But no, I get the girly tears.

Men will never take you seriously in their world if you break down and cry when things get hard.

The minutes stretch on, but I don't hear anything from Linc or Rett. For all I know, they're punching each other's lights out in the gym right now.

Fear rips through me, and the need to go out and check on them is almost too much to bear. But in the end, I focus on myself. I might have screamed at them that I'm an adult who can look after herself, but so are they.

If they need to fight this out, then who am I to stop them?

I need to talk to someone, though, so I drag myself from my bathroom floor and trudge through to my bedroom. After finding my cell at the bottom of my purse, I take myself back to the bathroom, close and lock the door, and then find my best friend's contact.

"Heloha," Casey says softly.

I try to fight it, but the second her voice hits my ear, I shatter.

"Parker? What's wrong?"

"I don't...Rett...Fuck. Linc and I—"

"Okay, you need to take a breath. Do you need me to come get you?"

"No. NO. No, don't do that. I'm hiding in my bathroom."

"Okay. Did you want to tell me why?"

I take a few calming breaths while I try to gather my thoughts.

"Linc and I...we're—"

"Fucking?" Casey finishes for me.

"Umm...well, that specific act hasn't actually happened yet, but—"

"You're hooking up?" she asks hopefully.

"Do you have to sound so excited about this?" I complain.

"Parker, I love you, you know this, but Linc has been in love with you forever. You're just too blind to see it."

"And you never thought to mention this before?"

"You wouldn't have believed me. You've always been too dead set on hating him to see anything else."

"Hmm."

"What does that mean?"

Guilt knots up my insides.

I have only ever kept one secret from Casey. And it's been eating at me for six years.

"Linc and I slept together on prom night," I say so fast, the words all blur into one.

Silence follows my confession.

"I'm sorry, that sounded like my best friend just told me that she slept with Linc on our prom night."

"Yeah, that...happened."

"What? When? How?"

"After I caught Seth cheating, I...uh...called Linc to come and get me. I didn't want to go home and deal with questions from Mom, so he took me back to his place. One thing led to another and...well, yeah."

"You gave Lincoln Storm your V card, and I'm only just finding out about this now?"

"I'm so sorry, Casey. I never meant to keep it a secret, but I knew if I so much as mentioned it, it would feel real and…I walked away. I promised myself that I'd put it, and him, behind me. I'd had a crush on him for so long, and I knew it wouldn't last. He was Lincoln Storm, you know?"

"Parker," she whispers. "You don't need to apologize to me. You're allowed secrets, especially if they're to protect your heart."

I sniffle as I fight to keep my tears at bay.

"We'll circle back to all of that in a bit, because you can bet your ass I have a million and one questions, but…what's happened tonight?"

I give Casey a rundown of recent events, and she listens to every word, giving me her undivided attention despite the fact she has her own man who I'm sure would like a little bit of it.

We're on the phone for almost an hour before I finally let her go, promising that we'll catch up tomorrow to continue dissecting the situation.

My ass has long gone dead from sitting on the hard, tiled floor when I finally get back to my feet.

After brushing my teeth, I crawl into bed, pull the sheets up to my neck, and stare up at the ceiling.

Now I'm in the bedroom, I can hear the deep rumbling from Linc and Rett's voices, and despite wanting to be strong, I end up crying myself to sleep.

Because tonight for the first time in a long time, I'm going to have to sleep alone, and I really don't like it.

69

LINCOLN

"Don't," I bark the second Rett looks like he's going to follow Parker.

Pain rips through my chest as I think about what I just said.

I didn't mean any of it.

I don't want her looking for another apartment and moving out. I just said what I had to say in the moment.

The only place Parker belongs is right here with me.

It doesn't escape my attention that I probably should have said just that.

Fuck the consequences. We should have been honest.

"The fuck?" Rett snaps back. "She's my fucking sister."

"And she's my..." Girlfriend. "Roommate. Just give her some time to calm down."

"Since when did you become her keeper?"

"I'm not. I just know she needs a moment." His eyes narrow as he studies me, hopefully thinking about the times when we were younger, when she lost her shit and needed to vanish. If I got the chance, I'd go after her. But it wasn't always possible. If I could go now, I'd be there in a heartbeat.

You only promised not to hurt her a few hours ago, and now look...

I shake that thought from my head.

We agreed to keep this between us for now. When we're ready, we'll tell the world...Rett...but that time isn't now. Especially the night before a game. The team needs me not to be lying in a hospital bed because Everett Donnelly put me there before we even stepped foot on the ice.

Rett's shoulders bunch around his ears as he looks back toward my guest bedroom with concern etched into his expression.

He cares a lot about Parker. He never intends to hurt her, and he also doesn't mean to make it worse once he has, but he has this way of riling her up. He always says the wrong thing, and the whole situation spirals. He's better out here.

"So, what the fuck are you doing here already?" I ask, pulling two bottles of water from the fridge and passing him one as I make my way to the couch.

It fucking kills me to do it, but what other choice do I have?

"I took an early flight."

"Your coach approved that?"

"Well, obviously, or I wouldn't be here," he snarks.

I shake my head, muttering, "Asshole."

"Honestly," he says, his voice taking on a more serious edge, "they were glad to be rid of me for the night."

I frown, not liking a single word that just fell from his lips.

"I think Coach is hoping that a night with my family might help."

"Help how?" I ask, concern for my best friend growing.

Sure, we've slipped further and further apart in the time he's been up in Seattle, but we still talk regularly.

"You haven't been online much then?"

"Uh..." Honestly, between work and Parker, there hasn't been much time for anything else. Plus, I know that the media is full of bullshit fake news, and the less I read it the better. "No. Why? What have you done?"

He shrugs. "Just...you know, being me."

I groan because I do know him.

When things aren't going his way, or life is a bit dull for whatever reason, he always goes out and finds the excitement —much to the delight of the media, and the dismay of the PR Director over in the Bandits' front office.

"The season is going to shit. We don't stand a chance of making the playoffs and…I'm fucking over it, you know. Losing is not the same buzz as winning."

"Rett," I groan, dragging my hand down my face and rubbing my jaw. "You gotta learn to take the rough with the smooth, man."

"Don't. You sound like my therapist."

"Maybe that's because I'm right?" I point out. "You need to get your ass in line and focus on your job."

"You think I don't know that?"

I stare at my best friend. Together, we might be a bit of a nightmare, but it's not a secret that he's the worst. Maybe if it weren't for him and his wild ways, I would have been brave enough to fight for Parker all those years ago.

Rett's always had stars in his eyes despite having Clark in the background, trying to keep him tethered to the ground.

He lives for the fame, the girls, the parties.

He also lives for the drama.

I swear, if there aren't at least five stories about him circling online, he gets the jitters that he's going to be forgotten.

Fuck knows where it all comes from. He grew up in one of the most stable homes I know—if you ignore Clark travelling for work. His parents are solid. They've given him everything he could possibly want. He's got the career of his dreams, but for some reason, it's just not enough.

"You know they'll trade you if you do too much damage," I point out.

I'm pretty sure the words are unnecessary, but I say them regardless. He needs to hear them. Maybe they'll hit differently coming from my mouth.

He just shrugs, making it look like he doesn't give a shit, which I know is far from the truth.

He loves Seattle, and he loves his team. He's worked too fucking hard there not to. But at the end of the day, it doesn't matter how valuable a player is on the ice if their behavior off it is hurting the franchise.

Conversation turns to tomorrow night's game before we dive into the Vipers' season so far and their chances for the cup this year. Despite Rett being a Bandit, the Vipers are his team. We were wearing green and white before we even knew what it meant.

He follows our season just as closely as he does his own.

He's never voiced it, but I know for a few seasons at least, he was bitter as fuck that I managed to find a place on the Vipers' roster and he didn't.

Maybe one day there will be a place for him. I know Coach respects him as a player. How could you not? He's one of the best defensemen in the league. He just comes with a lot of baggage and drama, and Coach isn't down for that. I should know; he's ripped me a new one a few times when I've got carried away on a night out in the past.

"I guess you're staying here tonight?" I ask when Rett begins yawning.

"That was my plan. Although I wasn't expecting you to already have a house guest."

"It's Parker," I say. "She's always been as welcome here as you."

He studies me, a small frown between his brows.

"I thought you hated each other."

A laugh tumbles free. "Rett, I've never hated your sister."

"Right. Well, good, because she's awesome."

I nod, terrified that if I open my mouth, I'll say too much and give myself away.

Before I risk doing any more damage, Parker and I need to come up with a game plan. And before we can do that, I really need to apologize.

"I guess I'll take your box room then," he mutters, getting to his feet.

"Oh, hardly," I scoff. There isn't a single room in this place that can be compared to a box. "See you in the morning."

"Yeah," he agrees as he walks off.

As he stops to pick up the small carry-on he abandoned in my hallway when he first arrived, he looks back over his shoulder. "Thank you for looking out for her. You were right earlier. I'd have fucking killed you if you didn't."

I smile in acceptance, knowing that he's probably going to kill me anyway.

Watching the seconds tick around on the clock, I wait.

And wait.

There is only one bedroom I want to spend tonight in, and I need to make sure Rett is staying put before I even attempt to slip into her room.

I shouldn't. I should be good and go to my own room.

But I can't.

Not only am I addicted to sleeping beside her, but I need to talk to her about earlier.

She looked utterly defeated as she marched from the room with her shoulders slumped and her head down.

I did that.

It fucking kills me.

With my patience withering, I push to my feet, abandon my empty bottle in the kitchen, and after making a stop in my bathroom, I silently slip into Parker's bedroom.

The fact that she's fully closed the door wrecks me. She's actively choosing to embrace her fear in order to put a physical wall up between us.

I guess I should be grateful there isn't a lock on the door because, if there was, I have no doubt she'd have used it.

The room is silent as I make my nightly journey around the bed.

It annoys me that she sleeps closest to the door. Not because it's my preferred side, but because there's a caveman inside me that wants to have that side so I can protect her. I'm not sure what from, but it feels right. Just one of many things I never used to consider before that are now a big part of my life.

Her breathing is shallow and even. I hate that she's fallen asleep with my words spinning around in her head.

Gently, I lift the sheets and slip under. It takes every ounce of my self-control not to groan loudly as the heat from her body hits mine.

"Linc," she mumbles as I wrap myself around her like I have done every night we've slept together.

I know she's asleep; she's too pliant, too relaxed.

The second the fog lifts and reality comes back, her entire body stiffens.

"What are you doing?" she hisses.

"Go back to sleep, pretty girl," I whisper.

She jerks in my hold, attempting to get away.

"You need to leave."

"Yeah, that's not happening."

"Linc," she argues, still trying to free herself. "I'm only here temporarily, remember? I'm moving out."

"Fuck that, babe. You're not going anywhere. I'm sorry," I say, rolling her onto her back so I can gaze down at her. "I didn't mean any of what I said. I was just...fuck. I was panicking. Rett was standing there, and I was rocking a semi. I didn't...fuck, Parker. I wasn't expecting to find him standing there, watching us. I didn't know what to do."

She falls silent for so long that if I didn't know better, I'd think she's fallen back to sleep. "Do you want to tell him?" she finally asks softly.

"Babe," I sigh, pressing my forehead to hers and staring into her eyes. "I want to tell the world, not just your brother. But I don't want to rush into it just because he's turned up. We do this our way, yeah?"

She nods, but even in the dark, I can sense that she's holding back.

"What is it, babe? You can tell me anything."

"I...uh...I've told Casey."

A laugh erupts.

"Why is that funny?" she asks, almost sounding offended.

"Because I assumed that she's known this whole time. You tell her everything."

She shakes her head. "I only told her tonight. I needed to talk to someone and...you were busy."

"You'd have chosen me over Casey?" I ask, my mind blown.

"Hearing you say all of that, making out like I wasn't important, hurt," she explains, ignoring my question. "I freaked out. I'm sorry."

"Hey," I say, cupping her jaw and kissing the tip of her nose. "You have nothing to apologize for. After the game tomorrow, we'll tell him. Just don't have too much to drink because you might need to drive me to the ER."

"He was angry earlier," she muses.

"Yeah, but I can handle Rett, babe. For you, I'll handle anything."

70

PARKER

Movement beside me wakes me up, and I open my eyes, already knowing what I'm going to find.

"Morning, pretty girl," Linc breathes, his voice still raspy from sleep.

Desire pools between my thighs as memories from last night flicker in my mind.

Rett's here.

I close my eyes again as I remember everything Linc said to me in the dark after he slipped into my bed.

The second I felt him, I knew it was stupid of me to assume he'd sleep in his own room. He's played incredibly well the last few games; I highly doubt he's going to risk messing that up by changing his routine again. Especially when he's going up against Rett. Neither of them is more competitive than when they're on the ice together.

"Hey," he says, reaching over and cupping my cheek. "Give me those beautiful eyes, babe."

I want to fight him and refuse his demands, but I can't.

My eyelids flutter open again, and I find his blue eyes gazing down at me.

"There she is," he muses.

"What time is it?" I ask.

"Early."

"You couldn't sleep?"

He shakes his head. "Can't stop thinking about last night. I'm sorry, Parker."

"It's okay. I won't lie—it hurt me at the time, hearing you talk about me like I wasn't important, but I get it. It's the way it had to be."

"I hate that he ruined our evening."

"Enjoying that new table, huh?" I tease.

"Like you wouldn't believe. Best purchase I ever made." The wide smile he gives me makes my stomach clench. "I just wish it had the happy ending I was hoping for."

I roll my eyes.

"You know you'd have been up for it," he teases. "How are you feeling today after your shift on the ice yesterday?"

I stretch my legs out, testing for aches and pain.

"Surprisingly okay."

"We're gonna need to do that more often, babe. Best foreplay I've ever experienced watching you handle a stick."

"Christ." I laugh as he snuggles closer.

"Sexiest thing ever, watching you out there with my teammates," he confesses, his lips brushing mine in the softest, sweetest kiss.

I moan as his tongue dances over my bottom lip. Without thought, I open for him. His tongue instantly pushes into my mouth, stroking mine.

I shift beneath him, needing to be closer still.

As our kiss continues, Linc's hand begins to roam.

Tingles follow his palm's journey across my body. My blood begins to heat, and my pulse picks up speed.

"Can't get enough of you, pretty girl," he muses against my lips as he pulls back slightly.

I whimper, unable to respond with words.

"Can I taste you?" he rasps.

Oh god.

My thighs clench, heat surging south at the thought of him down there, his tongue against my heated skin.

I nod, my teeth holding my bottom lip captive.

He lifts the covers and climbs fully on top of me.

His hips press against mine, forcing me into the mattress beneath me.

Resting on his knees with only his head visible from the sheets, he slides his hands up my side, pushing his shirt higher.

Ducking down, he kisses up my stomach, following the fabric as he exposes me.

By the time he gets to my breasts, my chest is heaving.

He groans as he licks up the underside of my needy breast and then sucks my hard nipple into his mouth.

I cry out as pleasure shoots through my body and straight to my clit.

Linc's hand shoots up and covers my mouth, cutting off any noise.

"You're going to need to be quiet, pretty girl."

My eyes widen as reality slams back into me.

"Rett?" I whisper the second Linc's hand slips away.

"In the guest room," Linc explains.

It's on the other side of the apartment. If he's sleeping, he won't hear a thing.

Linc switches sides and flicks my other nipple with his tongue. This time, I slap my own hand across my mouth to keep my moans in.

"Desperate for you, babe. I want you to come on my tongue. Can you be a good girl and do that for me?"

I nod frantically, widening my thighs in offering.

He chuckles as he kisses back down my stomach, disappearing beneath the sheets.

"Oh god, please," I whisper, desire coiling inside me.

"Fuck, you smell so fucking sweet," he groans, making my cheeks burn red hot.

Reaching down, I thread my fingers into his soft hair, gently pushing him toward where I really need him.

He doesn't say a word, but a push of air rushes over my heated skin.

"You're such a tease," I hiss when he kisses down one of my thighs.

"Want to make sure you're ready," he muses.

Lifting the sheets with my other hand, I look down, watching.

I can't see much, the room is still pretty dark, but what I can see is everything.

My body starts trembling as his lips close in on my core.

"Lincoln," I moan, my fingers tightening in my hair when he switches to my other thigh.

He chuckles, but I don't find it very fucking funny.

I'm desperate. He's teased me with a good time, and now I need it more than I need my next breath.

This time, when he gets to the sensitive skin between my thigh and my pussy, he doesn't stop.

Yes. Yes. Yes.

He licks me, entrance to clit, and I practically levitate off the bed.

Lying his forearm across my lower stomach, he pins me to the mattress before sucking on my clit.

Dropping the sheets, I cover my mouth with my hand again and cry out.

He teases me, learning what I like and what I don't as he builds me higher and higher.

In record time, I'm balancing right on the edge. But just before I fall, he pulls back, leaving me gasping for air and chasing my lost release.

"You're an asshole," I hiss.

"It'll be worth it," he shoots back before diving back in. Only this time, he slides two fingers inside me, and as he laves at my clit, he finds my G-spot.

My body trembles violently, and I'm pretty sure I pull his hair clean from his head as I hold him in place.

"Yes, yes, yes," I chant into my hand, my body like an inferno as my imminent release grows in intensity.

I lose sense of the noises I'm making, too lost in the pleasure that's about to explode.

And the second it does...fuck.

I swear the world shifts on its axis as lights flash behind my eyes and my body convulses as he works me through the orgasm.

I'm just coming back to Earth, swimming in an ocean of pure bliss, when everything changes.

My brain doesn't compute what happens; it's like it's in slow motion as the sheets are ripped from us, cool air rushing over my burning skin before Linc is dragged from the bed and thrown against the wall.

"You fucking asshole," Rett bellows before he pulls his arm back and slams his fist into Linc's face.

"Rett, no," I scream, scrambling from the bed as Rett pins Linc to the floor, his fist flying again.

I jump on my brother's back, wrapping an arm around his throat and holding tight. It's the only way I can think to stop him.

"Stop it. Please, just stop."

Rett's body vibrates with anger.

"Rett, please," I sob, my voice cracking as I picture what Linc might look like right now.

My brother is powerful; he can cause real damage with just one punch.

But Linc isn't exactly weak. He can hold his own.

As I cling to my brother, I realize that he isn't retaliating.

"Get off him, please," I beg.

"Fuck," Rett grunts after a few seconds, and thankfully, his shoulders relax.

As he climbs from Linc, I release my hold and slide down his back to the floor.

The air is thick with tension and unsaid words.

"Oh my god," I cry the second I see Linc on the floor with blood spilling from his nose and his eye already swelling.

"What the fuck, Rett?" I cry, grabbing a box of tissues from the vanity and dropping to my knees with a handful to try and clean him up.

"He was...you were...fuck. I fucking knew it," Rett bellows, his deep voice bouncing off the walls surrounding us. "How long? How long have you been fucking my sister behind my back, Storm?"

Linc takes the tissue and stumbles to his feet.

A million and one words dance on the tip of my tongue, but none of them break free.

"It's new," Linc confesses. "Although my feelings for her aren't."

Rett frowns, his fists clenching and unclenching at his sides. He's just waiting for a reason to go all over again.

"What?"

Linc shakes his head. "I've had feelings for her for years, Rett. You've just always been too blind to see it."

Linc's honesty floors me.

After last night, I guess I expected him to try and cover up the truth—if that's even possible, after being caught in the act.

Oh god. My big brother stormed in while his best friend was eating me out.

"No. You both hate each other," Rett argues, refusing to believe it.

Linc chuckles as if he hears a joke that no one else can.

"We tried hating each other," Linc explains. "But we never really have. She's the only girl I've ever truly wanted. No one else comes anywhere close to her."

Reaching out, Linc entwines our fingers together and tugs me into his side.

I go easily despite Rett's hard glare.

His brow is furrowed like he's trying to solve a math problem that doesn't make sense.

"And everything you said last night about her just staying here until she gets herself her own place?"

Linc shrugs his other shoulder. "It was true when she first moved in. Before we—"

"Started fucking."

"We haven't fucked," I blurt like an idiot.

Now Rett looks equally confused as he does disgusted.

"Don't lie to me, Parker. I know what I just saw. What I heard."

I stand a little taller. "I'm not denying that we were doing something. But we haven't fucked. Not yet."

"Why?" he asks before he realizes what he's asking and quickly backpedals. "Wait, no. Do not answer that."

"We're taking it slow," Linc explains, making Rett's brow shoot up as he glances at the bed beside us. "This isn't some hookup that we're going to walk away from and never think of again. It's...real. Serious."

"Fuck off. You want a serious relationship about as much as I do."

"With anyone else, yeah. But with Parker...I want everything with her. I always have."

"Why?"

"Because...because I'm in love with her."

71

PARKER

S ilence fills the bedroom as Linc's words echo in my ears.

Did he...did he really just say—

"You're in love with her?" Rett asks, his voice softer, calmer all of a sudden.

"Yeah," Linc agrees as easily as he would if Rett were asking if he wanted another beer.

"In love with her, like... you want to marry her and make babies with her?"

My heart slams against my ribs.

Things have moved so fast here that I haven't taken a moment to think about the future. I've been so focused on the now, of the possibility of losing my job, of being the laughingstock of the NHL, that where this could be leading has escaped my attention.

But marriage.

Babies.

That all sounds really freaking serious.

"Yeah, all of that and more. There isn't anyone else I want. There hasn't been anyone else I've ever wanted."

"But...it's Parker."

"Yeah," Linc says, holding me tighter and turning to kiss my forehead. "And she's perfect in every way."

My eyes burn as tears flood them.

"Fuck," Rett breathes, looking between the two of us with the same confused look on his face. "I...uh..." he mutters, combing his fingers through his hair. His knuckles are red and angry, but I can't find myself to care all that much. He shouldn't have been throwing them around in the first place.

Linc's face, however, is what I am concerned about. He needs ice, and I need to make sure his nose isn't broken.

"I need to get out of here. Promised Coach I'd be at the hotel when the rest of them arrived."

When neither of us says anything, he begins backing toward the door, his eyes still darting between us.

We let him go without saying another word. He closes the door behind himself, and the second it clicks, I exhale.

"Holy shit," Linc mutters, lifting the bloody tissues in his hand to wipe his nose before turning to face me. "Are you okay?"

"I...uh...I don't...you love me?" I ask, my brows pinching.

A wide, hopeful smile spreads across his swelling face.

"Yeah, babe. I do." He cups my face in his giant hands and closes the space between us until our noses brush. "I think I always have. I just...I didn't understand it before."

I try to swallow the huge lump that crawls up my throat, but it's pointless.

I blink up at him, trying to find some words to respond with, but I can't get any.

"It's okay," he soothes, sensing my anxiety levels rising. "I'm not expecting you to say it back. Maybe one day, but not yet."

I nod. It's all I'm capable of right now.

"Rett is right, though. I need to get moving as well."

He gives me the briefest of kisses before stepping away. The second I lick my lips, the coppery taste of blood hits me.

"No, wait," I cry, stopping him from going too far. "I need to check you over. Your nose. It could be—"

"It's not broken, babe," he says with the kind of confidence only a hockey player who's experienced his fair share of broken noses can.

"Then you need ice for your eye. You won't be able to play later if you can't see out of it."

He wants to fight it, but the longer he stares into my determined eyes, the more it drains from him.

"Okay, I can give you fifteen minutes to play doctor and nurse."

"This isn't some kinky roleplay," I chastise.

"Oh, what? So you don't have a slutty little nurse's uniform hidden in here somewhere?"

"Behave," I warn, as I move around the room. "Lie on the bed. I'll be back." I rush toward the door and pull it open. "And don't get blood on the sheets," I shoot over my shoulder before darting down the hallway.

It isn't until I get to the kitchen that I think of Rett. Nerves rattle through me that he's about to appear and tell me what he really thinks of what just played out in my bedroom.

Suddenly, I've hyper-aware of the fact I'm still not wearing any panties.

Not wanting to flash my brother should he appear, I bend over gingerly to pull an ice pack from Linc's freezer.

But as I make my way back to the bedroom, there's no sign of him. I can only assume he's already left.

Regret tugs at my insides. We should have been more considerate. We should have spoken to him before we did anything reckless.

But it's too late to think about all of that now.

Rett knows about it, and soon, the entire world will too.

I take a few calming breaths before I push my bedroom door open and step inside.

As ordered, Linc is lying in the middle of the bed with his

boxers resting low on his hips and the rest of his body on full display.

"See something you like?" he taunts, lifting his arms and tucking his hands behind his head, knowing that it makes his torso even more defined.

"You know, it wouldn't hurt you to pretend you're not God's gift to women every now and then," I tease as I crawl onto the bed beside him.

"I don't care about being a gift to women, Parker. Only you."

"On second thought, maybe it is a good thing you're hot with lines like that."

"You think I'm hot, pretty girl?"

"Meh, probably a seven out of ten on a good day."

He laughs at my blatant lie before he hisses as I press the ice pack to his eye.

"Rett isn't in a good place," he says, his tone much more serious.

"No, I saw that. He's always the same whenever his team is on a losing streak," I explain, remembering some of his worst moments as a teenager. "The Bandits will find their feet again, and he'll turn a corner."

"I hope so. It's been a while since he's been this bad."

My concern for my brother grows. There is only one person on this Earth who knows him as well as I do, and that's the man looking back at me. Both of us are too far away to really do anything, especially during the season. We can be there at the other end of a phone whenever he needs us, but when Rett is like this, he shuts himself off. Sometimes, he's impossible to reach unless we physically turn up and force him to talk.

"And here we are, making it worse," I mutter sadly.

"We can't stop living our lives because Rett is in a bad place," Linc says, taking my hand and lifting it to kiss my knuckles. "We knew he wouldn't like this. But we are not responsible for his reaction."

"I know," I sigh. "I just hate hurting him."

"Me too. And I must admit, him finding out while I've got my head between your thighs probably wasn't ideal."

"We should have told him last night."

"Well, he knows now. He's just going to have to figure out a way to deal with it because it's not changing anytime soon."

"I'm going to talk to HR today. Speak to Coach and Jarad and get everything in place."

Linc nods, aware that it needs to happen sooner rather than later. We have to be ahead of the gossip, and if Rett doesn't cool off before the game later, I fear the media might just put two and two together, and all hell will have broken loose by the morning.

ONCE LINC'S allocated fifteen minutes were up, he climbed off the bed and plodded to his room to get ready.

I did the same, and only thirty minutes later, we're descending through the building and toward his car.

My knee bounces the entire journey as my nerves about telling everyone what's been happening between us get the better of me.

Linc keeps telling me that it'll be fine, and a part of me believes him.

But what if it's not?

What if I'm effectively signing my resignation by confessing to being in a relationship with him?

This is my dream job. Everything I've worked so hard for.

But he's Lincoln Storm.

The only guy I've ever truly wanted.

If I had to make a choice...if I could only keep one...

Fuck.

I can't even think about it.

The second he pulls his car to a stop in his space beneath the arena, he kills the engine and turns to me.

"Do you want me to come with you?" he offers.

"No, you need to go and get dressed for practice," I say, holding my head high.

"Coach won't mind," Linc argues.

"I think we both know him well enough to know that he will. It's a game day, Linc. A big one, too. You need to be focused."

"I won't be while you're up there worrying."

"I'm fine. Everything is going to be fine."

He sighs. "Okay."

"I'll be rink side before you know it. And please, please try not to injure yourself any more than you already are," I beg.

"I'll see what I can do. Come here," he says, wrapping his hand around the back of my neck and dragging me over the center console to meet his lips.

He kisses me until I'm breathless and my concerns over how today is going to play out have lessened.

"I meant what I said earlier. I love you, Parker. And I have every confidence that all of this will work out."

I want to believe him, but until I hear the right words from the powers that be, I'm not sure I will.

Together, we climb out of the car, and side by side we walk into the arena. But instead of heading to the trainers' room, I continue to the elevators that'll take me to the front office.

By the time I walk into the HR office, I'm a wreck.

The young woman sitting behind the reception desk smiles at me, but it falters when she takes in my expression.

"Uh...hi...I was wondering if Esme was free?"

"Let me just see," she says before tapping on her computer.

Behind me, a set of heels click-clack down the hallway, and before the receptionist can respond, the woman I'm dreading to see appears beside me.

"Good morning, Parker. Is everything okay?"

"I...uh...I was wondering if you have a few moments?"

"Yes, of course. Come on in and take a seat."

"Ma'am, you have a meeting in ten minutes," the receptionist calls.

"I'm aware, thank you," Esme sings before closing the door behind us. "So, Parker, what can I do for you?"

I stare across the desk at Esme. She's perfectly put together, her brown hair pulled back in a sleek ponytail, her makeup flawless, and a soft, friendly smile playing on her lips.

She's the picture of perfection, and I'm sitting here feeling like I'm falling apart.

"I need...I need to tell you that I'm involved in a personal relationship with a player," I blurt.

She sits back in her chair, her smile growing wider.

My suspicions instantly rise.

Why isn't she more surprised?

Why isn't she asking me who it is?

Why isn't she shouting at me and telling me that I've abused my position and that I should be ashamed of myself?

"Parker," she says softly. "The organization is already aware of your relationship with Lincoln Storm. They have been since before you walked in here on your first day."

"I...I'm sorry?" I stutter, sitting forward as if that'll help me hear better.

Esme's smile continues to grow.

"The day that Lincoln came in here to tell me that you'd be moving in, he also ensured we were aware that the two of you weren't just friends."

"B-but...but we were," I argue. "Hell, I'm not sure we were even friends. He's driven me crazy for years. I went out of my way to annoy him just so he would leave me alone," I ramble.

"Well, it seems that Linc may have seen things a little differently. It's already noted in your file. Everyone who needs to know does, and everyone is happy, provided your relationship doesn't influence your judgment or ability to provide objective care."

I slump back in my chair again as if the wind has been knocked clean from my lungs.

"Everyone knows?"

"Everyone who needs to know, yes."

"And no one thought to tell me?"

Esme laughs. "Had we known that you weren't aware, we may have considered mentioning it."

"Wow, okay. So...what happens now?"

"Now, if you don't have anything else you need to discuss with me, then you get your butt back downstairs and do everything in your power to ensure our boys beat your brother tonight."

I have my fingers wrapped around the door handle ready to leave when I pause.

"Esme, before I leave, I'd like to make a formal complain about a member of staff."

72

LINCOLN

My thoughts are fully on Parker as I shove the locker room door open and step inside. My face might ache, but I'm more than used to living with aches and pains. And a black eye isn't anything out of the ordinary.

But the second the guys spot me, that all changes.

"Fucking hell," Killer announces. "I know Parker is strong, but damn, that's a mean right hook she's got on her."

"Ha, ha, you're funny," I state as I move closer to my stall, ready to get dressed for practice. "It wasn't Parker."

"But you went home after leaving us last night, didn't you?" Handsy asks, trying to piece it all together.

"Oh shit," Kodie gasps. "You've seen Rett already."

I drop to my stall and rest back with my face tipped up to the ceiling. Suddenly, my eye and nose ache more than they did when I first walked in here.

"Yeah," I groan. "I've seen Rett."

"I didn't think they were flying in until this morning," Killer says.

"Rett came alone to surprise us."

"How'd that work out for you?" Handsy asks with a smirk.

"Wonderful," I mutter.

"Is he going to be a problem for us tonight?" Fletch asks.

Kodie snorts. "When isn't Donnelly a problem for us?"

"Fair," Fletch muses. "But if he's pissed at Linc, tonight could be a bloodbath."

"Looks like it's already started," Monroe adds, clearly listening to our conversation.

"I can handle Rett," I state.

"So, does he look as bad as you right now?" Kodie asks, a knowing glint in his eyes.

"Uh..."

He shakes his head. "Oh yeah, you're going to handle it."

"I think I already caused enough damage," I mutter. "He was well within his rights to hit me. But he's done that now, so we can just focus on the game."

"Wow, I know you can be a lot of things, Storm, but I never had you down as delusional," Handsy muses.

"It's going to be fine. We all know how to handle Rett Donnelly. And if he's distracted by what this asshole has been doing to his sister, then all for the better. The Bandits are having their worst season for years. With their best D man on his own personal mission, we could secure an incredible W tonight."

"They've still got Westly and Petrov," Monroe points out.

"Maybe so. But do you know what they don't have?"

Monroe shakes his head. "All of us."

"Fuck yeah," Killer shouts. "And we're motherfucking winners."

Those who weren't involved in our conversation finally look over, and as his enthusiasm ripples through the room, they all join in chanting.

By the time we're all dressed and heading out of the locker room to warm up for morning practice, adrenaline pumps through my veins.

I might be in the wrong when it comes to Rett, but all my teammates see is an opportunity to increase our points and our position at the top of the division.

The second I step onto the ice, my eyes scan the space, looking for my girl. But she's not there.

Despite me telling her a million times that everything would be okay, I knew she didn't believe me.

A laugh tumbles from my lips as I think about what Esme will have said to her.

"You good, man?" Fletch asks, skating up next to me.

"Yeah," I say, a wide smile spreading across my lips. "I'm really fucking good."

His smile grows to match mine. "It's all worth it, isn't it, when you find the right one?" Just as he says the words, there's movement over his shoulder, and when I look up, there she is.

Fuck, she's so beautiful.

The second she notices my attention, she shakes her head, but there's a grin playing on her lips.

"Yeah," I muse, barely aware that Fletch is still standing there. "So fucking worth it."

I take off with my sights set on only one person.

Fuck, it's been that way for years; I just didn't know what it all meant.

It doesn't matter how long I've known her, how many years have passed. If she's in the same room, I always seek her out. If she's close, I always gravitate to her.

She's...she's my home. I just had no idea.

Having turned around to organize some paperwork, Parker startles when I crash against the board in front of her.

But the second she looks over her shoulder and I catch a close-up of her dazzling smile, it's like everything falls away.

We're not standing here in the arena surrounded by people; it's just the two of us.

"Hey, pretty girl," I shout, probably loud enough for people to hear, but I'm done caring.

She ducks her head, her smile turning coy.

"What did you do, Lincoln Storm?"

It's rhetorical. She knows exactly what I did all those weeks ago when I went to Esme.

Was I being presumptuous? Massively.

But was I also a hopeless fool with a teenage dream I was hoping might finally become a reality? Also yes.

But I figured, what was the harm?

If nothing happened, Esme would be discreet about it. And if it did? Well, I was already armed with everything I needed to ensure we both had long futures here with the Vipers.

Should I have told her before now to stop her worrying? Maybe. But it would have been too soon. She needed to be ready to take the next step herself. I knew she'd get there. Just like I know she'll tell me she loves me when she's ready. I know she does. I'm pretty sure, like me, she always has. I feel it in her touch, see it in her eyes.

"You're mine, Parker Donnelly. Nothing is going to get in the way of that."

I cringe as a whistle blows. "Storm, get your ass over here," Coach bellows.

Parker laughs, and it's like music to my ears. "Go," she encourages, waving me off.

I blow her a kiss before pushing backward and skating toward where everyone else is waiting.

"Fucking hell," Coach groans when he sees the state of my face. "Anything I should be worried about?"

"Nah, Coach. I've got this all under control."

***

"HAVE YOU HEARD ANYTHING FROM HIM?" I ask Parker the second she joins me in the car later that afternoon.

"Nope," she says, popping the P. "And I didn't go looking for him, either. I figure he needs to focus. Me turning up during their practice time wouldn't have gone down well."

"Pfft, what does he have to focus on? He already knows he's losing tonight."

"Linc," Parker warns.

Reaching over, I take her hand in mine and twist our fingers together.

"I know, babe. I know. Rett's gonna figure this all out, you'll see."

"I hope so. I just hate knowing he's hurting."

"Same, but I refuse to put our happiness on the line because of it."

"I can't believe you told Esme we were together weeks ago."

I smirk as I take the next left, pressing my foot to the gas to get her home as fast as possible. "I was feeling optimistic."

"You're something else, you know that?"

"Well, when I want something…"

"What if this had never happened?" she muses.

"Then I guess I'd have had to admit defeat and get Esme to take it out of our files. But I wouldn't have given up without a fight. This might have been years in the making, pretty girl, but it was inevitable eventually."

"You really are sure of yourself."

"Sometimes, you've just got to back your chances with the things you want most in life. And Parker, you've always been at the very top of my list."

"I thought that was hockey," she counters.

"It takes a solid second place, but it will never, ever come above you."

"So what happens next?"

"We beat the Bandits' asses, and then we celebrate the fuck out of it."

"What about after that? Esme said that I can still treat you as long as we keep it professional."

"What?" I ask.

"You didn't know that?"

"No. I mean, the fact that I was still assigned to you even after she knew gave me a clue, but she never said anything about it. So I don't have to go to Mitchell?"

"Apparently not. I mean, as long as you don't feel me up on the table."

I can't help but laugh. She has no idea how long I've had to hold myself back from doing just that over the years. "Me? What about you? You know you're going to be too distracted by my dick to focus on your job."

She scoffs. "As if. I doubt it's worth the hype."

My brows lift. "There's hype surrounding my dick?"

"Don't be obtuse, Linc. You know full well that there are a million and one stories out there spouting praise for it."

"I might be aware of such stories. I'm intrigued to know that you're aware, though. Have you been reading them?"

When I glance over, I find red staining her cheeks.

"Hell, no. I didn't want anything to do with your dick or the bunnies you were sticking it in."

"And what about now?"

"Fuck the bunnies." I can't help but snort at the disgust in her tone.

"Jealous, babe?"

"No," she mutters. It's cute as hell because she's lying through her teeth.

"Good. You have no reason to be. I'm over every single other woman on the planet, bunny or not. You're the only one I see, and you're the only one who's going to benefit from my magical dick."

"I never said it was magical."

"It's been six years; you've probably forgotten." She laughs. "But don't worry, babe. I have every intention of reminding you very, very soon."

"How soon?" she asks quickly.

"Oh, babe. Are you feeling a little desperate?" I tease, releasing her hand and sliding my palm up her thigh. My pinkie finger grazes over the fabric covering her pussy.

"No," she states. "Just wanted to know for planning purposes."

"Sure you do," I muse as I pull into our underground

parking garage. The second I kill the engine, I turn to her. "I love taking this slow with you, Parker. I love learning all the things I didn't know about you. But don't mistake my speed for lack of wanting." Tugging her hand over the center console, I press it against my hard dick. "You're all I can think about."

She gasps, her fingers curling around my length.

"I want everything to be perfect. I want to be worthy of you and give you everything you deserve."

"It is, you are, and you already do," she says, her eyes glassy with tears.

"Do you trust me?"

She nods, and I swear my chest expands to double its previous size.

"Good, now are you going to help me nap before our game tonight?"

"Nap?" she asks in surprise. "That isn't where I thought that was leading."

"We only have a couple of hours. When the time comes, we're going to need so much more than that."

"Whoa, that's a big promise."

"You know I'm good for it," I say as I kill the engine and climb out. "Come on, babe. We've got a game to prepare for."

"I'm scared," Parker admits as we walk into the elevator.

"I know. I'm worried about him too. But he will figure this out. I have faith."

"As much as you had in us when I first moved in?"

"Almost," I agree, leaning over to kiss her forehead. "This is still Rett Donnelly we're talking about. He's a wild card."

"And what am I?" she counters, gazing up at me with her large, golden eyes.

"Mine. All fucking mine."

73

PARKER

"What the fuck," I scream, making Jarad, who's standing beside me, jump as we all watch Rett slam Linc into the boards.

Multiple times today, I've opened my conversation with my brother and typed out a message. I haven't sent a single one, though.

In the hours before a game, hockey is Rett's only focus.

He's probably already pissed that Linc and I fucked up his morning.

But maybe I was wrong. Maybe I should have sent one of those messages. Hell, maybe I should have gone and sought him out so we could talk.

It's been like this since the very first puck drop. Rett has already been in the penalty box twice, but still, he isn't letting up. And it's not just Linc he has his sights on, either.

The Vipers are currently winning three to zero, and the Bandits are losing control, although no one seems to have lost their grip quite like Rett.

Linc's words earlier about my brother figuring shit out seem so far from the truth right now that they're laughable.

The Vipers' fans go wild when a penalty isn't called, and play resumes once Linc has righted himself.

At the other end of the bench, Coach Watson—Casey's dad—glances back at me with concern etched on his face.

I wince, unable to do anything to rein my brother in but wishing I could.

As the seconds count down to the end of the second period, we all watch with bated breath as Monroe steals the puck from Westly and quickly shoots it to Linc, who takes off down the left side of the ice with his eyes set on the goal.

We might be up by three, and he may have had two assists, but he's yet to find the back of the net, and I know he's desperate for it.

Behind him, Rett is like a machine as he closes in. His face is set with a determination that makes my stomach twist up tight.

Rett, no. Please. Please don't do this, I silently beg.

I stop breathing as Linc pulls his stick back and prepares to shoot, but he never gets to make contact because Rett collides with him, sending him flying backward.

I swear to God, the entire arena gasps as Linc hits the ice.

"Oh my god," I whimper, my eyes locked on Linc's unmoving body.

Play stops as the referee speeds toward Rett. I'm vaguely aware of him finally being ejected from the game, but I don't pay him any mind as he sulks off. My focus is on Linc.

Dr. Phillips, our lead physician, races toward him, but with the crowd of players surrounding Linc, it's hard to see what's actually happening.

There's movement beside me before a heavy arm wraps around my shoulders. I know from the stench that it's a player, and when I glance over, I find Killer with his eyes also locked on the ice.

"He'll be okay. He won't let Donnelly take him down. He's got too much to fight for."

A sob erupts, and I just about manage to catch it.

I swear, time seems to stop, but in reality, it's probably only a minute or two before Linc sits up, and the second he does, his eyes find mine.

"I'm okay," he mouths.

"He's okay," I breathe, tears burning red hot.

You're at work. Do not cry.

Do. Not. Cry.

You are a professional, and right now, Linc is just an athlete.

"See," Killer says, giving me a squeeze as Fletch and Kodie help him to his feet.

My breathing is labored as they slowly make their way over.

"Excuse me," I blurt before ducking under Killer's arm and racing ahead of them. I need to be there when he gets him on a bed to be checked over.

There is a small team of people in the room watching the game on a TV screen, and the second I race inside, they all jump into action.

"Oh," Nathan Cromwell, our head PT, says when his eyes land on me, not a broken hockey player.

"Sorry, they're just coming."

He frowns as he takes me in. I can only imagine what I look like right now.

Thankfully, there's a commotion behind me and when I spin around, there he is.

"You can let go of me now," he complains, attempting to shake off his minders.

"You can barely hold your own weight. Now isn't the time for showing off for your girl, Storm," Fletch chastises.

Eyes burn into me, but I don't look away from Linc. I can't.

Only a few seconds later, they have him sitting on the edge of the table.

Dr. Phillips follows, and both the guys step back to allow him to look over Linc.

"I'm fine," he spits.

"Let me be the judge of that," Dr. Phillips mutters, more than used to treating hard-headed players who'd rather play until they die than admit defeat.

"The hit just winded me a bit. Nothing's broken or dislocated. I'm good to go next period."

"Linc," I cry. "You can't go back out there."

"Why not? Rett's just been ejected."

Concern for my brother ripples through me as Linc begins to strip his uniform off so Dr. Phillips can check him over, much to his displeasure.

My breath catches at the bruises that are already darkening his skin from the repeated hits tonight.

Battle wounds are common. I'm not sure I've ever seen Linc's body without some kind of cut or bruise somewhere, but this is beyond anything I've seen before, and it's only just happened. Tomorrow he's going to be black and blue.

"I'm going back out there. The game isn't over. We haven't won yet."

"Storm," Fletch starts, but all it takes is a scathing look from his winger to stop him from saying anything else.

"Come on, man. Let's leave them to it," Kodie says before turning and leading Fletch away.

I stand there, silently watching, achingly aware that I should be in the trainers' room doing my job as well. The guys need me. But Linc—

"You're right. Nothing seems to be broken," Dr. Phillips confirms as he steps back.

Linc smirks at him, and I roll my eyes just in time for him to look my way and catch the reaction.

"Babe, you need to go. The guys need you."

My mouth opens and closes to argue.

"I'm okay. I promise."

With Esme's words from this morning ringing in my ears, I give him a quick smile before running from the room and into the one I should be in.

"About time," Mitchell snarks as I step up to where Monroe is waiting for me. I ignore him and get to work.

"Is he okay?" Hayden asks quietly.

"Yeah. I'm pretty sure his ego is hurt worse than anything."

Hayden laughs as I set to work on his shoulder.

"Rett's pissed, huh?" he muses.

"Yeah," I agree.

"He'll get used to it. I remember the first time my sister went out on a date. I wanted to flatten the guy just for looking at her."

I can't help but laugh. Hayden Monroe might be a D man, but he's not like the others. He's certainly not like Rett. He's not as violent or hot-headed. He's gentler, more thoughtful. A real golden retriever, and he only gets sweeter when he talks about his sister. He may have only told me a little about her, but every time he even mentions her name, he lights up.

"What?" he asks with a frown.

"You're cute."

"You'd better not let Linc hear you say that."

"Too late, asshole," a deep voice growls from behind me.

Shaking my head, I look back over my shoulder.

"Shouldn't you be resting?"

"I told you, I'm fine. Just needed to catch my breath. My groin is tight as fuck, though. Could do with a bit of work before the third period."

Hayden snorts a laugh.

I glance around the room. "It looks like Jarad is just finishing up," I point out.

"Fuck that. I want you or nothing. Now, are you going to let me go back out there like this or what?'

"I don't think you should be going out there, full stop, but what do I know?"

Linc stands there while I finish up with Monroe, and the second my table is free, he's on it.

"You're a pain in my ass, Lincoln Storm," I mutter as I get to work.

"Maybe so, but you wouldn't have it any other way."

No, apparently, I wouldn't.

THANKFULLY, the final period is less dramatic than the first two, but there is still plenty of action. Much to the Vipers' dismay, both Westly and Petrov score, but it's not enough, and we take the W three to two.

Linc plays his shifts, but he's nowhere near as fast as he was at the beginning of the game. He might like to pretend that he's okay after taking those hits, but I can see the truth. He's struggling.

As our players lap up the praise from the fans filling the stadium, Linc breaks away from the group with one destination in mind.

Me.

My heart jumps into my throat as he closes the distance between us. His eye is swollen and purple, but he's still hot as hell.

"What are you doing?" I ask, panicked as he stops just before stepping off the ice and gestures for me to come closer.

"What I should have done a long time ago. Made sure the world knows that you're mine."

"Linc, no—you can't." But despite my protests, he grabs me the second I'm in reaching distance and crashes his lips to mine in front of the entire arena.

Instantly, the tension drains from my body. The only thing I can think about is him.

Us.

It's not until he pulls back that the cheers and hollers around us finally filter through my ears.

"What about keeping it quiet for a bit?" I ask, staring up at him in surprise.

"I'm fed up with hiding how I feel about you, pretty girl. It's been too fucking long."

My heart clenches at his words.

"Storm," Coach barks from behind me. "For that little stunt, you're on post-game press. Hell knows the world has questions about tonight."

"I'm pretty sure I just answered them all, Coach."

"You kids are gonna give me gray hair."

"It's already gray," I point out with a laugh.

He mutters something under his breath before demanding that Linc get changed and fast before stalking off.

"Love making Coach proud." Linc laughs.

"He loves it really. You're all like his adopted kids."

"You too," Linc says with a smile. "He's been on our side this whole time, you know that, right? Apparently, you're a good influence on me."

"Maybe that's what Rett needs. A good influence."

"Not sure he'd know one if it hit him in the face," Linc jokes. "Have you spoken to him?"

"No, not yet. I'll go and find him after I'm finished up with the guys."

"He'll be okay."

"You keep saying that, but things seem to be getting worse. He's going to be savage about being ejected."

"That's on him. Not us. He didn't need to come out all guns blazing tonight. He took his shot this morning; it should have all been done by the time he left our apartment."

"Our apartment?" I question, choosing to ignore the rest. He's right, but it doesn't make any of it any better.

"Yeah, if you want it to be. I know you only moved in temporarily, but I don't want you to leave."

The thought of packing up my stuff and starting over somewhere else really doesn't sit right with me. I'd do it if he wanted me to. But I can't say it's what I want.

"I know it appears like we're moving fast, but really, we're going slow as fuck. I've been waiting for this since I was a teenager. I can't wait any longer."

My heart pounds and three little words dance on the tip of my tongue, but I swallow them down.

Not yet.

Not here.

But soon.

Really freaking soon.

PARKER

I stand at the back of the press room with butterflies rioting in my stomach. Fletch, Coach and then Linc file into the room and take their places.

I've only attended these events a handful of times in the past, and they've almost always been for Dad back in the day. I've certainly never attended one where I'm almost certain that at least half of the questions about tonight are going to be about me.

I almost didn't come. The temptation to distract myself by tidying the closet of messy athletic tape and other equipment in the trainers' storage room was almost too much to deny. That or heading up to the friends and family box, where my parents and Casey are waiting.

My stomach twists again at the thought of my parents. I'm pretty sure they figured out what was going on between us when we met them for dinner the other night. They were at least suspicious enough to warn Rett that he should have called first.

Coach welcomes everyone before opening up the floor for questions.

"Congratulations on your win tonight," the first reporter says. "It was an exciting game to watch, and of course, we all loved your celebration at the end, Lincoln. It seems that congratulations are in order all around." Linc nods as bile rushes up my throat. I love being a part of this world, but the thought of being at the center of any of it makes me want to run and hide.

The moment I allowed this thing between us to develop, I knew I was opening myself up to this.

"Is this new relationship between you and Parker Donnelly the reason for Rett's rough play tonight and his eventual ejection from the game?"

A ripple of silence goes around the room as everyone waits with bated breath for what comes next.

"Yes, Parker and I are in a relationship. Thank you for your well wishes. I can't talk for Rett, however. His game tonight was his own. As for our game, we knew it was going to be a close one, and we pulled together really well as a team, leaned on our strengths, and brought home the W." I watch Linc with awe and pride as he so easily swerves the conversation away from both me and Rett. I know he's had media training, but even still, watching him up there doing this blows my mind.

"I think the entire country gasped as you hit the ice earlier," another reporter starts. "How are you feeling after that hit?"

"Well enough to go back out there and secure our win. It took the wind out of my sails for a moment, but it'll take more than that to stop me."

"You and Rett have played together for years. Have you always been close with Parker?"

"Parker and I have always been great friends. I'm honored that she's finally given me a chance to be more. We're both very happy and ask for privacy as she navigates this new chapter of our lives together." His eyes find mine through the crowd, and his smile grows until it meets his eyes.

The heat of numerous people's attention burns into my skin, but as much as I might want to hide from it, I can't look away from him. He's lured me in and is refusing to let me go.

"Does anyone have any questions about tonight's game?" Coach asks.

Laughter rumbles around the room before someone directs a question at Fletch.

Hoping that my involvement in his press conference is over, I nod at Linc, letting him know that I'll see him soon, and duck out of the room.

I can't keep the smile off my face as I make my way to the friends and family suite.

Linc just announced our relationship to the world, and while I might be fucking terrified, I'm also incredibly happy. All the things I dreamed about as a teenager are coming true. It's almost too good to believe.

The excited chat and laughter hit my ears long before I get to the door to the suite. The second I step inside, I hear an excited squeal before a blur of green and white runs at me and wraps me in a hug.

"I'm so fucking excited for you," Casey cries in my ear.

"Thanks," I muse, squeezing her back.

When she pulls away and looks at me, she's got tears filling her eyes.

"I can't believe it. After all this time, you two have finally figured it out."

I frown. "What do you mean?"

"Oh, come on, I never believed the 'we hate each other' thing. I always knew it was a cover."

"Hell no. For a while there, I really did hate him."

Casey shakes her head. "Sure, whatever you say. Come on, everyone is waiting."

She takes my hand and leads me toward where my parents, Freya, her dad, and Sutton and Kodie's mom are waiting.

"You really know how to end a game, huh?" Freya teases me before also giving me a hug.

"Can't say it was planned. I thought we were keeping it under wraps for a while longer."

"What was the point?" Mom asks, beaming from ear to ear. "As soon as anyone sees the way that man looks at you, they'd know."

"Mom," I warn, blushing furiously.

"What?" She laughs. "The second you walked up to the table the other night, we knew. And I won't lie; we've been waiting a long time for it."

I sigh. "And you couldn't have stopped Rett from barging in?"

"Baby, you know as well as I do that we can't stop your brother from doing anything."

"How is Linc?" Dad asks. "Rett didn't go easy on him tonight."

"He says he's okay, but—"

"He's lying." Dad laughs as he fondly remembers old times.

"Yeah. Tomorrow his going to hit him hard."

"Speaking of tomorrow," Casey pipes up. "We're going for mani-pedis after work."

"Mom too?" I ask when she glances over at her.

"Of course, I'm not missing out on girl time."

"Me neither," Kodie's mom adds with a wink.

Why do I get the feeling that I'm going to get grilled all afternoon?

As we stand there chatting, players begin arriving, and the volume in the room only increases.

The second Kodie appears, Casey takes off, practically running across the room to jump into his arms, Sutton right behind her.

I watch with a smile as he lifts Sutton, propping her on his hip and kissing the top of her head before he turns and does the same to Casey.

"He looks good on her," Mom muses.

"They both do," I agree. "I've never seen Casey so happy."

"Or Kodie," his mom pipes up. "I'm so glad they found each other."

Sutton is deep into her game analysis when the three of them come over.

"That referee, though, Daddy. What was he thinking?"

Everyone chuckles at the disgust in her tone.

"I know, Peanut. He should have called it," Kodie agrees before greeting everyone.

The rest of the team, and a few of the Bandits, filter into the room, but we continue to wait for Linc, Coach, and to see if Rett is going to show his face. I have no doubt he's about to get reamed by the Bandits' coach for his performance tonight. I wouldn't be surprised if he just slinks off back to their hotel to drown his sorrows. It certainly wouldn't be the first time he's bailed.

The moment Linc steps into the room, a few of the guys cheer.

My heart jumps into my throat as I watch him scan the room. The moment his eyes land on mine, everything around me falls away.

A smile curls at his lips, and he surges forward.

My temperature increases with every step he takes, and by the time he gets to me, I'm burning up.

"Missed you, pretty girl," he muses before wrapping his hand around the back of my neck and pulling me in to kiss me as if we're the only ones in the room. Hell, we might be. He's the only one I can see.

"Whoa, tone it down. Child in the room," Kodie teases as Linc kisses the tip of my nose, his eyes locked on mine.

"Oh, please," Sutton sasses. "As if you and Casey are any different."

Everyone laughs as Linc tucks me into his side and finally turns to greet the others.

"Great game, son," Dad says, shaking his hand. "How are you feeling?"

"We got the win. I'm feeling great."

Dad eyes him suspiciously but doesn't question him further.

"How was the press conference?" Kodie asks. "Anyone interested in the game, or just your love life?"

Linc laughs. "A few had hockey-related questions. Most just wanted to know about this one," he says, dropping a kiss on my head.

"Be prepared for there to be a lot of that. Might be wise to stay off socials for a bit," Kodie advises.

"We've got a meeting with Hailee tomorrow," Linc informs everyone.

"We do?"

"We do. Probably a day late, but whatever," Linc says with a shrug.

"Bet she loves us."

"Nah, this shit is what she lives for."

"Storm," Sutton warns the second he swears.

"Sorry, Lil Riv."

As the conversation around us continues, Linc doesn't so much as loosen his hold on me. It's something I could very easily get used to. But despite how relaxed I feel pinned up against his side, I can't forget about Rett.

My cell burns a hole in my pocket, but I know messaging him would be pointless. If he doesn't want to talk, then he won't.

I'm distracted in conversation with Mom, almost thirty minutes later, when Linc's grip on me tightens and his body tenses.

I don't need to look up to know who's just walked in, but I do regardless.

My breath catches when I find Rett standing in the doorway. He looks wrecked.

As he surveys the room, another man steps up behind him.

Coach Watson wraps his hand around Rett's shoulder and squeezes gently.

Finding us, Rett nods at Coach before stalking over.

Mom instantly pulls him in for a hug. His arms

immediately wrap around her as if he needs her embrace more than he needs air.

"Tough game tonight, son," Dad says softly.

I didn't think it was possible, but Rett's shoulders get even tighter. My fingers itch to reach out and give him some relief, but I doubt he'd welcome that right now.

"There's no need to sugarcoat it; I sucked tonight. I was too up in my own head. I wasn't a team player. I just...well, I fucked it all up."

"Everett Donnelly," Sutton chastises with her hand on her hips and a fierce look on her face.

"Shit. Fuck. I mean...I didn't—Jesus Christ," he says, dragging his hand down his face.

"Ignore her, she's just yanking your chain," Kodie says reassuringly.

"I'm sorry about tonight," Rett says as he stares at the floor, not making it clear who he's talking to. "And about last night, and this morning," he adds before lifting his head, his eyes locking on Linc's. "I was out of line. And I apologize."

Briefly, Rett looks over Linc's shoulder, and when I glance over, I find Coach Watson looking our way.

Suddenly, Rett reaches out, holding his hand out for Linc.

The air crackles as he waits to see if Linc will accept his peace offering.

It takes a couple of seconds, but Linc's arm finally moves and his palm slides against Rett's.

"Really, I should be thanking you."

"Oh yeah?" Linc asks.

"Yeah. There isn't any other man out there that I trust with my little sister more than you." My breath catches at his words, and tears burn the backs of my eyes. "Just...don't break her heart, okay? I'd really hate to spend the rest of my days in prison because I had to bury your ass."

Linc swallows almost nervously as he nods at Rett.

"You have my word."

75

LINCOLN

I stand in the middle of a storage unit I've rented and take in everything we've done.

"She's going to lose her mind over all of this, you know that, right?" Rett states beside me.

His flight leaves in just over an hour, so he really needs to get moving, but he wanted to come and help with this. I think it's his way of apologizing for the past couple of days.

He may have accepted that Parker and I are a couple now, but he's still in a dark place.

"It's nothing," I muse, nerves already running rampant as I think about Parker's reaction.

"No, Linc. It's everything. She's going to love it. And hey, you never know, you might even get laid. Shit...no. Fuck. Forget I said that," he rambles as he combs his fingers through his hair. "Fuck."

I can't help but chuckle.

"I do really love her," I confess, the words tumbling out of me without instruction from my brain.

"Yeah," he muses, dragging his hand down his face. "I can see that. She loves you too."

"I hope so," I say with a shrug, which I pray looks less vulnerable than it feels.

I hate being out of control. All my life, I've known exactly what I've been doing. Playing in the NHL was the goal, and my sights were firmly set. But suddenly, everything is different. Sure, the game is still there, along with the strict schedule and traveling, but Parker is there too, and she changes the dynamic of everything.

For the first time in my life, I don't really know which way is up, and I fucking love it.

"What did Coach say to you last night?" I ask. The question has been nagging at me since the moment they appeared together in the friends and family suite.

James has always been somewhat of a mentor to all of us. Growing up, he was there for us with advice just as much as our fathers were.

Rett shrugs one shoulder. "Just some shit I really needed to hear."

"Care to elaborate?" I hedge.

"Just the usual stuff." As he says the words, I know he's lying. But I don't push for more. Rett will talk when he's ready and not a second sooner. We just have to be patient and hope he doesn't make us wait too long. The sooner he gets himself over this hump, the better.

"You should probably get going, or your coach will be ripping you a new one."

A self-deprecating laugh erupts from him. "What's new there?"

"Aw, he loves you really," I tease.

"Hmm," he mumbles as he gathers his stuff.

"You're going to turn it around before the end of the season," I tell him, trying to leave our time on a positive note.

"Maybe, but it's a bit late now. We have no chance at the playoffs from the bottom of the division."

He's right. But there's always next year.

"You guys are going to do it, though. It's about time the Vipers got the cup."

"Hell yeah, it is," I cheer, only able to imagine what it'll be like to live out that childhood dream. It's just a shame we won't do it together like we always talked about.

"Right, well. I'll...uh...see you soon, I guess."

"Yeah," I mumble, my mood instantly souring.

Rett stalks toward the roller door we've opened with his duffel swung over his shoulder.

I watch him go with a heavy heart. I hate that he's suffering and that there's nothing I can do about it.

He's about to walk out of the storage unit when I call for him.

He looks back, and his eyes widen when he sees me racing toward him.

"Wha—"

His question is cut off when I wrap my arms around him.

He tenses in my hold, but I don't let go.

"Love you, man," I say.

The last two days might have been some of the worst our friendship has seen, but how I feel about him will never change. One day soon, he might become my brother-in-law, but really, he's always been my brother.

After a few seconds, he relaxes, and his arms wrap around me.

"Love you too, bro," he says before we part.

His words have a lump of emotion crawling up my throat.

"I know you'll take good care of her, and not just because I'll kick your ass if you don't."

I scoff, but if the last two days have taught us anything, it's that I'll let him get his punches in if he deems them necessary.

"Thanks, man. I'll do everything in my power to make her happy."

I glance at my watch briefly. "Shit, you really need to go."

"Jesus," he mutters as he checks his cell and books a rideshare. "Talk to you later, man. Don't do anything I wouldn't do."

The second he's gone, the nerves really kick in.

"Fuck," I breathe.

Casey and Alison picked Parker up from work earlier and have taken her out to a spa I booked for some pampering. As far as I know, both of them have kept the secret and are going to be delivering Parker here in a few minutes.

I lower the roller door so she can't see in the second she arrives, before spinning on my heels and taking in the scene before me.

I really hope Rett is right and that she loves it.

Needing to keep busy, I tidy up again and shuffle a few things around, but before long, my cell buzzes with a message from Alison, letting me know that they're two minutes out.

"Jesus Christ," I breathe.

Get it together, Storm.

It's just Parker.

That's the thing, though. She's never been just Parker.

She's Parker.

She's...everything.

Standing by the door, I wait with my heart in my throat, and it only gets worse when the rumble of an approaching engine hits my ears.

Three car doors slam next, and then soft, female voices float in the air.

"What the hell are we doing here?" Parker asks, confusion thick in her voice.

"It's Kodie's," Casey lies. "He just wants me to pick something up."

The door rattles as someone grabs the handle, and my mouth waters. Shit, I'm going to vomit right here and ruin everything.

"We'll just be a minute," Casey explains. "After you..."

The second Parker steps inside, I stop breathing.

She gasps, her movements freezing the moment she sees me.

"Linc, what—"

"Okay, I'll see you guys later. Have fun," Casey calls as Parker continues to stare at me.

The door closes behind her, and silence falls.

Parker leans slightly, looking around me at everything.

"Linc, what have you done?"

"I promised you that I'd take care of everything," I explain.

"B-but...behind you. That's...that's my apartment."

"Yeah, babe. Well, some of it. Not everything could be salvaged."

She moves closer, her eyes darting between me and her things.

"But...how. It was trashed."

"I found a company to clean it all up."

Tears flood her eyes, and she shakes her head in disbelief.

"I knew you didn't believe me."

"W-what?" she stutters.

"When I told you that I'd do anything for you."

I move closer to her and take her face in my hands.

"Parker," I say, my voice low and serious. "Nothing will ever be too much for you."

Finally, her tears spill over, racing over my fingers that cover her cheeks.

"You really did all this?"

"Well, I had some help. The guys and I cleared your apartment, then a company took everything and delivered it back here."

"Thank you doesn't feel like enough."

I brush my thumb over her bottom lip.

"Do you want to see it all?"

"Yeah, but first I need—" I cut her words off with a kiss.

The second I lick across her bottom lip, the saltiness of her tears hits me, and I lose my mind.

My tongue pushes past her lips, seeking hers out as I hold her tight.

I kiss her like I've wanted to every single day for the last six years.

By the time we part, we're both breathless.

"Do you want to see now?"

She blinks up at me in a daze as she battles to remember where she is and why she's here. But the second she rips her eyes from mine and sees her couch just behind me, it all comes flooding back.

She steps around me and takes it all in.

We've set it up like an open-plan apartment. We've got a living, dining, and sleeping area displaying all her things.

She trails her fingertips across the back of her couch before walking over to her bookcase, her eyes scanning her photographs that span all her life.

"I can't believe you managed to save all of this. I thought it was all gone."

I follow, my eyes glued to her as I take in her reactions.

"Open your closet," I instruct, and watch as she walks over.

"Oh my god, my clothes," she cries happily when she finds them all hanging from the rail.

Spotting something on the bottom shelf, she drops to her haunches and reaches for it.

I was curious about the box with the little padlock on it when I first found it, but now that she's reached for it, I'm even more desperate to see what's hiding inside.

She carries it over to her bed and lowers it down beside her. After rummaging inside her purse, she pulls her keys out and then unlocks it.

"What's in there?" I ask, waiting for her to open it.

"Come and see," she says with a smile.

I take a seat on the other side of the box as she flips the lid.

Inside, there's a stack of books in all different sizes and colors. Each one has a school grade written on the front.

"I didn't know you kept a diary," I say, guessing what they are.

"I don't anymore," she says as she begins looking through the pile.

When she finds the one with senior year on the front, she pulls it out. Clearly looking for something specific, she flicks through the pages. Inside, each page is filled with multicolored writing, little doodles and stickers.

Discovering the page she wants, she opens the book wide and brushes her finger over her neat script.

"Here," she says, passing it over.

I take it but don't look down straight away.

"Are you sure?"

Parker may no longer be an eighteen-year-old high school senior, but this still feels like an invasion of privacy.

"I have nothing to hide from you, Linc."

Accepting her words, I look down.

Dear diary,

Yesterday was both the worst and best day of my life.

It was my senior prom.

And just like I planned, I lost my virginity.

But it didn't go how I expected it to.

Seth…Seth cheated on me, and this is the last time I'm ever going to write his name in here.

So, who did I spend the night with?

I can't believe I'm about to write this, but…

I lost my virginity to Lincoln Storm.

Squeeeee.

Can you believe that?

The Lincoln Storm.

It was incredible.

Linc was everything I've always hoped for and dreamed of.

He was sweet, and gentle, and caring.

He didn't mind that I didn't know what I was doing, and I wasn't embarrassed when he undressed me and saw me naked for the first time.

It was everything I ever wanted.

But I've messed it all up.

I did something this morning that I know I'll regret for the rest of my life.

I walked away from him.

I told him it couldn't happen again.

I'm scared, and deep down I know I've done the right thing, but...it's Linc.

I've loved him forever, and now he thinks I hate him.

"Parker," I breathe, my eyes burning with tears.

"You'll find your name written in every single one of these books, Linc. You'll probably also find a good number of doodles of things like Mrs. Parker Storm and PD loves LS," she confesses shyly.

"Do you still regret that morning?"

"Yes and no."

Pushing the diary aside, I shake my head as I reach for her hand and tug her into my lap.

"You shouldn't. We weren't ready back then."

"And now?"

"Now I'm ready to make you mine in every single way. I love you, Parker. I alwa—"

Her kiss cuts off my words, and I fall back, taking her with me.

"I've got another surprise," I confess when she breaks our kiss.

"Oh?"

"Yeah, but we're going to need to get up."

"I don't know, I quite like it here."

She circles her hips, grinding herself against me, and I grunt.

"Yeah, same. But I'm not making you mine in a storage unit, pretty girl."

She giggles. "It would be a great story for the grandkids."

Her words light something up inside me, and for the first time with a woman, I can see it. A future with a family. A life together.

Fuck. I want it.

I want it so fucking much.

"I've got an even better one waiting for you."

"I'm not sure you're able to top this," she says, looking around again.

"Well, let's see about that..."

76

PARKER

"What are you doing?" I laugh when Linc steps behind me, cupping his hands over my eyes, a beat before the elevator doors open to his apartment.

"It's a surprise, remember?" he tells me. His warm breath tickles down my neck, making me shudder.

My head is still full of images of that storage container full of my things. He promised me that we can go back whenever we want, and that anything I'd like to add to the apartment is okay with him.

Honestly, I'm struggling to take it all in.

I knew some of it could be salvaged, but he's managed to recover so much.

Even those diaries.

I smile as he leads me forward. I can't believe I showed him those. He is definitely going to want to read all of them. My cheeks heat, knowing some of the things less-than-innocent teenage me wrote about him. But all of it is true. And now it's not just a fantasy. It's my reality.

I wrap my hands around his forearms, needing to touch him.

"We're nearly there," he assures me.

We're in the living room—I've figured that much out, at least. And there is food. The scent of something delicious is floating around, making my mouth water, although I can't pinpoint exactly what it is.

"Are you ready?" he asks.

"Yep."

Excitement flutters wildly in my stomach that he's planned all of this for me. In my head, I'm picturing a romantically laid table with flowers and candles. So when he drops his hands and I get to see everything before me, I'm shocked.

"What the—"

The couches have been pushed together to make a kind of nest. There are pillows and blankets everywhere.

On a tray in the middle of the nest is takeout waiting for us, and there is a bottle of wine in a chiller. All the main lights are off, leaving only side lamps and flickering candles to illuminate the room. And on the television is a movie waiting to start.

The Kissing Booth.

I stand there with tears in my eyes and my hand over my mouth in shock. It is the most romantic thing I've ever seen.

"Do you...do you like it?"

"Linc," I breathe, barely able to find any words to express how I'm feeling right now. "It's...it's perfect. I can't believe you did all this."

"Well," he says, nervously, rubbing the back of his neck. "I may have had a little help."

I shake my head in disbelief.

"I have also taken the liberty of selecting our outfits," he explains as he walks over to the couch and grabs a couple of items of clothing I didn't notice before.

"For you," he says, holding out one of his jerseys.

"Of course," I mutter, rolling my eyes, but my smile never falters.

"And for me." A laugh tumbles from my lips as he holds up a pair of gray sweatpants. "And there is a no-underwear rule."

"Thank God," I muse, already knowing how hot he's going to look the second he pulls them on. Would it be weird to demand he also wear a backward cap while we watch a movie? That really would be all my teenage fantasies rolled into one.

"Go and get ready. We're starting in ten minutes."

Instead of grabbing his jersey and rushing away, which is what I think he's expecting me to do, I reach up on my toes and take his stubbly cheeks in my hands.

"You are incredible," I tell him. "I'm sorry I ever made out like I thought otherwise."

He shakes his head gently. "It's okay. I never believed that."

I laugh. "Good to see your ego is intact."

"Always, babe. Now, go get ready. I'm excited for my first date with the girl of my dreams."

I continue to stare up at him.

How?

How has this happened?

I lean forward to kiss him, but he presses two fingers against my lips, stopping me.

I frown, unimpressed by his move.

"If you kiss me now, we're never going to stop. I want to at least attempt this date before we get distracted."

I bite down on my bottom lip. "But getting distracted sounds so good."

I'm so ready for what comes next for us. My body is desperate for it.

I want him. All of him. And my patience is running out.

"Go and get ready, pretty girl," he demands. His voice is rough, and it makes my core clench with need.

"Okay," I breathe before finally snatching the jersey from his hand and rushing toward my bedroom.

I strip naked in record time and take the fastest shower

known to man to freshen up, and in exactly ten minutes, I'm back in the living room wearing nothing but his jersey.

Linc is leaning against the kitchen island, wearing just his gray sweats and staring down at his cell with a small frown playing on his brow.

"Is everything okay?" I ask in concern.

His eyes lift a beat before they widen, a smile spreading across his lips. "Fuck," he grunts, taking me in from head to toe. "Everything is absolutely perfect. Turn around for me."

Unable to deny his request, I spin on the balls of my feet.

"Lift the hem," he demands when my back is to him.

Hooking one finger around the fabric, I pull it up, letting him see my bare ass beneath.

"Fuck. I think I just came."

I giggle and glance back over my shoulder.

The expression on his face is everything. I wish I could bottle it and keep it forever.

That one look alone makes me feel so loved, so cherished, so beautiful.

Marching forward, Linc grabs my hand and tugs me toward the couch.

"On you get," he demands, slapping my ass the second I bend over to crawl on.

He growls, rumbling deep in his throat, and I put a little extra wiggle into my hips as my jersey begins to ride up as I crawl forward.

"Goddamn, Parker," he groans.

I flip over and find him still standing at the end of the couch, his hand massaging his neck and a tent in his sweats.

I did that.

I make Lincoln Storm lose control.

With my eyes locked on his fabric-covered cock, I make a show of licking my lips.

He groans again, but this time, he drops to his knees and crawls toward me.

What a fucking vision.

His body is a work of art, from the ink to the muscles, even down to the colorful array of bruises he's sporting thanks to last night's game.

He is just beautiful.

He moves right over my body, hovering over me with his hands placed on either side of my shoulders.

"Hey," I squeak quietly.

"Hey, pretty girl," he muses, his eyes bouncing between mine. "You look really fucking good in my jersey. I hate that you can't wear it to games."

He ducks lower, his lips brushing over mine, stealing any response I might have.

Dropping his weight to one elbow, his other hand lands on my waist, the heat of his skin burning through the fabric, making my temperature soar.

Wrapping my leg around his waist, I try to tug him down on top of me, desperate to feel his weight, his hardness between my legs. But he holds firm.

I whimper into our kiss, and he chuckles. Asshole.

We're both breathless when he finally pulls back.

"We need to eat," he tells me, his eyes almost black with desire. "We're going to need the energy."

My core clenches again at his unspoken words.

"O-okay," I breathe.

The second he pushes himself off me and sits at my side, I miss him. It's ridiculous; he's right there.

"Everything okay?" he asks, watching me with a smirk playing on his lips.

"Uh-huh. Yep. I'm good," I mumble as I push myself up.

"Good. Shall I hit play?" he asks, nodding at the screen.

"Go for it," I say as I begin pulling lids off of the take-out containers.

The waft of food gets stronger, and my stomach growls loudly, making Linc laugh.

As the movie plays, we sit side by side, filling up on

delicious Chinese food while sipping on the bottle of wine Linc had chilling.

As dates go, it's by far the best I've ever had.

About halfway through the movie, Linc pauses it to clear up the empty containers, and when he returns, he wraps his hands around my ankles and tugs me down until I'm lying amongst the cushions. He crawls next to me and pulls me into his body.

I think we only last another ten minutes before we're thoroughly distracted.

Our kiss starts innocent, but that soon changes. His hands slip under my jersey, grabbing and teasing everywhere he can. And I can't say I'm any better.

My hands gently trail over his shoulders and chest, being careful of the bruises, before I skim down his stomach, my palm bouncing over his abs until I can grasp him through his sweats.

He groans, his length jerking in my hold.

"I need you," he rasps, his lips kissing down my throat.

"God, yes. More."

I roll my hips in offering, and he smiles against me as he pushes himself on top of me.

"You want more, babe, you're going to have to ask for it. Tell me what you need. Tell me where you need me."

"Oh god. Everywhere, I need you everywhere."

"First place."

Dragging my jersey up, I expose myself to him.

His eyes drop, and all the air rushes from his lungs as he gazes down at me.

"Fuck, you're so hot," he muses.

"Yours."

"Fuck."

"Tits, Linc. Kiss me, lick me, suck me. Anything. Just please, give me something."

"As if I could say no to that." He shimmies lower, bringing his head right over my chest before teasing one nipple with the tip of his tongue and then wrapping his lips around it, sucking until a potent shot of desire heads straight between my legs.

"Lincoln," I cry out, my fingers twisting in his hair as his giant hand palms my other breast. "Yes."

"This is only the beginning, babe," he promises, his eyes locked on mine as he switches sides. "You remember how good we were together last time?" I nod, unable to create words. "Well, this time is going to be even better."

I want to mock him about his ego, but when the heat of his mouth surrounds me again, I lose all train of thought.

He teases me until I'm gasping for air and desperate to rub my thighs together for friction, but he's sitting between them, holding me open.

I'm so wet for him, I have no doubt I'm making a puddle on the blanket beneath me, but I can't find it in me to care.

I just need more of him.

Of everything.

"P-pussy," I blurt. "I need…"

"Tell me what you need, pretty girl."

"Your mouth. Eat me…eat me out, Linc. Let me come on your tongue."

"Fuck, you're a filthy girl, Parker Donnelly. I fucking love it."

My heart is pounding against my chest as he kisses down my stomach. My fingers twist in the blankets beneath me. He hasn't even touched me there yet, and I'm losing my goddamn mind.

I cry out the second he blows a stream of air across my sensitive skin.

"Look at you," he muses. "So wet and ready for me. So pretty."

"Please," I whimper. "I need you, Linc. I've always needed you."

"Christ. I never thought I'd hear you say that."

"I'm sorry I lied, that I pretended I didn't. All I've ever

wanted was you. A repeat of that night. Foreverrrrr," I cry as he drops to his stomach and latches onto my clit. "Holy fuck."

Gone are the slow and gentle licks from yesterday morning. This man is on a mission, eating me like I've never been eaten before.

"Fuck, fuck, fuck," I chant when he pushes two fingers inside me, his tongue not letting up on my clit.

He groans, and the vibrations of his deep rumble hit me exactly where he intends. My orgasm crashes through me like a tsunami. It approaches fast, hitting me almost out of nowhere, but it rocks me to my very core.

"That's it, pretty girl," Linc muses as he sits up, his face glistening with my juices and his fingers still slowly bringing me down from my release. "Give me everything."

"It's yours. Everything. It's yours."

77

LINCOLN

I lick my lips as I climb back up her body, taking her in. The second I get to the bunched-up fabric of the jersey around her shoulders, I reach out and tug it over her head.

I might want to fuck her while she's wearing it, but that can wait for another day.

Today, I don't want an inch of her covered.

The second it's free from her head, I throw it aside and duck down to kiss her.

She moans as her taste explodes on her tongue, but she doesn't back away.

Her hands slide down my back until her fingertips hit the waistband of my sweats. Her touch is so gentle as she tries not to put pressure on my bruises. It makes my skin prick with goose bumps.

"Parker," I moan into our kiss.

Her hands push my sweats over my ass before she wrestles them over my hips, letting my aching dick spring free.

Helping her, I kick the fabric off, leaving me as bare as her.

"Fuck," I gasp as she wraps her hand around my length and slowly starts stroking me.

Precum leaks from the tip, and she gathers it up before rubbing it around the head.

"I've never needed anything in my entire life as much as I need you," I groan, resting my forehead against hers and staring down into her eyes.

"Please," she whimpers, wrapping both her legs around my waist and tugging me down.

My cock grazes over her pussy, and we both gasp at the sensation.

"I need you, Linc."

"What do you need, pretty girl?" I taunt, wanting her to say it.

"You. I need you inside me."

Christ. This woman wrecks me in the best kind of way.

"You're sure?" I ask. "Because after this, there is no going back, no walking away, no changing minds. Once I'm inside you again, that's it. It's us. Forever."

She nods without hesitation.

"I'm never walking away again. Our time is now."

I squeeze my eyes closed as I try to keep my shit together.

I've waited so fucking long for this.

"Reach up and grab my wallet," I say, jerking my chin toward where it rests on the sideboard behind the couch.

Parker frowns, but she does as she's told and feels for it.

The second she wraps her fingers around the leather, she brings it between us.

As she holds it, her hand trembles lightly, letting me know that this is affecting her just as much as it is me.

"Behind the photo of me and Nova," I say.

She opens it and looks in the pocket.

"There isn't a condom in here," she says, her frown deepening.

"I know. Pull the picture out."

As she does, the front photo of me and my sister a few years ago at a Vipers game stays put while another one slides free.

I know the second she sees it because her breath catches.

"Linc," she whispers, staring at the small photo as if it can't be real.

"That's been in my wallet since that day."

"N-no," she sobs. "Why? I left. I turned my back on you and—"

"I wasn't giving up on you, Parker. I'd never give up on you."

I pluck the small image from her hand and look at it like I have done a million times over the years.

Parker stands with a wide smile on her face, wrapped in her stunning prom dress with the world at her feet. She was so beautiful that night. Hell, she's beautiful every night. But while she might have bad memories of her prom, it was hands-down the best night of my life. Well, it was until right now. Something tells me what's hopefully going to happen next will trump it.

"I've kept a little bit of you with me every day since."

She shakes her head and she loses her fight with her tears as they trickle over her temples and soak into her hair.

"I love you," she blurts.

Holy shit.

The words hit me like a bullet to the chest.

"Say it again," I demand.

"Linc," she breathes, gazing up at me with her big, watery eyes. "I love you."

My lips slam down on hers. I abandon the photo and my wallet and focus entirely on her.

"There are condoms in my room if you want me to—"

"No. I don't want anything between us. Please, Linc. Let me feel you."

Fucking hell. This woman...

"As long as you're happy with that," I force out.

"Please, Linc. I can't wait any longer."

"Fuck, yeah."

Shifting my position, I hitch her thigh up and drag my cock through her pussy, coating myself in her juices.

I hold her eyes as I fight to drag in the air I need.

Finding her entrance, I notch myself in just slightly.

Even that is enough to have me racing toward a release all too soon.

"Linc," she whimpers, sliding her hand up my arm and wrapping it around the back of my neck, anchoring us together. "I...I love you."

"Christ, Parker," I groan, pushing myself inside her, agonisingly slowly. "I love you too."

"It's okay. Keep going. Please. Keep going," she begs, assuming that I'm taking it slow for her comfort.

Of course, that is part of it. I never want to hurt her. But mostly, I need to take it slow to save me from blowing the second I'm fully seated inside her.

"I...I just need—"

She nods, understanding where I'm at without me saying anything.

Gripping my neck tighter, she drags my mouth down to hers.

As her tongue slips past my lips, I push deeper inside her.

She's so fucking tight I can barely stand it.

"Fuck, Parker. You feel so fucking good," I groan once I'm as deep as I can go at this angle.

"You too. I need...I need—"

"I've got you, pretty girl. I've always got you," I promise as I begin to move my hips.

Slowly at first, allowing us both to get used to it, but before long, she's clawing at my back and each of my thrusts is harder.

"Oh god, yes. Linc," she cries, throwing her head back and closing her eyes.

"Oh no. I need those eyes on me, babe. I need you to know who's doing this to you."

"I know. I know. Trust me, I know."

"Good."

My grip on her hip tightens to the point she'll probably be left with bruises tomorrow, but she doesn't say anything.

Our bodies move together as if they've done this a million times. It's hands-down the most exhilarating yet natural experience of my life.

"Oh shit, Linc. There. Right there," she cries as I lift her ass, hitting her that little bit deeper.

"Are you going to come all over my cock, pretty girl?"

"Yes, yes."

I reach down with my free hand and press two fingers against her clit.

She cries out, her pussy clamping down on me so tight that I know I'm not going to last.

"That's it, babe. Give me everything. Let me feel you milking my cock. I'm gonna fill you up so good, you'll forget anyone else was ever here."

"Linc. Fuck. Yes. Oh my gooooooood."

Fucking hell, if that isn't the most beautiful thing I've seen, then I don't know what is.

"Jesus. Fuck. Parker. Fuck," I groan as I spill inside her.

My movements slow as I drag out the final seconds of our releases before I drop to my side and pull her with me.

Wrapping her up in my arms, I nestle my head in her neck and breathe her in.

Mine.

All fucking mine.

I don't know how long we lie there entwined in each other. Time doesn't matter anymore. The only thing that does is the woman in my arms.

"That was..."

"Yeah, it was that and a whole lot more. Totally worth the wait."

Parker giggles at my words, and my chest expands with the love I feel for her.

"It's been a long six years."

"Yeah, but the good news is, we only have to wait like six minutes to go again."

I'm still inside her, so she's as aware as I am that six minutes is a push; I've barely softened.

"Six minutes, huh?" she asks, rolling her hips.

"Feeling greedy, Donnelly?"

"It has been six long years, Storm. You've got some time to make up for."

Rolling onto my back, I pull her with me so she's sitting astride my waist, my cock still buried inside her.

With my hands on her hips, I help her move, my eyes taking her in from her flushed cheeks and chest to her hard nipples and her glistening pussy. "Show me what I've been missing, babe. Then I'm taking you to my bed and spending all night worshiping you."

"All night?" she questions.

"All fucking night."

By the time we both find our next releases, the movie has long finished.

"I need to shower," Parker mutters against my chest, where she collapsed a few minutes ago. "But I don't think my legs will hold me up."

"That's what you've got me for."

Shifting us both to the end of the couches, I get to my feet and lift her into my arms.

"Ew, gross," Parker complains as I slip out of her.

"What?" I ask as I march across the room.

"You've just come in me twice and…and well, it's dribbling out."

"Is that right?" I ask, my legs suddenly moving faster toward my bedroom.

"Linc, what are you—" Her words are cut off as she bounces against my mattress.

Reaching out, I grab her knees and spread her thighs.

"Holy shit," I gasp as I watch myself leak out of her. "I'm pretty sure that's the hottest thing I've ever seen."

She cries out as I drag my fingers through my cum and push it back inside her.

"Sensitive, babe?"

"Uh-huh."

"You could come again though, couldn't you?"

She nods.

"My greedy little whore."

Pushing my fingers deeper, I curl them to find her G-spot.

"Oh god."

"Give me another one, then I'll carry you to the shower and clean you up myself."

In only a few short minutes, she's clamping down on my fingers, her body convulsing on top of my bed, my name like a plea on her lips.

I'm hard as fuck again as I do as promised.

I turn the water on, wait for it to heat with her head resting on my shoulder, and then step us both under it.

"You did so good, babe. Such a good girl for me."

She whimpers at my praise.

"Can you stand?"

She shakes her head, and I chuckle.

"Let me clean you up, then I'm going to tuck you into my bed."

"Mmm."

Lowering her to her feet, her knees thankfully hold out, and I make quick work of washing her hair—with her brand of shampoo I bought a while ago to ensure I was prepared for this night— and then I clean up her body before wrapping her in a big fluffy towel and carrying her back to my bed.

"Tonight was amazing," she tells me sleepily. "Thank you. For everything."

"Babe," I say, dropping my towel and falling onto the bed beside her. "Trust me, it was my pleasure," I say, rolling over and tugging her into my side.

"I love you, Lincoln Storm," she mumbles.

"I love you, too, Parker Donnelly."

78

PARKER

I wake the next morning, happy and sore.

Linc's arm is resting heavily over my stomach, and my skin tingles with his attention.

"I know you're awake, pretty girl," he whispers, letting me know I'm right. He's watching me sleep again.

"You're a bit of a creep, aren't you, Storm?" I accuse without opening my eyes.

"Creep, obsessed, whichever works."

My stomach flips with a mixture of excitement and disbelief.

Lincoln Storm is obsessed with me, and he watches me sleep.

Oh, and makes me come like no one else.

Christ, last night was something else.

And it didn't end just because I fell asleep in his arms. There may have been some middle-of-the-night-in-the-dark action, too.

My core clenches as I remember just how it felt to have him thrusting inside me, filling me so beautifully, and hitting that magic spot that had me seeing stars.

I'll always fondly remember our first time, but ultimately, I had no idea what I was doing. I was learning on the job. And as relaxed as Linc made it that night, it was never going to squash my nerves or anxiety.

But last night, the playing field had been leveled. We both knew what we were doing, and we were both confident enough to say what we wanted. Not that it was really necessary for me. Linc seemed to know exactly I wanted, what I needed. And it was hot as hell when he demanded for me to tell him what he already knew.

"Parker," he rasps. "You're thinking about my cock, aren't you?"

I can't help but giggle like a schoolgirl when he shifts a little closer and grinds said cock against me.

Oh god, I want it again.

"Maybe," I whisper, finally opening my eyes and looking up at him through my lashes.

"Is it wrong that I want you thinking about me and my cock every second of every day?"

"It is when I'm meant to be focusing on preventing you from injury," I point out.

"Yeah, but that still involves you thinking about my body, so I can take that."

"What about the other bodies?"

A jealous growl rumbles deep in his throat.

"You know, you're hot when you get all jealous."

His smirk tells me that he already knows how I feel about it.

"You're mine, Parker, and I want every motherfucker out there to know it."

"Don't worry, I'm pretty sure you've already achieved that."

I have no doubt that the photo of our post-game kiss the other night went viral before Linc even stepped off the ice. Add in everything he said at the press conference after, and then the statement Hailee and her team released after our meeting yesterday, and it seems the entire world is talking about us.

I've had to turn all my notifications off on my cell. It's just too much.

I've gone from twenty thousand followers on Insta to almost a million in barely forty-eight hours, thanks to being connected to Linc. It's insane.

People in the hockey world already knew my name. I'm Clark Donnelly's daughter, Rett Donnelly's little sister, Casey Watson's best friend. I'm one of the NHL's first female athletic trainers. And now...now, I'm Lincoln Storm's girlfriend. I don't stand a chance of moving in the shadows like I used to do. He's dragged me kicking and screaming into the limelight with him. And do you know what? I wouldn't have it any other way.

"Good. That was my goal." He rolls on top of me, caging my head in with his forearms on either side.

"How are you feeling?" he asks, his eyes holding mine.

"Amazing," I say honestly. "I don't think I've ever come that many times in one night."

"I hope you were counting."

"Uh..."

"How will we try to beat it if you don't know how many there were?"

"You're a menace."

"You love it."

"Umm...it seems I do."

I squeal as he drops his head to my neck and tickles my skin with his lips. But that shock soon turns to something else —something a hell of a lot more addictive.

"God, Linc," I cry when he sucks on the sensitive patch of skin beneath my ear.

"Are you sore?" he whispers, rephrasing his previous question.

"I think it would be impossible for me not to be. I've never been fucked like that before, Linc."

"Of course you fucking haven't. You haven't been being fucked by me. That all changes now."

He pinches my nipple before skimming his hand down my stomach and between my thighs.

I shamelessly spread my legs for him, allowing him to drag his fingers through my folds.

"Fuck, you're soaked," he muses as he teases me.

"Woke up next to you. Of course I am."

"Fucking love that, pretty girl."

I gasp when he circles my entrance with one finger.

"How's that feel?"

I want to lie and say it's fine just so I can feel him again. But he's going to know.

"Tender."

"Aw, did I wear you out, babe?"

I nod as he continues gently touching me. He hasn't even pushed the digit inside yet, and I can already feel a release building.

It makes me realize just what I've been missing out on all this time, hooking up with assholes online who think they know how to please a woman.

They don't know. They don't know anything.

Linc, though...he knows.

"I'm sorry if I was too rough," he says, a frown pinching his brows together.

"You weren't. I'm just out of practice. Gonna need a few weeks to get into shape if nights like that are going to be a regular thing in our future."

"Damn right they are. And in every city in the country."

Happiness flows through me as I think of all the experiences we're going to have together from here on out.

"I can't wait," I breathe before he disappears under the sheets. "What are you doing?"

He pokes his head back up. He looks adorable as fuck with his messy post-sex hair, a few days' worth of scruff, and a pillow crease down the side of his face. But that all changes as his eyes darken and the words, "Kissing you better," roll from his tongue.

Oh Christ.

"I...uh...I should clean up first."

"Why?" he asks from beneath the sheets. He opens me up with two fingers and blows a stream of air across me. "I know exactly where you've been."

Before I've even had a chance to argue, his mouth is on me, my back is arching from the bed, and he's going to town. And thankfully, this morning, we have the apartment to ourselves, so no one is going to be dragging him away until he's done.

***

"SOMEONE LOOKS HAPPY," Handsy remarks when he arrives in the trainers' room that afternoon for his session.

"Thanks. Things are good."

"I'm happy for you. Are you really sure about Linc, though? He can be a real asshole when he wants to be."

"I am right here," the man in question barks from the other side of the room, where he's stretching.

Handsy chuckles as he pulls his shirt off and lies face-down on my table, stating, "I won't say anything about anyone that I wouldn't say to their face."

"Lucky us," Linc teases before shooting me a wink.

I worked on him earlier, and by some miracle, he was the perfect patient. He didn't try to touch me once, nor did he make a single inappropriate comment. For a few minutes, I thought I was living in an alternate universe. But then I remembered Esme's words about being professional, and the bullshit that's being spewed online about our conflict of interest and questions over my ability to do my job properly. Of course, that barely scratches the surface of the bad press we've received in the past few days. As predicted, everything about my life and my career has been brought up. Questions about whether I'm even qualified to treat their beloved players, if I'm only here to get closer to the players. I've tried my best not to read it, but it's hard to avoid when it's the only thing that seems to pop up on my cell.

As soon as I figured out what Linc was doing, I respected him a whole lot more than I already do. He's trying, really fucking trying, to prove to everyone and anyone that I'm worthy of my position here.

Many of the guys have taken to the internet to fight in my corner, but quite honestly, they could stand out there naked and scream it until they're blue in the face. The questions will still continue. The women are jealous, and the men don't think I belong in their world. I get it. It's something I'm sure I'm going to be fighting as long as my career lasts.

Hopefully, it'll get easier. As more women step into roles like mine, the more normal it will become, but we've still got a way to go.

"Anyone invited you to the Valentine's gala yet, Parker?" Handsy asks after I've warmed my hands and started working on loosening his shoulder.

"Uh...no, actually. No one has. I wonder if any of the guys still need a date."

Out of the corner of my eye, I see Linc freeze.

"Any of them would be lucky to have you on their arm."

"I know what you're doing," Linc growls.

"Do you mind?" Handsy mocks. "I'm having a private conversation with my trainer."

"Parker will be coming to the gala with me."

I smirk, loving the possessive tone in his voice.

"I might already have other plans. No one has asked me yet," I taunt.

A chuckle rumbles through Handsy. "Parker, would you do me the honor of—"

"Do not finish that fucking sentence, Cole," Linc warns.

"Whoa, Storm is pulling out the big guns there with first names," Handsy laughs.

"Will you two stop?"

"Hell no. No one hits on my girl in front of me." Linc is on his feet now, glaring at Handsy—not that he can see; his head is shoved in the hole in the bed.

"I wasn't hitting on anyone. I was simply inviting her on a night out, seeing as her boyfriend has failed to do so."

"For the love of God," I mutter, aware that I'm not going to be able to stop this.

"Parker," Linc says, storming over with a determined look on his face. "Babe, will you go to the Valentine's gala with me?"

"Hey, I asked first," Handsy argues.

"No, you didn't." Linc scoffs. "And even if you did, she'd say no."

I raise my brows in amusement.

"Babe?" Linc prompts.

I pretend to think for a moment. "I'm not sure. How do I know I won't get a better offer?"

Handsy barks out a laugh as Linc growls in frustration.

"I'll buy you a pretty dress," Linc offers, as if that'll help. He should already know that there is no one else I'd rather go with.

"Hmm...how expensive are we talking? And will I get shoes and a purse as well?"

"You can have anything you want. I want you to feel as beautiful as I see you."

"Pussy," Handsy coughs.

Reaching out, Linc flicks him on the back of his knee. "Ow, motherfucker," he complains, twisting around to rub it.

"Parker?" Linc asks again, ignoring his teammate.

I shake my head, a soft smile playing on my lips. "Of course I'll go with you. And you don't have to spend a penny on me."

"What if I want to?"

"We'll talk about this later," I say, turning back to Handsy.

"Fine. But I'm buying you a dress," Linc states as he returns to his spot on the mats.

"Possessive asshole," Handsy mutters, making me laugh. Yeah, he is. And I freaking love it.

79

PARKER

"**Y**ou know you've ruined your career, right?"

I rear back as the words hit me, but I don't give him the privilege of turning to look at him.

"No one is going to be able to take you seriously after this. A few weeks into a job you only got because of your connection to the team, and now you're fucking one of the players?"

My teeth grind as anger burns red hot through my veins.

Mitchell has been itching to say something since the moment Linc kissed me on the ice a few days ago, but thankfully, we haven't been alone since. Unfortunately for me, he's managed to catch me alone in the trainers' room while the team is getting ready for tonight's game.

The arena is at full capacity, and the volume of the crowd is unbelievable. With every game the guys win, the busier and louder home games are becoming. Everyone is desperate to watch them go all the way this year, and they're doing everything they can to support them.

It's incredible to see, and even more exciting to be a part of it all.

"You have no idea, Mitchell," I say, continuing to clean down the table I was just using.

The moments before a game are the calm before the storm. The second the guys hit the ice, we're on full alert, waiting for the first sign of injury and treating everything we can to keep them out there doing what they do best.

His laughter bounces around the room.

I haven't heard anything from Esme since I put my complaint in about his behavior, but I trust she's doing her thing behind the scenes and that something will happen soon.

Worst case, he'll be pulled in for a disciplinary for his behavior and then sent back to work. He'll know immediately who put the complaint in, and I can only imagine how things will be between us after that. But then, there is the other option...

If others come forward, if there is more evidence than just my word, maybe, just maybe, there could be a successful outcome.

None of the guys like him. If they're spoken to, none of them will have a good word to say. But will that be enough?

My fists curl. The desire to spin around and throw one into his ugly face is almost too much to bear.

My chest heaves as anger like I've never experienced before erupts inside me.

"Don't tell me—Storm isn't the first or the only one you're fucking."

Unable to keep my back to him any longer, I spin around.

A gasp falls from my lips when I discover just how close he's standing.

"You have no idea what you're talking about," I snap.

The laugh he barks out sends ice rushing through me.

This man is fucking unhinged.

I have been nothing but professional since my very first day here. But that doesn't matter. Not to a misogynist asshole like him. The second he discovered I don't have a penis hanging between my legs, he hated me. Nothing else mattered.

"Sure I do. I've been dealing with women like you my

whole life. You think you can open your legs and it'll get you wherever you want to be."

"Is that why almost every member of the team here wants to be treated by me and not you?" I sneer. I shouldn't bait him, but I can't help myself. As much as I want to stand here and take it in the hope someone is listening, it's just not in my nature to shut up while someone disrespects me like this.

He scoffs. "They don't give a fuck about their treatment. They just want you."

"Bullshit. Not a single one of the team has ever been disrespectful to me. You are the only one with a problem. What's wrong, Mitchell? Jealous that I'm a better trainer than you'll ever be? That athletes actually feel a difference after working with me?"

"You fucking bitch," he roars, his face tomato red as he grabs my arm and throws me against the wall.

My shoulder screams in pain, but I don't cower. I will never cower to this asshole.

"Fuck you," I spit as he moves closer again. "I will not back down when I know I'm right."

Mitchell suddenly releases me, but his grip was so tight that I lose my balance and go crashing down.

There's some commotion, but I can't latch onto anything before my head collides with the floor.

"Oh fuck," someone bellows.

"Storm, no," someone else cries.

"Get her on the table," someone barks.

I hear it all happen, but it's almost like a dream.

Suddenly, I'm weightless as warm, strong arms wrap around me.

"I'm okay," I mumble, or at least I think I do. My body doesn't feel like my own.

There's more shouting, more arguing.

My head throbs. Keeping my eyes closed, I snuggle into something, needing to get away from it all.

"Parker? Babe?"

Warm hands cover my face, and I lean into it.

"Hey, pretty girl. It's me. Everything's okay."

I relax the second I recognize his voice and finally open my eyes.

I'm pressed up against a green jersey, but it isn't one that I know well. When I look up, I find Handsy's concerned face staring down at me.

"Babe, I'm here," Linc says, gently turning my face to look at him.

The second my eyes lock on his, I burst into tears.

I don't even know why. But the sight of him shatters something inside me.

Handsy passes me over, and Linc wraps me up in his arms, holding me while I cry.

There's movement and voices on the other side of the room, but when I try to look, Linc shields me from it all.

"W-what's happening?" I whisper, my voice barely audible.

"It's just security escorting Mitchell out."

Mitchell.

Shit.

My sobs come harder as I remember everything he said, what he was doing.

"It's okay, babe. We've taken care of it. He'll never step foot back in this arena again." It isn't until he says those words that I realize Linc is shaking.

Pulling my head from his padded chest, I look up at him.

His face is hard, his expression wrought, but he's okay. There are no new bruises or cuts.

But I know my man better than that. Twisting a little, I reach for his right hand.

His knuckles are grazed and covered in blood.

"Linc, you shouldn't have—"

"No one—and I mean fucking no one—talks to my girl like that. Hell, they shouldn't be talking to any girl like that, but especially not one who belongs to me."

If my head wasn't banging so hard, I might swoon at those words. But as it is, I can barely register them.

Resting my head back against Linc, I let him hold me. It could be seconds or minutes that pass, I have no idea, but I startle when a familiar voice speaks.

"Guys, I need you out there," Coach says hesitantly.

There are muttered agreements as the sound of their blade protectors tapping against the floor gets quieter as they leave.

Coach steps closer, his eyes on me before he glances up at Linc.

"I'll have Reeves start in your place," Coach explains, "but I'm going to need you out there tonight."

"No, I—"

"Casey is on her way back here. She'll take care of Parker. You have my word."

"B-but—"

"It's okay. You have to go."

"Fuck that, Parker. You're hurt. I don't need to do anything but be with you."

"I'm okay. Nothing a couple of Tylenol won't fix."

Linc gazes down at me, indecision warring in his eyes.

"Please, I want you to play. And I want you to win. Can you do that?" I squeeze his bloody hand. "Can you go out there and score a goal for me?"

"Fucking hell, babe," he breathes before pressing a kiss on the top of my head.

Footsteps race toward us, and a few seconds later, Casey bursts into the room with her little sidekick.

"What's happened? What's wrong?" she asks breathlessly, as if she's run all the way here.

"There was an incident," Coach explains, "but I need Linc out there. Can you take care of Parker?"

"Yeah, of course. Linc, you go. I've got this."

"No, I—"

"You have to," I beg. "We can't let that assho—" My eyes snag on Sutton staring at me with wide eyes. "Idiot win."

"Men like that never win, Parker," Coach assures me.

It takes a few more minutes, but eventually, Linc releases me and walks toward the door. Casey immediately hops up in his place and wraps her arms around my shoulder.

"I want a goal, remember?" I call.

"Anything for you, pretty girl," Linc says before forcing himself to walk away.

Silence settles between us all for a few moments before Sutton breaks it with a song.

"Lincoln and Parker sitting in a tree, K-I-S-S-I-N-G."

Casey, Coach, and I all fall about laughing. It makes my head hurt worse, but fuck, it does good things to my heart.

"Parker, I hate to ask this. But...we're a man down. Jarad isn't going to be able to cover—"

"I've got it, Coach. Just give me a few minutes to sort myself out. You can count on me."

"I know I can."

The roar of the crowd echoes through the room.

"I'd better get out there," Coach says, taking a step back. "I'm sorry, Parker. I never want a single member of my team to go through anything like that. I—I didn't know—"

"It's okay, Coach," I say, forcing a smile. "Onwards and upwards, right?"

His expression softens as he hears the words he used to say to us as kids when a game didn't go our way, or school was hard.

"Yeah," he muses. "Onwards and upwards. For what it's worth, Parker. I just need you to know how much of an asset you are to this team. The guys love you, and the number of injuries is down. Don't let anything that as—idiot said get to you. It was all lies."

"Thank you, I really appreciate that."

There's another cheer from the crowd.

"Go, Coach," Sutton demands. "You can't win a game from in here."

Coach nods before rushing from the room.

"Well," Casey muses. "I feel like I might have missed something."

Another laugh erupts from me. "I'll tell you everything later," I say, shooting a look at Sutton.

"Ugh, adult talk." She groans. "We can still watch the game, right?"

"Of course. Let me get some painkillers and we'll head right out."

"Out?" Sutton asks excitedly. "As in, down the tunnel?"

"Uh…" I hesitate, because I don't know if I can really take them down with me.

"Yeah, of course," Casey says for me. "Just this once, though."

"Oh my god," she squeals. "We'll be right in the action. Hurry, Parker, we need to get out there. We can't miss anything."

With a laugh, I slip off the table and walk into the office. The sight of Mitchell's messy desk exactly as he left it gives me pause. I shouldn't feel guilty that he's lost his job. That's on him though, not me.

After swallowing some tablets, I give myself a little talking to and head out.

As much as I don't need the noise of the crowd right now. I need to be out there. I need Linc to see me and know that I'm okay, so he can play without worrying.

But more than that, I need to be out there for me.

This is my job. My career. And despite what one pathetic little man might think, I'm damn good at it.

With my head held high and my shoulders back, I walk out of the room and toward the ice with my girls at my side.

We're barely there five seconds before Linc looks up and finds me. Relief instantly floods his face. He shakes his head, silently chastising me for coming out here, but before he takes off for the next puck drop, he blows me a kiss and mouths that he loves me.

And just like that, it's business as usual.

80

LINCOLN

By the time we get in the car after dealing with everything, Parker can barely keep her eyes open.

I want to demand she fight it. I saw her go down. I saw her hit her head. She could have a concussion. I know it's unlikely. The hit wasn't that hard, but still, concern for her floods through me as I drive.

The moment I stepped around the corner and heard what that cunt said to her will live with me forever. I'm pretty sure I can speak for the others when I say it'll be the same for them.

Handsy, Killer and I ran into the room so fucking fast, and fuck, am I glad I did.

Rage shoots through me, my grip on the wheel tightening enough to have my knuckles splitting open again.

I want to say that he was the only man I threw a punch at tonight, but that would be a lie.

Granted, he may have been the only asshole to deserve my wrath, but that's beside the point. My adrenaline was pumping, and getting in one of my opponent's faces was the only way I was going to expel some of it.

Fuck, it felt good as well.

"Almost home, pretty girl," I say, despite the fact she can't hear me.

Only a few minutes later, I pull into our underground parking garage, find my space next to her car, and kill the engine.

I turn to her, watching her rest just like I do every morning. Parker isn't wrong; it has turned into some kind of obsession. I can't help it, though. I wake up every morning thinking the whole thing has been a dream. But no, she's there, lying naked beside me. Knowing she's mine is the best feeling in the fucking world.

Reaching over, I gently drag my knuckle down her cheek. "Wakey wakey, sleepy head," I muse.

She stirs instantly, and only a few seconds later, she turns my way and opens her eyes.

"Sorry," she whispers. "I didn't mean to fall asleep."

"It's okay. It's been a long night. Stay there," I instruct as I throw my door open and climb out.

Miraculously, she does as she's told and remains in her seat, allowing me to open the door and help her out.

"I am okay, you know," she muses.

"It doesn't matter; I'm still going to take care of you," I tell her as I tuck her into my side and guide her toward the elevator.

"Thank you," she whispers.

She remains quiet as we rise through the building, and the second we're inside, I dump my bag and lead her to my room.

She's still silent as I undress her and tug one of my T-shirts over her head and then lead her to the living room to get her settled on the couch, one of the blankets from the other night over her.

"Where are you going?" she asks when I take a step back.

"I'm going to change, then I'm going to make you some food."

"I'm not hungry."

"You don't have to eat it. But I'm making it regardless."

She lets me go, but I don't make it very far before she asks, "What are you making?"

I smile to myself. I knew she was hungry.

"You'll have to wait and see," I tease before ducking into my room for another quick shower to hopefully wash away the final traces of tonight's game before I get to snuggle with my girl.

Only a few months ago, I'd have been out celebrating our win with the guys. We'd always start at the Fractured Compass before moving on to a club. Every time, the bunnies would find us and would be more than willing to take the party back to their place or a hotel room. Now, though, I can't think of anything worse. The only place I want to be is home with my girl.

When I make it back to the living area, I find Parker watching a reality TV program, although she quickly abandons it in favor of watching me in the kitchen.

Her eyes burn into my skin, ensuring that my blood is just below boiling point.

"Are you going to tell me what you're making yet?" she asks as I whisk my batter.

"Can't you guess?"

"Well, it's not ragu, I know that."

"Close." I laugh as I pull the waffle maker from the cupboard

"Grilled cheese?"

I continue to laugh as she throws out other ridiculous suggestions as I slice up some fruit and get a tub of ice cream out of the freezer to soften.

"Aren't you meant to be watching TV?" I shoot over my shoulder and find that she's completely turned her back on it now.

"I prefer watching you in those sweatpants."

I wiggle my ass at her, and she laughs. I wish I could bottle the sweet sound to listen to forever.

After loading up the waffles, I drizzle everything with caramel sauce and carry it over.

Parker's eyes go wide as she takes it all in.

"That looks incredible." She's practically drooling.

"Shame you don't want anything," I tease, lowering the plate to my lap.

"I'm sure I could eat a little bit," she says, shuffling closer. She sits on her knees beside me and gazes at the two spoons in my hand.

"Oh, did you want one of these?"

"It's a good thing you're so hot because you're not remotely funny."

"Lies." I laugh as I hand a spoon over.

Parker drags her spoon through everything before closing her mouth around it. She groans, and my cock jerks in response.

Down, boy. There's gonna be none of that tonight. We're taking care of our girl.

"Why didn't you tell me that you'd put in a complaint against him?" I ask. I hate to bring that asshole back up again, but I can't deny that hearing it hurt.

"Linc." She sighs. "I know you want to fight every battle for me, but sometimes you're going to have to let me do it myself."

I huff, filling my mouth with waffle and ice cream to stop me from saying something she won't like.

"Just because we're together, and just because we work together, doesn't mean that we have to do everything together. You'll have your issues, and I'll have mine. That's okay. I didn't want you getting involved because you have your own stresses and demands. Plus, I knew you'd go in with your fists," she says, raising a brow and glancing at my bloody knuckles.

"Well, sometimes it's the way things need resolving."

"And if he presses charges?"

"He won't," I say confidently.

"But what if he does?"

"Then I'll take the punishment. I don't give a fuck, Parker. The only thing I care about is you, and there was no fucking way that asshole was getting away with it."

A fresh wave of anger surges through me as I think about those few moments again.

"I'm sorry I—"

"No. Fuck that, Parker. You have nothing to apologize for. You did nothing but your job. All of this is on him."

"I know that. I just...I hate that you got dragged into it."

"Literally my job," I mutter before having another spoonful.

I don't want to toot my own horn or anything, but these waffles are amazing.

"Can we talk about something else? We've wasted enough energy on him tonight."

"Sure. What do you want to talk about?"

"Uhh..."

"Maybe about what kind of incredible sexy dress I'm going to buy you for the Valentine's gala?"

"Linc, I already said, I don't need—"

"And I already said I'm buying you whatever you want. Non-negotiable."

"You really are stubborn, aren't you?"

"I thought you'd learned that years ago, babe," I tease.

Together, we demolish the entire stack of waffles before slumping back on the couch with full bellies.

"I can't imagine that was on your diet plan." Parker laughs.

"Pretty sure I burned off enough calories tonight," I say, smacking my abs.

"Pilates in the morning?"

"That depends on whether you're my instructor or not."

"Not this time. We're going to a class."

I groan as if I'd forgotten, but I haven't. Not even close. I've been looking forward to watching her work out in those leggings since our last time.

"Do you need anything before we go to bed?" Parker asks, her eyes tracking over my body. "Anything feeling tight or—"

"I'm meant to be looking after you, remember?"

"I'm fine. I'll take some more painkillers before we sleep, and tomorrow it'll be like nothing happened."

"I'm fine too. If you're lucky, maybe I'll let you rub me down tomorrow after Pilates."

"Is that a promise?"

"UHH...WHAT THE HELL IS THIS?" Parker asks as we walk into her usual Pilates class the next morning. Only, there's a slight difference. There is no instructor in sight, and the people waiting for class to start...well, we know them all.

"About time," Fletch calls, where he's standing with Reese. Kodie and Casey are here too, with Freya, ready to get to work, along with the guys—Handsy, Killer, Brit, and Monroe. Brooke, Hailee, and Leah have joined with a few other girls from the front office. Even Coach has made an appearance.

Parker spins to me with confusion, twisting up her face. "What is happening right now?"

"Oh, didn't I mention? You're teaching the Pilates class this morning. And these," I say, gesturing to everyone in the room, "are your students. They are here to be tortured as you see fit."

"Uh...I didn't sign up for torturing," Killer barks.

"Well, tough," Reese teases. "You just don't want to be upstaged by us girls."

They all giggle.

"She's right," I announce. "This is hard as shit."

"We're all professional athletes. How hard can it be?" Handsy asks innocently.

"Oh, just you wait," I tease, walking Parker to the front of the room and passing her a headset that will connect her to the sound system.

"How and why have you organized this?"

"One, because you love hurting us. And two, because I thought you'd love it. I wanted to prove to you how much the guys love and value you. One mention of you running this class, and they all showed up. For you."

"Linc," she breathes, her eyes getting all glassy.

"You're up for it, right?"

"I mean, yeah. But a little warning would have been nice."

"You've got this, babe. Just pretend it's me in our home gym and you want to make me suffer."

She looks around the room, and a smile tugs at her lips while her eyes twinkle with something wicked.

"Those guys aren't going to know what's hit them," she announces.

"That's my girl," I say, kissing her forehead and walking back toward the reformer they've left for me at the front.

I've already warned the guys not to spend the entire class staring at my girl's ass. That is for me and me alone.

I watch with pride as Parker pulls the headset on.

"Right, is everyone ready?"

"Is it too late to change our minds?" Killer asks.

"Yes," everyone shouts back at the same time.

"Whoever gives up first is buying lunch," Parker warns before syncing her cell to the Bluetooth speaker and starting the music.

"Killer, I hope you brought your wallet," Handsy shouts.

"Fuck you, I'll wipe the floor with the lot of you," he says way too confidently.

***

FOR AN HOUR, Parker puts us through our paces. Coach taps out after thirty minutes, claiming that he is, in fact, too old for this shit.

Of course, we all rib him for it, but seeing as he's responsible for making us run drills, we let him off lightly compared to Handsy and Killer, who complain through the entire thing.

In the end, it's Handsy who ends up on the floor, claiming

that he's dying, and a couple of hours later, he takes one for the team and picks up our lunch bill.

With a few days off ahead of us, everyone is in good spirits despite how much all our muscles hurt. We spend the afternoon laughing, drinking, and eating good food like a completely dysfunctional family.

With my fingers entwined with Parker's, I glance at those around us and can't help but feel incredibly lucky to be surrounded by such amazing friends and colleagues.

There's just one person missing.

All our lives, Rett and I dreamed of playing in the NHL. We might have made it, but we're on opposing teams. Maybe one day that'll change, and I'll have everyone I love close by to keep an eye on.

But for now, this will have to do.

"Let's make a toast," I blurt, reaching for my beer and lifting it into the air.

"To the best goddamn hockey team this league has ever seen."

"Hear, hear," everyone shouts.

"And to the friends and loved ones we find alone the way."

We all clink glasses, but before Parker can take a sip of her drink, I wrap my hand around the back of her neck and tug her in to kiss me.

"I love you, pretty girl. Thank you for coming back to me."

EPILOGUE

Parker

Valentine's Day

"You look like you really need to drink this," I say, holding out another glass of champagne to Freya.

She takes it with trembling fingers, and despite mumbling, "I really shouldn't drink another," she instantly lifts it to her lips and takes a big sip. "I shouldn't be here. Why did I think this was a good idea?"

"Because it is a good idea," Casey calls from the vanity where she's reapplying her lipstick.

Tonight is the night of the Vipers' Valentine's gala, an event that Reese and her team run annually to raise money for our local children's hospitals. With games and travelling, it doesn't always land on the right day, but this year, Cupid has been on her side.

It's my first formal event both as a part of the Vipers' family and as Lincoln Storm's girlfriend, and I'd be lying if I said I wasn't nervous.

Linc and I may have had the spotlight on us for a week or

so now, but it's not becoming any more normal. Not yet, at least.

Freya stares back at me with wide, terrified eyes despite Casey's encouragement.

She made the mistake of mentioning that she no longer has any fun in her life or a reason to dress up. Casey took that as a mission, and well, she made it happen.

Tonight, Freya's is Handsy's unofficial date.

Freya tried to argue, but Casey was having none of it. And thankfully, forever-single Handsy was happy to spend the night with a beautiful woman on his arm.

"In my head, it was a good idea. Now I'm here, I'm not so sure." Freya looks down at herself. "Is this dress too much? It's too much, isn't it?"

She turns to look at herself in the mirror and frowns. How that's possible, I don't know. She looks stunning.

Her glittering silver gown is beyond beautiful, and her hair has been elegantly twisted up, pulling it back from her face, and her makeup is flawless.

The three of us have spent the afternoon relaxing and getting dolled up while the guys took Sutton to the arena to practice. I'm kinda disappointed I missed it, and I know Casey is, too. There is something very magical about watching a bunch of massive hockey players chase a little girl around the ice. She's got them all twisted around her little finger. Just the way it should be.

"No, Freya," Casey says firmly as she walks over and stands beside our much taller friend. "It is the opposite of too much. It's incredible, and you look like a knockout in it. Handsy is definitely not going to regret agreeing to take you."

At the mention of her date, Freya goes a little green again.

"It's going to be an amazing night. We're going to drink, have good food, laugh, and dance the night away. The exact kind of night out you need," Casey encourages. But despite Freya's desire to get out and live, I'm starting to wonder if she's pushing herself too hard.

Getting over breakups isn't easy. Each day is different from the last and it's impossible to know what the next one will be like.

"You've got this, Freya. And if at any point it gets too much, just bail to your room. No one will judge you for pulling your pjs on, ordering room service ice cream, and watching a rom-com."

"I know," she muses. "I just...I really want to be like the old me, you know? The version of myself that didn't overthink everything."

I wrap my arm around her shoulder and squeeze her.

"We know. And we also know that you'll get there. I know it sucks, but it just takes time."

"Now, drink up, because the longer we stay in here, the worse it's going to be. We've got three gorgeous men waiting for us downstairs. Shall we?" Casey asks after swallowing the rest of her champagne.

Freya finishes her drink and looks at herself in the mirror again. Unease comes off her in waves. I just hope that when she gets down there and is surrounded by the guys, she'll forget all about her nerves and enjoy herself.

"Ready to go see your man?" Casey asks as we move toward the door.

"Maybe," I tease, wiggling my brows.

The truth is, I can't freaking wait. Lincoln Storm in a dinner suit. Yum. Yes please.

We leave Casey's room and head for the elevator.

"Is your dad coming tonight?" Freya asks as we descend through the building.

"Nope, he's got a date," Casey announces.

"What?" I blurt. I have never, ever heard those words leave her lips before.

Casey laughs, and I'm immediately suspicious.

"Yep, and she's perfect for him. They'll spend the night talking about and watching hockey. His perfect kind of evening."

"He's babysitting Sutton, isn't he?" Freya guesses.

"Yep. He's on grandpa duties."

"What about Kodie's mom?" I ask. She's usually first reserve.

"She's gone out with the girls."

"Cute. Sutton is going to have the best time with your dad."

"Honestly, I think he was more excited than she was."

"Adorable," I breathe as the elevator doors open.

We're greeted by a mass of red roses and twinkling fairy lights.

"Wow," we all breathe as we step out.

"So pretty," Freya sings.

Turning to our right, we follow the low rumbling of voices toward the bar, where the men are waiting.

Handsy is the first to spot us. He pauses with his glass partway to his mouth. His eyes skim over me and Casey before finding Freya. His chin drops, and I just wish she saw it. But when I look over, she's too busy scanning the room, looking at everything.

Reaching out, Handsy backhands Linc and nods in our direction.

The second Linc's eyes land on me, my temperature soars.

Time seems to stand still as he takes me in from head to toe.

"Holy crap," Freya gasps. "Even I can feel the crackling in the air."

I'm vaguely aware of Kodie walking toward my best friend and Freya moving away from me as Linc closes in.

"Parker, you look...fuck," he rasps, his eyes everywhere.

My emerald-green dress is fitted everywhere it should be— it's low cut and elegant, and it makes me feel like a million dollars in a way any of the dresses I already had in my wardrobe wouldn't.

Linc was right; I needed this dress.

"It's the same color as your prom dress," he points out.

A smile twitches at my lips.

"You noticed," I whisper.

"Babe, I notice everything about you." My smile widens as my heart slams against my ribs. "I especially notice how fucking hot you are." His eyes drop to my exposed cleavage, and the blue darkens even more. "Do we have to go to this dinner? Can't we just go up to our room so I can peel this dress from your body?"

My cheeks burn red hot, and desire tugs at my lower stomach.

The picture he paints is so fucking tempting.

I lean a little closer. "Later," I whisper.

He groans as if he's in pain.

"Just wait until you see what I'm wearing beneath."

"Christ, babe. Do you want me to be walking around this event hard all night?"

My smile turns mischievous, and he shakes his head.

Reaching for my hand, he tugs me closer, until the warmth of his body burns down mine. "You are hands-down the best thing that's ever happened to me, pretty girl. Even when you weren't mine, you were still one of the best things about my life."

His words, and the emotion in his eyes as he says them, make me feel like the luckiest and most loved girl in the world.

"And now I'm yours?" I ask, unable to stop myself from digging for a few more compliments.

His hand slides up my bare arm, his touch making me shudder in the best kind of way until his fingers wrap around my neck, drawing me even closer.

Pressing his forehead against mine, he stares me dead in the eyes before whispering, "Everything, Parker. Now, you're my everything."

"Linc," I breathe.

One second he's there, and the next he's gone. With his hand holding mine, he tugs me toward where the guys are waiting for us.

"I've got a surprise for you," he says, keeping his back to the others, almost like he's shielding me.

He reaches toward one of the barstools before he reveals a clear box with a stunning ivory rose corsage with deep green detailing.

"W-what?" I stutter, confused.

"Six years ago, I'd have done anything to have been your date to your senior prom. I know this is very different, but I want to give you the kind of experience you should have had that night."

Emotion burns up my throat as he pulls the lid off the box and gently lifts the floral display from its home.

"Can I?" he asks, reaching for my hand with his free one.

Movement behind him catches my eye, and when I look up, I find our friends all watching us with smiles on their faces.

"This is going to ruin your reputation," I whisper.

"I don't give a fuck what anyone thinks about me but you, pretty girl."

My eyes drop to where he slides the corsage onto my wrist, the opposite one to where I wear the bracelet he bought me.

"I can't believe you've done this," I say, gently tracing the delicate petals with my fingertip.

"It's never too late for a do-over, Parker. Now, will you do me the honor of being my date for tonight?" he asks, holding his hand out for me to take.

I click my tongue, fighting my smile. "I mean...I did get a few offers, but...you are quite hot. And something tells me that you might know how to end the night on a high."

"Oh, babe, you can guaran-fucking-tee that."

He tugs me forward once again, and this time he brushes his lips against my stained ones in a sweet and teasing kiss.

"Do you want a drink?" he asks as he pulls back.

A laugh tumbles from my lips when I take in the lipstick that's transferred to him. "Red is your color," I tease, dragging my thumb across his bottom one to wipe it off.

"Yeah, I've been told that before." He tugs me toward our friends. "Champagne?"

"Sounds perfect."

"Ah, how nice of you to join us," Casey teases, lifting my hand to inspect my new accessory. "He's so sweet," she whispers while the guys begin mocking Linc.

"I never thought I'd see the day, but being pussy-whipped suits you," Kodie announces.

"It's really beautiful," Freya says, also inspecting my corsage.

As we enjoy our drinks, more of the team joins us.

Fletch appears with Reese at his side. Killer and Brit are flying solo. And finally, Hayden joins us with a beautiful woman on his arm.

"Whoa, has Marilyn got a girl?" Killer announces loudly enough for everyone in the bar to hear.

We watch as they take the final few steps toward us. Hayden looks incredibly handsome and a lot older in his tux, and the woman at his side is stunning. She's slim and has flawless porcelain skin. Her hair is dark like Hayden's, and her dress is the exact same shade of purple as the pocket square he has tucked into his jacket.

"Shut up, you idiot," Hayden mutters, his cheeks and the tips of his ears both pink with embarrassment. "Everyone, this is Rylee, my sister."

"I fucking knew it. No way are you ever pulling someone this hot," Handsy teases.

"Guys," Hayden warns.

"It's okay," Rylee says softly, gripping his upper arm. "I can handle your friends."

"Hey, Rylee. I'm Parker, and this is Casey and Freya," I say, introducing the most important people in our group. "It's so good to finally meet you. I've heard many, many amazing things."

A smile splits Rylee's face. "He talks about me?" she teases, glancing back at Hayden.

"All the time. I've even started reading some of your favorite books."

She instantly lights up. "Really?"

"Yeah. You've got good taste. Your book boyfriends are spot on."

"Uh…I'm sorry. What was that?" Linc asks.

I chuckle before turning to him and tapping his chest patronizingly. "Sometimes, you just can't beat a fictional guy."

He scoffs. "I beg to fucking differ."

Rylee laughs, instantly fitting in with our group.

"Can we get you a drink, Rylee?" Casey asks.

"Uh, yeah. A fruit juice would be great."

"You got it."

As we all stand there catching up with each other, I can't wipe the smile off my face. I have everything I ever dreamed of —the man of my dreams at my side, a job I never thought I'd land, and the best friends and colleagues I could ever ask for. If this is the best life can offer, I'll take it.

Two weeks later…

"Is this really necessary?" I ask as Linc slips a blindfold over my face.

"Yep, totally necessary."

"I told you that I didn't need anything but a night in with you for my birthday."

"Yep, I know that, too."

"So why are we going out, and why are you being all sneaky and shit?"

He chuckles before kissing my forehead and demanding, "Trust me."

I huff in fake annoyance as he closes the door. It might appear like I'm sulking, but deep down, I'm excited to see what he's done.

We've only been together a few weeks, but everything has been so incredible. I'm getting to discover city after city with my best friend, while we both do the jobs we were born to do.

The Valentine's gala was everything I hoped it would be. Linc was right; it wasn't anything like prom night. It was so much better. By the time we got up to our hotel room, my face and stomach hurt from smiling and laughing so much. But as fun as our friends were, I was so ready for some one-on-one time with my man. And boy, did he deliver. I have no idea who was in the rooms surrounding us, but I probably owe them an apology. And I have no doubt that whatever Linc has planned for tonight will be equally as awesome.

Okay, sure, I am a little concerned that I'm only wearing jeans and a Vipers hoodie, but I trust him. Not that I'm going to tell him that.

"You look cute," he tells me as he drops into the driver's seat and starts the engine.

"How far are we going?" I try.

He laughs. "I haven't kept this secret all this time to ruin it now."

"Hmm...sounds like a big secret."

"You have no idea, babe. It's just about killed me."

Curious as fuck about what he's up to, I try my best to relax while he drives to wherever it is we're going.

It's roughly thirty minutes later when he brings the car to a stop and kills the engine.

Ideas of what's half an hour from our apartment run through my head, but none of them feel right.

I really am clueless about this. Whatever he's planned, he's done a good job of keeping tight-lipped about it.

We got back in late last night from a road game, and as far as I knew, we were having a chilled evening at home.

"Can I take this off now?"

"Nope." A blast of fresh air hits me as he climbs out of the car. "Come on," he says as he takes my hand and tugs me from the car.

With his hands on my waist, he guides me forward.

I take a deep breath through my nose, hoping scents might help me identify my surroundings, but it doesn't help.

I'm clueless. Utterly clueless.

"Small step," he instructs.

The sound of distant traffic and the final bird song of the day fade as we head inside a building.

The scent is familiar, but I can't quite pinpoint it.

"That's it. Keep going," he says softly.

We take a few more steps before he brings me to a stop.

My heart thunders in my chest as I try to figure this out.

"Okay. Are you ready?"

"I literally have no idea."

Silence greets my comment.

"Three," Linc starts, his fingers hooking beneath the elastic around my head. "Two," he teases. "One."

"HAPPY BIRTHDAY!"

My heart is in my throat as everyone I know and love greets me.

"Holy shit," I gasp, my hand jumping to cover my chest to stop my heart from beating right out of it.

I look around, meeting everyone's eyes as I take in the fact that we're in Kodie and Casey's house.

Kodie hates having people over and hosting parties, and yet, here we are.

"Happy birthday, Parker," a little voice squeals as Sutton bursts through the crowd and wraps her arms around my waist, hugging me tightly.

My eyes turn as I embrace her and meet Casey's gaze.

"You," I mouth.

She grins innocently before pointing at Linc.

"What do you think?" Linc asks, almost nervously. He was so confident on our way over here, or at least, he seemed to be. But now...not so much.

"I think you and Casey are sneaky little shits for planning this, but I love you both for it. Thank you."

Everyone cheers the second I wrap my arms around my man. He kisses the top of my head before leading me closer to everyone.

Casey is next to greet me.

"I can't believe you did this?"

"Well, I've got to keep myself busy while you're all out of town," she mocks. "And anyway, the person who really needs all the credit is Freya. You should see the food."

Spotting her over Casey's shoulder, I wave her over.

My heart is so full of love as we make our way around the room. The entire team is here, a huge number of the medical team and the front office staff. My parents. The only person missing is Rett, and despite understanding why he can't be here, I can't lie, his absence is like a massive hole in my chest.

Things haven't really gotten any better for him. The Bandits are firmly at the bottom of the division, and watching them play is painful. They're trying to put on a good show, but somewhere along the way, they've lost themselves this season. There is story after story about my brother's antics circling online. I'm even more worried about him than I was when he visited last month. But there is nothing I can do but be there on the other end of the phone.

It hurts not to be able to do more, but when he's ready, I'll be here.

There is a pile of gifts on the coffee table in Casey's living room, but I don't make a move to open them—I'm more focused on spending time with the people in my life than I am on gifts. The food that Freya has made, on the other hand…I'm more than ready to dive into that.

I'm standing at the island with Casey, Freya, Mom and Sutton, grazing through the plates of mouth-watering food, when Linc marches over, announcing that he's got one more surprise for me.

A ripple of awareness and excitement goes through the room, and I figure there's another secret everyone else knows that I don't.

Everyone moves a little closer, ready for the big reveal, and I watch my boyfriend with curious eyes as he waits for everyone to settle.

"If anyone is expecting me to get down on one knee, I'll tell you now, you're about to be disappointed." A round of groans sounds out. "But don't think that's because I don't want to. I do. And one day in the future, it'll happen. So if anyone here thinks they stand a chance with my girl, I'm here to tell you that you absolutely don't. I waited years to make her mine, and that isn't going to change. Ever."

I laugh at him. We've had a few discussions about the future and where we'd like our relationship to go, and thankfully, we're both in agreement. We want to get married, have kids, and get a house with a picket fence, but for now, we just want to enjoy life. And that is exactly what we're doing. We have plenty of time for all the serious stuff in the years to come. Right now, we're making up for all the time we lost out on.

"Most of your gifts from me are at home," Linc confesses. "But I do have one very special one for you right here."

Ripping my eyes from Linc, I look around at everyone. Some people look as lost as I am, but others—mainly the team —seem to know exactly what's about to happen. Excitement and anticipation twinkle in their eyes.

"Will someone..."

"Oh, for the love of God. Again?" I cry when the blindfold returns.

"Sorry, babe. It'll be worth it."

People shuffle around and footsteps move closer.

For a moment, I think it's Linc standing in front of me. But as I breathe in, I know it's not. It's someone else I know just as well.

"Surprise," a deep, very familiar voice rumbles, and I rip my blindfold off long before anyone has a chance and jump into my brother's arms. "Happy birthday, PK." I squeeze him so freaking hard. Not that he probably feels it because the man is built like a tank.

"I can't believe you're here. How?" I ask as I pull back from him, lifting my hands to wipe my eyes.

"Well, there are these things called airplanes," he mocks.

Lifting my hand, I smack his shoulder, but the second my hand connects, I freeze.

My eyes drop to what he's wearing, and I swear my heart stops.

"Rett," I breathe.

"This might surprise you, but I'm not actually the surprise. Not really."

"What are you saying?" I ask, hoping that I'm not putting two and two together and coming up with eight.

"Look at your cell," he demands, his eyes holding mine firm.

"Uh...okay." I reach behind me and pull it from my pocket.

I hold Rett's eyes a little longer before I wake it up and look down.

Since Linc announced our relationship to the world, I've turned off almost all my notifications. My socials are too wild for that now, and mostly, I'd rather not know what's being said on them. But there are a few apps I still have alerts on for, and the one at the very top of my screen is the most important.

The NHL app.

And what's the top story right now?

Everett Donnelly has been traded to the LA Vipers.

"Holy shit, Rett," I gasp, my eyes flooding with tears as I read the words I didn't think I'd ever get to.

My vision is blurry as I stare up at him.

"You're coming home?"

"I'm coming home," he agrees, his voice rough with emotion.

"Turn around," I demand, desperate to see it.

He smiles and ducks his head before he spins.

And there, right before my eyes, is my big brother's childhood dream stretched across his wide shoulders.

Donnelly. Seventy-Seven.

Well, I guess it's true what they say. Dreams really do come true.

Freya

The sound of laughter fills the air as I move around Casey's kitchen a couple of hours later. The party has been incredible, and Parker has loved every second of it, but my social battery is depleted. There was a time not so long ago when every single day of my life was spent surrounded by other people. It never used to bother me too much back then, but I think that was more so because I didn't have a choice.

Now that I'm home and everything has changed all over again, I'm finding myself enjoying my own company in a way I was never able to before. I craved the excitement the buzz, but now...now I want to disappear and hide in any way I can.

After transferring all the leftover food onto a handful of plates, I stack the others and place them beside the sink.

I'm busy washing them all when footsteps move my way.

I don't bother looking back—it'll just be one of the guys popping in for round four or five. I swear, those guys never stop eating. I expect whoever it is to load up another serving and then disappear back outside to join the others. So when a deep voice rips through the air, I startle and nearly drop the plate.

"You know they have a dishwasher, right?"

Oh god. It's him.

My stomach knots and my mouth runs dry.

Cole Handley. Or Handsy, to everyone here. The infamous goalie for the LA Vipers.

Also, the man I spent Valentine's night with on an unofficial date.

My hands tremble, and I keep my eyes focused on them.

If I turn around, I have no doubt that I'll make an idiot of myself.

Of course I knew who he was before the Valentine's gala. I've been to games and watched him play. Hell, Dad talks about him all the time—him and all the guys. I even saw him in a pair of swim shorts at Coach Watson's house last year. But I didn't ever really think twice about him...until that night.

I was terrified.

I'd pulled on my very best dress and tried to channel my old self, but it wasn't really working. The new me was having a field day, questioning my every move and constantly telling me that I didn't belong there.

But Cole...he was the most perfect date. For a man with a notorious reputation, he was incredibly sweet and patient with me. Despite having me thrust upon him by our friends, he made me feel genuinely wanted. He also made me feel beautiful, which is saying something, because I can be the first to admit that my self-confidence is at an all-time low right now.

"Oh, I don't mind. I like being busy," I mutter nervously in the hope it'll send him away.

But it seems my words have the opposite effect, because not two seconds later, he steps up beside me.

His scent floods my nose, and I'm instantly taken back to dancing with him that night. For such a huge guy, he really can move. But then...I've seen his warm-ups. I know what those hips can do.

My cheeks burn red hot at my inappropriate thoughts.

"What are you doing?" I balk when he snatches a tea towel and picks up one of the dripping plates.

"Helping. You shouldn't be in here slaving away all night. You've already worked hard enough. The food was incredible."

I duck my head, unable to take the compliment.

"Thank you," I whisper like a little mouse.

"I mean it; those dishes are the best homemade food I have eaten in a very long time."

I squirm again. It's something I'm really going to need to work on if I want to make cooking my career.

I have all the information at home. I've even filled out the applications to go back to school. I just...I'm yet to pull the trigger.

"I'm glad you enjoyed it. I love coo—"

"Are you looking for a job?" he blurts, cutting me off.

"I-I'm sorry?" I ask, wondering if I misheard him.

"Freya." His deep, raspy voice flows around me, making my skin prickle and my blood heat.

I haven't reacted to a man like this in such a long time. It takes me back a little. But the way he says my name...

"Casey and Parker may have mentioned that you're at a bit of a crossroads right now, and if you're looking for a job, I think I might have something for you."

My head spins with possibilities.

"Go on," I find myself saying, my curiosity getting the better of me. I still don't look up at him, though. It's easier if I pretend that he's not really there or talking to me.

"I need a chef. I'm looking for—"

"Oh, no. I'm not a chef. I'm not even trained. I don't know what I'm doing, really. I just—" A gasp of shock cuts off my words as he wraps his fingers around my wrist and turns me to look at him.

"Your food is incredible, Freya. And more than that...I...uh...I trust you."

I stare up at him as his words repeat in my head. There's a small frown pulling at his brows as if he's as shocked by them as I am. But he doesn't take them back.

"Y-you think I could—"

"I don't think, Freya. I *know*."

His confidence in me throws me for a loop. I haven't

experienced that level of confidence or trust in...a very, very long time. And he doesn't even know me, not really.

"I promise you, if you cook like you have tonight, I'll be a breeze to work for. I'll pay you well, and you're only required to work when I'm in town. When I'm away on road games, your time is your own. It'll allow you to study," he offers, clearly having done some digging with my friends.

"I...um...I don't know what to say."

Reaching behind him, he pulls a piece of paper from his back pocket and hands it to me.

"What's this?" I ask, staring down at it as if it's about to bite me.

"An offer," he states, moving it closer, encouraging me to take it.

Hesitantly, I reach for it. The second I open it and stare down at the figure scrawled across it, I start laughing.

This has to be a joke.

Why would anyone in their right mind want to pay me this kind of money to cook for them?

"Shit," Cole curses. "Is that too low?"

He snatches it back, and before I can say anything, he's scribbled the figure out and doubled it.

"What the hell are you doing?" I shriek. "That's insane. I'm not worth that."

He stills, his eyes meeting mine. Something happens in that moment of eye contact, but I'm too lost in everything that's just transpired to try to figure it out right now.

"You're worth every single cent and more, Freya. Say yes," he begs, before tagging on a single word that stops me from walking away from this crazy offer. "Please."

Get ready, because Cole & Freya's story is coming December 26th with STPG!
Pre-Order your copy

Want to go back to prom night and discover what really happened?
Download the bonus scene now

Psst... Linc & Parker have an extra bonus over on Patreon. You can read this bonus scene and more, over in my Happily Ever After Book Club!
Become a member now.

BREAKING THE PUCKING RULES
SNEAK PEEK

Chapter 1
Casey

The second Dad's name pops up on my screen, I can predict what's coming.

"Hey, kiddo. I'm really sorry, but I need a raincheck on breakfast."

A sad smile pulls at my lips. I got too used to our Wednesday morning breakfast dates during the off season.

That's all over now.

He hesitates then adds sheepishly, "Any chance you could do me a favor, though?"

"You got it," I say.

"I left my bible on the kitchen counter..." he trails off.

A laugh spills free.

"Would you like a coffee as well?"

"You're too good to me."

"Someone's got to be," I tease.

"Love you, Care Bear."

The call cuts and I take the final turn toward the house I grew up in.

Killing the engine in the driveway, I waste no time in climbing out and finding my key.

The second I open the door, familiarity rushes over me. The scent of happiness and safety fills my nose.

I love this place. Always have, always will. I have so many fantastic memories here—my father being the main one.

As I step into the kitchen, I find the room in its usual state of chaos, and I can't help but smile. Dad isn't the cleanest or most organized of people, unless it comes to work.

Collecting a stray glass and mug, I dump them in the sink, doing my bit to help.

I'm twenty-three. I shouldn't care that he's busy and blown off our date. But the sad truth of it is that it's the only date of any kind I've had in...longer than I want to admit.

A loud sigh passes my lips.

Glancing around the room, I quickly locate what I came here for.

It's not a real bible. My father doesn't have a single religious bone in his body, unless you count his lifetime commitment to hockey. I'm pretty sure he's prayed to that puck a few times over the years.

His bible is his life. His calendar, his playbook...his everything.

He starts a new one immediately after the end of each season and begins filling it with notes for the next one.

By the time the season is upon us, it always looks like it does now: bursting at the seams, full of scraps of paper with plays scribbled on them, notes about players, and phone numbers. Women's phone numbers.

I shake my head.

Dad is a good-looking man. After years of playing hockey, his body is still something to be proud of. And as the single head coach for the LA Vipers, he is hot property with all the desperate women in a fifty-mile radius.

He's not interested, though.

He's too focused on his job, on his team, and on me.

Don't get me wrong, when I was a teenager, I loved that I didn't have to share him with anything but hockey. But now that I'm older, I do wish he could find someone to enjoy life with.

I lift the bible from the counter and tuck it under my arm before heading back to my car, placing it safely on the passenger's seat.

Walking through the arena is almost as familiar as walking into Dad's house.

It's my second home.

Some of my earliest memories are from here, watching Dad utterly destroying his opponents on the ice.

I loved it just as much then as I do now. Hockey isn't just a game. It's a lifestyle. One I can't imagine not living.

Sucking in a deep breath, I walk toward the rink where I have no doubt I'll find the man I'm looking for.

The scraping of skates on ice and men shouting get steadily louder, and my speed increases.

If I could, I'd spend all my days sitting in the stands watching them train. Watching Dad boss them around.

The second I turn the corner, my eyes fall on the rink, and without meaning to, they search out number fifty-five. It's been the same since he was traded here last season.

Kodie Rivers is a hockey god.

Always has been and always will be.

I'm honored to get the chance to watch him in action.

The truth is, I've been watching him for years. Since he first took to the ice in college.

Even in high school, he was the best, and that allowed him to have his pick of colleges. And things have only gotten better since.

Especially for me.

When it was announced that he was coming to LA, I thought all my Christmases had come at once.

There's just one tiny issue...

I'm the coach's daughter.

It doesn't matter how much I might obsess over a player; it's never going to happen.

They wouldn't risk losing the respect of my father. A night with me isn't worth it.

I get it. I do. And before Kodie joined the Vipers, it never really bothered me.

I saw them all as adopted uncles, big brothers, and friends.

But now...

I used to have photos of him stuck inside my high school textbooks. I'd have had them on my bedroom wall if I didn't think my dad would lose his shit over it.

I've followed Kodie's career, his life, ever since he first stole my attention all those years ago.

And now that he's here, I'm no less intrigued by him. If anything, I'd say my slight obsession is worse.

Managing to rip my eyes away from his form speeding across the ice, I spot Dad.

Determined to look like a woman in control of her life, I hold my head high, clutch his bible tighter to my chest and keep walking.

He's just a hockey player. Just a man.

No big deal.

But it is a big deal. He's Kodie fucking Rivers.

Gritting my teeth, I do my best to stuff down the excitable hormonal teenage girl who seems to pop up every time I'm anywhere near him and focus on the task at hand.

Noticing movement in his direction, Dad looks up. The second he discovers it's me, his entire face lights up.

"Care Bear," he mouths, making my cheeks burn red.

I'm not sure I'll ever truly feel like an adult when I'm in my father's company. Somehow, no matter how old I am or what I've managed to achieve, I still feel like a little girl.

I continue around the rink, and I've almost reached him when two players slam into the plexiglass beside me. A startled shriek rips from my lips as I twist around to see who it is.

My breath catches, my heart racing even faster when I lock onto a pair of mesmerizing dark brown eyes that I'd know anywhere.

I try to swallow, but my mouth has gone completely dry.

Never before have I been this girl. I've been surrounded by hot hockey boys all my life. Sure, I've crushed on a few, but none of them have caused the kind of reaction that Kodie Rivers does.

It should be illegal.

As much as I'd love for him to look excited to see me, the only expression on his face is one of irritation. I guess that's understandable when you've just been body checked by a teammate.

I have no idea if he recognizes me—I pray that he does, but I can understand that I'm probably not as big a part of his life as he is mine. He gives me a curt nod of acknowledgement, and that alone is enough to cause a riot of butterflies in my stomach.

Get a fucking grip, Casey.

I force myself to look away and at the much more amused-looking man behind him.

Lincoln Storm.

Now, if there was a player who would probably throw caution to the wind and be willing to hook up with the coach's daughter, it would be Linc.

He's been a Viper since his rookie year. He's a great player...in both senses of the word. He works hard and he plays harder.

The opposite of Kodie, who lives a much quieter life.

Linc smirks at me in accomplishment, and a beat before he releases Kodie, he winks. That should be the move to give me butterflies, but nope. There are none for him.

A deep growl fills the air as a shadow falls over me.

"Eyes off my daughter, Storm." The warning in Dad's voice makes my stomach knot. I risk glancing over and find Dad glaring daggers at one of his best players. "Drop and give me fifty," he commands.

Knowing he's fucked up, Linc instantly pushes back and drops to his hands on the ice.

Dad watches him for a few seconds, but once he's happy he's driven off any potential suitors, he turns to me with a soft smile playing on his lips.

"You're an angel," he says, his voice suddenly softer and calmer.

"It's not like it's out of my way," I tease, looking up at him and smiling.

Sure, he has a few more wrinkles and a couple of gray hairs at his temples these days, but James Watson is still a very good-looking man. I can't blame women for acting the way they do around him.

"Even still. Appreciate it, kiddo."

Linc finishes his punishment and he and Kodie take off across the ice again to join the rest of the team, who are watching with amused expressions.

After taking his bible and coffee, Dad promises to make up for missing breakfast by taking me out to dinner instead.

Not wanting to take up any more of his time, I stretch up on my toes to give him a kiss on the cheek and wish him a good day, and then I walk away from the rink without looking back.

The second I pull my car door open, something flutters into the footwell. It must have fallen out of Dad's bible.

With a frown, I reach over and retrieve an envelope. I'm about to turn back and take it to Dad when the messy, unfamiliar writing across the front steals my attention.

Coach Watson, I know you don't want to go, but here is your ticket. Please don't waste it.

It's signed by the team owner.

My heart rate begins to increase as I predict what's hiding inside.

Climbing into my car, I look around the lot nervously. It's deserted, but it doesn't stop me from slumping lower in my seat as I tuck my finger under the unsealed flap. My hand shakes as I pull out the single ticket inside.

My stomach twists with anticipation.

For years, the LA Vipers' fundraising department has organized a masquerade ball in the weeks leading up to the preseason.

Getting your hands on a ticket is like finding unicorn shit.

Every single year, my dad is given one. And every single year, he donates to the cause but refuses to attend, saying that it's not his thing.

I've begged for his ticket every year since I was seventeen, to no avail.

It's not that he's trying to keep me away from hockey. That would be really hard, considering I also work for the franchise. But it would be safe to say that he likes to keep me at arm's length from the team.

That wouldn't have been the case if I were a boy. Hanging out with all the hot hockey players would have been a requirement. I'm not sure it's fair that just because I was born with a vagina, I'm barely allowed to hang out with them.

It was fine when I was little. I was welcomed in as if I were one of their own kids. But as I hit my teen years, as I grew boobs, Dad started limiting my visits.

The team has changed a lot since then. There are only a handful of veterans now who remember me as a kid. I guess that's the issue.

I clutch the slip of paper tighter, feeling like the kid holding the golden ticket.

I shouldn't.

Dad will kill me if he finds out I've taken it.

He'll know, a little voice screams, but one look at the arena and I swallow it down.

Dad won't know. Every year that ticket goes in the trash.

It's a masquerade ball...what if no one finds out?

If I can secure a good enough mask and dye my hair, then no one has to know. Not Dad, not Gary, our GM, or any of the players.

For one night, I'll just be a woman at a party.

A party that a certain number fifty-five will be attending...

For more of Casey and Kodie's story, keep reading **Breaking the Pucking Rules**

- Steamy Contemporary Romance

- Second Chance

- Past Hurt

- Sports Romance

- Mental Health Rep

- Accidental Pregnancy

An all-new and addictive second chance, sports romance standalone from the USA Today & Wall Street Journal bestselling author, Tracy Lorraine.

The last time I saw Colt, I told him we were done. For good.

Our years of messing around were over.

The back-and-forth, the shattered promises and constant heartbreak, hoping he'd change his mind.

I was tired of being wrecked by a man I couldn't hold on to.

College was behind me.

He was chasing his NFL dream.

I was headed back to my small hometown.

That was the day everything changed.

The day I almost died.

Now, five years on, I've somewhat managed to restart my life after the accident.

I'm settled.

I'm... happy.

And I'm no longer the girl he used to know.

So, the last thing I should do when I get an invite to his football game is go... right?

But that's the thing about Colt—I've never known how to stay away.

Dear Reader,

Broken Saint is a second chance, sports romance. This book is part of the Seattle Saint series but can be read as a standalone.

Start the Seattle Saints Series today!

Hate You

- Enemies to Lovers

- Best Friend's Brother
- Tattooed Bad Boy
- Found Family
- Steamy Contemporary Romance

I loved to hate her...

She made it so easy. She was everything I wasn't—everything I didn't want to be.

A reminder that from the moment I was born, I was the outcast. The rebel.

I went against everything that was expected of me and created a life on my terms. I built my own empire, carved out my own destiny.

Then she shows up at my tattoo studio, representing everything I tried to escape.

She expects to just fit in... like she ever could.

Tabitha Anderson.

The posh girl trying to prove everyone wrong... that she can be something else—someone else.

She hates me because she knows I'm right. Or so I think.

Turns out this isn't the first time we've met, and our hate has history.

We have history. I might not have remembered, but I damn sure won't forget now.

Won't forget how her smile is always directed at everyone but me.

If everything changes and she proves she does fit in, will it still be hate I'm feeling or something else entirely?

And if I'm wrong, then she's right where she belongs... with me.

ABOUT THE AUTHOR

Tracy Lorraine is a *USA Today* and *Wall Street Journal* bestselling new adult and contemporary romance author. Tracy has recently turned thirty and lives in a cute Cotswold village in England with her husband, baby girl and lovable but slightly crazy dog. Having always been a bookaholic with her head stuck in her Kindle, Tracy decided to try her hand at a story idea she dreamt up and hasn't looked back since.

Be the first to find out about new releases and offers. Sign up to my newsletter here.

If you want to know what I'm up to and see teasers and snippets of what I'm working on, then you need to be in my Facebook group. Join Tracy's Angels here.

Keep up to date with Tracy's books at
www.tracylorraine.com

www.ingramcontent.com/pod-product-compliance
Lightning Source LLC
Chambersburg PA
CBHW021922220726
48287CB00019B/1115